A Dangerous Crossing

www.penguin.co.uk

A Dangerous Crossing

Rachel Rhys

Doubleday

LONDON · TORONTO · SYDNEY · AUCKLAND · JOHANNESBURG

TRANSWORLD PUBLISHERS
61–63 Uxbridge Road, London W5 5SA
www.penguin.co.uk

Transworld is part of the Penguin Random House group of companies
whose addresses can be found at global.penguinrandomhouse.com

First published in Great Britain in 2017 by Doubleday
an imprint of Transworld Publishers

A CIP catalogue record for this book
is available from the British Library.

ISBNs 9780857524706 (hb)
9780857524713 (tpb)

Typeset in 11.25/14.5 pt Adobe Garamond by Jouve (UK), Milton Keynes
Printed and bound in Great Britain by Clays Ltd, Bungay, Suffolk

Penguin Random House is committed to a sustainable
future for our business, our readers and our planet. This book
is made from Forest Stewardship Council® certified paper.

1 3 5 7 9 10 8 6 4 2

For Joan Holles and all the other women adventurers

4 September 1939, Sydney, Australia

SANDWICHED BETWEEN two policemen, the woman descends the gangplank of the ship. Her wrists are shackled in front of her and the men grip fast to her arms, but her back is ramrod straight, as if being held in place by the flagpole at the ship's prow. She wears a forest-green velvet suit, the fashionably slim skirt skimming the top of her calves, and black stockings that end in green leather shoes with a delicate heel. Around her shoulders is a rust-coloured fox-fur stole, the head hanging down at the front as if it is watching how her shoes kick up the dust as she walks. The outfit is far too warm for the seventy-degree heat and the small crowd of onlookers feel grateful for their cool cotton clothes.

A matching green velvet hat sits on top of hair that has been pinned neatly back. The hat has a veil that falls over her face. They have at least allowed her this modesty.

She stares straight ahead, as if imagining herself somewhere quite different. She does not look around at the docks, where ships hulk out of the water, grey and pointed, like overgrown sharks. She does not gaze beyond them to where the famous Sydney Harbour Bridge fans out across the mouth of the estuary, connecting the south side to the north, or back the way the ship has just come to where the sandy beaches are strung out along the coast.

She is seemingly unmoved by the smells and the heat and the lush green vegetation on the distant hills, all so different to where she's come from. The rasp of the seagulls overhead and the hum of the insects seem not to register, and when a fly lands briefly on the decorative brooch she wears just above her right breast, in the shape of a bird, its eye a tiny studded emerald, she appears not to notice.

There's a reporter shadowing the trio as they make their way across the quay, past the throng of family and friends who are waiting to greet the new arrivals and staring with undisguised curiosity at the policemen and their charge. The crowd have been standing for hours in the heat, and the unexpected drama provides a welcome distraction from the tedium.

The reporter is a young man with shirt sleeves rolled up to his elbows. He seems uncertain how to behave. He usually covers the dock-beat, greeting the great liners that arrive from Liverpool or Southampton or Tilbury, quizzing the migrants on how they feel to have arrived at last on Australian soil. He likes his job. Since the government, with the help of the Church of England Migration Council, introduced the assisted-passage scheme to encourage more young women to travel to Australia from the UK, there are always groups of girls disembarking, eager to meet a genuine Aussie, their normal inhibitions melting in the uncustomary sunshine. They are usually only too glad to talk to him about where they've come from and their hopes for the future. Most of them will go straight into domestic service in one of the large homes in and around Sydney, many of them British-owned, where they'll work as parlourmaids or cooks, for thirty-five shillings a week, with one day off, the shine of this brave new future wearing off rapidly in the dreary reality of domestic life.

He wonders if this woman is one of them, also destined for

domestic service. It's possible. In his experience, most of them choose their Sunday best for their arrival in this new world. He knows he should ask questions of her, of the policemen by her side. The rumours have been building since the ship docked. This is his opportunity to make something of himself, to grab the front page rather than settling for just a few column inches on page fifteen. Yet there is something about the woman that stops him, the way her face, under the green veil, is raised defiantly to the horizon, even while her hands, in their thin white gloves, shake.

He overtakes them and then turns back, so they cannot help but notice him. 'Can you tell me your name?' he asks the woman. He has his notebook out and his fingers grip tightly around his pen, poised to write, but she shows no sign of hearing him.

He tries addressing a question to the policemen who flank her. 'Who is the victim?' he asks, walking backwards ahead of them. And then, 'Where is the body?'

The policemen look hot and agitated in their heavy uniforms. One is young. Younger even than the reporter, and his fingers on the green velvet of the woman's arm are long and delicate, like a girl's. He looks determinedly in the other direction so as to avoid the reporter's questions. The other policeman is middle-aged and overweight, his square face red and shiny in the heat. He glares at the reporter through the half-closed, bloodshot eyes of a heavy drinker.

'Let us through,' he says brusquely.

Now the reporter is becoming desperate, seeing his chance of a career-making exclusive slipping away.

'Have you any comment to make?' he asks the woman. 'Why were you on the ship? What brings you to Australia? How do you feel now that war has been declared?'

The woman falters, causing the young policeman to all but fall over his own feet in their outsized boots.

'War?' she whispers through her veil.

The reporter remembers now that she has been at sea for more than five weeks, and that the last time she had fresh news would have been when the ship docked in Melbourne two days before.

'Hitler has invaded Poland,' he tells her, his voice betraying the eagerness of the giver of powerful news. 'Britain is now officially at war – as are we.'

The woman appears to sway. But now the police are propelling her forward again. Her back straightens once more as the trio brush past him as if he weren't there.

The reporter knows he should follow them, but he has lost the appetite for it. There is something about the woman that chills him. Something more than the rumours of what she is supposed to have done.

Afterwards, when he hears the truth about what really happened on that ship, when half the country's media is camped outside the prison, desperate for news, he will kick himself for not persevering. But for now he stands still and watches as she is led across the quayside and into the waiting car. The window is open, and his last glimpse of her as the car pulls away is her green veil fluttering against her face like a butterfly's broken wing.

1

ALL HER LIFE, Lilian Shepherd will remember her first glimpse of the ship. She has seen photographs of the *Orontes* in leaflets, but nothing has prepared her for the scale of it, the sheer white wall towering over the quayside, beside which the passengers and stewards scurry around like ants. All along the dock as far as the eye can see cranes stretch their long metal necks into the watery blue sky. She had expected the numbers of people, but the noise of it all comes as a shock – the harsh cries of the gulls circling overhead, the creaking of the heavy chains that hoist the containers from the docks and the jarring clang as they hit the deck, the shouts of the smudge-faced men who are supervising the loading and unloading. And underneath all that, the excited chatter of the families who've gathered to see loved ones off, dressed in their best clothes, their funeral and wedding outfits, to mark the momentous occasion.

There is so much industry here, so much activity, that in spite of her nerves she feels her spirits stirring in sympathy, excitement skipping through her veins.

'You won't be short of company, that's for sure,' remarks her mother, her eyes darting around from under her best linen hat. 'Won't have time to miss anyone.'

Lily loops her arm through her mother's and squeezes.

'Don't be daft,' she says.

Frank is gazing at a couple standing off to the right. The woman is leaning back against a wooden structure while the man looms over her with his hands resting either side of her head and his face angled down so that the lock of his hair that has come loose at the front brushes her forehead. They are staring fiercely at each other, noses just inches apart, as if nothing else exists and they can't hear the jangle of noises around them, nor smell the pungent mixture of sea and salt and grease and oil and sweat. Even from several yards away, it's clear the woman is very beautiful. Her scarlet dress fits her body as if someone has sewn it in place and her full lips are painted a matching colour, dazzling against the sleek black of her hair. He is tall, solid, with a moustache and a cigarette that burns, forgotten, between his fingers. Though the couple are oblivious, Lily feels awkward, as if it is they, her family, who are intruding.

'Fetch your eyes in off those stalks,' she tells her brother sharply, then smiles, to show she was joking.

Lily's family have visitor's passes so they can see her safely on board. Lily is worried about how her father will manage the steep gangplank, but he grips the rail and puts his weight on his good foot and ascends in this fashion. Only when he is safely at the top does Lily breathe again. They are getting older, she thinks, and I am leaving them behind. An acidic rush of guilt prompts her to blurt out, once they are all gathered on the ship's deck, 'It's only two years, remember? I'll be home before you know it.'

The ship extends far deeper than Lily has imagined. The upper decks are for first-class passengers, while tourist class is below, and beneath that are the laundries and the third-class cabins. F Deck, where Lily's cabin is housed in tourist class, is a warren of narrow corridors, and she and her family have to ask directions from two separate stewards before they find her cabin. Inside, there are two sets of bunk beds close enough together so that a person in one upper bunk could reach out a hand and touch the person in the other. Lily is pleased to see that her cabin trunk has already arrived, her name stamped on the end neatly in large capital letters, protruding from underneath one of the bunks.

There are two women already in the cabin, sitting on the bottom bunks. Lily guesses the first is two or three years younger than her, maybe twenty-two or twenty-three. She has a round, open face with pale blue eyes so wide and unfocused Lily suspects she ought to be wearing spectacles. The idea that she might perhaps be carrying a pair around in her bag but not wishing to wear them, in a small act of vanity, makes Lily warm to her on sight. Not so her companion, who looks to be at least a decade older, with a thin-lipped smile and a long, sharp chin.

The younger woman leaps to her feet, revealing herself to be above-average height, although she dips her head to the floor as if to make herself smaller. 'Are you Lilian? I knew you had to be, as there are only us three in this cabin. Oh, I'm so happy to meet you. I'm Audrey, and this here is Ida. And this must be your family. Australia! Can you believe it?'

The words gush out as if the girl has no control over them. Her voice pulses with excitement, causing the wisps of fair hair around her face to quiver in tandem.

Lily's parents are introduced, and her brother, Frank, whose eyes glide off Audrey's plain features as if they are coated in oil. Soon the ship will leave and I will stay on it with these two strange women, and my family will go home without me, Lily reminds herself, but it does not seem real.

Lily's mother is asking Audrey and Ida where they are from.

'We're chambermaids, working at Claridge's hotel,' says Audrey.

'Not any more,' Ida chips in curtly. She is wearing an old-fashioned, black, high-necked dress, and when she leans forward a sour smell comes off her that catches in Lily's throat.

'When we saw the advertisement about the assisted-passage scheme, we thought, "Well, why not?"' says Audrey, 'but we never really dreamed . . . That is, I never really dreamed . . .' She glances at her older companion and the words dry up in her mouth.

'Are you looking forward to seeing all the sights on the voyage – Naples, Ceylon?' Lily's mother coughs out the foreign words as if they are small stones she's found on a lettuce leaf.

'Got to be better than staying here, hasn't it?' says Ida. 'If we go to war –'

Instantly, Lily and Frank glance towards their father, who has stood all this while in silence, leaning against the wall.

'We won't go to war,' Lily breaks in, anxious to head off the conversation. 'Mr Chamberlain said so, didn't he? "Peace in our time," he said.'

'Politicians say a lot of things,' says Ida.

A bell sounds out in the corridor. And again. The air in the cabin vibrates.

'I suppose that means it's time for us to go,' says Lily's mother. And her voice now carries a thin note of uncertainty that it lacked before. I will not see her again for two years, Lily tells herself, as if deliberately pressing the sharp blade of a knife against her skin. The answering jolt of pain takes her by surprise and she puts a hand to her chest to steady herself.

'I'll come with you on to the deck to wave goodbye,' Audrey tells her. 'My own folks saw me off at Liverpool Street, but I want to get one last look at Blighty. You coming, Ida?'

The older woman narrows her little black eyes. 'Nothing for me to see there,' she says. 'Who'd I be waving to? A tree? A crane?'

On the way up to the deck, Audrey whispers in Lily's ear, 'Don't mind Ida. She's just sore because she didn't get the full assisted passage on account of her age. I hoped that might put her off coming, but no such luck.'

Lily smiles, but doesn't reply because of the pain which is flowering out across her chest like dye in water. She watches her parents' backs as they lead the way to the deck, noticing how her mother's head is bowed in its best black hat, how her father clings to the rail as he climbs the stairs, his knuckles white with effort.

'Is your dad always so quiet?' Audrey asks.

Lily nods.

'The last war,' she says.

'Ah.'

Now they are out in the open again and joining the line of visitors queuing to go down the gangplank. Lily imagines herself grabbing hold of her mother's arm. *I've changed my mind*, she'd say, *I'm coming home with you*.

'You look after yourself, mind,' her mother says, turning to face her. 'A pretty girl like you, there's some would take advantage.'

Lily feels her cheeks flame. Her mother has never told her she is pretty. Other people have, Robert's voice soft as butter – 'You're so lovely, Lily' – but not her mother. Too worried perhaps about giving her daughter a big head, the very worst of female vices in her view.

Mrs Collins appears beside them. She is a stout, pleasant-faced woman, appointed by the Church of England Migration Council to accompany Lily and the other seven young women travelling on the assisted-passage scheme to take up domestic-service employment in Australia. 'Accompany' is another way of saying 'chaperone', but Lily doesn't mind. They met her at Liverpool Street so had her company for the duration of the train journey. Lily could tell straight away that her mother liked her, and that that would be a comfort to her in the days to come.

'Don't you worry, Mrs Shepherd,' says Mrs Collins, and her wide, kindly face folds into a smile. 'I'll take good care of this one.'

Frank is the first to take his leave. 'Don't forget to write – if you have any time between fancy dinners and balls and love-struck admirers!'

Lily lands a soft pretend-punch on his arm, then pulls him into a tight embrace. 'Look after Mam and Dad,' she says in his ear. Her voice sounds lumpy and strange.

''Course.'

Her dad gives her a long, wordless hug. When he pulls away, his eyes are glazed with tears and she looks away quickly, feeling like she has seen something she shouldn't have.

'We must get off,' says her mother. She gives Lily a dry kiss on the cheek, but Lily can feel how rigidly she is holding herself, as if her body were a wall shoring up some otherwise unstoppable force.

'I'll write to you,' Lily promises. 'I'm keeping a diary so I'll remember every detail.' But already her parents are halfway down the gangplank, swept along by the tide of visitors coming behind them.

Audrey, who has been standing discreetly to one side, tucks her arm through Lily's.

'You'll see them soon enough. Two years will go like that.' She snaps her large fingers in front of her face. Her hands are coarse and pinkly raw. Lily is well aware how hard the lives of chambermaids can be.

Mrs Collins nods. 'She's right, you know. Now, hurry up, you two, if you want to get a space at the front.'

Passengers who have said their goodbyes are already arranging themselves along the length of the ship's railing. Lily's eye is caught by a flash of scarlet and she notices the woman they saw earlier on the dock. She is pressing herself against the railing with arms straight out on either side, steadying her. Lily is astonished to see she is wearing black-lensed sunglasses. Though she has seen them in magazines, it's the first time she's seen someone actually wearing them, and to her they appear alien, like a fly's eyes. The woman is scouring the crowd gathered on the dock, as if searching for someone. The rugged, moustachioed man she was with earlier is nowhere to be seen.

'Over here.' Audrey pulls Lily towards a gap in the crowd.

Again Lily is reminded of the sheer scale of the ship as she peers down at the quayside where the families and friends of the departing passengers are gathered in their sombre-coloured Sunday best, their pale, anxious faces turned up towards the deck. Lily scans them now, looking for her mother's soft brown eyes. Oh, *there*. There is her family. The three of them, craning their necks, looking for her. Lily shakes off Audrey's arm and waves her hand to get their attention. Her heart constricts at how small they appear, no bigger than her fingernail.

When he sees her Frank puts a finger in each corner of his mouth and whistles. Lily watches her mother give him a mock-slap. The sweet familiarity of the gesture brings a lump to her throat and she has to look away. Her eyes fall on a man she has not seen before, a few feet away from her family. He is wearing a cream jacket, which makes him stand out in that sober crowd. Also, unlike most, he is bare-headed, and his blond hair catches the weak sun as if he has been gold-leafed. Even from the deck she can see the perfect proportions of him, the wide shoulders and narrow waist. He steps out from the crowd until he is at the very edge of the quayside, where the wooden boards fall sharply away. Now he is closer she can see that his skin is burnished like his hair, his cheekbones smooth and sculpted. He is shouting something, his hands cupped around his mouth, face tilted upwards. Lily leans forward, straining to catch it.

'Stay! Please, stay!'

He is staring at a point to her left, and she follows his gaze until she finds the woman in the red dress. Still alone, she stands at the railing gazing down, impassive, at the golden young man, as if she cannot see his anguished expression or hear his heartfelt entreaty. Then, abruptly, she whirls around and begins pushing through the crowd behind her. For a second, she catches Lily's eye and Lily is sure she sees one of the woman's perfectly arched dark brows lift a fraction above the dark glasses, but then she is gone, heading back towards the entrance to the cabins and the upper decks.

Lily turns back to her family. Her father stands still, his face lifted towards her. From this distance she can't tell if he's still crying, and she is grateful for this. She tries not to notice how shrunken her mother looks and instead drinks in the trio on the dock as if trying to commit them to memory. She fishes around in her handbag for her neatly folded handkerchief, but the tears she feels she ought to be shedding don't come. Instead there is a treacherous flare of excitement. She is going, she thinks. She is really going.

The gangplank has been taken up, and now there comes a sudden, startling noise like a thousand bagpipes blaring at once. And then the ship is moving, the figures on the quay frozen into position like a painting in a gallery from which she is slowly backing away. She hardly dares believe that she is actually leaving it behind – her family, of course, and her home, but also the things she doesn't like to think of: Mags, Robert, that room with its peeling wallpaper and the green, blood-stained carpet. 'Are you running away from anything, dear?' that lady at Australia House had asked. Lily had said no, but she wasn't fooling anyone.

But now all that is past. Today a new life begins. For the first time in eighteen months hope bursts like a firecracker inside Lily's narrow chest. Still, she carries on waving her arm until Tilbury Dock is just a black smudge in the distance.

2

PREPARING FOR DINNER that first evening, Lily feels as if she has somehow stumbled out of her own life and into someone else's. Where is her little room in the Bayswater boarding house? Where are the stockings draped and drying over the open wardrobe door and the narrow bed in which she'd lie awake, listening to her neighbour coughing through the paper-thin wall? What has happened to the bus ride to Piccadilly Circus and the nine-hour shifts in the Lyons Corner House on the corner of Coventry Street and Rupert Street? How peculiar that a life can swing so completely around in only eight weeks.

She hadn't had any notion of escape when she picked up the newspaper that Sunday afternoon. It was just lying there on the padded train seat opposite, discarded by a previous passenger. Lily doesn't normally pick up things other people have left behind. She cannot bear the idea of being thought not able to afford her own. But the carriage was empty, apart from an elderly lady who had nodded off with her face almost buried in her vast bosom. Besides, Lily was restless. She'd made the journey from Reading to Paddington so many times she sometimes found herself lying awake, going through the stations like a litany: Reading, Maidenhead Bridge, Slough, West Drayton, Southall, Paddington. At night, their familiarity soothed her but during the day she felt as if she might burst with the sameness of it all.

The front page of the paper was full of Herr Hitler's latest provocations in Europe but Lily resolutely refused to believe the worst. The country had got to the very brink last year and stepped away again. Nevertheless, she flicked through those pages quickly, as if lingering might tempt its own bad luck.

On page four, her attention was caught by a headline. NEW GOVERNMENT SCHEME FOR MIGRATION TO AUSTRALIA, it read. Lily felt something stir, a tendril of excitement unfurling. Australia. The very word brought to mind unimaginable worlds. Cobalt-blue skies and emerald leaves against which exotic flowers bloomed. Lily has never been further than the south coast of England but she has seen newsreels of Australia in the cinema, and her uncle, who was a sailor in his teens, used to tell her stories of beaches and sharks, and spiders bigger than a human hand.

She read on. The government was subsidizing a scheme for young men and women between the ages of eighteen and thirty-five to travel to Australia with an assisted passage. Young women with domestic skills were particularly welcome. The large houses around Sydney and Melbourne needed staff, and British employees carried a particular cachet.

Lily has sworn she will never go back to domestic service, not after what happened with Robert. But as a means to an end? Could she? Would she?

And now here she is. When Lily and Audrey made their way back to their cabin earlier, with Lily's thoughts still full of that last image of her family on the docks growing smaller and smaller until they were black specks of dust, they'd been introduced briefly to the other five young women travelling under the scheme: two sisters from Birmingham and three others whose names Lily immediately forgot. Afterwards Mrs Collins showed them around the boat with a proprietorial air. The corridors and narrow staircase of F Deck hummed with the excited chatter of other passengers engaged in the same pursuit.

First the bathrooms. Though the cabins have their own washing facilities, there are bathrooms and toilets just along the corridor. Mrs Collins advised them to tip the bathroom steward at the beginning of the trip, as well as halfway through. There could be queues at busy times of day, she told them, so it was useful to have someone looking out for you. They'd agreed, all except Ida, who muttered that she wouldn't be tipping anyone before knowing they were up to the job.

'I've been around a bit longer than the rest of you. I know more about how the world works. There's no point tipping at the start, you have to make people work for their rewards.'

Later, Audrey had whispered to Lily that Ida couldn't help being bitter. She had had a fiancé who died of influenza, Audrey said. But Lily thought that a poor excuse for a lifetime of being miserable and spraying misery into the air like scent. They are only twenty years out from the Great War. Everyone has lost someone.

Next, a trip to the Purser's Office to store their money and valuables. Lily was relieved to hand over the fourteen pounds she has saved. It has to last her the whole voyage, as well as start her out on her new life when she arrives in Australia. Awareness of all that money had been weighing her down and now the purser has taken possession of it, painstakingly recording the amount next to her name in a large ledger, she feels immeasurably lighter. The Purser's Office is up on the first-class deck, and Lily had enjoyed peering into the dining room, which looked more like something you'd find in a luxurious hotel, and the sumptuous lounge, with its potted palm trees and velvet curtains.

Back in tourist class, they passed the swimming pool – much smaller than the one on the upper-class deck, but no doubt they'd be grateful for it once the weather got hotter. Then they looked in on the dining room, which was dotted with round tables set for six and topped with starched white tablecloths. There were lists of

21

table seatings, and Lily searched for her name anxiously, relieved to discover she would be at the same sitting as Audrey, if not the same table. Ida, to her own great annoyance, was on the earlier sitting.

Finally to the tourist-class lounge for tea, which was served with sandwiches and scones and cake. 'I shall be the size of an elephant by the time we dock,' Mrs Collins sighed, helping herself to another slice of cake. By then they had learned that she had been widowed some years before and that she had made this journey twice already, visiting her married daughter in Sydney. It was a way to have her passage paid, she told them. And she enjoyed the company.

The lounge was less formal than the dining room, with comfortable sofas in a dusky pink that reminded Lily of the curtains at home in her parents' parlour, where no one ever went. Neat desks were tucked into the alcoves, where passengers could write their letters home, and at one end a grand piano gleamed under the light reflecting off the crystal chandelier above. Windows ran the length of the room, through which the south coast of England was still just about visible, the dark obelisk of Eddystone lighthouse receding into the distance. Lily thought then about her parents, and wondered if they'd got back to Reading already. She imagined them letting themselves into the little house on Hatherley Road and how quiet it would feel, the hallway stiff with undisturbed air, and the thought made her momentarily morose.

But now it's nearly dinnertime and Lily's spirits are once again on the rise as she hurries along the passage to the bathroom. Mindful of Mrs Collins's advice, she offers five shillings to the bathroom attendant, informing him that she will be taking her bath before dinner each day and asking him to reserve her a bathroom. He is a young man, younger even than Frank, she guesses, and he smiles at her shyly.

'Of course, miss.'

For the first time in her life Lily feels like a person of substance, a person with choices. In her bath, she hums to herself, then stops when she remembers the attendant just outside the door. The water feels strange on her skin. Prickly. Mrs Collins has explained that they use treated sea water for the baths, and Lily is glad of the basin of heated fresh water that rests on a wooden board laid across the foot of the bath with which she is to rinse herself at the end. Once out of the bath, she looks down at her body, her pale limbs and the little swell of her belly. She thinks of Robert, and immediately covers herself up with her towel.

Back in the cabin a layer of anticipation and expectation coats the neatly made-up bunks and the few jars of cream and bottles of scent on the dressing table. It is tucked into the folds of the dresses on the hangers in the narrow wardrobe and the under-things in the modest chest of drawers. Audrey and Lily dress with care, Lily steering Audrey away from wearing her one evening gown. 'This is just dinner,' she advises. 'Save that one for when there's a ball.'

It feels good to be talking like this with another woman again. Since Mags, she has felt the lack of female intimacy keenly.

Lily decides on her midnight-blue silk with the white trim. It's an old dress which used to belong to the lady of the house, back in the days when she was a parlourmaid. But it's very good quality, and Lily has altered it so that it fits her perfectly.

'Oh, that looks so nice on you,' Audrey tells her. 'It brings out the colour of your eyes. Such an unusual shade they are. What would you call it? Toffee? Amber? If I had eyes like that, I should spend the whole day gazing at myself in the mirror.'

'It's just the light in here,' says Ida. 'Making everything look different. I expect it has had the same effect on my own.'

But Ida's black eyes seem not to reflect any light at all.

Ida is not pleased at being in the first sitting for dinner. 'Why have you two been put together and not me? I shall go and have words with the steward, see if I can swap with someone at one of your tables.'

Lily resolves to make allies of her fellow diners tonight and impress upon them that, if asked to give up their place, they must refuse at all costs.

Dinner is a four-course affair – soup, halibut, cold cuts of meat, strawberry mousse or fruit – but Lily is hardly able to concentrate on the choices on offer for curiosity about the others at her table. To her left sits a fragile-looking woman in her mid thirties who is travelling with her teenage daughter.

'I'm Clara Mills, and this is Peggy.' As she introduces herself, in a voice so small it's as if the effort of speaking has in itself depleted her, Clara's tiny hands flutter around her slender throat like paper caught in a rotating fan.

'We are travelling quite alone. I haven't slept in weeks for worrying. We're on our way to Sydney to meet up with Peggy's father, who has been setting himself up in business. We haven't seen him for over two years.'

'What kind of business?'

'Oh. He's a bookkeeper by trade.'

'Well, everyone needs accountants, don't they?'

'Yes. Except that isn't quite –'

'Papa has opened a sweet shop.'

Peggy has that doughy, unformed look peculiar to certain teenagers, as if she hasn't quite been finished off. She announces her father's new business endeavour with an air of triumph that takes Lily by surprise.

A deep pink stain blooms on Clara's chest.

'Yes,' she says faintly. 'It is rather a departure.'

The couple to Lily's right were down on the seating plan as Edward and Helena Fletcher. Engaged in conversation with the Millses, Lily got only a fleeting glimpse of them as they sat down, five minutes after the eight o'clock sitting began, but now the man turns to bring her into the conversation.

'We were just arguing about what we're going to miss most about home . . . Miss Shepherd, isn't it?'

'Yes, but please call me Lily.'

'Helena here thinks frosty mornings – you know, when your feet crunch on the pavement as you walk and you leave satisfying footprints behind – but I'm rather leaning towards jam-sponge pudding with custard.'

As Edward Fletcher speaks, Lily studies him covertly. He looks to be slightly older than her, but certainly no more than thirty. Though his complexion is chalky white and his cheeks hollow, he has a pleasant face, with widely spaced green eyes and a full, well-defined mouth that seems, even in repose, to be turning up at the corners as if at some private joke. She can see that some effort has been made to grease back his dark curls, but they are already escaping, springing back into life around his ears. He has narrow shoulders, and his wrists, where they extend from his lounge jacket and starched shirt sleeves, are long and graceful, their little nubs of bone as white and smooth as pebbles.

'Really, Edward, you're such a child,' says the woman sitting on the far side of him.

Lily is surprised to find Helena Fletcher so much older than her husband. She can see that she might once have been a beauty but now her skin is grey-tinged and there are violet shadows under her eyes. Her straight brown hair has been carelessly pinned up, as if done without access to a mirror.

'How about you, Lily?' Edward asks. 'What are you most sad to leave behind?'

'I shall miss my family, of course. And after that . . .' Lily's voice tails off. What will she miss? The cold mornings, where her breath clouded in the air above her bed, and the walls ran wet with condensation? The bus journeys home after a late shift when her feet ached from standing up all day and there was always one man with a pint too many inside him who imagined that, because she was out so late on her own, she must be looking for company?

'Well, mostly my family, I suppose,' she concludes lamely.

'Shall we have wine?' Edward asks, turning to Helena but not waiting for her reply. 'Yes, I think we should, to celebrate getting off all right. And leaving all tiresome things behind.'

He calls the waiter over and orders a bottle, making sure it is added to his bill. Lily is relieved they won't be expected to share the extra cost.

'What brings you on this voyage, Lily?' asks Clara Mills in her small, breathy voice.

'Yes, do tell us,' says Edward. 'Have you a pining sweetheart waiting for you at the other end?'

Lily searches his face for any signs that he is making fun of her, but his smile is open and gentle. For a moment she wonders about reinventing herself, making up a more interesting, more impressive story. But then she tilts her chin upwards. Domestic service was good enough for her mother and her grandmother. She ought not to feel ashamed. She explains about the assisted-passage scheme and the process that has led her here. The forms she sent off to the Church of England Advisory Council of Empire Settlement, the interview at Australia House on the Strand, with its grand entrance hall with the marble floor and pillars running the length of the walls. She leaves out the moment her interviewer, a kindly woman in her sixties, leaned towards her: 'Forgive me, my dear, but is there something you are running away from?' Instead she tells them about her yearning to travel and the uncle with his tales of adventure and giant spiders. She likes the version of herself she sees reflected back in their eyes. Spirited, independent.

'And you?' She addresses the question to Helena, anxious to

include her. The older woman hesitates, as if choosing her words from a densely stocked shelf.

'Edward has not been well,' she says. 'Tuberculosis.'

'Please don't look so concerned,' he interrupts, seeing Lily's expression. 'I am now quite cured.'

As if to demonstrate his newly robust constitution he pours four large glasses of wine from the bottle that has just arrived at the table and hands them out.

'The doctors believe the climate in Australia will be better for his health,' Helena continues.

Lily is struck by Helena's detachment. She does not look at her husband at all as she speaks.

All this while there has been an empty chair at the table, but now a man appears, in a state of some agitation, his eyes downcast and his cheeks flushed purple.

'I apologize for arriving so late,' he says, and his voice carries a hint of annoyance. 'I had to queue for the bathroom.'

The newcomer introduces himself to the table as George Price. He is going to New Zealand to help his uncle run his smallholding, he tells them. Like Edward Fletcher, he looks to be in his late twenties, but he is thickset, with square, meaty hands and a caved-in nose that looks to have been broken several times. When he is introduced to Lily, his small eyes dart to her face and then quickly away again.

Now George has joined them the conversation becomes stilted, lacking its earlier ease. He tries to engage them in talk of politics, of Germany, of war.

'Instead of making an enemy of Herr Hitler, we ought to be learning from him,' he tells them. 'You should read his book. It makes a lot of sense.'

George is fuming mad, he tells them, that the purser has confiscated his wireless radio and locked it away 'for safe keeping'. 'He asked me to imagine what would happen if war broke out during the voyage, with all the different nationalities there will be on board by the time we've passed through Europe – Ities, Germans, you name it. I said, "If war breaks out, I'd jolly well like to be prepared."'

Helena reminds him of the noticeboard, where, twice a day, world-news headlines are to be posted. 'Yes, but they'll keep quiet if it comes to war,' he says. 'At least till we're off the ship. Half the passengers would be our enemies!'

Lily is relieved when dinner finishes and the Fletchers invite her to take coffee with them in the lounge. One of the passengers, an elderly woman all in pink, is playing the piano and there is an atmosphere of cheery first-night optimism. Lily scans the room quickly to see if the woman in the scarlet dress might be there, or the man she was with on the quayside, but she isn't surprised not to see them. That dress hadn't come from the kind of stores Lily frequents, and she is sure the couple will be settling down for dinner in the more luxurious dining room of the first-class deck.

'George is a bit intense, isn't he?' Edward murmurs as they sink down on to one of the comfortable sofas. 'Hope he won't be ranting at us all through the voyage.'

'Just ignore him and keep out of his way,' says Helena sharply. Then she puts a hand to her head.

'I'm sorry,' she says, turning her clear grey eyes to Lily. 'I'm not feeling terribly well. I think I'll go back to the cabin to lie down.'

To Lily's surprise, Edward doesn't get to his feet to accompany her. Instead he blows her a kiss from the sofa. 'Sleep well, my sweet,' he says.

Now Lily feels awkward, unsure what is proper in this situation.

'I hope your wife will feel better in the morning,' she says eventually, her voice stiff.

Edward's pale, pinched face registers surprise, and then, bafflingly, amusement.

'Oh, you thought . . . How funny.'

Just as Lily is starting to feel affronted at being toyed with, he relents.

'Helena is not my wife,' he says. 'She's my sister.'

3

30 July 1939

THE FOLLOWING MORNING Lily awakes in her narrow bunk
and, for a moment, she cannot for the life of her work out where
she is, but then she glances over to the side and sees Audrey's fair hair
fanned out on the pillow. Her eyes drift lazily to the bunk below,
where she sees with a shock that Ida is awake and staring at her.

'You looked very cosy with that young man last night.'

Ida raises herself to a sitting position. Lily is transfixed by her
hair, which seems not to move with the rest of her, until she realizes
it is held back by a black net. 'Well? Are you going to tell us, or
what?' Ida smiles, her eyes narrowing to slits, and Lily feels a wave
of revulsion at the unwanted invitation to intimacy. Remember the
dead fiancé, she admonishes herself. Be kind. Yet still she does not
want to share confidences with Ida. Not that there are any confidences to share.

'I'm afraid there is nothing to tell. He and his sister are my
neighbours at dinner. We just chatted about the ship, really, nothing more.'

The effect of the rebuttal is instant. Ida swings her legs round.

'Well, you'd be advised to be a little bit more careful in future. I
can't think what Mrs Collins is about, allowing the young ladies in

her charge to gallivant around at all hours with strange men they've only just met.'

Lily is relieved the conversation is at an end, but she knows on some level that she has made a mistake in making an enemy of Ida.

Audrey is full of excitement when she finally awakes to the sound of the steward bringing round cups of tea, and wants to compare stories with Lily about the new acquaintances they made at dinner. There is a young girl on her table with whom she has already struck up quite a friendship. Lily is relieved. Though she finds herself liking Audrey more and more, she doesn't wish to be responsible for her. Besides, she is looking forward to getting to know Edward and Helena better and hopes to avoid feeling obliged to pair off with Audrey at every social event or stop-over. She knows she will never again let anyone get as close as Mags. It is not worth the pain.

On the way up to the dining room for breakfast Lily tries to quell the fizz of anticipation she can feel bubbling in her veins at the thought of seeing Edward Fletcher again. He was just being friendly last night, nothing more, she tells herself sternly. But still, when she sees him already seated at the table with his sister, she has a flush of pleasure, as if a warm flannel is being gently pressed to her cheek. In the daylight, his skin looks less ghostly pale and, in spite of her own warnings, her spirits leap when his face lights up in a smile at the sight of her.

'I'm so glad to see you up and about,' she tells Helena, although the truth is that Helena still looks unwell, her eyes red-rimmed and puffy.

'Thank you,' Helena replies. 'But I couldn't leave my little brother unattended. Someone has to keep an eye on what he's getting up to.'

She smiles, but Lily sees an odd look pass between the siblings that makes her uneasy.

Peggy Mills appears at the table, alone.

'Mama is ill,' she announces in a flat, emotionless voice. 'The steward had to give her some paper bags to be sick into!'

George Price, who has taken his seat at the other side of the table, freezes, a forkful of scrambled egg just inches from his mouth.

'Do you mind?' he says. 'Some of us are eating.'

Peggy shrugs but doesn't appear offended.

George catches Lily's eye and shakes his head, as if trying to draw her into his disapproval, but she looks away as if she hasn't noticed. For the rest of the meal Lily addresses most of her conversation to the motherless girl, to make sure she doesn't feel left out. So it is only afterwards, when Edward suggests a stroll around the deck, that she is able to talk freely with the Fletchers.

Outside, there is a cool breeze blowing off the sea and the sky is the grey of old porridge. Lily draws her cardigan around her. This isn't the weather she has been expecting.

'Are you cold, Lily?' asks Edward.

She shakes her head.

'I'm used to cold,' she tells them. 'My room in London had cracks in the window frames a mile wide, and it was so damp I once found mushrooms growing in my dressing gown!'

'Yes, the sanatorium was cold, too,' Edward says. 'Even at the height of summer it was impossible to feel warm there.'

His green eyes look momentarily cloudy, and Lily regrets having reminded him of what was clearly an unhappy time.

'Edward tells me your family are originally from Herefordshire,' she says to Helena, trying to move the subject on to something else.

Helena hesitates.

'Yes, that's right. Although we recently moved to the south coast. For Edward's health. I was working as a teacher there. Younger children, mostly.'

'And did you enjoy it?'

Helena's face relaxes, as if she has shed a pair of uncomfortable shoes, and now Lily can see that she's younger than she initially thought.

'Oh, I loved it,' she says.

'Helena is a natural with children,' says Edward, and he grabs hold of his sister's hand and squeezes it in a gesture Lily can't help but find touching. Now that they are all standing up, she sees more of a resemblance between the Fletchers. They are both of slight build and, with Helena's hair piled up on her head, there is little difference in height. Some of their mannerisms, too, are similar. They both have a way of covering their mouths with their hands when they laugh, as if to prevent their merriment from escaping.

On the other side of the ship, there are some low-slung canvas chairs, which are shielded from the wind by the lounge wall. Helena and Lily settle themselves down, and Edward volunteers to go in search of some blankets.

'Tell me, Lily. Have you left anyone behind in England? A sweetheart, perhaps?'

Lily is surprised at the question. Helena does not seem the type to encourage confidences. She thinks about Robert and the way one of his eyes looked different to the other, after an accident left one pupil permanently dilated, and how those eyes would travel lazily up the length of her when she came through the door until she felt utterly exposed.

'No. No one. How about you?'

'No. That is, not any more.'

And now Lily realizes why Helena introduced the subject – to give herself licence to talk.

'There was someone. In fact, we were engaged to be married. He was . . . is . . . a wonderful man. He's a teacher, and he writes poetry. Really very fine poetry. He has a very unique way of seeing the world.'

As Helena is talking, she appears almost radiant, her sallow skin flushing pink like dawn breaking.

'So what happened, if you don't mind me asking?'

Helena puts a hand to her forehead, and the colour drains from her face just as suddenly as it appeared.

'It didn't work out.'

'But –'

'Success!' Edward has reappeared, carrying warm woollen blankets for them to tuck over their knees. Lily's blanket is soft, red-and-white plaid and she has a sudden sense of wellbeing as she takes it from Edward's outstretched hand and wraps it around her. This is how it would be to be married, she thinks. Having somebody care whether you are warm enough. For your comfort to matter.

At teatime she meets up with Audrey in the lounge, which is crackling with life as the sound of passengers greeting old friends and chatting with new ones mixes with the clink of china cups hitting saucers and the tinkling of dainty silver teaspoons as they stir in the sugar. As with last night, there is someone playing the piano, a young man this time, softly picking out a melody Lily recognizes from a film score. Audrey is bursting with excitement about the ball that evening. This being the first full day of the crossing, there is to be a formal dance, with a band. An opportunity for Audrey to showcase her evening dress, of which she is most proud.

'I must say, I envy you your dinner companions,' she tells Lily. 'The youngest man on our table is about sixty-five and deaf as a post. When I asked him if he could pass the butter, he replied, "Not so well, unfortunately. The mattress is very thin." It's very hard to have a conversation. Good job I've got Annie to talk to. I can't wait for you two to meet, Lily. I'm sure you'll get on famously.'

'Hello, you two, I've been searching all over for you.' Ida has materialized, seemingly from nowhere. Her plate is heaped with sandwiches, as if to guard against a sudden reintroduction of rationing. Again Lily tells herself to be kind, but there is something about Ida that seems to suck the joy from the air.

'I was just saying to Lily that her table seems very jolly,' says Audrey, good-naturedly. 'The young man with the dark hair is particularly easy on the eye!'

'If you like that sort of thing,' says Ida dismissively. 'I prefer tall men with more meat on their bones.'

'Edward has been unwell,' says Lily, rushing to defend him. 'That's why he and his sister are moving to Australia.'

'Good of her to keep him company. I don't know if any of my sisters or brothers would do that for me,' says Audrey.

'She must have a poor excuse for a life if she's so ready to leave it behind,' is Ida's response.

Lily is taken aback. Now she thinks about it, it is strange that Helena has put her own life, and the job she loved, to one side in order to accompany her brother to the other side of the world. But then, perhaps after the heartbreak of her broken engagement, Helena might have been glad of the opportunity to escape. The Fletchers are clearly a close family. It is surely a good sign that they have not left Edward to face the journey alone.

Thinking about Edward's family reminds Lily of her own. She hopes her mother isn't worrying about her and realizes guiltily that she has hardly given them a second thought.

Her parents had been so shocked when she first broke it to them that she was going to Australia. 'Back to domestic service?' Mam had cried. 'After everything you said!' Of course, neither of her parents knew about Robert and Mags, but Mam wasn't stupid, she knew something bad had happened. Which is why she'd been so relieved when Lily got the head-waitress job. It was a complete change of environment.

But after a while Mam had relented. 'I know you've always had ambitions to do something different and see a little of the world,' she told her. 'You were always so bright, and I've always been sorry that you had to leave school so young to start earning.' Lily herself hadn't minded that much. She'd won a scholarship to what they all called 'the posh school' at eleven but, though she'd enjoyed the lessons, particularly English, at which she'd excelled, she hadn't much enjoyed the other girls' snobbery, or how her mam refused to come to the Christmas carol concert because her clothes were too shabby. And when she'd left at fourteen she hadn't looked back.

So in the end she had her parents' blessing to go to Australia, and this is how she repaid them – by forgetting all about them the minute they were out of sight. As a penance, as soon as tea is over, Lily installs herself at one of the little desks slotted into the alcoves in the lounge and, using the notepaper provided, impressively stamped with the ship's crest, she composes a long, colourful letter describing everything that has happened so far on the voyage: the people she's met, the food she's eaten, even the movement of the boat under her feet. Then she seals it in an envelope and takes it to the Purser's Office for posting at the next port, after which she feels much better.

Walking into the dining room later that evening, wearing the new full-length cream silk dress that cost her a good chunk of her savings and which Audrey insists makes her look like Greer Garson, Lily is surprised to feel her nerves popping under her skin like the bubbles in soda water.

Both Edward and George Price get to their feet when she approaches the table, but it is Helena who speaks first.

'How lovely you look, Lily. That colour is so good on you. And how clever to match it with that spray of silk roses.'

'You will be beating off admirers at the dance later,' Edward says. 'But don't worry, I will act as your own private police guard.'

There are two empty chairs at the table, as neither Peggy nor her mother appears.

'People are falling like dominoes,' says George, with some satisfaction. 'All my cabin mates are ill, and the steward says half the people on our deck have taken to their beds. First few days at sea will get you like that if you're not used to it.'

'I take it you've travelled before, then,' says Lily, grudgingly taking up the gauntlet that he has so obviously thrown down.

'Oh, yes. Europe. America. That's how I know so much about what's going on in the world.'

'Not the political manifesto again,' groans Edward in Lily's ear.

Luckily, Helena, seated to George's left, heads him off.

'America? How interesting. Where exactly have you been? Is it true Americans eat fried potatoes with every meal?'

After dinner there's a palpable frisson in the air as the band sets up. The dancefloor is an area between the lounge and the bar which is open on both sides to the decks. Lily is relieved to find the wind has dropped. She possesses an evening cape but would have been reluctant to cover up her new dress. Passengers who are on the other dinner sitting drift out to watch or gather in the bar. Though she hasn't had anything to drink, Lily nevertheless feels intoxicated. It's a mixture of the music and the beautiful clothes, the silks and velvets and chiffons, the peacock greens and sapphire blues, the russets and magentas; of the different fragrances, so recently applied, that mingle in the heady air – musks and florals and citruses, the woody smell of the cigar smokers. It's the tinkling laughter of women and low baritones of men, the crying of a baby, newly awoken and unhappy at finding itself somewhere unfamiliar. And, above all that, the awareness that they are here on this floating world, apart from all other worlds, all of them bound together by the country they have come from and the one they are going to, and by all the thousands of miles of travel that lie in between.

'You look like a princess from a storybook in that dress,' says Edward softly after they leave their table to stand on the periphery of the dancefloor. He is wearing a black dinner jacket, against which his skin appears almost pearlescent in the dwindling light. As ever, his shock of dark hair escapes all attempts at control and springs up from his head in defiant curls.

Lily is glad of the darkness as she feels her cheeks burn.

Helena is wearing a floor-length dove-grey gown that looks expensive, except that it is creased and the stitching has come loose at one of the seams. Not for the first time, Lily wonders about the siblings' background. Their clothes are well cut and they are paying full fare. Edward has told her he was training as a lawyer before he became ill. Yet here they are, travelling tourist class with her. She assumes their parents must be footing the bill for the voyage and for the initial costs of setting up in Sydney once they arrive. Yet neither has been forthcoming about their family back home. All Lily knows is that their father is something important in the civil service and their mother a housewife. 'Will they be coming to Australia to join you?' Lily had asked, and she hadn't imagined the look that passed between them before Helena said, 'We very much hope so, but Mother is not very strong so we will have to wait and see.'

When the band starts playing, Lily hopes Edward will ask her to dance. While she isn't a particularly accomplished dancer, she loves the glamour of it, the feeling of her body giving in to a rhythm not her own, the warmth of a man's hand resting gently on her waist as the lights and the music whirl around them. But Edward seems content to remain as they are, talking to Helena, and perhaps, Lily thinks, he does not want to leave his sister standing here alone.

'Quick, hide me,' she says, stepping behind the others as she spies Ida on the other side of the dining room in the brown dress she'd earlier fished out from her case. But when Ida eventually turns to walk off in the direction of the cabins, it's remorse Lily feels rather than relief. What would it have cost me to be kind? she reprimands herself.

The deck is getting very crowded as the passengers spill out from the dining room and the lounge. There's a noisy group by the bar which includes a woman with a loud, penetrating laugh that scrapes along each one of Lily's vertebrae in turn.

'That lot are down from First,' says George Price, who has wandered over to join them. 'Probably fed up with how stuffy it is up there – or just want to get a good look at how the rest of us live, I shouldn't wonder. I've seen it happen before.'

George asks Lily to dance and she can't think of a reason to say no. Up close, she can smell the alcohol on his breath.

'Are you looking forward to the voyage?' she asks, for something to say.

'It's a means to an end,' he says. 'It's pleasant enough at the moment but wait till we get to Toulon and Naples and the Jews and the Ities get on, trying to get away from Hitler. Then we'll all have to watch our backs.'

'I'm surprised you're off to New Zealand, when you're clearly so wrapped up in the political situation here,' Lily says tartly, not liking the direction the conversation is going. 'Wouldn't you prefer to stay in Europe, with everything that's going on?'

'My uncle needs help running his farm,' he says sullenly. His plump lips are wet and purple like raw liver. Now they are moving again, words coming out as if he can't stop them.

'Actually that's not the real reason. My father thinks there will be a war, so he's getting me out of the way.'

Lily is shocked. Not just because of what he's said, but because he's dared to voice it out loud. In her experience, people rarely talk openly of the probability of war, still less of how to avoid it. He stumbles now, as if also taken aback by his own admission, and she realizes how drunk he is.

When they go back on the deck Helena and Edward are nowhere to be seen. For a moment she thinks they have left her and, instantly, the joy drains from the evening. Then she spots them in the bar, queuing for drinks, and the scene springs once again to life.

'I thought I'd lost you,' she says, once she has pushed through the throng of people to get to them. To her great relief, George doesn't seem to have followed her.

'We decided to buy wine, but it's taking longer than we thought. Would you like a glass of something, Lily?'

It's warm in the bar, and claustrophobic. The loud group they'd heard earlier is still here, the same woman with the grating laugh. Now they are close up, Lily decides they are definitely from first class. It's in the cut of the women's dresses and the rustling sound they make as they move, and the languid stance of the men. Finally, Edward is served and hands them their glasses but, as they are pushing through the crowd, suddenly a roar goes up from the group at the side and a man steps back into Lily, spilling her drink all over her.

'I'm so sorry. How clumsy of me.'

Lily, who has been gazing down at her ruined dress, looks up with a jolt of recognition. It's the man from the quayside. The big man with the moustache who'd been standing with the woman in the scarlet dress. And now that everyone is gathering around, she notices that she is here too. The woman. Not in red today but in a duck-egg-blue gown that plunges at the front and wraps snugly around her narrow waist and hips before falling to the floor. Her black hair tumbles in waves over her creamy shoulders and her full mouth is the colour of ripe plums.

'Oh, Max, you are the most crashing idiot. Look what you've done. And such a lovely dress!'

Lily is astonished to hear that the woman is American. She had a few American customers at the Corner House, but somehow it doesn't fit with the picture she has painted of the woman in her head. How frustrating life is sometimes, pasting its own version of events over the top of the one you have already created, like a fresh billboard poster.

'Do forgive me. Please forgive me. What can I do to help? I am most abjectly sorry.'

To Lily's dismay, Max drops to his knees in front of her. A blonde woman with a long cigarette standing to his left lets out a distinctive shriek of laughter.

'Are you all right, Lily?' asks Helena, studying her face with her calm grey eyes.

'Well, I shouldn't think she is for a minute. Not with this great lummox splayed out on the floor in front of her,' says the American woman. 'Now, Lily. It is Lily, isn't it? You're not to worry about a thing. I'm going to take you to the powder room to get cleaned up and, in the meantime, my clumsy husband will buy you all another drink. Isn't that so, Max?'

Lily has no time to object because the woman is already holding her under the elbow and steering her away.

'She'll be back before you know it,' she calls over her shoulder to Helena and Edward in her strange, lazy, honeyed voice.

In the time it takes them to walk to the ladies' toilets at the back of the dining room Lily learns her companion's name is Eliza Campbell and that she and Max are travelling to Australia on a second honeymoon.

'Our first was in Paris and we had such an argument on the third day that I left him there in the hotel and took the train to Switzerland. It was the first train I could get on, and I arrived in Zurich with very little money and no clue what to do. Have you ever been to Zurich? It's quite the dullest place in the world, and he made me wait there three days before wiring me the money to get back!'

Eliza smells of late-summer roses and her ears sparkle with

diamonds. Lily feels ungainly by comparison. Unrefined. The spoilt dress that had earlier seemed so sophisticated now looks cheap to her eyes, the colour insipid next to Eliza's rich blue. She tries to think of something witty to say to match her tone to that of her new acquaintance, but everything sounds flat. In the Ladies Eliza wets a towel with hot water and dabs away at the discoloured silk until the worst of the stain is gone and re-pins Lily's spray of silk roses so that it covers the rest.

'Of course, you'll send us the bill for the laundry,' she says. When Lily tries to protest she presses a cool finger gently to her lips and Lily is shocked at the intimacy of it. 'If the next time I see you it's looking good as new, I'll know and you will be severely punished. You can't get away with anything on a ship, you know. Someone always finds out.'

When they get back to the bar Max is deep in conversation with Helena and Edward, their heads bent together so they can hear each other speak.

'Luckily Lily has been salvaged. I think you're forgiven, darling,' says Eliza, reaching up to kiss her husband's rugged cheek.

Lily smiles her agreement but, as she turns towards her dinner-table companions, her smile freezes upon her lips. Edward is gazing at Eliza with an expression of naked greed, as if she were an oyster he could swallow down in one deep, hungry gulp.

4

31 July 1939

WHEN LILY AWAKES, she feels different, as if the movement of the boat has entered into her body and now the blood inside her veins is swishing from side to side with that same lurching rhythm. She struggles down the ladder but, as soon as she tries to stand up, she is overcome with nausea and has to rush to the toilet, where she vomits up what seems like every little thing she has eaten or drunk over the last two days.

When she at last risks exiting, feeling hollowed out like a gourd, the young bathroom attendant tries to give her a sympathetic smile but she is too wretched to meet his gaze.

Back in her bunk, the world seems to be all off-kilter. When her eyes are open, the ceiling moves in and out of focus alarmingly, but when she tries to close them everything spins.

Audrey, too, is feeling unwell. They have paper bags tucked under their pillows which the steward has given them, and Lily remembers how Peggy Mills scoffed when telling them about her sick mother.

'I wish I'd never set foot on this boat,' says Lily when she is feeling strong enough to speak.

'And we have another five weeks or more of it!' Audrey replies, turning her head to face the wall.

Throughout that day and the next, Lily drifts in and out of consciousness. Her head feels like it is burning up and she throws off her blankets, only to be shivering minutes later, exposed to the elements. Mrs Collins comes in to see them, reassuring them that they are not, after all, about to die, but will feel perfectly fine in a day or so, when they acquire their sea-legs. Once, Lily even imagines Ida is there, laying a cool, dry hand on her fevered forehead, though afterwards she cannot tell if this, too, was just a figment of her febrile wanderings.

Towards the end of the second day there's a gentle knock on the door – well, more of a soft thud – and a young girl enters with the reddest hair Lily has ever seen and a face so crowded with freckles there hardly seems space for eyes and nose and mouth. She is wearing a yellow dress with tiny flowers on it that seems made for a much larger person and carries a small plate in one hand.

'Annie,' comes Audrey's voice, sounding much improved from the last time Lily heard it.

'I heard you've been poorly so I've brought you some dry biscuits to see if they might help. And for your friend, too, of course.'

She glances over at Lily's bunk. Lily hasn't the heart to tell her that the thought of putting anything in her mouth is enough to have her reaching for the paper bag.

Audrey, however, manages to eat a biscuit and subsequently declares herself to be feeling cautiously optimistic about the possibility of getting up.

'Are you sure you won't come with us, Lily? We can sit up on the deck under a blanket like a couple of grandmas. The fresh air might help.'

But Lily can no more imagine getting down from her bunk and making the journey upstairs than she can picture herself flying up to the moon. All through that evening and the long night that follows she lies in her bed while the air around her grows stale and her breath comes out hot and yeasty. People appear and she can no longer tell if they are real. Her parents are there, her father crying a torrent of silent tears. And now Edward is here also, his green eyes filled with so much kindness it makes her want to cry herself. She is visited by Robert and Mags, and by Eliza, who looks at her with amused pity and says, 'We must pay for you to get better. I insist.'

At one point Mrs Collins comes in to see her – although in Lily's fevered mind she might well be as much of a figment as the others. She brings with her the ship's doctor, who feels Lily's head, asks her some questions that she will later have no memory of, and gives her two tablets, which she washes down with water.

Finally, she sleeps. And when she next opens her eyes the world feels righted again, like a picture that has been hanging crooked but is now set straight.

5

2 August 1939

WEAK AFTER HER ILLNESS, she makes her way slowly up to the deck. Stepping outside, she is struck immediately by how much warmer the air is, as if someone is holding a hairdryer trained on the ship. The sun reflects off the white walls of the ship, dazzling after so long in the semi-darkness down below. She remembers the sunglasses Eliza was wearing the day they set sail and for the first time she understands what they might be for.

Canvas deckchairs have been set up the length of the deck, many of them occupied by people looking to be in much the same state as her. Some are wrapped in blankets, despite the heat, their greenish complexions and readily accessible stash of paper bags further giving their condition away.

Lily sinks gratefully into a chair, full of relief for the way the floor has stayed firm under her feet and her blood is no longer sloshing around inside her body like an overfilled bucket. She closes her eyes, enjoying the sun on her eyelids and the clean, sharp smell of the sea.

'Here you are at last!'

When Lily opens her eyes to find Edward sitting on the floor next to her chair, gazing at her with a mixture of happiness and concern, she wonders at first if this might be yet another hallucination. However, the touch of his fingertips on her forehead, checking for remnants of a fever, convinces her that he is real.

Though only two days have passed since she last saw him, he is looking noticeably healthier. His skin has lost its translucent appearance and no longer looks like it would tear if you touched it, and his cheekbones are less pronounced. Even his hair seems to have grown, though she quickly realizes that's because he has given up on trying to tame it so it falls naturally around his ears. He holds a cigarette in his hand, smoked almost to the end, and she thinks about his tuberculosis and wonders with a prick of anxiety if it's right for him to be smoking.

'I'm glad to see you. Mealtimes have been so dull without you.'

There's something new in his voice, something jarring, but she can't put her finger on it.

'Have I missed anything?'

Edward pretends to consider her question.

'Well, Mrs Mills reappeared for lunch yesterday, but she'd obviously been a little ambitious, and halfway through the salmon she had to bolt from the room with her napkin over her mouth. So then we had to babysit Peggy, and old George got into a dreadful sulk because she kept going on about how she should be sorry to miss a war if there was going to be one because she should like to see Hitler get what's coming to him. I don't know who she'd been listening to, but she had very certain opinions on it all, and because she's a child George had no option but to sit and listen. I must say, it was very satisfying.'

A shadow falls across Lily's face and she looks up, shielding her eyes with her hand.

'Well! Nice to see you up and about. I was starting to think you might be there for the duration!'

Today Ida has on a black hat with a large brim so her face remains shaded from the sun. Despite her thick black dress and stockings, she has the look of someone not quite warm enough. Cold-blooded, Lily thinks.

Lily has no option but to introduce Ida to Edward, and Ida takes this as an invitation to join them, pulling up an adjacent deckchair so close their knees are almost touching. She thinks we are friends now, Lily supposes, and the thought makes her feel cold.

'You were tossing and turning all night long,' Ida tells Lily, as though she might have done it on purpose. 'And the talking! Every time I went off to sleep you'd start shouting about something or other and wake me right back up again.'

'I'm sorry,' says Lily, helpless to know how else to respond.

'What was she saying?' Edward wants to know. 'Anything Mr Freud might be interested in?'

Again, she has the fleeting impression there is something different in his speech, but it's gone before Lily has a chance to analyse it. Besides, she has other things to think about because Ida is fixing her with her crafty smile and, before she even opens her mouth to speak, Lily knows what she's going to say.

'Who's Robert?'

'Pardon?'

Lily knows she should just make up a story, but she's so shocked to hear that name on someone else's lips that all thoughts go from her head, her mind washed as clean and smooth as a bar of soap.

'Robert. You talked about him a lot. And someone called Mags.'

It is insupportable. To hear Ida, of all people, tossing those names out as if they were apple pips. Lily puts a hand to her head.

'I'm not feeling so well.'

'You've overdone it. You must take it easy,' says Edward, concerned.

He glances over at Ida.

'We must leave her to rest,' he tells her, and gets to his feet, giving Ida no alternative but to follow suit.

After they've gone, heading in separate directions, Lily drops her head into her hands. The conversation has churned things up inside her so she fears, briefly, that the sickness has returned. She cannot help it. She has tried to brick up her heart, but one mention has the wall crumbling to the ground.

'Has she gone?'

Edward has reappeared at her side, approaching from the opposite direction to the one in which he went.

Lily nods, not trusting herself to speak, hoping he cannot tell from her face the surge of happiness that came over her at the sight of him.

'Ida is not exactly the tonic you need when you're recovering from a bout of illness,' she says.

He lowers himself into the chair Ida has just vacated. 'Think of me as your guard,' he says. 'While I'm here, no one else can bother you.'

For a moment or two Lily allows herself to indulge in this fantasy, closing her eyes and imagining him on permanent sentry duty, watching over her. But then she remembers Ida's voice saying 'Robert and Mags' and her eyes snap open again.

'Is there something troubling you, Lily?' says Edward, leaning forward in his chair so she can smell the cigarette on his breath. 'You look so worried.'

A flash of memory: Robert's arms around her, the surprising solidity of him, blood on a carpet. Screams.

'No, really, there's nothing. I'm still feeling a little weak.'

Edward nods, and leans back again. They sit in silence, gazing out through the rails of the ship to where the sea stretches out towards the horizon, glossy and smooth.

'Just think, this time tomorrow we will be arriving in Gibraltar,' says Edward, rolling the name around on his tongue like a lozenge. 'Do you know, I think this journey is going to be the most tremendous fun.'

And now Lily recognizes what is changed about him. For a moment there when he spoke he sounded just like Eliza Campbell.

6

LILY HAS SEEN photographs, but nothing has prepared her for the first sight of that great slab of rock looming up like a grey iceberg from the blue glass of the Mediterranean Sea.

'That's the most beautiful thing I ever saw. But then I guess I haven't seen much.' Audrey, as ever, says whatever is foremost in her mind. The more Lily gets to know her, the fonder of her she becomes, although sometimes she longs to coat her in varnish, as someone might French-polish a wardrobe to protect it from dents and scratches. She has discovered she is only two years older than Audrey, but she sometimes feels as if she is from a different generation altogether.

As they draw closer to the harbour Lily can see what looks like a flotilla of small boats and wonders if they are fishermen. But when the ship drops anchor and the boats surround it she notices they are full of local people selling everything from fruit to lace – items which they send up to the passengers in brightly coloured baskets. They smile and gesticulate and call to the passengers and to each other in a language that is as foreign to her as the shrieks of the birds circling above.

A woman sitting with her back against the wooden prow of her boat and a baby on her lap wrapped in an embroidered shawl catches her eye. 'Preeteemees!' she shouts, waving a silk scarf around in the air. 'Meespreetee!'

'That must be the Spanish word for scarf,' Lily says.

Helena Fletcher, who has just joined them, laughs; a low, musical sound that makes Lily realize how little she has heard it up till now.

'She's saying, "Pretty, miss."' Though whether she's talking about the scarf or you, I have no idea.'

Despite the air of sorrow that wraps itself around her, there is something deeply calming about Helena. Her wide-set grey eyes, so different to her brother's green ones, move slowly and deliberately from person to person and object to object, seemingly weighing each one up carefully and thoughtfully before going on to the next, giving each the full complement of her time, as if she is picking things up from a shelf and giving them equal appraisal. And she has a way of appearing to be both present and one step removed at the same time, both participant and witness. I should try to be more like that, Lily thinks. I should hold myself back. Yet she knows she does not possess that gift. Lily is one of life's plungers-in.

While glad of Helena's presence for her own sake, Lily cannot help looking around, alert for a sight of Edward. Though they have not made any concrete plans to go ashore together, she has been hoping for just this kind of opportunity. She did not admit it, even to herself, but she dressed with particular care this morning. Her white linen dress is lined and has long sleeves, so is really too warm for the day, but she likes the way it fits her body. And she has her favourite tortoiseshell combs in her hair. Just as she is trying to think of a way of introducing Edward into the conversation, he appears at Helena's shoulder.

'Isn't it splendid?' he asks, gesturing to the Rock and the boats and the deep navy blue of the sea.

Her eyes follow the graceful movement of his hand. It is. Splendid.

The launches go from the ship to the shore every half an hour and on board the air of anticipation is thick enough to be sliced through with a knife. Lily has an image of herself as she might appear from the outside, laughing with her friends, the light breeze coming off the azure sea blowing back her hair. Young. Carefree. Someone at the start of something. Someone for whom anything might be possible.

Stepping on to the dock, Lily has the queerest sense that her feet are still seeking out the motion of the boat, and she stumbles, only to find Edward's hand cupping her elbow, steadying her.

'It's always like that at the start,' he says. 'You'll soon get used to it.'

The harbour itself is frantic with life. Theirs isn't the only ship in the port, the launches come and go, plus the smaller boats of the hawkers, some of them looking scarcely more seaworthy than the old wooden crates that used to arrive at the Lyons Corner House packed with provisions. The ships are stocking up on fresh food and containers are being stacked up on the quayside ready to go onboard.

Lily already knew that, Gibraltar being a British colony, she wouldn't need to have her passport stamped. But still it feels strange to be somewhere so foreign, where even the air around her has a different, citrusy smell, yet still be in what is considered an offshoot of home.

Audrey and Annie want to look around the market stalls, so Lily, Edward and Helena form a trio to explore. First they head to Government House. Lily has already read about it in the literature she was sent before embarking on the voyage and is keen to see it for herself. 'It used to be a friary,' she tells the others when they arrive at the rather forbidding red-brick building. It makes a change for her to feel that she is telling them something new, rather than the other way around. She starts to show off.

'Apparently, it's haunted by a ghost the locals call the Lady in

Grey. The story is she fell in love with someone against her family's wishes and when she tried to elope with him she was found and, as a punishment, was walled up alive in one of the rooms.'

Lily is so caught up in her own story she doesn't notice Helena's pained expression until it is too late.

'I'm sorry,' she says, angry with herself for bringing up a story of lost love after what Helena has told her.

'It's fine,' says Helena, recovering. 'But can we please move on from here. There is something horribly sad about the place.'

They follow the road climbing upwards out of the town, winding around the Rock, in search of the famous monkeys. Lily tries to recapture that earlier exuberance, but something has been left behind at the stone portico of Government House. As the heat builds, reflecting white off the pale rock, so their steps become heavy and their conversation more laboured. Lily has dreamed of ascending to the very top of the Rock and seeing Africa spread out across the horizon, the Dark Continent exerting its own magnetic pull, but soon she can think only of returning to the town and the bustle and the life, and the cooling sea breeze. An irritable silence falls over the little group. Lily can feel blisters forming on her feet from her leather shoes.

As Edward and Helena stride ahead, each lost in their own world, Lily sits down on one of the benches that line the route and slides off her left shoe, rubbing her sore foot. From the corner of her eye she sees a movement. Then another. Now something is touching her shoulder. She twists around to find herself staring into the clear green eyes of a tiny macaque. 'Oh!' she exclaims. She is about to call out to the Fletchers when another larger monkey appears, clambering on to the arm of the bench, and, without further ado, starts pawing at her hair. A third joins them and, before she knows it, the three monkeys are gathered behind her, pulling at her hair with their sharp little hands. She tries to stand up but, with one shoe off, she can't balance. Panic overwhelms her.

'Ow! Stop!'

She finds her footing and stumbles away from the bench, turning around just in time to see the monkeys disappearing back into the undergrowth, two of them clutching her precious tortoiseshell combs like trophies.

Helena and Edward arrive at her side, alerted by her shouts and furious with themselves for going on ahead and not seeing the monkeys. Lily tries to explain how it felt, the monkeys' rough hands scrabbling at her skull, but it sounds comical rather than sinister and they declare themselves even more annoyed to have missed it.

To her relief, they agree to head back. As they descend Lily attempts to dispel the agitation the monkeys have stirred up in her by finding out more about her new friends. She longs to be able to place Edward in a context, to learn a little about his childhood, his home, his parents; to weave together the threads of him. But though the Fletchers answer her questions politely, their answers are unsatisfying, never quite giving her the full picture she craves. They seem fond of their mother, and afraid of their father. That is normal. Lily knows she has been lucky like that.

She gathers, after some persistent questioning, that they have money enough from their parents to spend some time looking around when they get to Australia before deciding where to settle. There is an aunt in Melbourne, they tell her, and a couple of younger cousins. But when she asks if they will be stopping in to see them when the ship docks there they are vague. The family live a distance from the town, they tell her. There is unlikely to be enough time.

Helena talks of her plans to go back, eventually, to teaching. 'The educational system might be different in Australia,' she says, 'but children are children in the end, don't you think?'

Lily is glad when they get back to the base of the Rock, where the market-sellers are lined up at the side of the road under the welcoming shade of the trees. Still shaken by her encounter with the monkeys, and conscious of her wild, combless hair, she wanders into a shop to buy some colourful postcards and afterwards stops at a stall where a dapper little man in a faded blue shirt and a wide-brimmed straw hat is selling silk scarves in every conceivable shade from vibrant red to the palest grey.

'This one very good for you,' he says, holding up a beautiful gold scarf embroidered with tiny birds in shades of orange and rust.

'Oh, no, I don't think so.'

Lily has brought money but is well aware of how long her savings will need to last her and how much of the voyage still remains.

'Yes. Good for eyes. Look!' The man holds the scarf up to Lily's face, as if even without a mirror she will be able to see how the gold picks out the amber in her eyes.

'No, really, I don't –'

'She'll take it,' says a man's voice over her shoulder.

Lily whirls around and is shocked to find herself looking into the very amused face of Max Campbell.

'You can't –' Lily begins, but he cuts across her.

'Oh, but I can, and after spoiling your lovely dress the other night it's the least I can do. Anyway, he's right. It is very good for eyes.'

He is looking so intently at her, as if he could stare right through her pupils and into her very mind, that Lily feels for a moment as if she cannot breathe. Certainly, she cannot swallow, for there is a lump in the back of her throat as large as the Rock in whose shadow they are standing.

The man in the straw hat is delighted.

'Is good you buy for your beautiful wife.'

'Oh, but I'm not –'

'You're quite right,' says Max, turning the full heat of his smile on the market-seller. 'My beautiful wife deserves beautiful things.'

He asks the price, and makes no attempt to bargain the man

down, reaching into his pocket and handing coins over without seeming even to glance at them.

Lily feels her cheeks erupting with tiny jets of heat, like liquid wax from a sputtering candle. She keeps hearing Max say that phrase 'my beautiful wife', the laughter threatening to bubble right out of his voice.

'You don't mind, do you? Please tell me you don't. You're doing me the most awfully big favour if you take this because, otherwise, I shall just have to keep on thinking of other ways to repay my debt and it will keep weighing on me until the entire voyage is ruined.'

He is holding the scarf, which is now wrapped up in paper, out towards her and she has no choice now but to look into his broad, handsome face, which houses the most extravagant smile as if he knows there will always be more smiles where that came from – so much to smile about – and he can afford to be generous.

'Thank you,' she says at last, reaching out for the package. But when her fingers close around it he doesn't let go, at least not immediately, so their hands touch, skin upon skin.

'You've found Lily! How clever of you, darling!'

At the sound of Eliza's voice Lily snatches her hand back as if burned. Eliza is wearing a pair of cream linen wide-legged trousers and a loose white peasant-style blouse that comes very low on her shoulders. Her black hair is tied back from her face and she has her sunglasses on again, so Lily can't see the expression in her eyes.

'We've been hoping to come across you, haven't we, darling? Everyone else in First is so horribly stuffy it's like being cooped up with a whole load of dusty old library books.'

'Surely there must be some young people? How about the group you were with in the bar the other night?'

Eliza makes a dismissive *pah* sound.

'Debutantes and dolts. Library-books-in-waiting.'

Edward arrives, breathing heavily, as if he has rushed over.

'Been shopping?' he says, eyeing Lily's package.

'Just a scarf,' she replies, looking at the ground.

'Now we must all have that drink,' says Eliza, hooking her arm through Edward's as if they are the best of friends.

Lily is confused. It's as if the wind has blown the pages of a book and she has jumped ahead of where she thought she was.

'We played a game of cards with Eliza and Max when you were ill in bed,' explains Helena, who has come to find them.

'Which I won, and, as the winner, I demanded that we all go for a drink in Gibraltar,' says Eliza. 'Victor's spoils.'

'I warn you, Eliza is an awful card shark,' says Max. 'And she absolutely hates to lose.'

A look passes between them, which Eliza's sunglasses render impossible to judge.

The five of them head towards a hotel which Lily had noticed earlier but dismissed as too grand. Eliza and Max and Edward are in high spirits, talking nineteen to the dozen. Walking behind with Helena, Lily sees how Edward has come alive suddenly, like a clockwork toy wound suddenly into action. He was so silent, up there on the Rock, she thinks. And now just look at him.

'Poor Lily had an alarming encounter earlier on,' says Edward, turning to her with a smile, 'with some monkeys.'

He is making a joke of it, to amuse his companions, yet to Lily it still does not feel like a joke. Tiny hands clawing at her head, yanking her hair.

'Scotch is very good for shock,' Max tells her. 'We shall get you a double.'

He winks and smiles his overflowing smile.

'Actually, I think I'll head back to the ship,' says Lily, stopping still. 'I have postcards to write. If I'm quick, perhaps I can even get them posted while we're here.'

There is a chorus of groans and 'no's.

'Please come, we won't stay long,' says Helena. Lily wavers, and looks at Edward. If he asks her to stay, she will change her mind.

'Well, if you're sure,' he says.

Lily makes her way back in the launch through the flotilla of little boats, and the shouts of the vendors: 'Miss! Miss!' *Mees, Mees.* She is glad of the breeze. And the solitude. She has been silly, she thinks, to become so attached so quickly.

Back on board, she goes straight to the lounge and sits herself at one of the little desks and writes to her parents and to Frank, before taking out her diary and filling the pages with everything that has happened. When Helena and Edward finally appear she bends her head over her desk and pretends she hasn't seen them.

7

4 August 1939

THE FOLLOWING DAY dawns clear and bright and still, as if it is
the first day in a world wiped clean. Lily is embarrassed by her
sulk of the previous afternoon. After all, Edward and Helena are nothing to her really, just pleasant people she has only recently met.
Strangers, almost. She resolves to expand her social horizons and be
open to new people. She has been too much in the Fletchers' pockets.

With her new silk scarf wound loosely around her throat and
Eliza Campbell's remark about the first-class passengers being like
dusty old books ringing in her ears, she resolves to visit the ship's
small library. She might have left school at fourteen but she has
never lost her appreciation for reading, has even nurtured a secret
dream of writing something herself one day. When she was in
domestic service she usually had a book by her bedside. Mrs Spencer
had thought it an odd request when she asked if she could borrow
something from the house's well-stocked library but she had been
happy to grant it, even turning it into a running joke with her
friends: 'I'm sure Lily will bake us one of her legendary apple
cakes – if we can tear her away from her reading!'

Mags used to shake her head when she woke up in the night and
saw Lily's lamp still on and her nose bent over the pages, eyes

straining to read the print. 'What do you see in it?' she'd ask. 'Just a load of old words, one after the other.' Her heart-shaped face peeping up from under her blankets, fair hair all tangled from sleep.

Enough.

She settles herself into a deckchair outside the library with her chosen book, a recent Agatha Christie called *Appointment with Death.* She is not a big fan of mysteries, but she is intrigued enough by the fact the book is set in the Middle East and thinks it might be suitable to read in the heat of the Mediterranean sun. She uses as a bookmark the letter from her mother she found lying on her pillow after the ship had pulled away from Gibraltar. The letter does not say much, a few lines about their journey back home from Tilbury Docks, a bit about Frank getting a promotion at Huntley & Palmers, the huge biscuit factory by the river in Reading where he's been grudgingly working for eighteen months. The real meaning of the letter is in the writing itself, the uneven, blue, slanting words that climb unsteadily up to the right of the page, the effort Lily knows it costs her barely educated mother to form them.

The sea is perfectly still. Above it, sounds are suspended in the unmoving air: the squeals of childish excitement from the swimming pool on the upper deck, the tick-ticking of a tea trolley as a steward does his rounds. Time washes pleasantly over her like a warm bath until, looking up from her book, she sees Ida further up the deck, heading for the lounge. Before she can duck her head Ida spots her and changes direction, failing to notice the wooden leg of a low-slung canvas chair protruding where it has been moved forward, out of line with the others. *Oh.* Lily makes a noise that is louder than an exclamation but falls just short of a warning as Ida launches full length through the air, landing with a sickening crash as her head hits one of the pillars that hold up the ship's awning, her skirts and petticoat lifted, pipe-cleaner legs in yellowing wrinkled stockings shamefully on display.

Lily's mind urges her forward to help pick Ida up, even while her feet remain fixed to the ground as if stuck there by glue. She knows how much Ida, with all her straight-backed pride, will hate being brought down like this in public. Eventually she forces herself to move but finds someone else has got there before her. A woman has jumped up from one of the chairs close by and is kneeling on the grubby deck next to Ida's prone body.

'Please allow me to help you,' she is saying, in a strange, thick accent. 'You know, I did just the same thing myself only yesterday, and I didn't fall nearly as gracefully as you.'

Lily can tell she is trying to lessen Ida's embarrassment, but Ida is having none of it.

'I shall be quite all right, thank you very much.'

Ida deliberately ignores the woman's outstretched hand as she pulls herself to her feet, using the pillar as support. Lily sees how humiliation has set her narrow face hard and wishes she could warn the woman to step back. Yet she persists.

'Are you sure you're not hurt? You took quite a fall.'

'I am completely fine, I assure you.' Ida's mouth snaps shut like a trap.

'Shall we sit down here while you recover?' Lily finds her tongue at last. But if anything, Ida looks only more affronted at Lily's interjection.

'What would I need to sit down for? I was on my way to my cabin. I have several chores to complete.'

It is a lie. But, still, as Ida rushes off, Lily feels light-headed with relief.

She sinks down heavily into the nearest chair and the woman who'd tried to help Ida reclaims her own seat next to it. They exchange a glance which seems to encompass all the complexities of the scene that has just passed. Now Lily has a chance to look at her companion properly she sees that she has a long face, with long, thin features to match. Her close-set eyes look out through a pair of round tortoiseshell spectacles and her thick black hair is piled on top of her head like a cloud of cushion stuffing. Yet somehow the overall effect is pleasing rather than off-putting, the various odd-shaped components slotting perfectly together like a particularly satisfying jigsaw.

The woman introduces herself as Maria Katz. 'I hope I didn't offend your friend,' she says. 'Not friend,' says Lily, and is embarrassed by her own sharpness. Maria has a novel open on the table next to her, the new Daphne du Maurier, which Lily has already read, and soon they are deep in discussion. Lily is astonished at the number of books Maria has read and how engagingly she talks about them, as if they are old friends rather than inanimate objects, until Maria reveals that she grew up in Vienna in an apartment with 'a library as big as a ballroom'.

After this revelation she grows quieter, her thin lips pressing together as if to stop words from coming out.

'My father does not want to leave his books behind,' she says softly. 'That's why they are still there.'

Now she explains to Lily that her family is Jewish. Lily has heard whispers of worrying things happening to the Jews in Germany and Austria and now Czechoslovakia, but it has never seemed real to her; it's been something quite removed. Listening to Maria describe how she and her sister and her sister's family fled first to Prague and then, when that too fell under Nazi control, to London, leaving behind their beloved parents and their home, Lily is ashamed of her ignorance. No, not ignorance, because that would imply she had never been presented with the truth rather than her choosing not to see it. She is ashamed of her own lack of curiosity.

'I have not heard from my parents for more than two months now,' says Maria. 'The not knowing is very hard. I have nightmares sometimes, where I hear footsteps behind me. Chasing. Always chasing.'

Maria's sister is staying behind in East London. Her little nephews have started school. They are becoming settled there. They have a small apartment. Even a piano. But Maria, like Lily, has a thirst for adventure.

'When you have to give up everything that is important to you, it is awful, obviously. But in a way it is also liberating. In Austria we had a great many things. Beautiful things. Paintings, books, furniture, clothes. I had a dog, too, an ugly little creature with a face like this.'

She uses a finger to push the tip of her nose up like a snout and goggles her eyes comically, making Lily burst out giggling despite herself. Then she resumes:

'Those things – the books, the ugly dog – kept us rooted in our home, so much so that my parents could not leave. Even though . . .'

Maria stops. Inhales deeply. Releases.

'Now I have nothing. But I am free.'

A cousin of Maria's has started up a small publishing company in Melbourne and sent her money to join him there as his assistant. Maria flushes when she tells Lily of her hopes that one day she might write a book. 'How else to make sense of this strange, changing world, if not to write about it?' she says. For a moment Lily thinks of confiding her own writing ambitions but at the last minute she stops, afraid of putting into words something she has never told anybody. Instead Lily tells her about the assisted-passage scheme and the domestic work that awaits her in Sydney. 'I hope not to do it for long,' she can't help adding. 'Just while I'm settling.'

Maria smiles.

'New starts for us both,' she says. 'And in the meantime we sit in the sunshine and eat lovely food and listen to music and read books. It's not such a bad life.'

'I feel very frivolous,' Lily tells her, honesty compelling her to speak, although she regrets her choice of word. 'My reasons for leaving home are so selfish compared to yours.'

Maria fixes Lily with her eyes from behind her spectacles and Lily can see they are rich brown like treacle.

'On a boat like this,' she says, 'everyone is running away from something.'

At lunch Lily tells Helena and Edward about her encounter. George Price listens with an expression of growing disgust.

'The Jews have brought it on themselves,' he says. 'Growing richer while everyone else starved. Hoarding their money and their art without loyalty to the countries they live in. This ship is crawling with Jews. I never expected they would be here, in the same class as all of us.'

Lily wants desperately to respond but does not know how. She wishes now that she was better informed so she could knock George's remarks straight back at him. Her 'Well, she seemed very nice to me' sounds shallow and weak.

George follows her out on to the deck after lunch. She had been hoping for a chat with Edward and Helena but instead she finds herself stranded by the railings with George blocking her route back.

'I can see you're a well-meaning sort of girl,' George tells her, 'but you haven't seen much of the world. You don't know the history of these things. I would hate to see you being taken advantage of. So I'm advising you to stick with your own kind. I'm happy to show you the ropes, if you like.'

Lily thinks of the way Maria's face looked when she talked about her parents still in Vienna, and her dog and her books.

'Thank you, George,' she says, 'but I'm quite capable of choosing my own friends.'

And now George's face is passing from red to purple, the blood flowing thick from his wounded pride. Robert was like this, she remembers suddenly. Not in the things he said, obviously. Or the person he was. But in the certainty of being right. And the dislike of being challenged.

'Can I borrow Lily for a while? We need her to make up a four for cards.'

Edward has appeared at George's shoulder. For a second George glares at him, as if minded to say no, but there is nothing about Edward's mild demeanour or slight stature to allow purchase for his anger and he reluctantly steps away.

They have gone several yards before Lily allows herself to relax.

'Thank you,' she whispers. 'I thought I should be stuck there for the rest of my life. It was a good ruse. The cards, I mean.'

'Oh, no, that's not an excuse. Well, what I mean is, it's a very fortuitous excuse as I could tell you needed rescuing. Eliza and Max have asked us to join them upstairs for a game of cards. Helena is resting. She's not feeling well, so we are missing a fourth player. You will come, won't you?'

Lily hesitates, remembering Max's wink from the day before, her own unease. Then she checks herself. Isn't she here on this ship seeking adventure? The Campbells are so different from the kind of people she would normally mix with. This is an opportunity to open her mind.

Edward is still gazing at her uncertainly, and she sees suddenly how he might have looked as a child, wanting to be sure that everything is all right, that all is well.

'Of course I'll come.'

On the way up to the first-class deck she wishes she'd changed first, or at least brushed her hair, windswept from standing so long next to the railings. She regrets wearing the new gold silk scarf. What if Max Campbell reads some kind of message into it? She has on her midnight-blue dress with the white trim and worries it is too dowdy. As if he can sense her thoughts, Edward turns to her. 'How well you look now your skin has caught the sun a little. Everything about you is the colour of honey.'

Lily knows that it is not uncommon for tourist-class passengers to be invited to the upper deck. Some people she has met have friends travelling in First and regularly join them for after-dinner coffee. Yet still, when they join Max and Eliza in the sumptuously appointed lounge, she cannot shake off the notion that everyone is watching them. It takes her back to being at school again, the looks that mean her clothes are wrong, the way her parents speak is wrong.

Eliza is in yellow today. A summer dress with a tight-fitting bodice and a skirt that flares out from the narrow waist. The dress has a square neckline under which the ridges of her collarbones protrude, smooth like ivory.

'I'm so glad you came, Lily,' she says, leaning forward to wrap one of her cool hands over Lily's. 'I was so worried we'd driven you away yesterday. My husband can be very overbearing sometimes. I hope you didn't think he was going to hold you down and pour Scotch down your throat against your will!'

'No, of course not.'

Eliza's eyes are the most curious colour, by turns navy and then appearing almost violet, like a taffeta gown that changes shade according to the light.

Lily has been nervous about seeing Max again, but he is in a subdued humour and barely seems aware that she's there. Ever observant, Edward notices the difference in him. 'Are you well, Max?' he asks.

'Yes, fine.' Max practically snaps the words out and Lily senses Edward stiffen on the sofa next to her. He will not like being rebuffed in front of Eliza, she thinks.

As they start playing cards the atmosphere lightens, although

Lily is still painfully aware of the curious stares from the other passengers. Her hand goes to her hair, smoothing it down. She tightens the scarf around her throat.

'It suits you,' says Max. 'I knew it would.'

He is sitting opposite her, smiling, and his eyes are like chips of blue glass from a broken vase. Lily can sense Eliza watching her and her mouth feels suddenly ash-dry.

Edward tells the Campbells about rescuing Lily from George Price, and then of course Lily has to explain about meeting Maria on the deck that morning.

'A Jew?' says Eliza. 'Oh, we have those.'

Seeing Lily's bafflement, she elaborates. 'In the States, I mean. I befriended one once, mostly to scandalize my father. He was frightfully clever – the Jew, that is – but such a bore. Could never go out on a Friday night. I'd say, "Can't you just take one Friday off and do your praying, or whatever it is you do, on a Monday or Tuesday to make up for it?", but he never would.'

'I don't think it quite works like that,' laughs Edward.

The afternoon passes, as such afternoons do. Groans when the cards are bad, exclamations of delight when a hand is won. When Eliza loses three hands in a row her interest ebbs.

'Cards are so dull, aren't they?' she says, shaking out the skirt of her egg-yolk-yellow dress. 'So many petty rules and regulations.' And then, a few minutes later: 'I'm so glad we're stopping at Toulon tomorrow. These games are intolerable.'

Two hands later, when she loses again, she rounds on her husband.

'Watch out for Max. He's the most terrible cheat.'

The first-class lounge is much larger than the one on the lower deck. The sofas are soft and plump and thickly upholstered in velvet of a deep claret colour, and in addition there are chaises longues and armchairs. A string quartet plays in the far corner, the searing notes of the violin rising above the hum of chatter. Stewards walk around bearing silver trays on which balance drinks and teapots and cigarettes. Two small girls in identical dresses, their sunburnt faces betraying the reason they are in here and not splashing in the swimming pool with the rest of their peers, play pattercake on a sofa, their small hands slapping rhythmically together.

While they play cards, people come and go around them. First a young couple, she with a noticeably rounded belly, then three elderly women already hungry for their dinner, and still later a family who sit in silence, conversation either exhausted or unnecessary. Yet despite the montage of changing faces Lily cannot shake off the uncomfortable sense of being stared at. It is only after the game finishes and she and Edward take their leave that something makes her look back as they reach the exit to the deck – some need, perhaps, to commit the scene to memory so that she might describe it better in her letters home – and she makes a most perplexing discovery.

It isn't, after all, she and Edward who are the objects of the other passengers' relentless narrow-eyed scrutiny.

It is the Campbells themselves.

8

5 August 1939

L ILY IS AWOKEN by the clinking sound of the cabin steward delivering tea. To her dismay, she realizes even before opening her eyes that the sickness is back, although this time it seems as if it is her head rather than her stomach that is at the centre of things.

She raises herself on to her elbows, hoping that the dizziness will right itself, but though she feels less queasy than before, her skin is clammy, her temperature lurching within the space of a minute from freezing to boiling and down again.

'Just another hour or so and we'll arrive at Toulon,' says the steward, a perpetually cheerful man with a round face from which his two ears protrude on either side like the handles of a Toby jug. In addition to the tea cups that crowd his tray, there are also leaflets, which he distributes to Lily, Audrey and Ida, on which there is a map of the area and directions from the wharf to the town.

'Will you be getting up, miss?' he asks Lily, concerned. From her vantage point on the top bunk she can see he has a bald patch on the top of his head the size of one of the saucers he is handing out. 'It might do you good to be on solid ground again. And we pull in right to the wharf so you only need to walk down the gangplank and you're there.'

Audrey declares that she and Annie will look after Lily when they go ashore, which immediately prompts Ida to retort that Annie doesn't look capable of looking after a goldfish and that Lily will be in much safer hands if Ida herself takes care of her. Ida has made no secret of her low opinion of Audrey's new friend, who was late starting in paid work, having stayed at home to help take care of her younger siblings, and so has never progressed beyond kitchen maid.

Eventually, it is decided that the four of them will go ashore together. Lily is too weak to resist and only grateful that, by sticking with Audrey and the others, she won't risk being swept up by the Campbells, but by the time she is dressed and making her way slowly down the steep gangplank, one hand clutching the rail and the other holding on to Audrey's arm, Lily already knows it is a mistake. Though the sun is hidden by a bank of high grey cloud and there's a persistent breeze that causes goosebumps to pop up like tiny bubbles on the skin of her arm, Lily's forehead burns.

This time, when she steps on to solid ground, she is expecting that sensation of her body still imitating the movement of the sea. Even so, she sways for a few seconds until Ida, of all people, puts a hand on her arm to steady her.

'Still feel like you're rocking? When you've travelled as I have, you don't notice it any more.'

Ida has not mentioned her fall the previous day, and Lily knows better than to bring it up.

Some of the passengers have prearranged coach tours to Nice. As she watches them file on to the waiting buses, Lily is grateful she isn't one of them. Just the thought of spending hours on a coach negotiating the hairpin bends she has seen on the map makes her feel nauseous. Instead, they follow the rest of the passengers and head in the direction of the town. To the surprise of the others, Ida announces that she speaks French but, when they stop some local women to ask directions to the post office so that they can mail their letters home, Ida's speech is sparse and halting, and the women at first shrug their shoulders before launching into a torrent of incomprehensible words.

'They said this way,' says Ida, pointing up ahead, but Lily has seen her expression and knows she is guessing.

After Audrey approaches an elderly man and shows him an envelope, pointing to the space where the stamp should be and miming the question 'Where?', they make it to the post office and, after that, to a small café. As they thread their way across the terrace, Lily's eye is drawn to a folded newspaper someone has left behind on a table. The headline is in French, so she cannot understand it, but there's no mistaking Hitler's furious stare in the accompanying photograph, and a chill passes through her. The four women settle themselves down and try to order tea but, on being met with blank looks from the waiter, a good-looking young fellow with a strutting walk, switch to lemonade instead.

The first sip feels wonderfully cooling to Lily's fevered head but, by the time she is halfway through the glass, she is already shivering.

'That waiter is looking at you, Lily,' whispers Audrey. She and Annie glance over towards the bar and giggle.

'I'm sure it's not me he has his eye on,' says Lily. 'I don't think anyone would be looking at me in the state I'm in now. Except maybe a doctor wanting to study me for medical research.'

They all laugh, but Ida fixes Lily with her black eyes, glittery as marbles.

'Nonsense. You're an attractive girl, Lily. In fact, I'm quite surprised you haven't left anyone behind. A husband or sweetheart. How old are you? Twenty-five? Twenty-six? You're not getting any younger.'

Despite her physical debility and feelings of self-pity, Lily nevertheless finds herself fighting a sudden surge of laughter at

Ida's bluntness. She puts her hand to her mouth as if to stopper it up.

'Oh, Lily, I hope we haven't upset you,' says Audrey, misinterpreting her gesture.

After Lily reassures her that this is far from the case, Audrey returns to the subject, shyly, as if she is testing thin ice to see if it will hold.

'So has there been someone, Lily? Someone special?'

In anyone else this might seem like prying, but there is something so artless about big, ungainly Audrey, with her mess of fair hair, and those blue eyes so pale, like they've been washed too many times, Lily can't find it in herself to object.

'Please tell,' says Annie, sweeping a lock of red hair from her face. They want romance, Lily thinks to herself. Girls like these are alive to it.

'Any proposals?' adds Annie eagerly.

And now, here in Lily's fever-fuelled mind, she is sitting with Robert in the park while he ties a blade of grass around her ring finger. 'We will get married,' he tells her. 'One day.'

'No,' she says abruptly, snapping closed the shutter to the past. 'None.'

Ida has been watching with her usual intense stare, as if Lily is a rare bird she wishes to inventory and tag.

'Well, I think there's someone on the ship who has taken quite a shine to you,' she says now. Ida has a way of talking as if she is calculating the weight of each word as she goes along.

'Who?' Sniffing a love story, Annie is desperate to find out more.

'That one from her dinner table.' She turns to Lily. 'I've seen the way he looks at you.'

She makes it sound like something unsavoury, something Lily has invited that she should not have. But still it doesn't stop the rush of pleasure Lily feels, piercing her aching bones, her heavy, broiling body. All through her incarceration in bed, she had not allowed herself to think of Edward Fletcher. She remembered how taken he'd seemed with Eliza Campbell, and told herself it was as well she had discovered that now, before she allowed herself to get carried away, imagining things that didn't exist. But Ida's words have ignited a treacherous flare of hope.

'I really don't think Edward has any interest in me,' she says.

'Edward? Is he the one with the dark curls? Oh, he's very handsome,' says Annie, smiling, so that the freckles over her nose join together to form one continuous brown stain.

'Not him.'

Ida makes a movement with her hand as if swatting a fly.

'I'm talking about the other one. Him with the squashed-in nose and the raspberry cheeks.'

And, just like that, the pleasure drains from Lily as suddenly as it arrived, leaving a hollow in its place where the cold now gathers. They are sitting at an outside table but the sun is still masked by cloud and Lily shivers when the gusts of cool breeze hit her skin.

She wishes she could go home. Not to that narrow bunk in that airless, constantly moving cabin. Not even to the damp room in Bayswater. But to the terraced house in Reading where her mother would sit on the side of her bed and stroke the damp hair from her eyes and tell her that soon she'd be right as rain.

'I think we should get you back now,' says Ida, and, not for the first time, Lily has the disconcerting idea that the older woman can read in her face exactly what she is thinking. Such a strange mixture she is, this Ida. Astute but intrusive, tactless but sensitive to things others do not seem to notice.

As they get to their feet and make their way out of the café Ida's fingers curl tightly around Lily's arm, as if she might crack it like a nut.

9

7 August 1939

H OW QUICKLY ONE becomes accustomed to an alien reality until it is the old, familiar world that now seems unreal. It has been scarcely more than a week, but when Lily thinks about her life in London – the buses, the fog, the crowds at Piccadilly Circus on a weekend night – it has the feel of something imagined from a book or remembered from a film, not anything that touches her personally. Instead, what is real is this: the clean brightness of the day as she steps out on the deck in the morning, the gentle movement of the boat under her feet, the way she feels cleansed by that first breath of fresh, salty sea air.

Lily makes her way to the railing and leans out, enjoying the cool patter of the spray on her face, the endless blue carpet of water stretching in every direction.

'Can you see Italy yet? Not long until Naples,' comes a voice from behind.

She turns and sees Maria Katz seated in a deckchair, her cloud of hair tethered down by an emerald-green headscarf, a book open face down on her lap.

Lily looks again. Now that Maria has mentioned the possibility of Italy, Lily starts to doubt her own vision. Might that not be land? That dark streak on the horizon?

She pulls up a chair next to Maria.

'You have been ill once again, Lily?'

Maria has a way of angling her head down when she talks to you so that her eyes are looking up into yours and her brow is raised as if in a perpetual question or wonder.

Lily finds herself telling Maria all about the ill-fated trip to the café in Toulon, about Ida and Audrey and the staring waiter. When she mentions the folded newspaper and Hitler's face, Maria grows still.

'Do you mind if I join you?'

Helena Fletcher stands by the empty chair next to Lily. Today she is wearing a severe black skirt with a plain white blouse. It is an outfit Lily's mother might have worn. Why does Helena insist on being old before her time? Lily asks herself again. She supposes it has to do with lost love and with nothing seeming worth the effort now that he is no longer there to see.

Lily makes the introductions between Helena and Maria and is pleased to find that they seem instantly to take to one another. They have a similar quiet intelligence. And both have suffered, though Helena wears her suffering wrapped around her like a blanket, buffering her from the world, while Maria's is like a hair shirt that only she knows to be there.

The two discover they have something else in common. Maria, too, has taught children, though she had to stop when she came to England. They talk happily together, comparing amusing stories about naughty pupils and demanding head teachers. While they talk, Lily leans back in her chair and allows the sun to warm her face, burnishing her closed eyelids orange. She remembers how Edward had said, 'Everything about you is the colour of honey,' and how the corners of his mouth lifted up and tiny lines appeared around his eyes like tucks in a skirt.

'Have you seen my brother today, Lily?'

Lily starts. Has she been speaking aloud? The thought makes something tighten in her chest.

'No. I've only just got up.'

Helena frowns. There are deep purple grooves at either side of her nose that are visible only when she lets her face fall. Lily watches as she worries at one of them with the end of one of her long fingers, rubbing the pad hard against the discoloured skin.

'You are looking for the man who is always with you, Helena.'

Lily is beginning to realize that, when Maria makes a statement, it is just as likely to be a question. Something lost in the translation from German to English, she imagines.

'Forgive me. I don't wish to sound like a spy, but I like to observe people.'

'Maria is a writer,' Lily tells Helena, with a degree of pride.

'Lily is too generous. I am someone who wishes to be a writer. I have seen you and he often together, Helena. He was here earlier, sitting very close by. But then he went up to the top deck.'

Lily has been listening alertly to this exchange, but now her spirits flatten into disappointment. It seems to her as if Eliza Campbell believes she can summon him like a little dog. She pictures her now, with her taffeta eyes and that heavy floral scent and her intoxicating, lazy way of talking. Why wouldn't he come running? she thinks.

Helena's thoughts appear to be following the same lines. Her grey eyes look slack with worry and a deep vertical line has appeared on her forehead.

'Was he with Mrs Campbell?' she asks. 'The lady with the black hair?'

Maria shakes her head. 'No, it was a man. Big, with a loud voice and a moustache.'

Helena doesn't seem much comforted by the news.

'I wish he would keep away from there,' she says, her grey eyes darting up in the direction of the upper deck, as if she might be able to see him through the decking and the railings and the rugs and the velvet and the curtains.

'I worry that they aren't very kind people. The Campbells,' Helena tells Maria. The words come out in a rush, as if she hasn't had time to consider them. 'Edward is too trusting. He gets involved with people too quickly. He isn't well, still.'

She addresses this last to Lily.

'But he's cured, surely?'

Lily seems to have taken a leaf from Maria's book, her question emerging from her lips as a statement of fact.

Helena raises her hand to her hair, which is again piled haphazardly on her head, seemingly without care.

'I fear he won't ever be completely cured,' she says.

Lily wants to ask more but a shout goes up from a child standing by the railings.

'Land! I see land! Italy!'

The three of them get to their feet and join the other passengers peering over the side of the boat. And oh, but it is beautiful. Lily's unasked questions die on her lips as the boat draws nearer and they can make out the towering cliffs, some topped with green trees, others studded with houses clinging perilously to the sides. The city of Naples itself is slung across the bay like a hammock, and there, hulking in the distance, the dark mound of Vesuvius, silhouetted against the blue sky.

Edward appears behind them.

'Isn't it wonderful?' says Lily, for once not caring if she gives herself away as a sheltered girl from the provinces who has seen nothing of the world.

'It is, Lily,' Edward replies, smiling. He rests his hand briefly on her bare arm – she is wearing a short-sleeved blouse today with her navy linen skirt. Her skin burns under his light touch.

Lily has booked in advance to go on a tour of Pompeii. She remembers sitting down with her parents with the information the shipping company had sent spread out on the table in front of them, deciding which trips to take, and how her mother had pored over the photographs of the destroyed city. 'I can't believe my daughter will be seeing all these things for herself,' she'd said. 'All these wonders.'

To Lily's delight, it transpires that the Fletchers and Maria are also booked on the tour. After much fussing and to-ing and fro-ing to cabins for cameras and watches and jackets, they assemble on the dock, along with another fifteen or so passengers. Lily feels guilty when Audrey and Annie walk past with Ida tagging behind, and Audrey makes a face as if to say, *Look who we're lumbered with!* Their guide, an excitable Italian called Antonio who speaks impeccable English with a musical accent, assures them they are about to see one of the greatest sights in the world.

'You will be astonished, I think,' he tells them. Lily repeats the words in her head. *Aston-eeshd.*

After leaving the wide, open space of the docks, where the sun sparkles off the sea and the sky seems never-ending, the coach turns into the city, where the roads grow shabbier and darker and peeling 'Viva Il Duce!' posters are plastered over the lamp posts and walls, until they reach the backstreets, so narrow Lily doesn't know how in the world the driver manages to pass through them, with washing strung out across the top of them like tattered vines, from the windows on one side to the windows on the other.

'I didn't realize it would be so poor,' Lily tells Maria, who is sitting next to her, as they pass two undersized children dressed in rags sitting on a step, watching the bus with impassive faces. She has seen poverty in London, of course, but somehow this seems more unpalatable, butting up grey and ugly against the glittering jewels of the coast.

'Poverty is always shocking,' Maria says. 'And if that stops being the case, then there's no hope for any of us.'

Lily is relieved when the bus starts to wind its way up out of the city, leaving the grime and the grubby, sharp-boned children behind. As the bus climbs higher, she becomes aware of an unpleasant smell, like bad eggs.

'If you are smelling something at this moment and hoping it will go away, you need to get used to it, because this is sulphur,' the guide tells them, explaining how poisonous gas that had built up inside Vesuvius caused it to erupt, burying the city under volcanic ash and pumice.

When they arrive at Pompeii itself, Lily is silenced by the feel of the place, the bones of the city so perfectly preserved, its secrets open to view nearly two thousand years after it was destroyed, and by the sinister, looming presence of Vesuvius in the distance, belching out smoke. As the relentless sun beats down, she and Maria follow Edward and Helena in the shadeless dust through what had once been streets teeming with life, looking into houses, many still with their intricate mosaic floors intact. They see the plaster casts of people frozen for ever in time by the molten lava and ash, their bodies contorted by fear. There is a man reclining on a marble slab, naked apart from a fig-leaf posthumously applied to cover his modesty. There is even a little dog, which Lily gazes at for a long time, wondering whether it knew something was about to happen to it, whether it was scared.

For some reason the little dog makes her think of Mags, and how frightened she was. Scarcely more than a child. Her eyes stretched wide, locked on to Lily's own. *Am I going to die, Lil?* And Lily shaking her head. What else could she do?

'If the ladies would like to enter into that house there, you will find some cooking things that might interest you,' says Antonio, the guide. Wilting with the heat, Lily watches as he then leads the men, including Edward, into another building a short distance away.

When they reconvene, some of the men are smirking, but Edward looks embarrassed and doesn't meet her eye.

'What was in there?' asks Lily, desperate to know, but he just shakes his head.

'Nothing you'd want to see.'

When everyone else has gone on Lily doubles back and ducks inside the two-storey building the men have visited. At first she cannot see what might have deserved such interest, then she notices the walls of the largest room are covered in frescoes. On closer inspection these are revealed to be pictures of naked men and women engaged in sexual relations of a type and variety that make Lily clasp her hand to her mouth. Couples, groups, even animals. Though she knows she should leave, Lily stands rooted to the spot, like the stone villagers themselves, and despite the coolness of the interior she blazes with heat. One picture in particular holds her attention. In it a powerfully built man kneels up behind a pale woman who is leaning forward on her hands and knees, her face almost on the floor. Though his face is indistinct, in the long seconds before she finally tears herself away, she clearly sees Max Campbell's features superimposed on it.

'You found the brothel then?' whispers Maria, amused, when Lily rejoins them. Lily feels instantly as if she will dissolve in a pool of embarrassment. She has heard of such places, of course. She is not naive. Not any more. But she has never heard the word said out loud. And by a woman!

'I had no idea,' she says, noting how Maria's amusement seems to grow in step with her own mortification. 'How did you—?'

'I researched it before we came,' Maria says. 'It's lucky that London has such excellent public libraries.'

There is a small shop on the way back to the coach, selling

exquisite cameos carved either from shells or from Mount Vesuvius lava. Though they are too expensive for her, Lily runs her fingers over them, enjoying the smoothness of the finish and the delicate bumps of the reliefs. By the exit, Edward and Helena are deep in conversation with Maria. Still unsettled by what she saw in the ancient brothel, and by her own reaction to it, Lily lingers, glad of a few moments of solitude.

'Excuse me.' The voice belongs to an elderly woman wearing a velvet suit in a deep plum colour that looks good quality but in which she must be, Lily thinks, roasting on a day like this. The woman has on a matching hat, beneath which her cheeks, as if affected by the proximity to the rest of the outfit, have taken on a similar red-wine shade.

Lily gives a hesitant half-smile.

'I recognized you from the other day,' the woman goes on. 'You and your husband were in the first-class lounge playing cards.'

'Oh, he's not my husband.'

Lily doesn't know why it should feel so important that she explain herself to this stranger, but she cannot bear the idea that Edward might overhear and think she is deliberately misrepresenting herself – and him.

The woman raises her eyebrows and pulls back her chin so that it nestles in the cushion of her neck.

'I see. Whatever the case, I feel I must speak to you.'

She saw me in that building, Lily thinks, hot-faced.

'I'm sorry if I –'

It is as if she hasn't spoken. The woman ploughs on, cutting right through the middle of Lily's sentence.

'I don't know how much you know of the Campbells, but I must tell you that in society – that is, polite society – they are very much avoided. There was a terrible scandal.'

'Josephine!' A disgruntled man is bearing down on them, irritation exuding from every one of his large pores. 'I've been waiting outside in the blasted sun for so long it's a wonder I haven't got heatstroke. Are you coming?'

He hardly glances at Lily. The woman takes his arm to leave, but hesitates.

'You seem like a nice girl. Trusting. I couldn't live with myself if I hadn't warned you. They might seem glamorous and exciting, but the truth is the Campbells are very dangerous people.'

Lily makes her way back to the coach in a state of agitation and is relieved to see that the woman and her husband are not joining them but have hired a private taxi and guide. Still, she cannot shake off the memory of those mottled cheeks and the way she'd said that phrase, 'terrible scandal', in a voice so loud it might have awoken even Pompeii's two-thousand-year dead.

In one way the new information clears up a few mysteries. It explains why the other passengers were scrutinizing them so intently and also the Campbells' frequent appearances on the lower deck. Not because the company in first class is so stuffy but because they are excluded from it. But while it answers some questions, it creates still others. What scandal could have made the Campbells so thoroughly ostracized? And why are they dangerous?

Maria also seems preoccupied as the coach begins its descent back towards the streets of Naples, the fingers of one hand worrying at the skin around the nails of the other.

'Just think of it,' she'd said to Lily as they walked to the gift shop, 'a whole community obliterated.' And Lily knew she was thinking of her own home in Vienna and her parents still clinging stubbornly on while the city empties around them.

Lily is in a window seat on the wrong side of the coach, where the sun blazes in and there is no hiding place. Edward and Helena are two rows ahead, and she finds herself staring at the back of Edward's head, where his hair curls over his collar and at his narrow shoulders, so expressive when he is talking, like an extension of his hands. Her mind flits, before she can stop it, back to one of the frescoes in the brothel in which a naked woman was lying back with her legs spread wide and there in the centre was the back of a man's head, with dark, curling hair, just like Edward's.

No, she tells herself firmly. No, I must not.

And yet.

She remembers Robert and how his hands had worked their way under her skirt, his fingers thick and probing. 'It's all right,' he'd said, his breath uneven against her ear. 'I'll be careful. We'll get married.' But Lily had thought of her parents and her job and her friend Molly, the only other scholarship girl in her class, forced into a marriage at sixteen with a boy she didn't really like because there was a baby on the way. Of her mother's shame. And she'd pushed Robert's hands away. Though she hadn't wanted to.

What if that is to be her only experience of sex? Those fumblings with Robert that left them both panting and unfinished? She closes her eyes against the fierce sun so her thoughts are painted orange. They turn to the frescoes again, and she remembers how that one had seemed like Max Campbell, broad and bronzed and overspilling with lust. And now she's seeing again the back of Edward's hair, but the woman whose legs it is buried between is no longer the woman in the painting but Eliza Campbell, head thrown back in pleasure.

'Are you all right, Lily?' Maria is looking at her curiously. 'You fell asleep and cried out.'

'Yes, I am fine,' Lily says, the words snapping out sharply.

Maria leans back in her seat and looks away.

When they arrive at the ship the dock is crowded with people, many of them carrying large bundles. 'The new Italian passengers. Our steward told us they'd be boarding at Naples,' Helena whispers as they make their way through the voluble crowd.

'There seem to be a great many pregnant women,' Lily observes.

Maria explains that most of the Italian women will be going to join their husbands, who are working as cane-cutters in Queensland, so they time their crossings to make the most of the ship's doctor. The four of them fall to speculating about what nationality the children would be, born of Italian parents onboard a British ship, and Lily begins to relax. She wonders whether she should tell Edward about her strange encounter in the shop in Pompeii but she doesn't yet trust herself to talk collectedly about that place. I will tell him at dinner, she thinks, imagining an amusing conversation where they will all take turns at guessing what the Campbells might have done, this 'terrible scandal'.

But when dinner arrives Edward seems in no humour for conversation, amusing or otherwise, sitting wrapped up in his own thoughts two seats away, while Helena takes the place next to Lily.

George Price is in full flow, holding forth about the ship being overrun with 'Ities', even though, as far as Lily can tell, there aren't more than thirty on board, and their cabins are on a lower deck even than tourist class, with a separate, smaller dining room all of their own. 'You'd better keep an eye on your valuables,' he says. 'They're like magpies. Known for it. And don't any of you ladies let yourselves get in a situation where you're on your own with an Itie man. They simply have no self-control when it comes to that sort of thing.' He glares meaningfully at young Peggy Mills, as if stopping himself saying more on her account.

Clara Mills, who looks even more fragile and bird-like than she'd first appeared after her long bout of seasickness, makes a gasping noise.

'If I'd known the voyage would be so fraught, I'd have insisted my husband come back to accompany us,' she says. 'It's so hard being a woman alone.'

Then she glances at Lily and Helena. 'What I mean is a woman alone in charge of a child.'

Throughout all this, Edward remains silent and, though he smiles at Lily when he catches her eye, it lacks its usual warm energy. Lily remembers what Helena had said that morning about him never being completely cured and worries that he has overdone things. The day has been so long and the sun so strong, and the plaster figures twisted in fear were indisputably disturbing.

Finally, he speaks.

'I wonder what the Campbells got up to in Naples today. It feels strange to have no word from them this evening when we have all been so much in each other's pockets these last days.'

So this is the cause of his despondency. The absence of the Campbells. Lily feels her spirits deflate.

'It certainly makes a change,' Helena says, 'to have a day to ourselves. Don't tell me you haven't enjoyed it. Remember the stillness up there in that ruined city, that sense of history.'

'But everything is so much more fun when Max and Eliza are around,' says Edward, and once again Lily gets a hint of Eliza's voice and intonation in his speech.

'You don't need fun, Edward.' Helena says, perhaps more loudly than she intended, because she softens her voice for the next sentence. 'What you need is calm. Do you want to end up back at the sanatorium?'

Edward has been examining the back of his hands but at this his head snaps up. He's terrified, Lily senses now. Up until now she hasn't thought properly about how it must have been. To be so close to death for so long, and surrounded by people whose lives hang similarly in the balance so that each newly empty bed is a horrible reminder of your own mortality.

What an enigma he is, this Edward. So full of contradictions and complications, light and shade, softness and strength. He is unlike any man Lily has ever met. She wishes she could tell him now, about the Campbells and the information she was given in the

Pompeii gift shop. But as soon as the thought occurs to her she realizes it would make no difference. Edward is intoxicated by Eliza. Lily recognizes that feeling only too well. It's how she once felt about Robert.

That night, when she sleeps, she has a terrible dream in which she and Edward and Robert and the Campbells are transfigured into stone, trapped for eternity. Ida shakes her awake. 'You're shouting,' she says. 'In your sleep. How are any of us going to get any rest with that racket going on?'

Alert now, Lily lies in her bunk, turning the events of the day over in her head and listening to the sea whispering outside the cabin porthole. Glancing down, the fine hairs on her arms stand up in shock when she sees the whites of Ida's eyes glinting through the darkness.

10

8 August 1939

WHAT A COMMOTION.

Lily has gone down to the laundry with a modest pile of clothes to wash, only to find the place in disarray. Normally, the laundry rooms, which include a dedicated ironing room, are well ordered and calm and Lily hasn't minded saving money on paying to use the ship's laundry service by doing it herself. But this morning everything is different. The Italian women who came aboard the previous afternoon have brought down great bundles of washing, with which they are filling and refilling the tubs. Washing belonging to the other passengers, which had been discreetly hanging on the drying rails, has been swept on to the floor, where it lies shamefully exposed.

The Italian women, and their enormous bellies, have arranged themselves around the rooms and are chatting away to each other, quite content and seemingly unaware of having caused offence, while several of the original passengers huddle together, discussing in animated tones how to deal with this outrage wreaked upon their petticoats and underthings.

'Have you seen?' says Clara Mills, spotting Lily in the doorway. Once again her tiny hand flutters at her throat, like a baby bird trying to take flight. 'George Price did warn us, but I never thought . . . Oh, to think I'm to do this whole voyage completely alone, with no one to protect me and Peggy!'

'I'm sure it's a misunderstanding,' Lily says, although she is mortified to spot one of her own brassieres among the muddle of ejected clothes in the middle of the floor. 'They don't know yet how we do things.'

But Clara and the others won't be mollified. A deputation is despatched to talk to the captain and reappears after ten minutes in the company of the purser and two stewards. The purser is an austere-looking man of around sixty with silver hair and a regal posture to complement his impressive starched uniform. As he addresses them in their own language, the Italian women listen quietly. After a while they start muttering and a couple start to speak, only to be silenced once again by his air of authority.

He comes over to join Lily and Clara and the others.

'They have been given an hour to clear the laundry and told that, from now on, they will only be allowed to do their washing between four and six in the afternoon. At all other times the laundry is reserved for the other passengers.'

Behind his back the Italian women have started talking excitably among themselves and gesticulating towards the others.

'They seem very angry about it,' says Clara.

'That's as may be,' says the purser. 'But they are on a British ship and they must respect the British way of doing things. The sooner we make that clear to them, the better.'

The scene leaves Lily feeling disconcerted. For the last week and a half the ship has been like a world within itself, a vast floating city outside of normal rules. But the longer the journey continues, the more confined it is starting to feel, deck upon deck, passenger upon passenger, all of them churning around each other without anywhere to go.

It doesn't help that it is getting so hot. Not just the burning midday heat of Naples but a permanent dampness that coats Lily's skin, causing her cotton blouse to stick to the small of her back and sweat to pool behind her knees. She makes her way to the small swimming pool, where she takes off her shoes and dangles her feet in the cool water. There are two young girls in the pool. Normally, the children are looked after by the stewardesses in the onboard nurseries, where there is organized entertainment to keep them amused, so it makes a pleasant change to watch these two splashing around with naked delight. She wonders whether they will look back one day when they are fully grown, grandmothers, perhaps, and pluck a memory out of the air of a boat and a swimming pool and a cloudless sky. I will be dead by then, she thinks, and the thought is an unexpected punch in her sternum.

Alerted by a shout from the front of the deck, she makes her way, barefoot, to see what is happening. 'There,' says an Italian man, pointing off to the left, where a volcano rises steeply out of the water like a giant pyramid, smoke swirling around its peak.

'Stromboli,' the man says. As if reacting to its own name, the volcano belches out a flame into the air.

'He is angry,' the man says, and smiles, revealing several missing back teeth. The ship will soon be sailing into the Straits of Messina. Already, Lily is in mourning for the quarter of the voyage that is behind them.

At lunch, Helena is once again absent. 'The trip to Pompeii exhausted her,' says Edward.

'Is she ill?' asks Lily. 'She seems always to be having to rest.'

'I think it is just her heart that's ill,' says Edward. 'And that is my fault. It's for me that she had to leave everything . . . everyone . . . behind.'

'You couldn't help that,' says Lily, leaping in to defend him. 'You couldn't help getting tuberculosis. You can't blame yourself.'

Edward sighs and then smiles. 'You're so kind, Lily. But you must know by now that guilt is another of my many unattractive features.'

Despite this exchange, Lily is pleased to see that Edward seems, on the whole, to be in a lighter mood today. Even George Price trying to get them to join in his damning condemnation of the events in the laundry that morning doesn't seem to dent his mood. Edward is attentive to her, almost to the point of making her embarrassed. When Audrey bumps into her in the Ladies, she says, 'And now you have two admirers at your table. It's so unfair,' and when Lily gets back she cannot look Edward in the eye.

Afterwards they sit in the shade on the deck and Edward fans Lily with a straw hat he bought in Gibraltar. 'I'm so glad you came,' he tells her. 'You're the best thing about this whole crossing.'

It is as it was that first evening, and Lily is enjoying Edward's company so much she is almost irritated when Maria appears and asks if she can join them. But before long they are chatting, the three of them, about Pompeii and the scene at the laundry room, and the infernal, unrelenting heat.

'How can they bear to be wearing all those clothes,' asks Lily, pointing out a small group of Jews further down the deck, the men dressed in dark suits and collars and ties. She has noticed before that many of the Jewish women wear the same dress day after day, regardless of the changing weather.

'That's all they have,' says Maria. 'Many of those who have come directly from Germany or Austria or Czechoslovakia had to leave with only the clothes they were standing up in. I am lucky that I was able to work in England, so that I can treat you all to my wonderful collection of haute couture outfits.'

She gestures with a flourish to her dress, a drab brown thing that looks to Lily to have been made for a woman much bigger in the bust than Maria.

'And why do the men carry their briefcases around all the time?' Edward wants to know. 'Are they doing some sort of business here?'

Maria takes off her spectacles and cleans the lenses on the material of her skirt.

'Some of these men were doctors or lawyers. I've even met one who was a composer. Another who owned a string of factories. And now here they are with nothing. The briefcases, even empty, as many of them might be, are all that connects them to the people they once were.'

Lily tries to imagine how it would be to know she was never going home. Never again to walk through the front door in Reading to give her mam a kiss, or argue with her brother. Never again to be the person she had always been. She can see how she, too, might feel impelled to clutch on to whatever object might link her to her past.

'So here's where you're hiding!'

Eliza Campbell has stepped out from the lounge and is looking at them over the top of her black sunglasses. She is wearing a coral-pink dress that cleaves to her body, leaving her arms and the tops of her bosoms bare, and white shoes with narrow straps.

'I've been looking everywhere for you two. Doesn't this heat make you just want to dissolve?'

Lily waits for Edward to reply, for his attention to swing automatically from her to Eliza, but he does not spring to his feet as she might have expected. Hope stirs, treacherous, inside her.

'Well, now I've found you I am not going to let you get away. I insist you two come up to the top deck and play cards with me and Max. Otherwise, one of us is going to end up killing the other and you will be entirely to blame.'

Lily tries to introduce Eliza to Maria, but Eliza's eyes slide off her, as if she were just a part of the ship itself, or a chair or a wall.

'I would invite the three of you, but it's only a game for four. I'm sure Maria won't mind if I borrow you for a little while, not when she has this wonderful view to look out on.'

Lily is about to say no when Edward gets to his feet. 'Come on, Lily,' he says. 'It will be a relief to have a change of scenery.'

'And we have far better fans,' says Eliza. 'Lovely, delicious, cooling fans.'

'You go,' Maria tells her. 'I shall be quite happy here reading my book.'

Still, Lily hesitates, but at the same time wants to be with Edward and is already imagining how the cold air from the fans will feel against her skin.

'I will see you later,' she promises Maria, but she walks away with an unpleasant taste in her mouth.

Upstairs, and subjected once again to the stares of the other passengers, she is immediately reminded of her encounter with the ruddy-cheeked woman in the shop in Pompeii.

Now that Lily knows about the 'terrible scandal' she can see how isolated the Campbells are. No one catches their eye as they head towards Max, who is sitting at a table in the lounge, playing solitaire and smoking a cigarette. No cheerful 'Good afternoon's or 'Isn't it hot?'s. She recognizes the group of young people who were with Eliza and Max in the bar that first night they met. They are splayed out in armchairs near the entrance to the room and look away as Eliza passes.

'Have you done something different to your hair?' Max asks Lily as she sits down. 'You look so well.'

'It's because she's caught the sun,' says Eliza. 'I wish I had the kind of skin that went golden, instead of being pale and boring all the time.'

She makes a face like a little girl having a sulk, turning out her lips, which are painted a coral colour to match her dress.

'Shall we have a drink? Oh, I know, let's have a cocktail. Max, what's the name of that one we were drinking at the Savoy all last summer?'

The name is remembered. The cocktails are ordered. Someone is playing the piano, a soft melody of notes that gently ripple across the room. The fans are on full, cooling Lily's skin down for the first time that day, and through the big wall of windows, the once monstrous Stromboli grows ever smaller. Max smiles his bountiful smile, Eliza charms and pouts and tells funny stories. And just like that Lily finds herself being drawn back into the circle of light that surrounds the Campbells, warming her hands around their fire.

They start playing cards, a new game that Lily has never played before and has to have explained at length, until Eliza gets bored and says, 'Let's just start – you're bound to pick it up.' This time, Eliza wins, but even so she is easily distracted, keeping up a commentary on the other passengers: 'See him, he puts his false teeth in a napkin on the table while he eats'; 'She keeps a bottle of something in her handbag – watch how she reaches in to take a swig when she thinks no one is looking.' More cocktails are ordered. And more again. Pink Ladies, they are called. They have a sweet flavour that makes Lily think of ice cream in the park on a summer afternoon.

After the next hand, which Edward apologetically claims, Eliza jumps to her feet. 'Lily, I have the perfect dress for you. I can't imagine why I didn't think of it before. You must come to my cabin. I can't wait to show you.'

Lily demurs, embarrassed. She does not like the way everyone is staring. Does not like the suggestion that she is in need of charity. Eliza appeals to her husband.

'Max, you know my peach silk? Can't you just imagine it? With Lily's hair and eyes?'

And now Max is appraising her, his eyes passing up and down her like he is tracing a map.

'I don't think . . .' says Lily. She glances towards Edward, appealing for help. He looks closed off, tense. He doesn't want Eliza to leave, Lily thinks. The unwelcome realization makes her angry, and bold. She stands up. Eliza claps.

'Come, come.'

'Just to look,' Lily says. 'I have quite enough clothes of my own. Thank you.'

She allows herself to be led away, pretending not to notice Edward's pained expression or the other passengers' curious stares. Until now, she and Edward have been confined to one section of the first-class deck. Now she and Eliza pass the formal dining room with its circular tables and polished wood panelling, and up ahead the swimming pool, so much larger, even from this distance, than the one below.

She has no intention of accepting a cast-off from Eliza but she is curious to see Eliza's cabin. She has heard that a single first-class berth costs seventy-five pounds and a state room closer to a hundred. Such amounts seem inconceivable – a hundred pounds for a journey that will end in a few weeks! Lily's mother rarely discusses money and, when she does, it is always in lowered tones, as if it is not quite nice, but when Lily's uncle bought his house in Edgware last year – the first of their family to buy his own home – she told Lily proudly that he had put down a two-hundred-pound deposit and borrowed the remaining one hundred and fifty pounds, so Lily knows a little of the price of things. The notion that two first-class cabins could cost almost the same as a house – well, it makes no sense.

In the event, Eliza and Max's cabin is almost a disappointment. Not that it isn't luxurious, with a dressing room and a private bathroom and a huge bed, which Lily tries to ignore, but because Lily has already imagined it to be the size of a palace and festooned with velvet and furs, so that anything less seems somehow unsatisfactory.

'Oh, the staff have been in tidying again,' says Eliza with a frown, surveying the neat satin counterpane on the bed and the orderly dressing table, with scent bottles lined up in order of height. 'Now I won't be able to find a thing!'

She disappears into the dressing room, flings open the door of one of the vast wardrobes and starts riffling through the hangers, impatiently tossing garments aside that get in the way. Finally, she locates the dress she is looking for.

'Here!' She holds it up. 'Wasn't I right? Isn't it perfect?'

'No. Really. I couldn't . . .'

Lily's protestations die on her lips. The dress is the most beautiful thing she has ever seen, a wisp of peach silk, fine as a cobweb. Eliza thrusts it into Lily's hands and it spills over her fingers like water.

Still she tries to give the dress back.

'It's lovely but I –'

'Nonsense. Try it on. Come on. I insist. Just to make me happy.'

Eliza throws herself down on to the bed and sits up against the padded headboard, her arms folded, as if waiting for a show to start. Lily has a horrible thought that Eliza is expecting her to get changed right in front of her. Though she had shared a room with Mags and thought nothing of walking around half dressed, the idea of taking her clothes off in the full glare of Eliza's scrutiny is too disturbing to contemplate.

'I'll use your dressing room,' Lily says. 'Just in case Max comes bursting in.'

Even though she pulls the door to, she wriggles out of her clothes as discreetly as she can, feeling exposed even in the semi-darkness. The wardrobe is still open and she notices the red dress Eliza was wearing the first time Lily saw her. Eliza must have pulled it off the hanger while she was looking through her clothes just now, and it lies pooled like blood on the wardrobe floor. There's something else lying next to the dress, which Lily, at a first startled glance, mistakes for a live animal, before realizing it is a fox stole, rich russet and white. The head is still attached at one end and, as she picks it up to replace it on the hanger, the fox's dead eyes lock on to hers and she shudders.

As soon as she has the peach dress on Lily knows, even without seeing it, that it is perfect. The way it slips lightly over her body as if it were spun from air and skims her hips before flaring slightly at the hem, the way the slender straps show off her shoulders and the back dips daringly low. It is the first dress she has ever worn that is cut on the bias, and she can tell immediately that it's a style that suits her slim, small-chested figure. Eliza is a couple of inches taller than Lily, so the dress falls just above the ankle rather than mid-calf but, when she closes the wardrobe door so that she can look into the full-length mirror, Lily sees that the longer length looks good on her. She gazes at her reflection for a long time. She looks like someone else entirely.

'Aren't you ready yet?'

A petulant note has crept into Eliza's voice and Lily hurries out, smoothing the dress down over her hips.

'I knew it! Didn't I tell you? You look utterly ravishing. Oh, I am clever, even if I say so myself.'

Eliza crawls forward across the satin counterpane on her hands and knees so that she can stroke the silk over Lily's ribcage, and Lily steps backwards in shock.

'Come here, and let's have a chat,' says Eliza, pulling Lily down on to the bed beside her. 'This is what I love about boats. That there are no silly social barriers and we can all just be friends with whomever we choose!'

Sitting stiffly on the end of the bed, Lily looks around the expansive suite and thinks about the tourist deck down below with Audrey and Ida and the Jews huddled down one end wearing their one set of 'good clothes', and below that the Italians, the women heaving their huge bellies around across the laundry room, their crossings grudgingly paid for by the owners of the sugarcane plantations where their husbands work. Is this truly what Eliza believes? she asks herself. That here on the ship we are all equal?

Eliza quizzes Lily about herself and her background and, though at first wary, Lily finds herself becoming more garrulous. It feels good to be talking about her family, describing her mother's quiet stoicism and her brother's youthful impatience. Even telling her about her father's war injury and how he has struggled to work since doesn't upset her.

'I love the sound of them all,' Eliza declares. 'You're a lucky girl, Lily.'

When it comes to talking about her own family, Eliza is less exuberant. She picks at a seam on the counterpane and seems to be choosing her words with care rather than tossing them out into the air as she usually does. Her mother died when she was a child, she tells Lily. She remembers very little about her – a pair of pale blue shoes with ribbons attached and high heels which the little Eliza would totter around in, a smell of verbena. Lily has never even heard of verbena. She rolls the word around in her head, enjoying its languorous sound.

'She killed herself,' Eliza says, gazing right at Lily as if daring her to refute it.

'Oh!'

Lily has never known anyone to say such a thing out loud. In Lily's world, suicide is referred to obliquely, as if even to formulate the word is a sin, and always in hushed tones, whispered into someone else's ear.

'Her grandmother did the same thing,' Eliza goes on. 'It's part of our family legacy. I dare say I will end up doing the same, too, one of these days. My father married again, with such indecent haste one has to consider the possibility that the new Mrs Hepworth was in the picture while the old one was still very much alive. My step-mother hated me from the first time we met and the feeling was very much mutual so it was boarding schools for me from then on!'

Eliza is struggling to regain her usual brittle tone and Lily's heart softens. She may have beautiful dresses and jewellery and the money to waft around the world at leisure like a leaf on the breeze, setting down and picking up on a whim, but still Eliza lacks what Lily has, a loving family. A home.

Now Eliza is asking Lily about sweethearts and whether she has ever been in love. Still touched by the honesty of her revelations about her mother, Lily tells her about Robert.

'I did think I loved someone once, but we broke up.'

'Oh, my poor Lily. I knew there was a dark, tragic secret in your past.'

Lily looks up sharply, unsure if she is being mocked, but Eliza's expression is one of concern, so Lily finds herself adding, without even meaning to: 'He was the son of the family I worked for when I was last in domestic service. So of course it would never have worked out. But I was a lot younger, and naive enough to believe it might.'

'And he threw you over because of that? How spineless!'

Eliza is outraged on her behalf, and Lily tries to explain.

'No, not because of that, and it was my choice to end it.'

She is wishing she hadn't brought up Robert's name, hadn't revealed this confidence. The horrible images she tries to keep at bay are prowling like wolves around the edges of her consciousness. No. In her panic to change the direction of the conversation she speaks without thinking.

'Of course, you must be used to men falling in love with you, Eliza. I think Edward is completely smitten.'

Eliza, who has been leaning forward on her elbows with her face in her hands, now sits up abruptly. Through the hot rush of her own embarrassment, Lily registers that the news seems to have come as a surprise – or else Eliza is a very accomplished actress.

'In love with me?' Eliza laughs. 'Really, Lily, are you completely blind?'

Lily gazes at her without comprehension until finally her meaning sinks in, bringing with it a fresh flood of discomfiture, mixed with acute pleasure. She feels her chest burning under the wisp of the dress.

'Oh, I don't think . . .' she says. Then, 'But he's given me no reason . . .'

Eliza looks at her strangely, and then laughs again, that same lacquered laugh Lily is used to, which shatters the quiet intimacy of the last few minutes.

'Well, of course he's in love with you. Who wouldn't be? Look at you, you're lovely. Even Max is quite besotted. Better not let him see you in that dress. Who knows what might happen!'

She reaches out and pulls up one of the straps which Lily hasn't even realized has slipped down her shoulder. Her fingers are cool like marble against Lily's burning skin.

Lily leaps hurriedly to her feet.

'I'd better get this off before it creases.'

Eliza's laugh follows her to the dressing room and breaks against the closing door.

11

9 August 1939

Now that there is no let-up in the heat even after darkness falls, warm air pressing down on you like a hundred woollen blankets, the stewards set up camp beds in pairs on the deck for the passengers to sleep on. One side of the deck for the men and the other for the women.

Lily has never slept outside and finds the idea both intriguing and nerve-wracking. After all those nights in the airless cabin, with Ida's intrusive presence lending an extra, unwelcome weight, just the thought of sleeping in a place without walls or ceiling, with the sea and the sky stretching infinitely in every direction, fills her with a sense of lightness and longing. But to be surrounded by all those people, many of them strangers, in a place which isn't her own?

In the event, Lily's need for space overcomes her fear of the unknown.

'You will sleep next to me, won't you, Maria?' she asks her friend, finding her leaning against the railing after dinner, gazing out at the reflection of the moon on the water, shiny as a new shilling.

'I don't know, Lily.'

Maria looks down the length of the deck to where the Jews are gathered, as usual keeping largely to themselves.

'Please say you will. Audrey wants to stay down in the cabin and Helena is still unwell, and I should feel so much better if you're nearby.'

Maria smiles in assent, transforming the shape of her long, thin face.

'It will be an adventure, won't it? I have never been camping!'

As Lily moves around her cabin, collecting various items for her sojourn outside, Ida's eyes follow her like a sniper's rifle.

'I don't think you should be up there on your own,' she says. 'I will come with you. We can get beds close together.'

'There's no need. Maria is sleeping next to me.' Even as the words escape her, Lily knows she has spoken too quickly, too eagerly.

Ida presses her lips tightly together, as if she is squashing something between them.

'You haven't travelled much before,' she says at last, 'so you haven't experience of these things, but I must warn you that it doesn't look good for you to be spending so much time with that woman.'

'Because she is Jewish?'

Lily's anger takes them both by surprise.

'There are a lot of people on this ship who aren't keen on those people. You're young and you don't understand but there's too many of them in England now, taking over perfectly good neighbourhoods – houses, schools. They're not the same as the rest of us. They don't fit. And the ones on here are no different. Look how they keep themselves separate, like they're too good for the rest of us. And then wearing the same clothes day after day.'

Lily turns her back on Ida, pulling her trunk out from under the bottom bunk in search of the satin pyjamas she has not yet worn.

'You're not making yourself too popular round here,' Ida tells her, as Lily crosses to the cabin door. 'All that hobnobbing with first class, giving yourself airs and graces, and now keeping company with that Jew. People don't like that kind of thing, Lily. People don't like it at all.'

And now Lily has Ida's thin, one-note voice lodged like a mosquito's whine in her ear. Climbing up to the deck, footsteps clanging on the metal staircase, her blood pulses with the things she ought to have said. She has never liked confrontation, picking her way around it as though stepping around a puddle, so often it is only in afterthought that she becomes brave enough to say what she thinks, stand up for what she believes to be right.

She has no knowledge of what it is the Jews are supposed to have done. Maria is the first she has ever got to know. But she resents Ida telling her who she can and can't get close to. Ida, of all people, who has not made a single friend on the voyage.

Up on deck, Maria is already waiting on a camp bed near the end of the row. Lily wonders whether she chose that position on purpose, feeling safer somehow nearest to an escape route. Lily understands that feeling. After Mags, she slept with the light on for weeks. She waves to Maria. As she makes her way towards her, she passes Mrs Mills with her daughter, Peggy, heading in the opposite direction, towards the cabins.

'Aren't you tempted to spend the night out here, in the fresh air?' asks Lily, although in truth the air cannot be described as fresh, only less turgid than the air down below.

Clara Mills shakes her head.

'I shouldn't feel safe,' she says. 'With all the' – here she lowers her voice – '*foreigners* we have roaming around the ship.'

'Please, Mama,' whinges Peggy. 'It's so suffocating in our cabin. Sometimes I wake up in the night and feel like there's an elephant sitting on me, smothering me, and I just can't breathe.'

Peggy has put on weight over the last two weeks, Lily thinks. The breakfasts, the lunches, the dinners, the tea and cakes, and sandwiches before bed. And no exercise beyond walking from cabin to dining room to lounge.

Clara looks as if she might burst into tears.

'I'm sorry, darling,' she says, 'but I cannot take the risk. A woman travelling on her own with a child is just the sort of person they would target.'

Maria has saved Lily the bed next to hers. Though the makeshift camp is under an awning, once they're lying on their backs they can look straight up and see the stars pricking the black velvet sky with light. Now that everyone has settled for the night, they can hear the gentle, reassuring slap of the sea hitting the underside of the ship and the dull rumble of the engine. Someone is whispering to someone else further along the row, and the shushing sounds hang for a moment before dissipating into the breezeless air. The wood of the deck itself is creaking in its own soft rhythm, while from the men's side of the deck comes a low growl of snoring. Somewhere in the kitchen, beyond the dining room, Lily can hear the far-off clinking of the night dish-washer finishing his shift.

'Doesn't it make you feel small?' she asks Maria. 'Knowing that here we are, two little specs of nothing on this tiny boat, surrounded by this vast ocean under this endless sky?'

But Maria is already asleep, her glasses folded on the pillow next to her head, white sheet pulled up to her chin, with one slender arm lying over the top.

This is me, Lily reminds herself. This woman lying under the stars in a boat skimming the coast of Africa. It scarcely seems possible.

As if unwrapping a secret treasure, she allows herself to think about Edward, sleeping just a few yards away, looking out on the same stars. She remembers how Eliza had said, 'Of course he's in love with you,' as if it were the most obvious thing in the world. After Robert, she swore she would not lose her heart again. But

Edward is as different from Robert as it is possible for two men to be: kind, where Robert was often thoughtless; considerate of others, where Robert was so consumed with himself. When at last she closes her eyes Edward's face shines through her thoughts as bright as the moon and she dreams of being in a small boat with him and Maria, the three of them drifting oarless and engineless away from the ship.

She is awoken some time later by a scream that seems at first to be pulled out from her own dreams. There is a muffled thud of footsteps, then another scream that wrenches her fully into the present.

Sitting up, she looks wildly around, surprise at finding herself outside soon giving way to concern as she sees Maria standing, dishevelled, by her bed, with her sheet wrapped around her and her hair standing out like dark foliage around her pale face.

'What?' Lily urges. 'What happened?'

Around them, other people are stirring, whispered words carrying over to them. *What's going on? I heard a scream.*

'Someone was here,' Maria says, and her voice is choked and lumpy. 'Someone . . . touched me.'

'What do you mean, "touched" you?' asks Lily.

Mrs Collins, the chaperone, has arrived, summoned by the commotion from wherever she has been sleeping. She is wearing a long white nightgown that reaches to the floor and carrying an old-fashioned oil lamp. Her round face is slack with worry.

'I suspect your friend means she was touched *inappropriately*,' she says.

Maria has by this time slumped down on to her bunk and is hunched forward, hugging her sides with her arms crossed, crying silently.

'Did you see anyone?'

Maria shakes her head. 'I woke up feeling hands on me, touching me *there*. There was a dark shape crouching next to me, and I screamed and he ran. Oh, Lily, it was so horrible.'

Lily sits down next to Maria on her bunk and puts her arm around her. She can feel her thin shoulders shuddering under the thin sheet. Lily's own heart is racing inside her, chasing away the last vestiges of sleep. 'I'm here,' she tells Maria, not knowing what else she can say. 'I'm here. It's all right.' She tries to forget that she has said these words before to someone else, in different circumstances, and it proved to be a lie.

A steward appears and Mrs Collins takes him to one side, relating to him in lowered tones what has taken place. He is a portly man and his ruddy face first registers shock, but it seems to Lily that when he sees who the victim is his outrage subsides into something more resembling duty.

'I'll need to ask you some questions, miss,' he says. 'And the purser will have to be informed.'

His voice is polite but distant.

Lily offers to go with Maria, who has stopped crying, although her body still shakes, in spite of the sultry night air. And Mrs Collins insists on accompanying them both: 'You are in my charge, Lily,' she says. 'Your mother would think me a poor supervisor if I let you go through this alone.' Lily thinks it strange that Mrs Collins is lavishing concern on her while it is Maria who has been assaulted.

They sit in the lounge while the purser is summoned. Mrs Collins seems anxious to assign blame. 'Perhaps you recognized something about him, Miss Katz? Was he known to you?'

Maria shakes her head. 'It was dark. I didn't see. I only felt his hands on me.'

Mrs Collins sighs, looking pained, as if Maria is somehow remiss in not being able to shed further light.

Finally, the purser arrives, his silver hair sleek and neat as ever, his manner calm and unruffled. Lily relaxes, feeling as if, finally, here is someone in control.

'A very unfortunate business,' declares the purser after hearing what Maria has to say. 'I offer you my apologies that this should happen on our ship. Rest assured, I will be making full investigations in the morning and, in the meantime, I will station stewards on both ends of the ladies' deck so that there can be no risk of further incidents.'

They return to their camp beds. Maria says she would prefer to sleep in her cabin but she doesn't wish to disturb her cabin mate, an older woman she does not know well. A few feet away, at the end of the row, a steward lowers himself into a deckchair, rubbing his eyes as if recently woken from sleep.

Lily lies awake, watching the stars, but now the sounds of the slumbering ship no longer seem reassuring but, rather, ominous. The creaking of the deck sounds like someone creeping towards her bed, the tossing and turning of restless passengers becomes the scuffle of retreating footsteps. Next to her, Maria gulps, as if choking back a sob. When Lily turns towards her, she sees that her friend's face is glazed with tears which glisten in the moonlight.

12

10 August 1939

'JOHN, GET OUT of bed, you lazy lump. Come look!'
The shouts of the thickset woman standing at the railings wake Lily with a start. For a moment she thinks she is in her own cabin and wonders who the woman is, then the previous night's events come back to her and she swings around to look for Maria, only to find her companion's bed empty, the sheet neatly folded on the end, as if no one had ever been there.

Light-headed from lack of sleep, she makes her way over to the railings, where more people have now gathered, some still in pyjamas and shaking off the last clinging vestiges of dreams. 'Didn't I say it was worth seeing?' says the thickset woman, hearing Lily's gasp of surprise.

Sometime over the course of the dark night the ship has arrived at the entrance to the Suez Canal. The place is awash with ships and boats of all sizes and, beyond them, splayed across a peninsula of land, are the houses of Port Said, their next destination, fronted by a distinctive white colonnaded building with arched porticoes and domed roofs. The water that stretches between the ship and the land is dotted with hundreds of other ships, some of them belching out black smoke.

'Bet you never saw anything like that,' says a bald-headed man, who Lily decides must be John.

He gestures towards the quayside on their left, where a huge ship is berthed and, next to it, a long string of men with blackened faces are running with enormous sacks on their backs towards the ship and then back in the opposite direction once their sacks are empty, all keeping pace with one another in an endless human chain.

'Coal steamer,' says Probably John. 'Those are Lascars, Indian sailors, loading their ship with coal so it can get to the next port. Dirty old business, isn't it?'

Lily wonders what it would do to a man's back to be running up and down bent under that weight of coal, what the men think about as they scurry after the heels of the man in front. Or does the nature of the work allow them no space for thinking of anything apart from 'Run, run, nearly there; back, back, and again'? How tenuous is this matter of birth that sees some born into a life of luxury, paying a hundred pounds to travel in a first-class state room from London to Sydney, and others running up and down a quay-side with bent backs and coal-grimed faces.

Lily tears herself away from the sight of the port in order to go down to her cabin and prepare for going ashore. As she reaches the stairwell that leads down from the deck she sees Ida getting up from one of the camp beds further along, a dressing gown pulled tightly around her middle.

'I thought you were staying in the cabin?' Lily says, remembering with a jolt of displeasure the altercation of the previous evening.

Ida shrugs, her bony shoulders rising up and down like piano keys.

'I changed my mind.'

In the cabin, Audrey is agog with excitement.

'I cannot believe that we're about to land in Africa,' she says. 'If only my parents could see me. They wouldn't believe it.'

'The place is teeming with Arabs,' declares Ida. 'I, for one, won't be going ashore.'

Thank heaven for that, thinks Lily.

Audrey wants to know how Lily's night under the stars went, and Lily explains, in the broadest of terms, what happened to Maria. 'You were sleeping up on deck,' she says to Ida. 'Surely you must have heard something?' It seems inconceivable to Lily that such a momentous happening might have passed straight over the other passengers' heads.

But Ida insists she slept 'like a baby'. 'I don't like to say "I told you so",' she says, 'but I did warn you about consorting with all sorts.'

There is an organized tour leaving from Port Said. It will travel to Cairo and then take in the Pyramids before picking up the ship at its next destination, Port Suez. When the details were first announced Lily's heart had skipped like that of a child on a hopscotch grid, but the price – nearly six pounds – was out of her reach, as it was for most of the other tourist-class passengers. She must manage her expectations, she knows this. Already she has done more than she could have dreamed possible a few months ago. She must learn not to ask for too much.

For those not on the trip, the ship will be docking only for a few hours. Time enough to load up with fresh food and provisions and pick up the waiting mail. Time enough to take in the noise and the activity, to smell the coal-thick air and have photographs taken at the place where Africa and Asia collide.

The *Orontes* berths right up at the quayside so the passengers need only descend the gangway to be upon Egyptian soil. As they gather on deck, vendors start massing on the docks, clutching their wares. Lily is fascinated by their long nightshirts and turbans, their dark skin and the strange, throaty language that carries upwards, harsh as gulls' cries.

'It's as if I went to bed in Europe and woke up in a different world,' says Helena, who is finally over her sickness, although she still looks pale, her white skin fragile as the shell of an egg. Lily was so happy to come up on deck and find Edward and his sister looking for her. She is wearing a different dress today, made of pale green cotton that feels daringly skimpy with just her brassiere and knickers underneath. As she put it on, she had thought of Edward, trying to see it through his eyes. And it was worth it to hear him say, 'Lily, how well that colour suits you.' Like his sister, he was also looking wan, she noticed, and full of solicitude for her.

'I heard something happened last night,' he said. 'And then I saw you and Maria being led off to the lounge. Is everything all right?'

So Lily filled them in, and there were gasps, and 'Oh, no's, and Helena's hands were clasped to her mouth. They looked around for Maria but could not see her, and when Lily approached the woman who shares Maria's cabin she was told her friend was 'resting' and treated to a long, unsmiling stare, the meaning of which she could not decipher.

As they prepare to descend the gangway there is a stir behind them. Not a noise exactly but a sense of movement, of new alertness, a smell of roses, a frisson travelling like an electric current from person to person.

'Lily! Edward! Thank God! I'm so glad to see you two.'

Eliza has pushed through the scrum of waiting people and has arrived by their sides in a blur of motion and ill will from those displaced in the queue behind them. Max ambles after her, a benign smile on his handsome face, as if to say, *I know, but what can you do? What can you do?*

'Where have you two been? We've been going out of our heads with tedium. We even had to play cards with each other – and you can imagine how that turned out! We didn't make it past the first hand before having the most enormous row.'

'Well, you were cheating, my darling,' says Max.

'Nonsense. You just don't know the rules.'

Eliza is wearing the yellow dress again today, and she draws attention like the sun.

'I jolly well hope you three are coming on the trip to the Pyramids,' says Eliza, and the word 'jolly' sounds odd in her American accent. Forced. As if she's reading a line from a play.

'Particularly you, Lily,' whispers Max. 'At least then I'd have something nice to look at, instead of a load of old stones in a desert.'

He is leaning in so close to her that she can almost feel the bristles of his moustache scratching her skin. He smells of smoke and sweat and something else that she cannot put her finger on. Instinctively, she pulls back.

'Leave poor Lily alone, darling. You're practically smothering her.'

Eliza is smiling but her voice is flint-sharp.

Lily glances over at Edward in time to catch a frown darkening his face. Pleasure creeps over her like a rash.

When the Campbells hear that no one else is to join them on their trip they are volubly upset.

'But you must come!' says Eliza, linking arms with Edward as they proceed down the gangway. 'If it's a question of money, don't even think of it. We will buy you the ticket.'

'I wouldn't hear of it,' says Edward.

When they arrive on land they are instantly surrounded by hawkers, many of them carrying trays of trinkets. The air is oven-hot. They flock around Eliza in her canary-yellow dress as if magnetized there and she, in response, clings more tightly to Edward. She glances around and catches Lily's eye, and gives her a strange half-smile. Lily is confused, thinking back to Eliza's cabin and how she'd allowed Eliza to glimpse her feelings for Edward – yet now she seems to be going out of her way to claim him for herself.

'Max!' Eliza calls. 'Will you please tell Edward that he has to come with us?'

Max gazes at his wife with his ice-chip eyes. Something unsaid passes between them. Then he steps forward and hooks his arm around Edward's shoulders, steering him away from his wife.

'Of course you must come, old chap. And the two ladies, too.'

Helena, following on with Lily, shakes her head so violently two of her pins come loose, causing a hank of straight, mousy-brown hair to fall down her back.

'No. I don't want to. That is to say, it's very kind of you, Mr Campbell . . . Max . . . but I should be far happier staying here. I haven't been well. And my brother, too.'

To Lily's surprise, Helena grabs Edward by the arm and yanks him towards her. She's taking her older-sister role too far, Lily thinks. Edward's furious expression indicates that he feels the same.

Lily, too, starts to protest, even though she is not entirely convinced the Campbells aren't toying with them. Wouldn't it be just like Eliza to toss out a statement like that just for the amusement of seeing them all flustered?

'I'm perfectly content to stay in Port Said and visit the bazaars,' she tells Max, although the pressing of the vendors around them, all of them talking loudly, in that strange language with its harsh, throaty sounds, is starting to make her nervous. She looks around for Eliza, who seems to have become separated from them, and briefly glimpses through the throng a flash of sunshine yellow before the crowd closes in again.

A hawker tries to press something into Lily's hands – an exquisite hand-carved bird, fragile as spun sugar.

'No,' she says, dropping her hands to her sides. 'No, thank you.'

The hawker's eyes are impassive as he once again thrusts the bird towards her. She shakes her head. 'No,' she says. More loudly. And steps back into a tray of intricate, inlaid music boxes which clatters to the ground. The vendor whose tray it is thrusts his face close to hers, shouting so that her cheek is sprayed with spittle. 'I'm so sorry,' she says as he drops to his knees to retrieve his stock, but he only glares up at her.

There is a whir of yellow and Eliza appears, waving something aloft like a trophy.

'It's all taken care of,' she says. 'Two extra tickets. Helena, I know you would prefer to stay and, of course, that's entirely your choice. But Lily and Edward are coming with us, even if we have to kidnap them and load them on to camels ourselves.'

Lily, still shaken from the altercation with the music-box vendor, is aghast at the thought of sitting on the coach with all the passengers from first class. Them knowing they are there because of charity. She cannot say this to Eliza, so instead she says, 'I have nothing with me. No clothes.'

Eliza scoffs.

'It won't take you a minute to run back to your cabin. It's only one night, for heaven's sake! Will you please leave me alone!' She is addressing a young boy who has been tapping her insistently on the shoulder. He looks momentarily sorrowful, then begins again. Tap, tap, tap.

'Oh, please, hurry up, you two, so we can get out of here.' Eliza raises her voice, glaring at the boy.

Lily glances at Edward, helpless. He shrugs.

'Look, you might as well come, otherwise the tickets will just go to waste,' says Max, swatting off an eager vendor as easily as if he were a fly.

'Well, in that case,' says Edward, 'I suppose there's nothing to say but thank you. You really shouldn't have, but I should so like to see the Pyramids. Lily, shall we?'

He turns towards the ship, and Lily finds herself meekly following him back up the gangway, pushing past the tail end of the disembarking passengers. In her cabin she is in such a state of shock she cannot focus on anything apart from gathering up a few things and cramming them hastily into a small overnight bag. She does not dare ask herself how she feels about going, or think about how it might be. I will visit the Pyramids, she tells herself. I will see the Nile. It seems as little connected to her reality as if she were announcing her intention of travelling back in time.

Ida bursts in and stops short, surprised to find her back.

'I'm going on the coach tour to Cairo,' Lily tells her. 'I will be back tomorrow. Please tell Mrs Collins where I am.'

Ida narrows her black eyes, waiting for the explanation that never comes.

Out on the deck, Lily sees Edward and Helena waiting by the gangway. They are deep in conversation and do not hear her approach. 'I'm begging you, Edward, do not do this.' Helena looks fevered, some of her hair still hanging loose at the back. 'You owe this to me. Have you forgotten how much I've given up for you?'

'Not given up. Given up implies you did it voluntarily. Out of choice.'

Edward has been glaring at his sister, but now he looks up, noticing Lily for the first time. Instantly, his tone softens.

'Shall we go?' he asks her.

Lily nods but hesitates at the top of the gangway.

'I wish you were coming,' she says to Helena.

Helena sighs.

'You take care of yourself, Lily,' she says eventually. 'And take care of him.' She nods in the direction of Edward's retreating back.

'It's only one night.'

'A lot can happen in a night, Lily.'

On the coach, Lily is silent, looking out of the window at the dust-blurred fields where peasants labour in close-knit rows in the searing heat. 'Oh,' she says, spying her first glimpse of a camel, kneeling in the dry earth and being loaded with sugar cane. Next to her, Max Campbell follows the direction of her gaze. 'Stupid-looking things, aren't they?' he says. 'With those humps on their backs, like old women.'

Lily still can't quite work out how they came to be sitting in this configuration, with Edward and Eliza in front and her jammed into the window seat beside Max, who seems not to notice how much space he is taking up, with his broad shoulders and his legs spread apart.

The orange dust outside the window gives way to lusher, green vegetation. 'The Nile Delta,' announces someone sitting behind, as if that should be quite explanation enough. They pass a man herding goats and sheep by the roadside. He raises a weather-beaten hand to shield his eyes and follows the coach's progress without change of expression.

But Lily is finding it hard to concentrate on the scenery, so anxious does she feel. Though she saw a couple she recognized from tourist class getting on to a separate bus, this coach is exclusively first class, with the exception of her and Edward, and she cannot shake off the sense of being watched and judged.

Then there is also the fact of the money the Campbells have paid for her to join them. Lily has never stopped to wonder how rich they are, presuming only that their presence in First presupposes a certain standard of living, but now she finds herself dwelling on it. Perhaps the twelve pounds they have paid out for her and Edward to join them is nothing to them, like the small change her father carries around in the pockets of his trousers and jingles when he's feeling nervous.

But still, that does little to stave off the humiliation that buzzes gently but insistently around her ears and, worse, the heavy fug of obligation. I didn't ask to come, she reminds herself. But this knowledge fails to improve her frame of mind or dispel her unease at being, whether she asked for it or not, in thrall to the Campbells.

Edward, for his part, shows little sign of being similarly beset with doubt. He and Eliza have their heads close together, sleek black hair next to unruly dark curls. Edward says something, and they both laugh, Eliza throwing her head back so that her laughter escapes to the roof of the bus, like Stromboli belching smoke into the sky.

I am not being entertaining, she thinks, panicked. Max Campbell is not getting his money's worth.

Through the window, the sight of buildings, gradually increasing in density, indicates they are arriving in Cairo. The streets are once again dusty, the houses narrow and tall. But as they progress further into the city the roads open out, becoming wider, some tree-lined, and the buildings more impressive. The coach overtakes horses and carts ambling alongside the motor cars.

'Ladies and gentlemen, we are arriving at the Shepheard Hotel,' says their Egyptian guide, a good-looking young man with very straight black hair that falls across his eyes and smooth brown skin that gleams like the casing of a freshly shelled conker.

Lily is surprised and slightly thrilled to find she shares a name with the hotel in which they are to stay but, just as she's about to remark upon it to the others, she glances past Max, out of the far window, and stifles a gasp. The hotel is enormous, taking up a whole block of the street, and impossibly grand, with its pale stone façade and its rows of shuttered windows and the glass-roofed portico supported by the slenderest of pillars and flanked by palm trees in the most enormous pots Lily has ever seen. A row of awnings runs along the base of the hotel, behind which shopfronts are visible, though Lily cannot tell what they are selling. At the very top two flags droop, listless in the breezeless air.

Inside it is more intimidating still – a vast vestibule, its high ceiling held up by immense marble columns. There are velvet armchairs in which people sit, reading the newspaper or drinking tea, under the watchful gaze of two scantily clad statues. An imposing staircase rises up at the far end before dividing into two separate branches that turn back on themselves.

If only Lily could relax enough to appreciate her surroundings, committing the details to memory so she can re-create this room exactly in her next letter home. *I can just imagine what you'd have to say, Mam. 'Not exactly homely, is it?'* But, instead, her nerves are being plucked like harp strings. Surely she isn't going to be given a room of her own here, in this place. How much would that cost? How much will she owe?

As if reading her thoughts, Eliza turns to her. 'We have two double rooms between us – that's all that was left.' Then, seeing Lily's face, she breaks into a laugh.

'No need to fret. Your honour is perfectly intact. You and I will share our original room and Max and Edward can have the other.'

Edward has his face turned away but Max doesn't bother to hide his displeasure at finding himself cast out of the marital bed.

'Can I have a quick word?' he says, steering his wife away by her elbow and leading her to the edge of a vast Persian carpet, where a turbanned waiter dressed all in white stands immobile as one of the statues behind him.

'He doesn't seem very happy,' Lily whispers to Edward as they watch Max Campbell gesture angrily to his wife, who gazes away into the distance, as if bored.

Edward doesn't reply and Lily notices that his face is paler than ever and his long fingers claw at each other as if he is trying to knit them together. She wonders if he is regretting the scene with Helena on the boat. She wonders if he, too, wishes they had never come.

They stand together, stiff and mute. The statues gaze out, haughtily, over their heads; the miniature palms flare from their pots. The musical clink of bone-china tea cups on a tray and the occasional rustle of newspaper pages turning are muffled by the rich velvet curtains and the soft ply of the Persian carpet. It is the most glamorous building Lily has ever been in and yet she can scarcely remember feeling more miserable.

13

THE ROOM LILY is to share with Eliza faces the front and has two enormous windows with slatted shutters on the outside. A fan is suspended from the centre of the ceiling, rotating at a stately speed with a gentle whirr, while a few feet away hangs a large hook from which a sheer white mosquito net tumbles like a spider's web over the king-size bed. They have only half an hour to freshen up before the afternoon's trip to the Pyramids, so there is hardly time to take in the luxurious en-suite bathroom with its enormous claw-foot tub or admire the paintings on the wall or acknowledge the *thump thump thump* of her heart as she considers the strangeness of her position and asks herself again what she is doing here.

Downstairs, Edward has picked up a British newspaper. There are two spots of high colour in his otherwise pale cheeks. Lily hopes he is not getting ill. She remembers again how Helena had said 'he won't ever be completely cured'. Perhaps this might be the very worst thing for him – the extremes of temperature: passing from the heat outside to the coolness of the hotel lobby; the awkwardness of the situation. He glances up anxiously when he senses someone approaching, then visibly relaxes as he sees it is her. He must like me a little, Lily thinks, if I can make him smile like that.

'What is the news from home?' she asks.

'Things with Germany are grim. Hitler has told the Polish government that by refusing to co-operate with his demands to annex Danzig, he considers them to have invited Germany to invade. And, if that happens, we're more or less committed to going to war with Germany ourselves.'

Lily feels cold fingers of fear wrapping themselves around her throat. So far, all the talk of war has been entirely theoretical to her, a dark cloud that has floated above her head but which she long ago stopped believing would release rain.

'But Chamberlain wouldn't allow it. Surely there would be another treaty, as over Czechoslovakia.'

Edward shrugs. 'Perhaps. But there is also all this business with Japan.'

Suddenly, the newspaper is snatched out of his hands.

'No war talk. It's too boring for words. Here we are in one of the world's most glorious hotels and you two are discussing politics? For heaven's sake!'

Eliza holds the newspaper behind her back and glares at the two of them in mock-admonishment. Next to her, dressed in white linen trousers and a pale blue shirt, Max stands with his hands thrust deep in his pockets, gazing off into the distance. The tension between the spouses hums angrily in the air.

'Sit with me on the coach, Lily,' urges Edward as they follow the guide out of the hotel. 'Please?'

They push ahead so they are ensconced into a double seat before the others arrive. Lily is flushed with pleasure at Edward's request, until she notices him shooting covert looks across the aisle to where Eliza has settled sulkily with Max. But soon all thoughts of Edward and of Eliza are wiped from her mind as, having followed a dusty road out of the city, they emerge from the built-up area to be greeted on one side by a row of distant palm trees and beyond them the River

Nile and on the other a vast, sandy plain. And there in the distance, the unmistakable triangular humps of the Pyramids, silhouetted against the hazy sky.

As she gazes at the astonishing sight, Lily thinks suddenly of her gentle, silent father. How much she should like to have him here by her side, seeing this with her, his large, soft hand holding hers. The thought, taking her unawares, gives her a savage stab of pain. Almost as if he can sense her sadness, Edward slips a hand through her arm.

'Doesn't it make one feel small?' he says softly. 'Imagining all the people who have looked on this same sight over the last five thousand years, and all the ones who will come after us? Makes all one's personal, private horrors seem insignificant, don't you think?'

Lily is stopped from prying further into what horrors he is talking about by the good-looking Egyptian guide, who has launched into a potted history of the site.

'Incredible to think that a hundred thousand men worked for thirty years to build the structures you see here,' he tells them in heavily accented English. 'But how did they bring the millions of blocks of stone from those cliffs' – he points through a window to the hills that rise up steeply on the far side of the Nile – 'across the river and the desert? And how then did they manage to construct, without the modern tools we have today, these monuments, which measure up to four hundred and fifty feet high? It is one of the greatest mysteries of all time.'

As they troop off the coach it is the sand that hits Lily first, getting into her eyes and nostrils, settling in a fine spray on her lips so they feel grainy and strange. And now comes the heat, pressing like an iron on her skin. They are at the base of the Great Pyramid, the largest of the structures, and Lily, like Edward, feels that sense of being dwarfed by history, of being just a speck of sand on the surface of time. Even the Campbells seem awed by their surroundings, listening in uncharacteristic silence while their guide talks to them in his melodious voice about kings and pharaohs and tombs and gods.

Inside the pyramid, they climb up a steep, narrow passageway. By the time they emerge into a grand, vaulted gallery twenty-six feet high, but also on a steep slant, Lily's heart is pounding. Her cotton dress sticks to the backs of her thighs as they progress onwards through the ancient hall. Now there is a great stone step, its surface worn almost smooth, to navigate, by way of two metal rungs. She peels her dress off her legs before stepping on to the first rung, aware of her hair hanging damp around her face and the sweat trickling down her neck. Now comes a second, very low passageway, also rising steeply and stuffy with stale air. Max is behind her. As she waits for the woman in front of her, who has stopped to catch her breath, Lily is horrified to feel Max pressing on her from behind and something hard against her buttocks, and his breath hot in her ear. Ahead of her, the woman starts once again to climb and Lily propels herself forward, not daring to look around.

They come to the King's Chamber and Lily quickly steps to the side, her chest tight. Immediately, she is doubting what she felt. It was so close in that narrow passageway, everyone piled on top of everyone else. Probably Max had himself been pressed forward by the crush behind him. Gradually, her breath, which has been coming out in shallow bursts, calms and she risks looking for the others.

Eliza and Edward are deep in conversation, their dark heads close together like Siamese twins. Max is standing to the side with an expression of benign calm. He does not look shifty or furtive or even leering. She has imagined it all.

The room in which they find themselves is smaller than the great gallery, and far less ornate. The only adornment is a huge granite slab at one end. This, the guide informs them, is the king's sarcophagus, a stone coffin. Lily is relieved to hear that grave robbers have long since stolen any remains from within. Nevertheless, something about the room chills her, some malign presence that hovers above their heads, where the huge granite blocks are held in place as if by magic, not even a hair's space between them.

Their guide tells them that Napoleon Bonaparte once spent the night in here and was by all accounts left shaken by whatever transpired. More recently, a British philosopher and traveller had managed to arrange to have himself locked in the chamber for a night and claimed to have undergone a profound spiritual experience in which he became completely detached from his own body and roamed freely around the various hidden parts of the pyramid.

'I would not care to do that myself,' the guide says, shuddering in a theatrical way. 'I believe the dead must be allowed to rest in peace.'

And now comes into Lily's mind an image of Mags, her own Mags. Her face as it was the first time they met in the kitchen of the Spencers' house overlooking Ealing Common. Her eyes set wide apart, the palest, softest blue and ringed by navy, as if a child had outlined them in ink then used a sooty pencil to fringe them with dark lashes. Pale cheeks, still with the blurred, unfinished look of adolescence, and a shy smile that seemed to question her right to be smiling at all.

'Oh!' She has said it aloud and, instantly, Edward is by her side.

'Are you all right, Lily?'

'Yes, perfectly all right.' She is embarrassed and forces herself to laugh to show that she is not in the slightest perturbed. 'It's just the heat and the climb.'

But as they make their way along another narrow, steep passageway, through a second, less impressive chamber, and then down again, almost crouching, until they finally reach the entrance, Lily cannot shake off the oppressive sensation she'd felt in the King's Chamber, something dark pressing down on her, nor the image of Mags's face superimposed over it, like a double-exposure photograph.

Outside once again, she breathes in great gulps of hot, sand-saturated air. 'I should like to spend a night in that room, wouldn't you, Lily?' asks Eliza, coming to find her. 'What bad luck they've stopped allowing people to do it. It would be a hoot. We could have a little party. Why do I always seem to arrive places just as the fun is finishing?'

'Oh, I don't know, darling,' says Max, strolling over. 'You don't seem to do too badly when it comes to fun.'

As the group gathers outside figures emerge from the dust-hazed air and converge on them, holding out souvenirs – carvings, necklaces. Their guide, whose name, one of the other passengers has ascertained, is Anwar, makes a flapping motion with his arm and talks in that throaty language that makes it seem, to Lily, as if every word is threatening some violence.

'Ladies and gentlemen, if anyone is feeling as if they have not yet exercised sufficiently' – there is a dutiful groan at Anwar's little joke – 'it is possible now to climb a little on the outside of the Great Pyramid. The rest of us will rest a while before moving towards the next pyramid and, of course, the world-famous Sphinx.'

A couple of the younger men break off from the party and begin to scale the monstrous blocks. Lily, still agitated, gazes around. A second group of passengers from the ship, who have travelled on a different coach with their own guide, has joined them. Lily feels her already heated cheeks burn when she spies among them the elderly woman who had approached her in the gift shop in Pompeii to warn her about the Campbells. The woman is carrying a parasol and looking pained, as if the visit to one of the Wonders of the World is something to be endured rather than enjoyed. She catches Lily's eye and purses her lips in disapproval.

Eliza has now made her way over to Anwar and is engaged in animated conversation. She throws back her head and laughs at something he says, and the sound travels through the dust and sand, arriving gritty in Lily's ear. Max stands watching, arms folded, his presence, tall and broad as he is, suddenly almost as overwhelming as the pyramid that looms up behind them. Lily remembers how his body had felt pressed up behind her in the passageway.

'I think I'll go for a climb,' she tells Edward.

He looks startled and immediately glances around the company, his eyes coming finally to rest on Max. He does not want to be left here alone, the only outsider, Lily realizes, recognizing his thought processes as if they were her own.

'Why don't you . . .' he starts, but she is already pulling herself up on to the lowest block, and then up again, her need to get away from Max and the confusion he brings out in her overcoming her fear of standing out and her worry over her cotton dress revealing her bare legs as she lifts her feet from step to step. Lily has always been athletic. With a competitive younger brother, she understood early she had either to learn to be interested in the things he liked – running, football, tennis – or resign herself to playing always on her own. She is already thirty feet up before she becomes aware that Edward is following her, and struggling to keep pace.

He came after me, she thinks. The thought breaks over her like a warm bath.

'You could have told me you were related to the mountain goat,' he gasps, arriving finally on a level with her. Damp with heat, he looks down and briefly closes his eyes. 'Please tell me we're high enough now. We're practically airborne.'

Lily follows his gaze to the knot of people below. There's Max, staring upwards, though she cannot see his expression. And Eliza, still standing beside Anwar, her hand on his arm, her yellow dress blooming like an unlikely flower in the desert.

'Not yet,' she says, and begins once again to climb, on impulse grabbing hold of his hand to pull him along with her. His palm is pillow-soft, the bones of his fingers fragile as twigs. Immediately, she is embarrassed. She drops his hand and stares fixedly ahead.

They climb for five minutes. For more. The hazy sun makes the dusty air shimmer. Up ahead, the young men from their party have disappeared from view, in competition to reach the very top. Down below, so far away they are just dots in the vast, sandy landscape, the rest of the tour group is moving away, even Eliza's bright dress now swallowed up by the sea of beige sand.

She stops on a wide block, aware of the aching muscles in her calves and the backs of her thighs, of her hair, damp and curling with sweat and heat. Leaning back against the warm stone of the block behind, she waits for Edward to catch up. Closes her eyes. She senses him beside her, panting from his exertions. So close to her the fine hairs on her arm rise up to meet his.

'Lily?'

Opening her eyes, she finds his face just inches from hers. His eyes are cool green pools she can sink into and feel washed clean. Who makes that first move? It is impossible to say. His mouth is suddenly on hers, and it's as if her entire being is concentrated at the point where their bodies meet. She parts her lips and his tongue is there, gently seeking out her own.

How different from those kisses with Robert, his mouth a gaping hole that would swallow her whole, his big hands roving over her as if he were checking over a cut of meat.

They pull apart. Slowly, Edward opens his eyes. 'Oh, Lily,' he says softly, tracing her face with his fingertips as if she were made from Braille. 'Lovely Lily.'

Then he drops his arm to his side and his expression changes. 'I'm sorry. I should never have . . .' He leans forward and puts his head in his hands.

Lily is awash with confusion.

'Edward, it's fine,' she tells him. 'I wanted to.'

He looks up at her, his hands still resting on his knees, and she is alarmed to see how stricken he looks.

'What is it?' she asks. 'Are you unwell?'

And then, the thought pricking her like a needle: 'Is there someone else?'

Eliza dances across Lily's vision in her yellow dress.

There is a noise from up above, the sound of feet slapping on stone, and the young men who preceded them up the pyramid come back into view. 'I say, is that as far as you got?' calls one, triumph perhaps making him garrulous. 'We've been all the way to the top. There's the most marvellous view. You can see practically back to Blighty!'

'I think we will take your word for it,' says Edward, straightening up. 'Are you ready to head back down, Lily?'

She nods, not wanting to speak for fear that, if she opens her mouth, the lump that has formed in her throat will fall out like a lozenge.

They begin their descent, dropping down in silence from one ledge to another. At one point, where the cement between the blocks has crumbled to loose stones, Edward offers her his hand, but Lily lowers her head and pretends she has not seen. All the time, while the voices of the young men just ahead of them echo off the stone, she is trying to make sense of what happened, but now the kiss is blurring with the heat and the strangeness of the day into a sensory maelstrom where nothing is distinct and everything hurts.

Reaching the bottom, they set off in search of the others, and Lily is glad of the swaggering presence of the two young men, so buoyed up from conquering the summit of the pyramid they don't notice the heavy atmosphere that has settled over their newly encountered companions like a cloud of dust.

Dinner in the Shepheard Hotel is impossibly grand. A vast hall with pillars that prop up an ornate vaulted ceiling, starched white tablecloths to match the long, white robes of the waiters. Max and Eliza, however, are irritable, too wrapped up in their own squabbles to notice the subdued moods of their guests. At least, that's what Lily thinks, until Eliza turns on her abruptly.

'Such a dark horse you are, Lily. So quiet and meek and then suddenly hitching up your skirts and clambering up the rocks like a native. How many other secrets are you keeping from us? I wonder.'

Lily feels her face flame.

'I grew up with a brother,' she says.

'I think it's admirable,' says Max, looking Lily over until her fingers, under the table, pluck at the chiffon of her midnight-blue dress. 'I like a woman who knows what to do with her body.'

'Max!' Eliza glares at him, though whether in earnest or in mock-anger Lily could not have said.

'I was talking about sport,' says Max, and his lips, under that moustache, widen into one of his outsized smiles.

After dinner Lily tries to say she is tired. She is dreading the intimacy of sharing a room with Eliza and hopes that by retiring early she can be already asleep by the time her room-mate arrives.

But the Campbells will not hear of Lily leaving early. 'We did not kidnap you and bring you all this way just so that you can go to bed at nine o'clock,' says Eliza. She is smiling, but Lily can't help feeling like a pet monkey, expected to perform for its keep.

They repair to the Long Bar, which Eliza informs her is now known as St Joe's Parish in honour of the legendary barman Joe Scialom. One of Eliza's friends, who was here earlier in the year, has told her she simply must try one of Joe's signature cocktails.

'We'll have four Suffering Bastards,' Eliza asks the dapper man in the white jacket and black bow tie behind the bar.

Lily gasps, but the man behind the bar merely flashes a gleaming smile and begins mixing up a seemingly lethal combination of gin, cognac, lime cordial and ginger beer.

'Divine!' Eliza declares, draining hers and instantly ordering four more, even though Lily has not had more than two sips. Though she is used to wine and the occasional beer, Lily rarely drinks spirits, and she can already feel an unfamiliar warmth seeping through her veins.

Seeing Anwar, the guide, standing at the bar talking to one of the hotel staff, Eliza calls him over and insists he join them for a drink.

'I'm afraid I don't drink alcohol,' says the guide, but while his words are apologetic, his eyes, travelling over Eliza in her coral silk dress, are anything but.

A band starts playing as the barman mixes Anwar a cocktail made from fruit juices and cordials, and Eliza moves closer to him so she can hear what he is saying, their conversation drowned out for the others by the sound of a saxophone.

Max looks at his wife's back, which is now fully turned towards them, the spine gracefully curved as the frame of a harp, and Lily sees how a muscle is moving at the side of his cheek. She glances over towards Edward, hoping he might step in to end the awkward silence, but Edward is frowning into his drink, his expression closed. Already she is doubting what happened up there on the pyramid. Could this man with his dark head bent over his glass really be the same man who pressed his lips, his tongue, to hers?

Max snatches Lily's glass out of her hand and slams it down on the bar, together with his own empty one.

'We'll dance,' he says. And it's not a question. Lily has the sense of things being expected of her, payment due in kind for the fact of their being here in this bar, in this hotel, in this strange, exotic city, instead of back on the boat tucked up alongside Ida and Audrey, or giving moral support to Maria, as they chug through the darkness in the Suez Canal.

Even so, she hesitates, throwing a helpless look to Edward, who gives her a small, tight smile and raises his glass.

On the dancefloor the band breaks into a popular swing number that Lily has heard before. She usually enjoys dancing, but now she cannot seem to find the rhythm. Max's hand on her waist burns through the thin material of her dress until she feels certain it must leave a scorch mark on her skin. Please let this be over, she thinks, as she lets herself be led around the floor, her gaze fixed on Max's white bow tie so she won't have to look up and catch his eye.

Edward stands to the right of the dancefloor, drinking and following their movements intently. She imagines how different it would feel to be holding his soft hand in hers instead of Max's.

'You're so stiff, Miss Lily Shepherd,' says Max. 'You need to relax. Let yourself go a bit.'

'I'm quite relaxed, thank you. Maybe just a little tired.'

'I'm not surprised, after all your exertions up that pyramid.'

Lily's heart stutters in her chest. Did he see what happened between her and Edward? The thought of it makes her feel weak.

The song finishes, to Lily's immense relief. She is just turning away back towards the bar when the band strikes up again. This time it is a slow melody which she recognizes as the Fred Astaire and Ginger Rogers hit 'The Way You Look Tonight'. Max tightens his grip on her hand and around her waist and pulls her towards him so that their upper bodies are pressed together. She remembers the passageway inside the pyramid, something hard against her back.

'You're blushing, Lily. Are you hot?'

It is as though he can read her body's responses, just as Edward so often seems able to read her mind. Robert was the same, although she was too young then to recognize it. Something brushes the top of her forehead and, from the warm, damp breath that accompanies it, she knows it to be Max's moustache, and that his mouth is just a hair's breadth from her skin.

There's a peal of laughter from behind, and Lily is surprised to turn and see Eliza in the arms of Anwar, the young guide. Such a blurring of lines here – the guests dancing with the staff. But then again, is it any more strange than her being here, with the sort of people to whom she used to serve tea, whose houses she once cleaned?

The sight of his wife seems to effect a change in Max. He pulls Lily closer and his fingers tighten over hers until they are all but crushing them. When he speaks his voice has lost its tone of cool amusement.

'I love my wife. You understand.'

More of a croak, in fact, than a voice. Has Lily heard him correctly? She is about to ask him to repeat it when he suddenly erupts.

'Why must he stare so? He is growing tiresome.' Lily follows Max's gaze to Edward, who is still watching them from the shadows beyond the outer limits of the dancefloor.

Joy flares briefly and, instantly, she becomes protective, unable to bear the idea of this fragile thing that exists between her and Edward being held up to Max's ice-blue scrutiny.

The song finishes, and Lily pulls away, wresting her hand free.

'I really am feeling terribly tired. It's been such an exciting day. I'm very grateful to you and Eliza.'

Max, marooned on the dancefloor, makes an impatient movement with his hand, as if slapping away a fly.

'Save your gratitude, little Lily,' he says. 'It's so boringly bourgeois.'

Back in her hotel room, Lily clings to the outside edge of the bed. The events of the day are playing through her mind like a loop of newsreel and she despairs of being able to sleep. Nevertheless, she must have dropped off because she is awoken some time later by voices outside the door.

'Let me come in with you.'

'Goodness, you're tiresome when you're drunk, Max. You know Lily is in there.'

'So. It's not as if you haven't done it before.'

'Don't be a pig.'

There's the sound of something moving, a grunt, a muffled 'Don't'. Then Max again.

'Bet you wouldn't say "Don't" if it was that greasy guide who had his fingers in your –'

The sound of the door opening and quickly closing again. Eliza's breath heavy in the thick darkness.

'Bitch.'

Lily flinches at the word, the violence of it, even through the thick wooden hotel-room door.

There's a swish of satin, and the sweeping of the mosquito net along the floor, and then the mattress dips. 'Are you awake, Lily?' asks Eliza, in a voice that sounds surprisingly untroubled.

Lily is tempted to feign sleep but she can't shake off the notion that Eliza would be able to tell.

'Yes,' she says, yawning, hoping her tone sounds suitably sleep-soaked. 'Although I'm awfully tired.'

'Really? I could have danced all night, except that the orchestra packed up and Max was being such a bore. You go back to sleep, though, and if I start pushing you out in the night, just roll me right back to my side. Max maintains I'm the greediest bedmate ever. I like to colonize every single bit of the mattress, like this.'

Eliza stretches out her arms and legs in a star shape. Lily forces herself not to recoil when she feels one of the other woman's warm feet brushing her leg.

She closes her eyes and tries to slow down her breathing. For a while the only noise in the room is the gentle groaning of the ceiling fan and the whine of a mosquito over by the window.

Then comes a whisper in the darkness: 'Lily?' Lily grunts, as if she already has one foot into sleep.

'Lily, do you ever feel as if you only exist when you see yourself reflected back in someone else's eyes?'

Lily remains still, keeping her breathing even. Eliza sighs, a sound as delicate as sea mist. And now the mattress moves again, and there is once more the sweeping of the mosquito net, this time followed by the padding of footsteps.

Eliza will be going to the bathroom, Lily thinks. So she is surprised to see a shaft of light fall across the room as the door to the corridor opens, and then hear the soft click of the latch as Eliza closes it behind her.

14

11 August 1939

ILY IS SO happy to see the *Orontes* waiting by the dock at Port
Suez she almost bursts into tears. It feels as if she and Edward
have been away for weeks, rather than twenty-four hours. She can't
wait to see Audrey and Helena and have a conversation where she
doesn't always feel as if there is a second conversation going on
underneath the first that she isn't party to. And she wants to check
how Maria is. She feels guilty at leaving her so soon after she was
assaulted. The memory of it shocks her all over again.

But mostly she wants to get away from the Campbells, with all
their confusing complications, and even from Edward, who has
been curt and moody ever since they all gathered in the hotel lobby
at six o'clock that morning. Max, who pronounced himself as
having the beast of all hangovers, has also been monosyllabic. Only
Eliza, who had slipped back into the hotel room just half an hour
before they were due to get up, is bright and breezy. Lily doesn't ask
her where she was. Better not to know.

On the way from the coach to the ship they are followed by a
group of children, who seem especially interested in Eliza.

'Meeses Seeempson,' they chant, pulling on her arm and smiling
up into her face then bowing deeply.

'You remind them of the lady who stole King Edward,' says Anwar, who is accompanying them to the gangway. He is different this morning. Subdued. Unable to meet anyone's eyes.

'Wallis Simpson?' laughs Eliza. 'That's hardly a compliment!'

'It is only your hair,' mutters Anwar.

When he takes his leave of them at the edge of the quayside Anwar shakes each of their hands in turn and only when he comes to Eliza does he finally raise his eyes from the dusty floor. There is something in them that Lily cannot read, some question which hangs in the air until Eliza turns away and starts up the gangplank.

'Max, make sure you give Anwar a nice, fat tip,' she calls over her shoulder.

Back on board, Edward and Lily stop on the tourist deck, where the staircase continues up to First.

'I really can't thank you enough,' Edward says, addressing a spot somewhere between Eliza and Max. 'I shall remember my trip to the Pyramids for the rest of my life.'

Lily hopes her face does not give away the flush of embarrassment she feels when he mentions the scene of their kiss which, already, is seeming as if it happened in another life.

'The same goes for me,' she tells them. 'I am really so grateful.'

'Nonsense,' says Eliza. 'You did us a favour. Without you we should literally have died of boredom. Shouldn't we, Max?'

Max says nothing, but the look he shoots at Edward before he follows his wife up the staircase is unexpectedly cold and Lily wonders if he resents them having muscled in on what should have been an intimate night away with his wife.

'Right. Well, I think I'll go and drop my things at my cabin.' Lily makes to leave, but Edward puts his hand on her arm.

'Lily? I just wanted to say, about yesterday. I should never have –'

'Don't worry. Really. It's forgotten. It was the heat.'

'It's not that you're not utterly wonderful, it's just that I haven't been –'

'I know. You haven't been well. And the last thing you need is a complication. It is the same for me, too. We just let the sun and the place carry us away.'

How pompous she sounds. How stilted. But she cannot bear to stand here, not daring to look at him for fear of the pity and embarrassment she should find in his face, not wanting him to see how her hand is shaking.

'We're still friends, Lily, aren't we?'

Such appeal in his voice. How badly he wants for everything to be all right again, for yesterday's kiss to be forgotten. What can she say, except: 'Of course. I'll see you at lunch.'

And now she is released, and hurrying down to F Deck, where she carefully puts her overnight things away, and then climbs the ladder to her bunk, curls up facing the wall and sobs without making a sound.

She is disturbed by the cabin steward bringing letters that have been picked up in Port Suez. If the man wonders at her swollen eyes or rumpled appearance, he doesn't show it.

'Good to have you back, miss.'

She has a letter from Mam, and a second one from Frank. She reads Frank's first, smiling at his careless writing, the characters all different sizes and liberally decorated with ink splodges. The letter is typical Frank. He starts by telling her how boring it is at home, and how his job at the biscuit factory isn't much better and he hopes there is a war because then he would at least get to travel, then he launches into a long-winded and confusing anecdote about his best mate, Geoff, and how he had too much to drink in the pub and then tried to liberate his elderly neighbour's racing pigeons on

137

his way home, before ending abruptly with 'Mam's just put my tea on the table so I'd better go.'

Her mother's letter is longer and just seeing her laboured writing on the page makes Lily long for home so acutely it's like a cold needle passing between her ribs. She thanks Lily for her last letter and tells her they are all following the progress of the ship in the atlas they have at home. She likes the sound of Edward and Helena Fletcher, she says, and warns her not to get on the wrong side of Ida: 'She seems the sort would hold a grudge.' She tells Lily that they are still optimistic that war will be avoided and that Chamberlain 'hasn't the appetite for it'. She describes her most recent visit to her sister Jean in Basingstoke and how Jean's daughter-in-law had visited with her toddler. 'Jean calls her "bonny" but quite honestly, Lily, I think "fat" would be more truthful.' She talks about Lily's dad and how the daily talk about war is affecting him badly.

Lily was only two years old and Frank just a baby when a grenade went off just feet away from her father, tearing off the bottom part of his right leg and sending him into a coma, from which he emerged two weeks later, suffering nightmarish flashbacks and with no memory of his earlier life.

Gradually, with the help of Lily's mother, the flashbacks went away, and he'd learned to walk using a prosthetic leg. But he'd had to relearn his entire life, and he'd never spoken again. 'Is it because he can't or because he won't?' Lily would ask her mother as a child. One of the older neighbourhood children had once told her his tongue had been cut out by the Germans, and for weeks she'd kept that horrible thought to herself, hardly daring to look at her father when he ate or yawned for fear of seeing some disfigured stump in his mouth, until, finally, she told Frank and he told her mother, and her mother had her father stick his tongue out to show them it was still all present and correct.

She's never got a proper answer from her mam on the question of whether her father's muteness is self-imposed, and now his silence is as much a part of the fabric of her life as the little terraced house in Reading or her mam's old brown leather handbag.

When Lily comes to the end of her letters, she reads each one again, slowly, homesickness building in her throat. Just as she is readying herself for another bout of crying Audrey bursts into the cabin, with Annie following on like a red-headed shadow.

'You're back! I thought you must be when I saw everyone else getting on board. The Pyramids! You lucky thing. I feel like I might explode with jealousy. Tell me everything. Don't leave a single thing out.'

Lily looks at Audrey's wide, good-natured face and is instantly flooded with shame. What right has she got to be feeling sorry for herself when she is having the adventure of a lifetime? She remembers all the nights in her lodgings in Bayswater when she'd let herself into her room after a late shift and the cold and damp would be waiting in the dark to meet her like a reproachful husband, and her heart would shrivel a little as she wondered, *Is this it? Is this all?* And now here she is on a ship, with Africa on one side and Asia on the other, surrounded by interesting people, having just spent the night in Cairo's most glittering hotel and visited one of the Ancient Wonders of the World.

I'm an idiotic woman, she thinks.

Taking a deep breath in, she places the letters between the pages of her diary and climbs down the ladder and joins Audrey and Annie sitting on the spare bottom bunk, where she talks them through the events of the last twenty-four hours, leaving out only the kiss with Edward and the dance with Max, and Eliza's footsteps padding out of the hotel room in the early hours of the morning.

By the time she finishes she is feeling much cheerier and resolves to put all her confused feelings behind her and focus solely on what is in front of her. Back up on the scorching deck, she stands at the railing for as long as she can bear, watching the coast of Egypt roll past with its ridge of sandy mountains, reflecting almost pink in the hazy heat. The ship is passing slowly through the Red Sea on its way to its next stop, Aden, and all around there is a sense of life suspended, of people waiting out the heat. Regrouping.

She locates Maria at one end of the ship, sitting with a circle of Jewish women talking in German.

'Lily!' Maria exclaims, and gets up to greet her, but not before Lily has sensed a hesitation.

'How are you?' Lily wants to know.

Now that she sees Maria's face, with purple shadows under her eyes and a line down her forehead that wasn't there before, Lily feels more wretched than ever about having left her, but when she tries to apologize Maria quickly shuts her down.

'Lily, if you had given up the chance to see the Pyramids on my account, I should never have been able to speak to you again, and that would be a terrible tragedy. Now, tell me all about it.'

And once again Lily gives an account of the journey to Cairo and the Pyramids, which, already, is starting to take on the quality of a dream, or something that happened to someone else.

As she talks she and Maria parade up and down the deck under the shade of the awning. From the dining room comes the clatter of cutlery being set out for lunch, while from the passengers draped listlessly over deckchairs there's a quiet hum of chatter, broken by the soft thump of cards being laid down on tables or the rustle of pages being turned.

'And how did you get along with Edward Fletcher?'

Maria glances sideways at Lily, a smile twitching at her lips, and Lily is hot with embarrassment. Is it that obvious? Does everyone know? Anxiety makes her more abrupt than she intends.

'We're friends, of course.'

Maria says nothing, just waits, and soon Lily gives in.

'There was a moment when I thought, perhaps, we might be more than friends. But . . .'

She tails off. Once again Maria waits in silence, not pressing Lily for more information but leaving a space for her to be more expansive if she needs to.

'Well, I think, after a night to think it over, he had second thoughts.'

'And you don't know why?'

Lily shrugs miserably.

'I'm just not the right person for him. I know he likes me, but he doesn't . . . well . . . look at me the way he looks at Eliza Campbell, for instance. But really, that's fine. I'm not looking for an onboard romance.'

Her intention of injecting a note of firmness and finality into the last sentence is thwarted by her cracking voice.

Maria reaches out for Lily's arm and draws it through hers.

'Did it ever occur to you, Lily,' she says eventually, speaking slowly, as if deliberating each word before delivery, 'that it might be a question of – how to put it? – class? Helena told me her family are professionals. Her father is in the – how do you say this? – service of the government. Edward himself was studying to be a lawyer before he became ill. Please don't be offended, dear Lily, but you are travelling to Australia in order to go into domestic service. Might his parents not have been expecting what they might consider to be a better match?'

Lily stops still, conscious suddenly of the overwhelming heat and the new burning sensation at the back of her eyeballs. Now that Maria has mentioned it, she can see that it must be so. She has allowed the ship, with its blurring of social boundaries, to convince her that they are all on the same level, but now she realizes how naive that is. Even though Helena and Edward are travelling in tourist class, just like she is, back in England they would move in completely different circles. How would Edward ever be able to write to his parents and tell them he had an involvement with a housemaid?

'Of course, you're right, Maria. I hadn't thought about it like that. How silly of me.'

Now Maria looks stricken.

'Lily, it was not my intention to make you upset. I merely wanted to make you understand that it might be nothing to do with how Edward feels about you.'

She wishes to cheer Lily up, but nothing can override the feeling Lily has of foolishness, of having allowed her schoolgirl fantasies to overrule her common sense. She'd been so sure that, after Robert, she would never again let herself be carried away by the notion of a real-life love story, and yet here she is again, as if she has learned nothing.

As they reach the stairwell leading down to the lower deck an anguished cry floats up to them, jolting Lily out of her self-absorption.

'Another Italian baby on the way,' Maria tells her. 'Our steward told us this morning.'

'That makes three so far. The ship's doctor must be exhausted.'

Fitting, nevertheless, to think of new lives beginning as old lives are being left behind.

Anxious now to steer the conversation away from her Cairo tour, Lily risks bringing up the assault.

'How is the investigation going? Have they found out who did it?' she wants to know.

Maria is quiet, gently pressing her lips together.

'I don't think there has been any investigation. When I saw the captain yesterday afternoon he said he was very sorry but there wasn't very much he could do. He suggested that if I'd been at the other end of the deck with "my group", it would never have happened.'

'Your group?'

'The other Jews, I think he meant.'

'But that's nonsense.'

Outrage has ground Lily to a stop.

'Someone attacked you, Maria. They have an obligation to find out who it was. They need to talk to everyone, in case anyone saw something.'

'It's fine, Lily. It's finished.'

'No, it's not fine. I'll find a steward. I'll ask him to draw up a list of who was sleeping on deck so they can start interviewing the other passengers.'

'Lily, leave it.'

Maria has spoken so loudly that a couple playing cribbage at a nearby table look over in their direction, frowning.

'It's fine,' she repeats, lowering her voice. 'It's forgotten.'

But all that afternoon Lily can't shake off a bristling sense of injustice. On some level she is aware that she is focusing on this in order to avoid thinking about Edward, but nevertheless she finds it intolerable that, instead of finding out who was responsible so that they might all feel safer sleeping outside in the future, the ship's authorities seem to be trying to lay the blame at Maria's feet.

It's the custom on board for the ship's captain to appear in the dining room once a week and go from table to table, making conversation with the passengers. It's designed, Lily supposes, to put passengers at their ease, knowing that the ship is in such capable hands. The captain is a short but nevertheless imposing figure with a calm, deliberate manner and a way of speaking that invests his words with instant authority. Tonight's dinner will coincide with his weekly appearance and she resolves to question him about what he is doing to investigate what happened to Maria, even though on the previous occasion she has found herself too awestruck in his presence to say much about anything.

She spends a good time getting ready, telling herself it is because of the captain and not in any way because Edward will be sitting just inches away from her. The bathroom steward is pleased to see her.

'I reserved your bathroom yesterday, as usual, miss, but you never came.'

Lily apologizes and makes a mental note to give him the other half of his tip, as they are almost halfway through their journey. He puts her in mind of her brother, Frank, with his touching mix of inexperience and cocky cheeriness. On a ship peopled with unfamiliar types it is reassuring to find someone who reminds her of home.

Sitting in the bath, she scrubs herself with the treated seawater, relishing how the sting of it makes her skin feel alive, as if it's washing off the dust and the dirt from the Cairo trip and the residual flakes of shame that seem to have attached themselves to her. Afterwards, she rinses herself well with the warm, fresh water from the basin at the foot of the bath. It's forgotten, she thinks, as she watches the water drain between her toes. All of it.

She wears her navy linen skirt, which is freshly laundered, together with a sleeveless white blouse and her gold silk scarf around her neck, noticing only when she is dressed that it is the sort of outfit a librarian might wear. She thinks for a moment of Eliza last night in her coral dress and almost changes but then stops herself. If she resembles a middle-aged librarian, so much the better.

At dinner, Helena insists on sitting next to her so that she can hear all her news. Lily is grateful to have Edward safely one seat away.

'He hasn't told me anything,' Helena complains. 'Just that the Pyramids were "big" and "old" and everything was covered in sand. Well, what a surprise – I think I knew that much already!'

So Lily talks a bit about the tour and Anwar and the way the coach had no sooner passed the last buildings of Cairo before the Pyramids appeared there, looming up on the city's very doorstep. She talks about the narrow passageways inside the Great Pyramid and the chill in the King's Chamber.

'And did you climb up the outside?' Helena wants to know. 'Up all those ancient blocks?'

Uncomfortably aware of Edward sitting to Helena's right, Lily tries to keep her tone light and breezy.

'Yes, a few of us climbed a little way up. It's harder work than it looks!'

'And the hotel?' asks Helena. 'Was it very grand? It must have cost a lot more than six pounds for you to have a room each.'

'Oh, we didn't have our own rooms.' Seeing Helena's eyebrows shoot up, Lily feels herself flush and quickly launches into an explanation of the sleeping arrangements, only to be interrupted by Edward.

'We drank the most wonderful cocktails. Suffering Bastards, they were called.'

There's an audible gasp from the other side of the table, and too late Edward remembers about Mrs Mills and her fifteen-year-old daughter, Peggy.

'Oh, I'm so sorry, please forgive me.'

In the ensuing fuss, the apologies and the protestations, the conversation about their brief sojourn is forgotten, to Lily's immense relief.

But now the captain is doing his rounds, and Lily steels her nerve to talk to him. George Price professes his own intention to make good use of the captain's ear. The Italians are too noisy, he informs them all. His cabin is directly over theirs and all night he is kept awake by their infernal yabbering.

The captain, when he arrives, listens in respectful silence to George's grievances. Then he summons a steward, who has accompanied him and is currently lurking near the door to the dining room.

'Mr Hodkin here will make a note of your complaint,' he says. 'Be assured, we will be looking into the matter most thoroughly.'

Afterwards, George seems mollified, proud even. He puffs out his barrel chest.

Now it is Lily's turn, but still it is only when the captain is just about to take his leave that she finally finds the courage to address him.

'I just wondered, Captain,' she says, 'whether there has been any progress with the investigation into the' – she glances at Peggy Mills then lowers her voice to say – '*assault* that took place up on deck the night before last. I am a friend of Maria Katz. The victim.'

The captain, whose gaze has before merely grazed Lily politely, now looks at her with interest.

'Miss?'

'Shepherd.'

'Well, Miss Shepherd, I'm afraid we have abandoned our investigations into the . . . *incident.*'

He really does have a voice that invites blind trust. She finds herself nodding, though there is nothing to nod about.

'We made enquiries among the other passengers who were sleeping on deck that night and I'm afraid we have it on good authority that there was no assault.'

Lily stares at him, uncomprehending.

'But I was there,' she says at last.

She tries to think back to that night. Waking up in the darkness, Maria's scream.

'I saw . . .'

But what had she seen? A shape? A shadow that could have been something or nothing.

'I heard footsteps,' she says.

The captain holds her gaze. 'Someone screamed. Of course there would have been footsteps.'

Still Lily cannot make sense of it.

'Whose authority?' she asks. 'You said you had it on good authority.'

'One of the other passengers who was lying nearby told my

purser that they were suffering from a stomach pain and didn't sleep the whole night. They were wide awake when Miss Katz started screaming and swore there had been no intruder.'

'Oh my,' says Clara Mills, her tiny hands once more on the move about her chest and throat. 'Are you saying she's an hysteric, Captain?'

'One must not try to guess what drives another person, Mrs . . .'

'Mills. It's Mrs Mills and this is my daughter, Peggy. We are travelling quite alone, which is why the news of the attack came as such a shock to me.'

'Well, now you need worry yourself no further.'

'But they must have got it wrong,' Lily says. 'Maria is such a sensible sort of person. She wouldn't invent something like this.'

The captain holds up his hand.

'As I say, Miss Shepherd, it's not up to us to ascribe a motive. It was very hot that night – perhaps the lady was suffering from some sort of heatstroke.'

'More likely she just wanted to stir up trouble,' says George Price. 'Her people are known for it.'

The captain raises his hand again, as if to halt the conjecture.

'I don't suppose we will ever know the real reason. The best thing we can do is put the whole unfortunate affair behind us. But be assured, ladies, the deck is perfectly safe for sleeping.'

After dinner Lily has coffee with Helena and Edward in the lounge. The shock news about Maria has temporarily pushed aside any lingering awkwardness about what happened in Cairo, and now the three of them can talk of nothing else except what a strange affair it all is.

There is some mistake. Lily is sure of it. Maria would not make up such a thing. She is not that kind of a person.

And yet, asks Helena gently, how sure can she really be?

'Think of it, Lily. All of us are thrown together here on this ship in such close proximity with no way of escaping and so much time to kill, and we become intimate much more quickly than we ever would in the real world. But what do we really know of each other? Only what we choose to share or to reveal. Maria could be anyone. So could we, for that matter. None of us has any way of knowing who the others are.'

Feeling deeply unsettled, Lily looks around the lounge. Most passengers are now familiar to her, even those she hasn't yet spoken to. There's the family from Kent over there with the three rotund sons who are always first in the queue for cakes and sandwiches at suppertime. And the newly-weds over in the corner who met just six months ago at a dinner-dance in Bexleyheath and are off to Australia to begin a new life, away from the interference of her parents. Might they all be inventing themselves? It hasn't occurred to Lily not to take her fellow passengers at face value. Has she been too trusting, believing in the tiny fragment they present to her, not realizing the full extent of the iceberg hidden under the water's surface?

One of the male passengers has sat down at the piano and starts playing a tune that Lily doesn't recognize. To her surprise, his two male companions join in, singing along lustily.

'They're Aussies,' says Helena, noticing her stare. 'They came aboard at Port Said and have already scandalized half the passengers.'

Lily turns to look again more closely. Two of the men are young, not much older than her, she guesses, with fair hair that looks quite shocking against their deeply tanned skin. The third looks to be in his forties and, while also brown as a polished nut, has brown hair, slightly greying at the sides. As they come to the end of their song there is a round of applause from the passengers nearest to the piano, and they retake their seats, laughing and making mock-bows.

'The older one keeps looking at you,' Lily tells Helena.

Helena's cheeks colour instantly. 'Don't be ridiculous.'

'He just did it again.'

'Lily's right,' Edward joins in. 'There was definitely a look.'

The three of them play a game of whist and Lily is glad things are seeming more normal between them. It's as if the kiss never happened, she lies to herself. After a while the band sets up and there's dancing out on the deck. Though it's completely dark outside, the air is as hot and sultry as if the sun were still beating down and the couples glide languidly around, hardly picking their feet up from the floor.

Lily wonders if Edward will ask her to dance and simultaneously longs for him to do so and dreads it happening. She watches him light a cigarette, holding it between his beautifully shaped fingers, and has to look away when he puts it to his lips. Just over two weeks ago she did not know Edward Fletcher existed, yet now she is aware of every single movement, every change of position, every soft, shallow sigh.

When she met Robert it was his voice she first responded to. He had a way of saying her name as if he were swilling it around his mouth like fine wine. Of course, she'd had no concept that first time they met that there could ever be anything between them. She'd already been working as housekeeper for his parents for six weeks when he came home from university for the Christmas holidays. They'd been friendly. Nothing more. But the following Easter, he'd sought her out more, talking to her in that way, as if everything they said to each other were a huge private joke. Saying 'Li-ly' as two separate musical notes, the first higher than the other. She'd known – obviously, she'd known – that it couldn't be anything, that *they* couldn't be anything, but his voice had been like a silken thread, too fine to see, that he'd wound around her again and again until, by the time she grasped what he was doing, it was impossible for her to get away.

Why is she thinking of Robert now, when she has come halfway across the world to escape from what he did?

Someone approaches, standing behind the sofa where she sits.

'Three is such an awkward number for cards, isn't it? Could I persuade you to accept a fourth player?'

It's the older Australian. Up close, Lily can see that, while he is not handsome, he has a kind face, with fine white lines in the outer corners of his eyes where laughter has prevented the sun from tanning his skin.

'By all means,' says Edward, and a look passes between the two men that Lily has started to recognize, an unspoken question – 'Are you a threat?' – followed by, in this case, an instant lowering of guard.

The newcomer introduces himself as Ian Jones. He and his two friends are engineers in the Australian military who have been in Egypt carrying out some sort of reconnaissance in the event of war breaking out.

'Don't worry,' he says, seeing Lily's face. 'It's just a precaution.'

In turn, they tell him a little bit about themselves, the potted histories they choose to define themselves by. Lily watches the lines around his eyes crinkle as he finds out Edward and Helena are brother and sister. So that's how it is. She is happy for Helena, hopes Helena can set her sadness aside, at least for the duration of the voyage.

After three or four hands, their motivation wanes. Despite the slowly rotating fans, the air is still soporifically warm.

'Would you care to dance?' Ian asks Helena in his strange, rough accent. *Wouldya keh ta dawnce?*

After a moment's hesitation Helena rises, reaching up to repin a lock of hair that did not need repinning, a nervous habit Lily recognizes from her own arsenal of similar tics. Ian puts his hand under Helena's elbow to lead her through the dancers. Edward and Lily are alone.

'I'd forgotten what Helena's smile looked like,' says Edward, watching after his sister until she has disappeared from view.

'Has she always looked out for you?'

Edward looks pained. Nods.

'I never asked her to. You know, Lily, sometimes love can be as great a burden as disinterest.'

Lily wants to ask him what he means, but finds she cannot. The word 'love' coming from his lips has sealed shut her own.

They watch the dancers until Lily feels she might burst from the silence.

'I think I might turn in,' she says, rising hastily to her feet. 'I did not sleep particularly well last night.'

Instantly, she wishes it unsaid. Might he think she is referring to the scene on the Pyramids?

'Nor I,' says Edward, and she sees, to her chagrin, that his cheeks are stained a dusky pink, suggesting that his thoughts have taken him along the very path she feared.

On her way down to her cabin, however, her mood takes a swing upwards. Didn't he say that he also had trouble sleeping last night? Might that not indicate that he also was replaying what happened in his mind? Then she remembers what Maria said about his family expecting more for him and her spirits plunge.

You are ridiculous, she tells herself. Going up and down, just like the ship itself. She resolves to be more level-headed. The voyage is nearly half over. She must be sure to enjoy the time she has left.

Even so, when she looks at herself in the mirror and realizes she's mislaid her silk scarf at some point in the evening, it's enough to make her lay her head against the bed frame and weep.

15

13 August 1939

THE SWIMMING POOL has become a lifeline, the only respite from the relentless heat. The passengers gather in listless knots under the awning, leaving the shade only to dunk themselves in the cool water for a few minutes, like hippos at the zoo, before retreating again.

Lily has lost the self-consciousness she felt at first at appearing in public in her bathing suit. Now it's being dressed that feels wrong, putting layers on top of her already burning skin.

All but the most stuck in their ways of the men have started wearing shorts, and the women waft themselves with colourful fans bought in the bazaars of Port Said. The older women who insist on corsets under their clothes stay in the lounge, beached on the sofas, complaining about the 'intolerable' weather. At mealtimes they all eat half the amount they did before, as chewing seems to require too much effort. Even the family from Kent with the three chubby sons no longer arrives in the lounge early to be first in line for cakes and sandwiches.

'Now I know how bacon must feel when it's cooking in the pan,' says Audrey. Annie giggles and Lily can't help thinking that if Audrey *feels* like bacon, Annie is the one who *looks* like it. Audrey's red-headed shadow is wearing a cloche hat tied under her chin with a headscarf to shield her white skin from the sun. She has already burned her shoulders, causing the skin to blister and then peel, revealing a shiny surface underneath, pink as boiled ham, and now wears a long-sleeved cotton blouse to stop it happening again. Whenever Lily looks at Annie's headscarf, she feels a pang of regret for her own lost silk scarf. Though she has asked around all over the ship, no one has found one, or had one handed in.

Ian Jones is telling them about Australia. They have already heard about his tough upbringing, working in the outback as a teenager and sleeping in a barn. But he assures them conditions have changed now and that all employees are paid an 'award' wage, which means there is a set minimum to how much a person can earn. He tells Lily that Lady Help, as apparently domestic servants are now called, should get at least thirty-five shillings or two pounds a week and probably a separate flat as well with their own bathroom.

Though Lily is pleased to hear it, the conversation makes her feel rather gloomy, reminding her that the voyage is not, in fact, reality but rather a lovely dream, a world where things like work and money have magically ceased to exist, and that when they get to Sydney they will be plunged straight back into real life. She will have to go back into service, which is something she swore she would never do when she closed the door on Robert's family's house that last time.

She and Mags had once had such ideas of what they might do with their lives. Office work to start with. Or maybe nursing. Save some money. Travel the world. 'I don't mind what we do, as long as we're together,' Mags had said. 'If I wasn't with you, I'd never have the nerve to leave the county, let alone the country.'

And now here Lily is. Seeing the world alone.

Edward is complaining about the taste of the salt tablets they've been given. At first Lily didn't understand why they needed them, but then Ida explained it was to replace salt lost through sweat, which made her wish she'd never asked. The salt tablets are left at their place settings at mealtimes. 'I feel embarrassed taking them, though,' Audrey has confided in Lily earlier in the day, 'because everyone will know I sweat.'

They are all arranged, as usual, under the awning next to the swimming pool. Lily was relieved, when she first came out, not to find Maria here. And then she was ashamed of herself for being relieved. Maria is her friend. She needs to have faith in her. Still, Helena's words echo around her head. On the ship, they don't know about each other's histories. They can't check up on each other's families. Or consult each other's neighbours or bosses. All they have to go on is what they choose to tell each other. But what if it's not quite the truth?

Lily is filling in her diary and finds herself posing just that question. Then she scores it out, hotly, in case anyone else should ever read it.

Helena gets up to go into the pool. Instantly, Ian is there beside her. Since they played cards the night before last, Ian has hardly left Helena's side. His infatuation is painfully obvious, and Lily finds herself half delighting in it and half wishing he would shield himself a little, not leave himself so open. Her experience with Robert at least taught her that much.

'Was it all lies?' she remembers asking Robert that last time she saw him. 'All those things you told me, all those things you promised me?'

And he had the grace at least to look abashed. 'I meant them all,' he said. 'At the time.'

One advantage of having Ian attach himself to their little group is that his presence has the effect of dissipating any tension between Lily and Edward. They are still, on the surface of things, friends, just as they were before. Most of the time, she can make herself forget about that sand-dusted kiss on the steps of the pyramid. And even when, in weaker moments, it comes unbidden into her mind, it already has that sense of being something once removed, something that happened to a different person or in a different life. Still, despite their best efforts, things cannot quite return to normal between them, something has become lodged, some gritty grains of sand, in the once smooth shell of their relationship.

As Lily is watching Helena and Ian she becomes aware of a disturbance in the torpor of the afternoon, a picking up of energy, a tensing of slack muscles.

A steward appears, a young, acne-ravaged man, looking stiffly self-important, closely followed by the most extravagantly brimmed straw hat Lily has ever seen. Attached to the hat is Eliza Campbell and she does not look happy.

'Thank heavens I've found you,' she says, coming upon Lily and Edward. 'I was beginning to think there was no civilized company left on this ship and I should have to hurl myself into the water and swim back to Cairo!'

Eliza has on her dark glasses again so it is impossible to judge her expression, but no one is looking at her face anyway. The attention of the entire population of the swimming-pool deck is focused on what Eliza Campbell is wearing. Or rather not wearing. She has on a red halter-neck top which completely reveals her shoulders, and black, tight-fitting, high-waisted shorts that stop at the top of her thighs and barely conceal her bottom. On her feet she is wearing high-heeled black pumps.

While many of the women, like Lily, have been wearing bathing costumes around the pool area, knitted garments that sag when wet, they would not dream of parading around the ship in them, and there is something intensely shocking about Eliza's tiny waist and the swell of her bosom, accentuated by the minimal halter, and her creamy bare thighs.

A chair is found and Eliza sits down, removing her hat, which would have struggled to fit into the confined space. Lily is aware of a lull in the chatter around them as the other passengers listen for what she will say, already rehearsing their own dinnertime conversations for later. *Did you see? Did you hear?*

Lily sees Maria Katz come to the edge of the pool area and peer in, as if looking for someone. When she sees Lily and Eliza, she waves but does not come over.

'Max is being impossible,' says Eliza, lighting the cigarette she has just taken from Edward. 'He is so bad-tempered – probably because he spends his life being either half-cut or hungover. Do you know, he's hardly said a word to me since we got back from Cairo. As if this filthy heat wasn't bad enough, I've also got to put up with a husband who acts more like a spoilt child than a grown man.'

'I think the weather is making everyone more irritable,' says Helena.

'This is nothing,' says Ian, laughing. 'Just try midday in January in Western Australia and see how you like that!'

Eliza pushes her sunglasses down her nose and peers at Ian over the top.

'What a treat,' she says. 'A native!'

Ian laughs good-naturedly and then flicks his eyes automatically towards Helena, which is when Lily has a most interesting revelation. Ian is utterly unaffected by Eliza. So far on the voyage, people have either been dazzled or appalled or fascinated by her, so Ian's indifference is something new. As if to test out her theory, she glances at Edward, who seems to have shut himself off since Eliza arrived, setting out a game of solitaire and snapping the cards down with particular force.

Eliza seems baffled by Ian's lack of interest, and fires questions at him, which he answers in the affable tone he uses with everyone. Even when Ian's two young Australian colleagues approach, eager to be introduced to her, it seems not to make up for Ian's own absence of regard. Eliza's eyes follow him as he turns repeatedly in Helena's direction. Finally, she pushes her chair back, so vehemently it clatters backwards on to the deck.

'I just cannot abide this heat a moment longer. Lily, I'm dying to see your cabin. I've never seen it before. Will you show me?'

Lily is taken aback. Imagining Eliza in the cramped cabin she shares with Ida and Audrey is like picturing an exotically plumed parrot in a pigeon loft. Still, Eliza is standing, waiting, and everyone else is watching. Lily gets slowly to her feet.

'I can't think you'll find much to interest you,' she says, grabbing hold of her cotton dress from the back of a chair and slipping it on over the top of her still-damp swimming costume.

'Nonsense. I just want to see where you live, so I can picture you when I'm stuck up there' – she raises her eyes to the upper deck – 'dying of boredom.'

As she and Lily move off she draws Lily's arm through hers. She has put the enormous hat back on, and the edge of the brim scratches Lily's face whenever Eliza turns her head, though she does not seem to notice.

'You don't mind me dragging you away, do you?' Eliza asks. 'I'm just not in the mood for company.'

They make their way along the row of deckchairs, all pulled well into the shade. Maria is sitting back in one, gazing off into the distance, a book, forgotten, over her knees. Lily stops, conscious of having neglected her friend.

'Are you all right, Maria?'

'Oh yes. I'm fine.' Maria smiles, but her gaze flits restlessly to Eliza and back.

'We are just –'

'We are going for a tête-à-tête,' Eliza breaks in, turning her eyes, behind those black-lensed sunglasses, towards Maria. 'We have so much to discuss. I hope you'll excuse us.'

And she leads Lily away before she can protest.

'I rescued you,' says Eliza. 'You owe me.'

Now, Lily does stop.

'Maria is my friend. I didn't need to be rescued from her.'

She has never been so outspoken to Eliza, and she feels her own heart quickening, but still she goes on. 'I don't care if she's Jewish.'

To her surprise, Eliza laughs.

'I don't care if she's Jewish either. She could be Hindu or Buddhist or Muslim or a devil worshipper, for all I care. I can even forgive her being so plain. It's her worthiness I can't stand, that air of intellectual superiority.'

'She's not like that.'

She has spoken loudly, and Lily notices the woman in the chair nearest to them raise her eyebrows to her companion.

Eliza scrunches up her face. Contrite.

'I'm sorry, Lily. I have no right to tell you who you should and shouldn't be friends with. Forgive me?'

Lily's anger dissolves in the heat.

'Of course. I overreacted.'

'No, you didn't. You're quite right. I get so possessive with people I like. I can't bear for them to have any friends apart from me. Max is forever telling me off.'

They open the door that leads down to the lower decks. The air in the narrow staircase is thick like tar. As they approach the door to her cabin, embarrassment prickles on Lily's skin. She wonders if Eliza will look at her differently once she has seen, close up, how Lily lives.

But Eliza doesn't seem put off, despite the sour smell that lurks in the turgid air, and the underthings drying over the end of Audrey's bunk.

'It's perfectly sweet,' she says, and flings herself down on the smooth counterpane of the empty bottom bunk.

'Sit down and talk to me, Lily. We never seem to have time to chat. I was hoping Cairo would have given us more opportunity, but things just seemed to get in the way, didn't they?'

Lily nods and sits down on the spot Eliza is patting.

'Tell me more about yourself, Lily. What do you want to do with your life?'

Lily hesitates.

'I suppose I'll stay in Australia a couple of years – if you go home any sooner you have to pay back your passage.'

'And then what? Back to England?'

Lily nods.

'I imagine I'll get married at some point. Have a family.'

It sounds so predictable, her life plan. So tame.

'How about you, Eliza?' she asks, longing for the focus to be somewhere other than her. 'Shouldn't you and Max like to have children?'

Eliza picks at a woven strap above her head that forms the base of the top bunk.

'I can't have children.'

Fire rushes to Lily's face.

'Oh, I'm so sorry I asked. How clumsy of me.'

'Don't be silly, Lily. You weren't to know. Anyway, who says I want to have children?'

'Do you?'

Eliza is quiet. Pick. Pick. Pick. She takes a deep breath in.

'I had a child, actually. We. We had a child.'

Lily freezes. Eliza and Max, parents? It does not seem possible.

'A little girl. Olivia. Oh, she was quite the most ugly baby, Lily. Completely bald, with such a chubby face. Max used to call her Oliver because he said she looked like Oliver Hardy – you know, from *Laurel and Hardy*? But I adored her, of course. Couldn't get enough of her, as it happens. Didn't even mind that she'd torn me up so badly being born – the big, fat thing – that I would never be able to have more children. She was enough.'

Eliza is speaking in a low, flat voice, completely unlike the way she usually sounds. It's as if someone has taken her normal voice and squeezed all the theatre out of it. Lily finds it almost unbearably touching and takes Eliza's hand, the first time she has ever made a spontaneous move towards her.

'You don't have to talk about her, if it's too painful.'

'Don't be a ninny, Lily. It was three years ago now. I have come to terms with it. Besides, I like talking about her. Max won't even have her name mentioned.'

'So what happened?'

Lily's voice is soft as ocean spray, and she wonders for a moment if she even uttered the words out loud. But then Eliza speaks:

'I used to bring Olivia with me everywhere. I loved her so. We had nannies, of course, but I wanted her just with me. She was so happy, you see. Never cried. Always smiling. We had a party, in our house in Mayfair. Olivia was with me, as always. I put her down on the floor. Just for a moment. Just while I went and fetched a drink for someone.

'She ate something. Something she shouldn't have. She was such a greedy little thing, always putting things in her mouth. She died two days later.'

'Oh!' Lily's hand is over her mouth. She does not know if she has ever heard anything so sad. 'But what did she eat?' she wants to know.

Eliza gazes at Lily, her astonishing eyes almost purple in the dim light of the cabin.

'Do you know what cocaine is, Lily?'

Lily shakes her head, already sure she does not really want to find out.

'It's a drug, Lily. Max has been taking it for years.'

'But is it legal?'

Eliza laughs out loud.

'If we only did things that were legal, life would not be worth living. Anyway, Max left a little bowl of cocaine on a coffee table. He always has to be so generous to his friends. It looks like little crystals of white powder. Olivia must have thought it was sugar.'

'But that's terrible. Poor Max, he must have felt so awful.'

Eliza snaps her head back, banging it on the upper bunk.

'Good. I hope he feels terrible for the rest of his life.'

'Don't say that, Eliza. Please. It was a mistake. A terrible mistake.'

Eliza glares at Lily, as if she might slap her. Then she looks away.

'You know, sometimes I hate him so much I want to kill him.'

Lily cannot believe she has heard right. And yet, at the same time, she knows she has.

'You don't mean that.'

'Don't I?'

But now Eliza is sitting up, gathering herself. Painting on a smile.

'You're right. Of course I don't.'

Her voice is different. Hardened.

'And now you, Lily. I've told you my innermost secret. Now yours. Who have you lost? And don't tell me about your dear old grandmother. I know you have a story. You wouldn't be here on this ship if you didn't. Who have you lost who properly broke your heart?'

Lily feels her heart pounding in her chest. She has never spoken of this. To anyone. And yet Eliza has been so open with her, so honest. It's almost as if she owes her this confidence.

'I had a friend,' she begins. 'Her name was Mags.'

Eliza sits up and leans fractionally towards her, as if listening with her entire body.

'She died eighteen months ago.'

'A close friend, obviously. How did she die, Lily?'

Lily sways. The cabin feels so hot suddenly, the air so close it is like cotton wool, stuffing up her nostrils, pressing on her eyeballs.

She closes her eyes, but that is worse, because now she sees that room again, with the mint-green carpet. The blood dripping down the wall. Mags screaming: *Am I going to die, Lil?*

'Lily, you know you can tell me anything. You know you can trust me.'

Lily nods. Presses her lips together. Begins.

'There was a man called Robert . . .'

But now there comes a blast of breeze as the cabin door bursts open. And here is Ida, her pointy face only made sallower from exposure to the sun, her heavy black dress marked under the arms by bleached rings of salt. She sees Lily first, sitting on the bed, her swimming costume making damp patches on her dress, her face heavy with the weight of her untold story.

'Lily?'

Only now does she see Eliza, sitting there in her shorts, with her legs and shoulders bare, all that soft skin on show.

'What's this?'

Ida's eyes look as black as her dress in the dull, heat-soaked cabin air. Eliza stares at her as if she were something nasty the wind has just blown in.

Lily gets to her feet and makes the introductions, but Ida looks as if there is something stuck in her throat. So much flesh, you can see her thinking as she looks over at Eliza.

'You're wearing your wet bathing suit under your clothes? You'll catch a chill.'

Ida does not seem to notice the heat that coats their skin like treacle.

'A chill?' Eliza laughs. Her old, brittle laugh. 'Now that would be a novelty.'

When Lily and Eliza make their excuses and leave the cabin, they gulp in the air in the narrow, stagnant corridor as if it were mountain-fresh.

16

14 August 1939

LILY SPENDS THE NIGHT up on the deck. The ship is due to arrive at its next port of call, Aden, at 5 a.m., with passengers allowed just two hours ashore, and she does not want to risk being late. She and the others who have the same idea sleep fully clothed in the camp beds so they will be ready when the ship docks. Helena lies next to Lily. Lily did look around for Maria before settling down for the night, remembering guiltily how Eliza had bundled her away from her earlier in the day, but she was nowhere to be seen. It's not altogether surprising. Most of the passengers have no appetite for such an early, short stopover in this hostile climate.

Unable to sleep in the sticky night heat, Lily goes over the conversation with Eliza. 'I had a child, actually. We. We had a child.' Now, finally, Eliza begins to make sense, the sharp edges of her. Pointed enough to hurt. Thin enough to snap. What would it do to a person to lose a child? What would it do to a marriage? Lily knows very little of babies but she has imagined, in her lowest moments, how it might feel to have someone depend upon you utterly and love you unconditionally. How it might give meaning and structure to a life that sometimes seemed lacking in both.

Robert had talked sometimes of the children they might have.

And because Lily was young and in love, and because her mother had always told her she was as good as anyone, she'd allowed herself not to think about what his parents might say. His family.

'Come on, Lil,' he would say, his lips on her neck, his body pressed up against her as hers was pressed in turn against the outside wall at the side of the house. The fingers of one hand kneading at her breast, the other working its way up under her skirt. 'We'll make the most beautiful babies.' The heat where their bodies connected, everything in her liquefying until she felt she must dissolve completely into the burning centre of him.

But always something had stopped her, some last vestige of sense. Her mother's voice in her ear. *Where's the ring, Lilian?* The knowledge that a blade of grass tied around her finger wasn't enough. But oh, how persuasive he was, with his words, and his tongue, and his hands. All of it pushing, probing, wanting. More, more, more. How different to that kiss with Edward in Cairo. The heartbreaking softness of it.

Shortly after 4 a.m. the ship pulls in to anchor. It is still dark and the buildings on the shore are indistinct black shapes against the inky sky.

By five, the light is grey and grainy, but still there is an oppressive atmosphere and everything on shore appears blurry as if seen through a grey filter. Lily can just about make out arid mountains crouching in the distance like brooding giants. They are to be taken to the dock by launch and, as they gather by the gangway, the passengers glance nervously upwards at the dense sky. There is an unpleasant, swollen feeling about the day that reminds Lily of summer storms at home when the heat builds until it must explode.

'Will we be needing umbrellas?' one of the women asks. The steward on duty laughs. 'You'll be lucky. Don't think it's rained here in years.'

Helena and Lily are joined by Edward and Ian Jones. It is

astonishing how quickly and easily the Australian has slotted into their group; it is as if he had always been there. Lily is glad of his cheerful, uncomplicated company. He seems to have a positive effect on Edward also and there is no sign of his bad humour of yesterday.

Despite the earliness of the hour, as soon as the launch lands they are swamped by hawkers, and the little shops along the shoreline are all open.

'Of course they're open, this is how they make their living,' says Ian. 'Either from the boats that pass through or from the soldiers on the British army base.'

Lily already knew there was a military base nearby. She got talking on deck one day to a young woman who was on her way to join her husband and become a military wife. Imagine coming to live here, she thinks, in this desolate place. But when the next launch pulls up and she sees the woman fly out of it as soon as it docks and hurl herself into the arms of a uniformed officer whose smile looks as if it might burst clear from his face, she changes her mind. Maybe love will be enough to overcome even this parched, grey place.

Aden has a reputation as the cheapest spot to buy merchandise such as cameras and lighters, and Edward is intent on buying a new watch, as his has stopped working after he accidentally wore it in the pool. Lily sticks by his side as he drifts from shop to shop. Everywhere they go they are followed by little Arab children with trays of trinkets.

Helena and Ian have gone on ahead, he with his hand constantly on her arm, half steering, half protecting.

'They seem so happy together,' says Lily, unable to help herself.

Edward looks up sharply.

'It certainly makes a change to see Helena smiling again. I thought for a while there she had lost the knack of it!'

He is joking, but there is a grain of hardness in his voice.

'What is it?' Lily asks. 'Surely you must like Ian?'

'Yes, of course. From what I know about him so far he seems a really good sort.'

'Then what?'

Edward is saved from replying by a young boy tugging on his sleeve. 'You want watch? I have watch.'

Lily leaves him and makes for a shop selling silk kimonos. The kimonos are exquisite – in jewelled colours, with intricate embroidery – and there are matching mules. A red one catches her eye, the same colour as the dress Eliza was wearing the first time Lily saw her. 'That would look lovely on you, Lily,' says Helena, who has entered the shop without Lily noticing.

The first price they are given is four pounds, but Ian soon manages to haggle that down to two pounds, ten shillings. It's still too much for Lily. She is very conscious of her limited pot of money in the Purser's Office and how long it might need to last her.

As she turns to go the young soldier's wife she'd met on deck comes through the door. 'Don't go,' she says. 'My husband will sort this out for you.'

She emphasizes the word 'husband' as if trying it out for size. Sure enough, the uniformed soldier Lily saw earlier on the dock now launches into negotiations with the trader until the price is knocked down to twelve and six. Delighted, Lily is just about to reach for her purse when the officer starts shaking his head and marshalling them out through the shop door. They haven't gone more than a few yards when the trader calls them back.

'I will make no money myself, and I have six children to feed, but I want so much to make the pretty lady happy.'

The price is fixed at eight shillings. The money is handed over, the kimono wrapped in paper. The soldier has the look of a conquering hero and his young wife hugs him as if they are celebrating the completion of a dangerous mission. Yet as they leave the shop Lily can't bring herself to look at the trader's sorrowful face. She can see that he would not dare get on the wrong side of the British military, who are permanently stationed here and whose trade must be essential to their livelihoods.

'Do you think he really has six children to feed?' she asks Edward.

Edward smiles. That sweet smile that presses dimples into his cheeks, as if with a giant thumb. 'Probably, Lily. But at least now he has eight shillings more to feed them with than he had an hour ago.'

Edward is in a buoyant mood, having bought a watch and a beautifully carved ivory-handled paper knife, which he unwraps to show her. In the grainy light, the handle looks like a bone.

Still Lily cannot shake off a sense of having wronged the man and his unseen family. Outside the shop the atmosphere is leaden and thick, the sky merging with the sea in a uniform greyness. She is glad they are staying only two hours. The place has a stifling feel, as if the air is being trapped by the hulking, parched mountains behind them.

And still the traders keep coming, seeming to appear from nowhere. Lily finds herself separated from Edward, surrounded by a gaggle of Arab women, all in black from head to toe, apart from their faces, which are covered with brightly coloured scarves, leaving only their eyes showing. They are carrying trays of beads, and Lily resolves to buy a couple of necklaces.

One of the women takes hold of her arm, gesticulating towards a shop at the far end of the front, clearly intending to propel Lily the entire length of the dock to show her whatever treasures lie inside. When Lily manages to get free she is alarmed to find herself quite a distance from most of the other passengers. Only George Price is up this end. Lily hasn't seen much of her table companion over the last few days, for which she is grateful. George struggles with the heat and seems to have spent a lot of time down in his cabin.

Now he is surrounded by children, all trying to get his attention or to force their trinkets on him. Each time he tries to pull away they follow him, sticking close to his side, blocking his exit. 'No,' she hears him say. And then, suddenly, he bellows, 'No! Get off me!'

But one boy is unafraid. He hangs persistently off George's arm, calling out random phrases of English. 'Please. Good day. Very nice wallet. You like. Very good.' He looks around twelve years old, but thin and small as they all are.

'Leave me alone!'

George always has a high colour, but Lily can see that his face is darkening into a deep, bloody red.

She moves towards him, thinking she might be able to intervene, when *Thwack!* George's hand catches the boy on the side of the head and the youngster is on the ground. Rather than take the opportunity to escape, George moves in and begins to kick the boy repeatedly. *Kick, kick, kick.* He kicks harder. *Oh! Oh, please don't.* The boy covers his face; his nose has begun to bleed. A deathly hush has come over the children and Lily is horrified to see George bend over the boy and draw his clenched fist back behind his head, preparing to punch. Without thinking, she breaks into a run and dives into the throng of children, positioning herself between George and the boy, who is curled in a ball, crying soundlessly.

'What do you think you're doing?' she screams.

George's face is still the colour of liver, his stretched-back arm trembling, his breath coming from him in short gasps.

'They won't go away. They won't stop touching me.'

'They're children. Just children.'

'You don't understand, Lily. They're not like British children. These are vermin. You have to be tough. That's what they understand.'

From the corner of her vision Lily sees dark shapes moving closer. The Arab women have noticed something is happening, are coming to find out what. She glances at the boy and is relieved to see him stirring.

There's a noise from the dock, a raised shout. The last launch is about to set off.

'We need to leave *now*,' says Lily, pushing away just as the women arrive, dragging George behind her by his arm. She does not dare turn around, but she hears the boy sniffing, a soft sound muffled by the dirt and the thick, paste-like air and the terrified whispers of the other children.

Now she is moving faster, her eyes focused on the launch and on the other passengers queuing to get on. She can make out the slight figure of Edward, wearing a white shirt rolled up at the sleeves. And ahead of him Helena. There's a shriek from behind her. Over her shoulder she sees a woman crouching next to the boy, gesticulating in their direction. Now everyone is turning towards them.

She turns back to the launch, where the last passenger has now boarded. They must not leave, she whispers to herself. They must not leave me here.

The woman is shrieking louder now, and Lily begins to run. She hears George's broken breathing behind her. Now the men are also shouting, and moving towards them. The shopkeepers come out from their shops to see what is happening.

'Wait!' she calls to the boat, where a steward is loosening the ropes. 'Please wait!'

A man grabs hold of Lily's arm. 'Lady,' he says roughly. 'Lady.' It appears to be the only English word he knows. She shakes free. 'I'm sorry,' she says, without slowing down. 'I'm so sorry.'

She hears George behind her. 'Get your hands off me. Leave me be.'

Finally, she is at the launch, where the steward is now standing, impatiently peering along the dock.

'What has happened?' asks Edward, getting up to greet her. 'Lily, are you all right?'

She nods, but tears are coursing down her cheeks.

'They frightened her,' says George, dropping heavily into a seat. 'Those people are like savages.'

As the boat pulls away from the dock through the grey, turgid water, Lily finally dares to turn around and sees the boy's black-clad mother, one arm around her weeping son, gesturing angrily with her other hand as if to summon them back.

'George is completely unstable. That's what he is. You can't strike a child like that.'

Edward is leaning forward in his deckchair so that his head is almost touching Lily's. Since disembarking from the launch this morning, he has barely left her side. She knows he blames himself for allowing her to become separated from them.

'He had a terrible look in his eye, as if he had quite lost control,' Lily says, shuddering to remember George's fiery cheeks, his raised, trembling fist.

'Well, we must just give him a wide berth,' decides Helena. She is on her own, for a change, Ian having gone to take a nap after their early start, and she appears strangely vulnerable. That's how quickly his constant presence has become a part of her.

Some of the passengers have set up an entertainments committee to help the stewards find ways to amuse the passengers throughout the voyage. Yesterday afternoon there was a magic show and today they are organizing a fairground, setting up makeshift stalls at the far end of the deck, using canvas and sheets procured from the stewards which they drape over drying racks and chairs.

Mrs Collins, the chaperone, is a member of the committee and is busy issuing instructions to some of the younger volunteers. 'Up a bit. A teeny way to the left. That's it.' Audrey and Annie are helping out, happily trailing yards of sheeting from the cabins to the deck.

Lily closes her eyes and leans back in her chair, suddenly exhausted. They have been told that, now they are leaving the Red Sea and entering the Indian Ocean, the weather will change, but so far there has been no let-up in the oppressive, dry heat. In her mind, she goes over the scene on the quayside at Aden, sees the boy's head jerk back as George's thick hand strikes his skull, sees him curled on the ground with the tears forging clear channels in his dirt-grimed cheeks. She remembers her shame when the boy's mother started shouting, knowing the Arabs would imagine she and George were together.

'I should have done more,' she says now to Edward and Helena. 'I should have stayed and helped the boy.'

'How could you?' asks Edward. 'You don't speak the language.'

'I could have tried. Instead, I was just focused on getting away. I wasn't thinking about the boy, just about how to get on to the launch before it left without me.'

Lily feels limp with despondency and self-reproach, and she suddenly has a great yearning to see Maria. If she cannot rid herself of her sense of guilt over failing to protect the boy, at least she can make amends for neglecting her friend.

She finds her at the opposite end of the deck to where the fairground will be, talking to a Jewish couple whom she introduces as the Neumanns. They have been discussing the situation in Austria and Maria is looking serious, her eyes behind her round spectacles blinking rapidly as if to ward off unwelcome thoughts. She looks older, Lily thinks. The voyage has aged her.

'Have you heard from your parents?' Lily asks, regretting that she has not thought to ask this question sooner.

Maria shakes her head.

'But this is not a surprise,' says Mrs Neumann, a tiny woman with deep lines scored down each side of her mouth like a ventriloquist's dummy. She has a very pronounced accent that means there's a slight delay in Lily's head between hearing the words and making sense of them. 'Austria is under German control and Germany is at war. Everything is in chaos.'

'Maybe they've left and you haven't heard from them because they are on the move,' Lily offers, desperate to give comfort.

Maria's eyes brighten.

'Yes,' she says quickly. 'This is what I am hoping. It would be very difficult for them to send letters while they are travelling.'

'Exactly,' says Mr Neumann. But Lily sees the look that passes between husband and wife and her chest feels tight.

After the Neumanns have gone Maria and Lily remain in their chairs, talking.

'I'm so glad to see you again, Lily. I thought I had done something to offend you.'

'No. Not at all. I have been . . . distracted. Tell me, how have you been?'

'You mean, after the assault on the deck?'

Lily nods, but she is conscious of her body stiffening. This is the conversation she has been dreading.

'I am fine. Really. But I don't think the captain and his staff really took it seriously. No one has come to talk to me about it.'

'Maria, could you have . . . Might you have been mistaken? Could it have been something you dreamed or just a question of the heat and the unfamiliar noises on the deck?'

Lily knows even as she is speaking that she should not be saying this. And one look at Maria's stricken expression only confirms what she already knows.

'You think I made it up, Lily?'

'No! I was only trying to see if there could be another explanation.'

'Lily, I know what happened. I was there. *You* were there.'

She sounds so anguished Lily quickly changes the subject and for a while they talk about books they have read or would like to read. Afterwards, they stroll in companionable silence to see the fairground at the far end of the deck. There is actually a breeze, coming from the sea. Lily holds her face up to it as they walk. The cooler air calms her. Already, that morning's scene on the quayside in Aden is seeming distant. When she thinks of it, she sees it in grainy grey, like a bad-quality cine film. And though there is still an awkwardness between her and Maria that was not there at the beginning, at least they are walking together, talking, not estranged.

The fairground has taken shape since the afternoon. The individual stalls have been set up using the sheets and drying racks, each one with its own oil lamp inside. One contains a table, arranged with individual lanes marked out in cutlery, down which five people at a time can roll a coin, the winner receiving a token for a drink from the ship's bar. Another has a large glass jar packed with liquorice allsorts. Whoever comes closest to guessing how many sweets are in the jar wins the lot. Lily has never much liked liquorice allsorts and Maria claims never to have heard of them and declares their appearance 'unappetizing'.

They go next door, to a booth with a curtain hanging down that has to be lifted before entering. There's a low table with an oil lamp that's covered with a colourful patterned scarf, giving out a red glow. A woman sits on a rug behind the table with a shawl wrapped around her head and face. She has black kohl lining her eyes, and though Lily thinks she seems familiar, she cannot recognize who it is.

Lily goes first, sitting herself down in the chair opposite the fortune teller, who starts wafting her hands over the lamp as if summoning a spirit. 'I see great adventure for you,' the woman says in a low, theatrical voice. 'And love, with a tall, handsome stranger from a foreign land. You will be torn about where to settle, but you will make the right decision.'

Lily laughs. Could there be a more predictable fortune for a young woman on a ship bound for Australia? But a hidden, foolish part of her is disappointed. Though she knows this isn't a real fortune teller but a passenger playing a role, nevertheless she was hoping for some insight into herself.

Now it is Maria's turn in the chair. She sits upright as a bookend as the fake fortune teller makes extravagant gestures with her hands over the glowing lamp.

'For you also, I see adventure,' she says, and Lily digs her fingers into Maria's shoulder. The fortune teller has run out of new ideas already, her fingers mean to say. But then the fortune teller adds, 'And great riches. However, I see also separations and goodbyes.'

Maria stands up abruptly and Lily can see her eyes blinking again. The fortune teller is confused.

'I'm sorry, have I said –'

But Maria is already tearing blindly at the sheet that curtains the exit and striding out.

Lily catches up with her by the railings. Maria is gazing out at the ocean, where the breeze has whipped up the waves so they ripple along the surface, a relief after all these days of flat, lifeless expanses where nothing moved and it was as if the world had lost all definition.

'Maria?'

Lily is tentative. Nervous. Uneasily, she recalls Clara Mills asking the captain if Maria was an hysteric. Nonsense, of course. But still.

'I'm sorry, Lily,' Maria says. 'I took it too seriously.'

'It's perfectly understandable. Given everything that has happened to you and your concerns about your parents.'

'We'll forget all about it,' says Maria. 'The fair is just a bit of fun. Everyone has worked so hard.'

Still, she makes no attempt to move, and the knuckles of her hands gripping the rail gleam white in the moonlight.

17

OVERNIGHT THE WEATHER changes, the ship rising and falling with the swell of the waves. Lily lies in her bunk and thinks about the depths of water beneath them and how far they are from home. Things have been strained between her and Ida since Eliza's visit to the cabin two days before, but in the morning, as Lily is dressing, the older woman starts up a conversation.

'I expect you're missing your silk scarf – that gold one with the embroidery.'

Lily doesn't understand. What does Ida know about her missing scarf?

'Do you have it, Ida? Is that where it's gone?'

Ida scoffs.

'What would I want with that?'

'You didn't find it, then?'

'No. But I know who did.'

Lily looks in the mirror, watching Ida's reflection, sensing how much she is enjoying this little crumb of power. Finally, Ida continues.

'It was him. The one off your table. The one that looks as if he needs a few good meals inside him.'

'Edward?'

Strange that Edward would have picked up her scarf and said nothing.

'When was this?'

'A few nights back. You'd left it behind in the lounge, on the sofa seat. I saw him pick it up when he thought no one was looking and hold it to his face like this.'

Ida takes up her discarded nightdress from her bed and presses it to her nose, inhaling deeply, then she strokes it gently against her cheek, as an infant might stroke its comfort blanket.

'I don't believe you.'

'Suit yourself.'

Ida sniffs and begins folding her nightdress, pinching the edges together between her bony fingers and then smoothing it flat.

'I'm sorry. I didn't mean anything by that. I just can't understand why he hasn't returned it to me, that's all.'

'As far as I can see, there's only one reason for a man to keep hold of a girl's personal things. Because he's sweet on her.'

Ida smiles out of the side of her mouth and Lily again has the discomfiting notion that she is being asked for a confidence. It's like an economic transaction. Ida has given her something and now Lily is being asked for something in return. And Lily tries. She really does. But.

'I don't think that's the case here.'

Ida looks disappointed, as if Lily is deliberately shutting her out.

'Don't forget, Lily, I've been around a lot longer than you. I have experience of young men.'

Lily remembers now about the dead fiancé. She realizes Ida has left the door open for her to ask about him, but she cannot find the right question. She wants to resist the intimacy Ida is trying to force upon her, even while she understands to her shame how lonely the older woman must be to be seeking her out like this.

'I'm sure he's just forgotten about it, that's all,' she says.

A while later, ensconced on deck, Lily leans back in her chair, letting the sunlight warm her face. Though it's still hot, the gentle breeze blowing off the ocean makes the temperature bearable, almost pleasant. A few feet away, a middle-aged couple are discussing the possibility of war in low, anxious voices.

'Archie wouldn't have to go,' the woman says, 'not with his eyesight being so bad.' She pauses. 'That's right, isn't it? They wouldn't make him go.'

'It won't come to it,' the man says. 'We've learned our lessons from what happened the last time.'

'And if it did, Archie would be okay, wouldn't he? On account of his eyes.'

Unease brings a bad taste to Lily's mouth. She thinks about Frank, thinks about how far she will be from home, about her parents with both their children gone. Then she rallies. The notice-board is still posting news twice a day and usually there is something positive. Hitler is looking for a peaceful solution. A British delegation is even now in Moscow negotiating for an alliance. No one has the appetite or the economic capacity for war.

'Can I sit here?'

The person standing in front of her is blocking out the sun so at first they appear just a looming black shape against the bright August sky. She blinks and gradually the features define themselves as those of George Price.

'Of course.'

She says it in a snippy way that makes it clear it is politeness speaking rather than warmth. But still he sits. She tries not to look at his flattened broken nose or the capillaries that have burst like purple fire crackers under the surface of his face.

'I think we should talk about what happened in Aden,' he says, not really looking at Lily, just at the wooden arms of her chair.

He has come to apologize, she thinks. And surprise makes her kinder.

'If you wish, George.'

She sees the Arab boy's head when it first jerked back, and the curve of his narrow back as he lay on the ground trying to protect himself from George's kicks.

'You do understand I had no choice. I did it for you.'

'For me?'

Now Lily turns her eyes to him.

George nods, violently, so his greased-back hair comes unstuck and falls about his face in lank strands.

'I could see you were being pestered and pawed by those women. I was coming to rescue you but those children wouldn't let me. They had their hands all over me to stop me coming to you. I had no option.'

Lily feels light-headed, her mind reeling. That's not how it was. That's not how it happened. But when she thinks back to the quayside already the sequence of things is growing blurry around the edges. Surely she was already free of the women by the time she came across George? Surely his arm was already raised and down before he saw her?

But sand and dust are blowing across the images in her mind, distorting her memories.

'That's not how I remember it,' she says.

'It was hot, Lily, and dusty, and there were so many damn people everywhere, and I bet you'd hardly slept. You just got the wrong end of the stick, that's all.'

'I don't think so. I'm sure. That is, I'm almost sure –'

George leaps in quickly.

'Almost. You see.'

Finally, he raises his sludge-coloured eyes to hers. Enthusiasm has lit up his face, making his heavy, thick features look almost child-like.

'The fact is, Lily, it really isn't wise for you to be walking around places like that on your own. An Englishwoman abroad, alone, can be a target for these kinds of people.'

'What kind?'

'The kind who have no education or manners, whose parents bring them up knowing only how to scavenge and pester and rob. It's not really their fault, you see. They have never been taught any better.'

Lily knows that he is wrong. She thinks back to the scene on the quayside and the woman who'd hurried over to the boy. How she'd raised her arm. Cried out, a mother's cry. *Stop*. But George is looking at her, wanting her to agree, his mouth, with its plump, wet lips, open as if to let his unspoken words – *You see? Am I right?* – fill the space between them. Lily thinks about arguing but loses momentum even before the sentences form in her head. What would be the point? He only sees what he wants to see. And besides, she is now doubting her own recall. The order of things is becoming jumbled in her head. Better to change the subject. Talk about something else.

'Are you excited to be going to New Zealand?' she asks, remembering that he is on his way to help his uncle run his smallholding.

The eagerness drains from George's face, like something drying up and desiccating in the sun.

'No. Why would I want to hide myself away in the godforsaken arse-end of the world? Excuse my language. It's my father's doing. He organized it all.'

'But surely you have a say in what happens to you. Couldn't you say no?'

George looks down at his thick fingers and Lily sees a purple flush creeping up from his shirt collar.

'You don't say no to my father,' he says bitterly. 'He's a deputy commissioner in the British Raj.'

'A government official? And he's sending you to New Zealand so you don't have to fight in a war?'

Outrage makes Lily's voice louder than she intended, and George looks around to see who has heard before turning back to her.

'I am an only child. He does not want my mother upset. If it was up to me, I'd be on the front line.'

'Against the Germans? I thought you admired everything about them.'

'Not everything. And I'm a patriot first.'

There's something about George Price that Lily finds terribly disturbing. Something beyond his moist, fleshy lips and his stubby, bitten-down fingernails and the way he seems to wear his anger like an extra layer of clothes.

It's his unpredictable volatility. That sudden, terrifying rage. The alarming sense of disconnect between what's happening around him and his reactions to it.

'Well,' she says, half standing, 'I really must be –'

To her horror, George suddenly grabs hold of her arm with his damp hand, pulling her back down into her chair.

'Do you think you might like me?' he blurts out.

'Pardon?' Lily tries to pull her hand away.

'You see, the thing is, Lily, I think you need looking after.'

Lily opens her mouth to protest, but George talks on over her intaken breath.

'I know what you're going to say, and it's true, I don't think my family, my father, would be much impressed with me consorting with a woman who works in domestic service. But, as you say, I'm a grown man. I make my own decisions.'

George's hand is still on her arm, her skin sticky underneath his palm. Shock renders her mute, slowing down her thought processes so she struggles to make sense of what has just been said. He is wanting to court her, which, she supposes, must be a compliment, and yet a compliment coated in an insult. His parents would not be impressed. Now it comes. Finally. The anger. Building up from the base of her stomach, spreading, spreading, spreading, through the tightly wound core of her.

George quickly turns his head, sweeping his eyes around the near-deserted deck. Then, just as Lily is preparing to explode, he leans forward and fixes his mouth on to hers as if he were plunging a sink.

Oh. But. No. No. His mouth is open like a basking shark, all that hot wetness, his fat tongue trying to prise her lips open.

Finally, her senses return to her and she tears herself away, gasping for breath.

'I'm sorry if I've given you the impression . . .' she pants, then stops. Why should she be sorry?

She feels his saliva still on her mouth and wipes it off with her hand. Sees him notice the gesture and narrow his eyes until they are only slits.

'I'm sure I should be grateful that you would even entertain the thought of . . . forming an attachment to me. What with me being just a lowly domestic servant and everything. But the fact is I don't share . . . that is, I don't want . . .'

Now it is he who is on his feet, his face dark as his shoes, his nostrils flaring.

'You're a tease. That's what you are, Lily Shepherd. I've met women like you before. All meek-looking and big eyes and "Oh it's my first time abroad." And really all you're doing is looking around to see who you can snare. Bet you think you can do better. Is that it? Don't hold your breath. You think that gutless Edward will stand up to his family on your behalf? Or maybe you think you can persuade your friend Mr Campbell to leave his wife.'

Lily gasps and he seems to take that as an acknowledgement that a nerve has been hit. When he starts speaking again he hisses through tight lips.

'You'd better watch yourself with those Campbells. You have no idea what they're capable of. If you knew what they'd done –'

'If you're talking about their child, I know all about that.'

For a second, George falters. Then he is all snarls once again.

'I know nothing about a child. But if you knew the true measure of them, then you'd realize they're toying with you. You really think he'd look twice at you? You have a very high opinion of yourself.'

'Lily? Is everything all right?'

Maria has come up behind her, placing her hand on Lily's shaking shoulders.

George Price, breathing heavily, flicks his puddle-coloured eyes from one woman to the other.

'Don't worry, I'm going. Just remember, Lily, you need to start choosing your friends more carefully.'

One more look, dark, as if all this were an illusion: the sunshine glinting on the water, the brave blue sky stretching in all directions as far as the eye can see, the sound of children's laughter drifting from the swimming pool. All of it a dream that the breeze whipped up and the only reality is George with his bitterness and his rage. And then he is gone. Turned on his heel and walking fast and furious along the deck, his shoulders hunched, head down. Passengers strolling in the other direction move fractionally to the side as he passes, as though afraid of catching something, some germs of ill temper.

Lily sinks back into her deckchair. Maria crouches down by her side.

'Has he upset you, Lily? What happened?'

It comes back to Lily now, the kiss, his mouth opening on to hers like he would suck her into him. For a moment, she feels as if she might be sick and again rubs vigorously at her mouth with the back of her hand.

She tells Maria what has happened, and Maria is horrified.

'Will you report him?'

An uneasy silence falls between them now as Lily thinks about what happened when Maria reported her attack and then wonders if Maria is thinking the same thing.

'No. I will just try to keep out of his way.'

She strives to sound matter-of-fact and hopes Maria cannot tell how the thought of sharing a table three times a day with George Price and all his intensity fills her with dread.

18

THIS EVENING THERE'S to be a gala ball. The passengers, bored after days of one another's company, seize upon the distraction like seagulls around a crust of bread.

All day there are excited whispers and conversations. Women troop in and out of each other's cabins, trying on dresses. Most of them have only brought one trunk with them and are conscious that their evening gowns have already been aired numerous times. The deck resounds with 'My blue shoes will go wonderfully with your taffeta' and 'This corsage of roses is just the thing for your yellow silk.' Even the men seem caught up in the excitement, fussing around, making sure white ties are starched and black tails are clean.

Only Lily is subdued. She hardly slept the night before, despite the improvement in the weather. Whenever she closed her eyes she felt George's mouth on hers and snapped them back open.

Is he right? she found herself thinking. *Am I a tease?*

It is not the first time that accusation has been levelled at her.

She remembers lying with Robert after dark on a deserted park lawn, kissing as if they would die if they stopped, hardly knowing where her body ended and his began, feeling his fingers working at the tops of her stockings. Wanting. But not wanting. Not like this. Not in the park. 'It's all right, Lily. I'll be careful. I know how.' And that being enough to make her pull away, straightening her clothes. He knew how because he'd done it before. She wasn't the first. How did she know she would be the last? 'I love you, Lily. I want to marry you.' But something holding her back. Something making her sit up straight, repinning her hair. And him, furious now. 'You're a tease, Lily. That's all. Well, if you won't, I'll find someone who will.'

Useless to tell him she did want him, just not like that, not there.

'I've been patient, God knows. But as soon as I ask you to do something for me you close up like a bloody nun. A man can only take so much rejection. I'm off to find someone honest. Someone prepared to finish what they start.'

And the person he'd found was Mags. Her Mags. Old enough now to turn heads as she walked but still too young to know how to say no to the boss's son.

Helena finds Lily standing at the railing, gazing down into the foam-tipped waves churned up in the ship's wake.

'You're not thinking of jumping in, are you?' Helena jokes. 'We missed you at breakfast.'

'I wasn't very hungry.'

Lily hadn't wanted to see George so she'd given the dining room a wide berth. As a long-term strategy, she knows this is flawed. She has to eat sometime, after all.

'Your Mr Jones not with you?'

Helena blushes.

'He certainly isn't my Mr Jones.'

'Come on, Helena. You'd have to be blind not to see that he worships the ground you walk on.'

'Lily. It's not as simple as you think.'

'Because you're still thinking of the other one? Your lost fiancé?'

A shake of the head. Vehement.

'You know, I haven't thought about him in days. I can honestly say I think I'm over him now.'

'So why not give Ian a chance? You two seem to get along so well.'

'Maybe that's true while we're on board. But.'

'But?'

'Oh, Lily, you must see that it's impossible long-term. He left school at fourteen. He worked in the outback cutting cane and doing goodness knows what else. My parents would never hear of it.'

'Helena, your parents are thousands of miles away. How will they even know?'

'Lily, you don't understand. They've written to say that they're coming to Australia, just as soon as they tie up some loose ends in England. And we rely on them, Edward and I. We don't have any income of our own. Not since Edward's illness. Anyway, Ian and I are from two different worlds. Maybe it would do for an onboard romance, but there can't be any future in it.'

Lily listens with growing frustration. Here it is. Just as Maria warned her. The real reason Edward seems to blow hot and then cold. She isn't good enough. Their parents would be appalled. Maybe she, too, would do for a shipboard romance, but nothing more. To her horror she feels hot tears building behind her eyes.

'It's a wonder why we bother, then, any of us,' she says, 'forming friendships with people who we would never speak to in normal life. Maybe we should all just keep ourselves to ourselves.'

And she turns away in the direction of the cabins, leaving Helena gazing after her, open-mouthed.

Lily skips lunch as well, prevailing on her cabin steward to bring her a sandwich instead, which she eats in a deckchair tucked away at the far end of the deck, scribbling in her diary, which she has neglected in recent days. In the afternoon Edward comes to find her.

'Helena said you were out of sorts this morning. I'm worried about you.'

'Well, you needn't worry. I'm just enjoying a little quiet time, that's all.'

Immediately, she regrets her harsh tone. It's not his fault. Edward looks hurt. Stands up, not knowing what to do with his hands.

'In that case –'

'No, please sit down, Edward. I'm sorry. I'm in a strange mood.'

She considers telling him about George Price but thinks better of it. The last thing she needs is Edward challenging George about it, further fanning the fire, when all she wants to do is forget it ever happened. Besides, she would not feel comfortable talking to Edward about kissing, not with the scene at the Pyramids so fresh in her mind.

'We're halfway through the voyage,' she says. 'I think it's just dawning on me that all this will come to an end, and then what? Back to domestic service. I really thought I'd left that part of my life behind.'

'Surely there are other jobs you could do? You're so clever, Lily. You could do anything.'

She longs to ask him. The words fizz on her tongue. *Would it make a difference? If I was in some other less shameful occupation, could you? Would you?* It even crosses her mind to tell him of her aspiration to be a writer, as if her dreams alone might elevate her. But of course she does not. Instead she tells him about the other jobs she has done in the past. The clerical office work she did in Reading after she left Robert's parents' employ. Then the move to London and the waitressing. The long hours on her feet, and the late buses home. She tells him about the scholarship to the girls' school and how she'd had to leave to help support her family. She tries not to be sentimental or self-pitying. It's important to her that he should not pity her, nor think badly of her family for expecting her to contribute to the household expenses.

As she speaks Edward's eyes stay focused solely on her face, as if studying her for a test.

'You make me feel ashamed, Lily,' he says at last, smiling his sweet, sad smile. 'I've achieved nothing in my life. A few years of studying for a career I never even really wanted, and then just lying in bed like a baby.'

'You were ill!'

He puts his head in his hands, so that his long fingers rake through his unruly dark hair. When he looks up again his expression is full of misery.

'What a waste, Lily. What a waste my life has been.'

What would have happened then if they hadn't been interrupted by a shout from further down the boat? Would Lily have leaned forward, as she wanted to, as she needed to, and taken his hand in hers and made him see himself through her eyes? Would the image Ida has implanted in her mind of Edward burying his nose in her discarded silk scarf have made her so bold?

'What on earth are you doing all the way down here? Are you hiding?'

Eliza is here again, wearing her shorts and a blue short-sleeved blouse that brings out the navy in her eyes. She is trailing something over her arm: the peach silk dress that Lily tried on in her cabin.

'Here I am come to do you a good turn and you have me marching up and down the whole length of the ship. If I expire from heat exhaustion, I shall hold the two of you entirely to blame.'

Eliza tosses the dress to Lily and then flings herself into a chair and sweeps her heavy black hair off her shoulders with her hands, holding it up over her head so that such breeze as there is can get to her neck. She is wearing blue sandals with a high heel and kicks them off theatrically, sending one skidding over to the railing.

'I thought you might want to borrow it for the gala evening tonight. It looked so divine on you.'

'Thank you. I was actually thinking of giving the dance a miss.'

'Nonsense. What the hell else is there to do on this endless, beastly voyage? I won't hear of it. You must come. Edward. Tell her.'

'You must come,' he parrots, laughing.

'You two have no idea what it's like up there.' Eliza gestures to the first-class deck. 'It's like a living death. You know those tombs in the pyramid we went to? That's what it's like. Being buried under a thousand tons of old dust and rock.'

Since the conversation with Eliza about her daughter Lily finds herself viewing her in a different light, prepared to consider her carelessness a result of having nothing more to lose rather than a lack of consideration for anyone else. Still, she wonders what it was that George had been about to reveal about the Campbells. If the scandal the elderly woman told her about in the Pompeii gift shop was nothing to do with the death of the Campbells' child, what could it relate to? Lily does not even like to think. She has the inbuilt aversion to gossip that only someone who has been on the receiving end can understand, which is what prevents her talking to Edward and Helena about it. Perhaps it's nothing, she decides. Just an old woman who wanted to feel important for a few minutes.

Eliza is again furious with Max. She'd been wanting to get off at Aden. Had been *desperate* for it, in fact, but when the steward had come in that morning to get them up as instructed, Max had sent the man away and then promptly gone back to sleep.

'I wouldn't mind, except he didn't bother to wake me up before he fell back into his drunken stupor, so I slept all the way through it and only woke up when everyone was coming back on board. And now I feel like I've been trapped on this boat with these ghastly people for ever. And we're not stopping again until Ceylon. I shall be crazed with cabin fever by then. Tell me everything that happened. Every last detail.'

Edward and Lily exchange glances. George Price looms up in

Lily's mind, standing over the boy, his arm bent back, fist clenched, and she snaps her eyes closed, blinking the image away.

'You didn't miss much,' says Edward.

Lily thanks Eliza for the dress and agrees, reluctantly, that she will make an appearance at the dance. She knows she can't avoid George for ever, so she might as well get the first meeting over with.

'Will you be staying on the upper deck?' she asks Eliza.

'What, so the old women can make disapproving noises at me while the young ones flirt outrageously with my husband? No chance.'

Down in her cabin, Lily drapes the dress on a clothes hanger hooked over the top-bunk railing. Even in such prosaic surroundings the dress exudes a glamour that lifts her spirits, despite herself. She does not like the idea of being beholden to Eliza or of accepting her charity, but she is only twenty-five years old, too young not to be affected by lovely things. She will wear the dress, just for a night, and just as the ship itself is not real life so the Lily who slips the peach silk over her head and dances under the stars on the surface of the Indian Ocean will also be an illusion.

When Ida comes in and sees the dress she is silent. Her eyes travel from the flimsy, floaty hem to the slender straps, hardly wider than silk thread.

'I'll wager you didn't buy that from those Arabs.'

'No, Mrs Campbell lent it to me.'

A noise. Could be a laugh or a snort. Impossible to tell with Ida. She steps forward and grabs hold of the dress, rubbing the silk between her thumb and one bony middle finger, and it's all Lily can do to hold back from knocking her hand away.

'It's a lovely dress, all right. Must have cost a pretty penny. What does she want in return, Lily?'

'It's not like that, Ida. She just wants to be generous. She doesn't want anything from me.'

Ida glances at her and Lily is surprised to see something akin to sadness in her companion's sallow face.

'Nobody gives you something for nothing, Lily, you mark my words.'

Later that evening, Ida's ominous response is forgotten as Lily enters the dining hall, everything about her feeling slightly altered by the dress she has on, from the way she walks, with a swishing looseness around the hips, to the way she holds herself completely upright, allowing the silk to fall low in the back as it is meant to. At the risk of appearing old-fashioned, she has on white gloves, freshly laundered, which end halfway up her arm and contrast startlingly with her skin, made tawny by the sun.

'Oh my word. What have you done with our Lily?' asks Helena as she approaches. Clara Mills declares it a 'complete transform-ation', which makes Lily wonder how bad she must have looked before. Edward gets to his feet and makes a deep mock-bow. 'You look like a princess,' he explains. 'I feel I should prostrate myself on the floor at your feet.'

Only George, already seated when she arrives, says nothing, beyond a curt 'Good evening'. She cannot help glancing at his lips, wine-stained now, like two fat, purple leeches, and the nerves that surround her heart shudder.

All through dinner Edward is attentive. He has bought wine and refills her glass the instant it empties.

'I love your hair like that,' he tells her, and she doesn't confess that it took her and Audrey half an hour to make it so, twisting and pinning and then untwisting and unpinning until they were both heartily fed up.

Afterwards they head out on to the deck. Ian has come to find them and volunteers to go to the bar 'before it gets mobbed', and Helena accompanies him to help with the carrying of drinks. Edward and Lily drift towards the railing and gaze out to sea in silence because the scene needs no commentary, not the moon, bright as a new sixpence in the inky sky, nor its reflection – a spill of silver paint across the glassy surface of the sea. They are so close Lily can feel the fibres of his tailcoat brushing against her bare shoulder.

He turns his face to her and she sees, or thinks she sees, that he is full of longing but also regret.

'I wish,' he says, and then stops, whatever it is he wishes wafting away on the gentlest of breezes.

I wish that I could unlock you like a safe, Lily thinks. Find out what's hidden away inside you.

A hand presses large and hot and heavy on her shoulder.

'Well, if it isn't the lovely Miss Shepherd.'

Lily spins around to face Max, and he looks her up and down as if she were a statue in a gallery.

'If that's what wearing my wife's dresses does for you, I shall insist she hands over the lot immediately.'

'Really, darling,' says Eliza, coming up behind him. 'I think the captain might have something to say about me parading around naked. Anyway, you're embarrassing the girl.'

'Lily? Are you embarrassed?'

Lily shakes her head, although she *is* embarrassed, not just because of what Max has said but also by the way he says it. As if it is only the two of them here and the others matter no more than that rail or that chair.

Helena and Ian return from the bar with drinks and Max has to stop Ian turning right round to buy two more for the Campbells.

'I insist on going myself. I'm afraid my wife has very expensive tastes.'

'I can only drink champagne,' says Eliza, who is wearing a dress that so nearly resembles her skin tone as to make her appear, as she had originally joked, almost naked. 'It's a medical issue.'

As soon as Max is out of earshot she says, 'I apologize in advance for my husband. He's already had a couple of large Scotches and I'm sure he'll take advantage of his trip to the bar to have a couple more. And he is the most boring drunk.'

By the time Max reappears, clutching a bottle of champagne in one hand and several flutes threaded through the fingers of the other, the band has started playing and a few keen couples are already moving around the dancefloor.

Ian Jones, who never seems at his most relaxed around the Campbells, ushers Helena towards the music.

'But I'm in the middle of my drink,' she protests, holding up her beer.

'Here. I'll help you.' He downs the glass in one.

The others stay by the railing, watching Helena and Ian take their places on the dancefloor.

'Don't you just love a shipboard romance?' says Eliza and, as so often, Lily cannot tell if she is serious or making fun. 'The really marvellous thing about them – shipboard romances, I mean – is that they don't count. You can do what you want on a boat, behave as badly as you like, and when you get to wherever you're going it's as if it never happened. When the ship sails away your sins go with it.'

Lily, standing stiffly beside Edward, is sure that her cheeks are burning and is glad they are in the unlit part of the boat so no one can see her. She glances at Max, who is scowling at his wife. Why was she talking about behaving badly? Was it some sort of message between the two of them?

Edward seems as uncomfortable as she is. She can see how his hand grips more tightly around his glass so that the knuckles protrude through the skin. He will ask me to dance, she thinks. And the thought soothes her. But when Edward does ask someone to dance, it is Eliza, not her.

'Now that I know you'll forget all about my terrible dancing as soon as we step off the ship, as if it never happened, I finally have the courage to ask you,' he jokes.

And then there are only Lily and Max left standing at the railing. Lily wonders if Max will feel obliged to ask her to dance. But he shows no inclination, pouring himself a brimming glass of champagne and trying to top up Lily's. Lily is not used to champagne and already feels the effects of the small amount she has had. She puts her fingers over her glass and some of the champagne splashes on to them.

'Sorry,' he says.

Lily turns to look out at the water, holding her face up to catch the slight breeze. She's conscious of Max's eyes on her, his unabashed stare.

'Tell me about yourself, Lily Shepherd.'

His voice is low and slow and he curls her name around his tongue like cigarette smoke.

'There isn't much to tell,' she says. 'I was a waitress. I'm going into domestic service. I have a brother, two parents. My life is very ordinary.'

'But what about *you*? What are your dreams? Your hopes? Are you wanting to meet a husband in Australia? Have lots of Aussie children?'

Lily feels the blood rush to her face.

'I have no intention of getting married out there. I'm only staying for two years, so I don't have to pay back my passage, then I'll be returning to England. That's where my family is. This is just a little adventure before I settle down. What about you, Max? Have you and Eliza any plans to stay in Australia?'

She is trying to deflect the conversation away from her. It feels too exposed here on the deck, where it is just the two of them.

Max swigs from his glass.

'Oh, I expect we'll stay a few months. And then Eliza will get bored. My wife bores easily, as I'm sure you've noticed.'

He pauses, looking over the water, so that the moon stripes his face silver.

'Has she talked to you about Olivia?'

'Your daughter? Yes. Yes, she told me. I'm so dreadfully sorry.'

'She blames me, you know.'

'I'm sure she—'

'I bet she didn't tell you she'd left her there for half an hour.'

'Where? I don't understand.'

'On the floor. Eliza put Olivia down on the floor because she was grizzling, and instantly forgot about her.

'What you have to understand, Lily, is that Olivia was like a dolly to Eliza. We had nannies – one for the day and one for the evening – but Eliza insisted on carrying her around as if she were a new bag or fur wrap. She even had dresses made up for Olivia to match her own. She started quite a craze, with all her friends following suit, taking their own babies out for lunch. Sometimes it was like feeding time at the zoo. 'Course, the nannies would step in when things got too raucous. Take them off their hands.'

'But she loved her.'

Lily is remembering Eliza's expression as she'd talked about her daughter. The way her features had softened, as if made from sand that the wind was blowing around.

'Oh, yes. Of course she loved her. More than anything she'd ever loved in her life. But with Eliza there are always limitations. It's to do with her background, her family.'

'Her mother, you mean?'

Max looks surprised.

'Oh, she told you. That is unusual.'

The band starts playing a new song, with a lazy saxophone melody that dissolves into the balmy night air. Lily waits for the others to join them, but no one arrives. When she glances towards the dancefloor she sees the dark heads of Edward and Eliza pressed together like two magnets, and she quickly turns her back to them.

'So what happened? At the party?'

'Olivia had been out of sorts all day. I think she was teething. I told Eliza to give her to the nanny to look after, but she'd had a little dress made, in pale green silk to match her own, and she wanted to show her off. So she sent the nanny to her room and brought Olivia downstairs. But Olivia wouldn't settle. She'd got to the age where she didn't want to be carried around like a little lapdog. She was starting to pull herself up on things – you know, getting ready to walk. So she was fidgeting and fussing and Eliza got bored and put her down in a side room, intending to go and fetch the nanny. Only she got distracted. By the time she remembered it was all too late.'

Lily does not know what to say. It's all so awful. And she can picture it so easily.

'And of course she blames me,' Max goes on, 'for what happened to Olivia. Because I left that stuff out. She never did like me taking it. You might have noticed, Eliza doesn't need anything to get her high, and she made no secret that she thought it a sign of weakness that I did. She hasn't let me make love to her since.'

'And you? Do you blame her?' The champagne and a desire to avoid the subject of the Campbells' love-making, or lack of it, makes Lily bold, the bubbles sending her thoughts fizzing unchecked to the surface. Max sighs. A forlorn wisp of a sound that drifts off on the breeze.

'I loved my daughter beyond life itself. And I love my wife. But something has been broken.'

There's a disturbance further down the deck, where the lights from the bar and the dancefloor do not reach. Lily can just make out two shadowy figures, a man and a woman, emerging from under the tarpaulin of a lifeboat. The man is carrying something that he drops on to a nearby deckchair. A blanket. The woman is straightening her skirt. As they pass Max and Lily they stare straight ahead as if they haven't seen them, and all of them are quiet, listening to the *click click click* of the woman's heels on the floor.

'How about it, Lily?' says Max softly after they have gone. 'How about we take a turn in that lifeboat, you and me, and make each other happy for a little while? We don't have to do anything. Just lie there and hold each other. I'm so damn tired.'

His eyes, in the moonlight, are no longer chips of blue but a faded grey in his broad, defeated face.

'I should so like to rest for a bit with you, Lily. Not because you're so lovely, although of course you are, but because you're kind. Couldn't we just go somewhere and be kind to each other?'

He looks so worn out and desolate that Lily, swaying in her champagne haze, allows herself to imagine how it would be if she gave in, how Max's strong, thick arms would feel around her. He's so similar to Robert in that way, tall and broad, with that illusion of solidity so you imagine you might be able to lean there for ever and be supported. Then he takes another swig from his glass and she realizes how drunk he is, and how drunk she is also, and she steps away just as the music changes once again, into something fast and jazzy, and Helena and Ian arrive, breathless and laughing.

'Helena is such a spoilsport,' says Ian. 'I was just preparing to show off my world-famous Aussie quickstep.'

'I'm heartbroken to miss it,' laughs Helena.

How young she looks in this silvery light with her eyes shining and her hair, for a change, tumbling down around her face in waves, as if she's pin-curled it overnight.

Be happy, Lily urges her silently. Don't let this slip away.

Now Eliza and Edward are also here, Edward's hand still on Eliza's arm from having steered her through the crowd. Eliza looks from Max to Lily and then back again, but doesn't speak.

Edward goes to the bar and comes back with another bottle of champagne.

'Edward!' Helena tries to disguise her exclamation as mock-stern, but Lily can see the worry creeping back into her face.

'It's a party, Helena,' says Edward. 'We're celebrating being here on this boat in the middle of the ocean far from home with our new friends. The world is so big, and we're all just tiny little specks, but here we are still, all together. Don't you think that's worth raising a glass to?'

Lily has never seen Edward in this mood. She supposes he must be drunk, too. He has a kind of edge to him, hard and sharp and brittle as a brandy snap. They drink more and then Ian asks her to dance, prompted, she guesses, by Helena. Still, she is grateful to get away from Max and the little knot of people by the railings, the constricting tension that seems suddenly to have wound its way so tightly around them. The band are playing an up-tempo number and it feels good to let herself be lost in the music and the laughter of the woman behind her and the woody smell of cigar smoke coming from the group of men by the bar.

'How come they're always down here, your friends, Mr and Mrs Campbell?' asks Ian in his usual forthright way.

'They claim the people on the upper deck are too stuffy. But I think there might be other reasons.'

'Such as?'

'Oh, someone else from First told me they had been involved in some sort of society scandal back in London that they had to escape from.'

'And now the other passengers are shunning them?'

Lily shrugs, regretting having spoken. Champagne has made her tongue loose.

'You don't like them much, do you?' she asks Ian.

He chews his lip, as if considering.

'It's not that I don't like them, I just think they're damaged. And damaged people are dangerous people.'

Lily is surprised to hear the bluff Australian talk like this. She had not imagined him capable of such deep thoughts. Or rather, she hadn't imagined him capable of expressing them.

'So we are embarked on a dangerous crossing?' she says, teasing.

Ian smiles, but he doesn't reply.

After two dances they head back to the railing, to find the others standing in silence, looking out to sea.

'Ah, here you are at last,' says Eliza, snatching Lily's hand and pulling her close. 'I thought you'd abandoned me.'

'No. Still here,' says Lily dully, and immediately wishes she could be more like Eliza, with her easy, throwaway remarks.

Max is holding a tumbler full of Scotch. He must have gone to the bar in their absence. Even in the dim light she can see that his face is darker than normal, the alcohol causing his blood vessels to dilate.

Ian is talking about a bar he goes to in Sydney where one of his friends once bet another that he couldn't sample every single drink behind the counter.

'He was sick as a dog,' he says.

Suddenly, Max drops his empty glass on to the floor, where it shatters into pieces.

'Sorry, sorry.'

Some of the tiny fragments of glass have sprayed upwards across the bottom of Lily's dress, catching on the fabric and winking like crystals where they reflect the light.

'Sorry,' Max repeats.

Ian goes to fetch a steward to clear up the glass while the rest of them move away from the scene of the accident. Max staggers as they walk and Lily sees Eliza roll her eyes.

'My wife thinks I'm an embarrassment,' Max announces as they arrive at the edge of the dancefloor.

'Don't be an ass.'

'Then dance with me, my darling.'

Max lurches towards Eliza, who sidesteps him neatly. He shoots her a look of unveiled fury. 'Don't you dare play games with me, Eliza.' For a seemingly endless moment they glare at one another. Then he turns, swaying towards Lily.

'You'll dance with me, won't you?'

But she is already backing away, holding up her hands, shaking her head.

'I'm not in the mood for dancing tonight.'

Really, she is not in the mood for Max. There was a moment, back there by the railings, where she'd finally felt she was seeing the real Max Campbell, stripped of his bombastic posturing and his too-wide smile. When he talked about his daughter his sorrow had been genuine and awful and it had seemed to come from a place buried as deep inside him as the King's Chamber in the Pyramid of Giza. And all that makes *this* Max, with his over-loud voice and his drunken arrogance all the harder to tolerate. Besides, he doesn't look capable of dancing. It's hard to see how he is even managing to stand.

Helena, as if sensing that she will be next to be asked, calls out to Ian, who is showing the steward the location of the broken glass.

'Come and join us.'

And he, reading the unspoken message hidden within her plea, comes to stand by her side.

Now Max is looking angry. His nostrils flare. He wants a turn on the dancefloor. He won't be denied.

'Well, if the ladies won't oblige, I shall have to look elsewhere.'

For a ghastly minute Lily thinks he means to proposition the other women around them, all of whom have been giving their party a very wide berth. But instead he lunges towards Edward, who, also perceptibly drunk, has been standing aloof from the rest of the party.

'Come, Edward, you'll dance with me.'

At first Lily thinks it is a joke. A poor one at that, but a joke nonetheless. And indeed, Max is smiling. That wolf smile back again. But when he grabs Edward's arm and propels him, too startled to resist, on to the dancefloor, she realizes he actually means it.

A gasp goes up from the onlookers as Max roughly pulls Edward towards him, with one hand around his waist and the other held up to the side, crushing Edward's fingers in his.

Lily expects Edward to laugh and push Max aside, but he seems to be in shock, his feet stumbling to keep up with Max's, his eyes wide and staring.

'A disgrace,' mutters an elderly man next to Lily as Max steers Edward in a clumsy foxtrot, barging into the couples around them. A young girl on the far side of the dancefloor giggles.

Max is being unnecessarily brutal with Edward, Lily thinks, observing how Max's fingers dig into the fabric of Edward's jacket and how he first pushes, then drags his partner around, as if he is a carcass of meat. Still Edward seems unresisting, almost in a trance.

Lily feels something brushing past her as Helena launches herself on to the dancefloor. Gone is the youthful-looking girl of earlier. In her place, a grim-faced, stiff-limbed woman reaches out to pull her brother free from Max Campbell's grasp.

'Come now, Edward! You can't do this. You can't.'

It's the kind of hissed whisper that carries. Edward is wrenched away and Helena hurries him off the floor. Lily expects them to stop, perhaps to laugh about it now the drama is over, but instead they push on past Lily, past Eliza and Ian, and on towards the door that leads down to their cabin, but not before Lily sees how Helena is trembling.

It was a joke, she thinks. Just a stupid joke.

Abandoned on the dancefloor, Max looks forlorn, as if unable to understand how it has come to this. For a moment or two he stumbles on by himself, like a chicken with its head cut freshly off. Then he starts to sag. Instantly, Ian is there, supporting his weight.

When they get to the edge of the dancefloor Lily expects there to be some kind of altercation between husband and wife, is braced for it. Instead, as Eliza looks at Max, her expression seems to soften from its usual detached amusement into something else. Pity, perhaps. Affection, even.

'Come on, old chap,' she says softly, in a mock-English accent Lily has not heard her use before. 'Let's get you back upstairs.'

She turns to Lily and smiles a regretful little smile, although what she might be regretful about, Lily cannot tell. Then, with Eliza on one side and Ian on the other, they half-carry, half-drag Max away. A shaken Lily watches as their dark figures, silhouetted against the moonlight, grow smaller and smaller until they merge with the shadows at the end of the deck.

19

17 August 1939

THAT NIGHT, in her alcohol-fuddled sleep, Lily once again dreams of Mags.

Mags is coming towards her in her good brown skirt. The one she wore to church and for visits home. Except now the bottom half of it is black with blood. Her blue eyes gaze out, baffled, from her little heart-shaped face, at only eighteen still half child, her character still only half mapped out.

'Help me.' Mags has her hands stretched out imploringly, and they, too, are blood-slippery. 'Lily, please help me.'

Lily awakes, hot and sticky with champagne and dread, to find it is Audrey, not Mags, who needs her help.

'She's burning up,' says Ida, who is standing next to Audrey's bunk, applying a damp towel to her forehead.

Lily is surprised by the tenderness with which Ida is discharging this duty, stroking the towel across Audrey's brow so gently and rhythmically she could almost be getting a young child off to sleep.

'This isn't seasickness,' Ida says.

'How do you know? It's not uncommon for people to get a second bout, even this late in the voyage.'

Ida shakes her head.

'It's something else. I lost two sisters to the Spanish influenza in 1918. I know the signs.'

Dread prickles at the back of Lily's neck.

She hauls herself out of her bunk and down the ladder. When she gets closer to Audrey she doesn't even need to touch her to feel the heat coming off her. Her fair hair is plastered to her head with sweat, and her skin is clammy, like cheese left out in the sun. Audrey opens her eyes and looks at Lily. 'Mum?' she says. 'Close the window. It's cold.'

The ship's doctor is summoned, and informs them there is an outbreak of something onboard but he does not yet know what. An elderly passenger in First is affected, and one of the Italian newborns. He gives Ida tablets, with instructions on when to administer them, and tells them Audrey must be kept cool. Annie, who has been moping around the corridor all morning, comes to sit on the empty bunk, gazing at Audrey as if she might cure her through goodwill alone.

Towards lunchtime there is a knock on the door, even though it is anyway ajar, to let in whatever breeze there might be. Edward stands in the doorway, looking pale and sheepish.

'I've come to find you. I hope you're not trying to avoid me, although I wouldn't blame you if you were.'

The cabin is hot and close, and Lily is conscious not only of the unpleasant smell of sweat and illness and stale air but also of Ida and Annie, both gazing at Edward.

'Let's go for a walk up on deck. I could do with the fresh air.'

Outside, the brightness feels hard and metallic after so long in the dim cabin. She blinks and stares out to sea, straining for some kind of new landmark. After all, it is not long before they are due to arrive in Ceylon. But it is still just the same as it was. A flat carpet of shifting, glinting lights stretching out in every direction.

Lily notices that some of the other passengers are staring at them, and a couple whisper as they pass. She hears the word 'dance' and then a giggle and isn't surprised when Edward leads them to the far end of the deck, where there are fewer people.

'Do you mind if we sit down?' he asks, reaching for a pair of empty deckchairs, nicely tucked away in the shade. 'I'm really not feeling terribly well.'

'I'm not surprised,' says Lily, then relents. 'To be honest, I'm not either. And having to nursemaid poor Audrey all morning hasn't helped either.'

'Lily, I'm sorry about last night. There you were, looking so lovely, and I turned into a drunken boor and spoilt your evening.'

Lily turns away so he won't see her pleasure at that word 'lovely'.

'I was far from sober myself, I can assure you. I'm sorry Max dragged you on to the dancefloor like that. You seemed to be almost in a state of shock.'

Now it's Edward who looks away.

'He was just horsing around. Helena is furious with me.'

'Why?'

'For not walking away. I embarrassed her.'

Lily is surprised that Helena should be so easily embarrassed, and even more so that her fury should linger beyond the night. Clearly, there is a lot she does not understand about the relationship between the siblings.

'He's an idiot, though.'

Edward blurts it out as if he hadn't even been aware he was about to say it.

'Who? Max Campbell?'

'Yes. Why do they have to keep coming down here? Why don't they stay upstairs, where they'd be more at home?'

Lily bites back the urge to point out that he hadn't seemed that unhappy about the arrangement when he was dancing all that time with Eliza. And now that reminds her of what Max was saying to her while the others were dancing, and once more she has to turn her head for fear of what her face will give away.

'They were involved in some scandal, I think. Back in London. That's what they're running away from, and that's why I think they're not made terribly welcome upstairs. Also . . .' She pauses, unsure whether to go on.

'The fact is, they had a baby daughter who died in rather horrible circumstances. I think they blame themselves. And each other. And maybe they think that, down here, no one will know and they won't have to talk about it.'

Edward has his hand to his mouth, and his eyes are round with horror.

'Oh, no wonder,' he says. And, 'Oh, how ghastly.'

They sit for a moment, contemplating the sea and the sky and the world, and the nasty, unpalatable reality of death.

'Poor Max,' Edward says softly. 'Poor Eliza.'

He closes his eyes and Lily begins to think he might have fallen asleep, but then he snaps them open and gives himself a shake, as if arriving at some moment of decision. Then he turns to her. How green his eyes are in this light. Like moss, or the smooth green glass one sometimes finds washed up on the beach. From the dining room comes the noise of cutlery clattering on to plates and people talking excitedly. The first lunch sitting must be starting. A woman shrieks with laughter and the sound seems to bounce off the metal railing in front of them and the white walls of the lounge. Still Edward looks at her, and it is a moment suspended in time.

'I like you so much,' he says, and she finds she cannot swallow for the lump that blocks up her throat. 'I wish I could be the one to make you happy.'

'Couldn't you be?' she whispers.

He studies her face. Here I am, she thinks. If you'd only see me.

206

'Maybe I could. I think I would like to try.'

He takes her hand and his fingers feel almost weightless around hers, so light is his touch. She leans in towards him, her body leading so her mind has no option but to follow on, and when their lips meet it's so familiar, as if this kiss is something she's always known, a part of herself.

Lily is the first to pull away as something occurs to her.

'Your parents would be horrified. I'm going into service, don't forget.'

Edward smiles.

'They're thousands of miles away. And besides, they'd be delighted with you. Who wouldn't be?'

They stay together on the chairs in a shrunken world that encompasses only the two of them, until Lily remembers Audrey and Ida and Annie, and tears herself away, using every ounce of willpower to haul herself to her feet.

She imagines Edward will drop her hand when they walk into the busier part of the deck, but to her surprise he clasps it even more tightly. Most of the other passengers don't notice, so used are they to seeing them together, but there are a few eyebrows raised, the odd elbow digging into a neighbour's ribs.

They pass Maria, walking out from lunch.

'Lily, I've been hoping to talk to you. Oh!'

Maria notices their conjoined hands, and Lily tries to detach herself, but Edward resists.

'Never mind. It can wait.'

Maria is smiling, but there's a hesitation there that Lily finds troubling. And now, to add to her discomfort, here comes George Price. Edward hasn't spotted him, so only Lily sees the startled look on his face when he notices her that turns so quickly to narrow-eyed spite when he takes in Maria and Edward and darkens to something else entirely when he sees Edward's hand in hers.

Before they go down to the cabin they stand by the railing one more time.

'You see that cloud?' says Edward, pointing to the one single white spot in the endless expanse of blue above them. 'That's now our cloud and, when it passes in front of the sun, we can both make a wish, and whatever we wish will come true.'

Waiting for the cloud to drift closer to the sun, George is forgotten and Maria and, God forgive her, poor Audrey, and Lily takes a note of exactly what she can see, and hear – of the warmth of the sun on her cheeks and how the smell of the salt coming up from the sea mingles with the stodgy, yeasty scent of the sponge they must have served up for pudding – trying to commit it all to memory so that in the future she can look back and think: *Here, I was happy.*

The cloud is inches away from the sun.

'Are you ready?' asks Edward, squeezing her hand.

But just as the world turns momentarily grey and Lily closes her eyes the better to will her wish into fruition a scream pierces the air, shattering into tiny pieces the scene she has just memorized. The scream is coming from below deck. Audrey, she thinks. And starts to run.

As she flings open the door that leads down to the lower decks there is another scream, more anguished even than the first, which reverberates around the narrow metal staircase until her ears ring with it. Audrey. Audrey, Audrey, Audrey.

By the time she arrives at their cabin she is crying. The door is closed, which she knows to be a bad sign. This is her punishment for that one, exquisite moment of happiness. This, too, will turn out to be her fault, just as what happened to Mags was her fault.

But when she bursts inside she does not find Annie dissolved into a weeping puddle on the floor, or Ida pulling a sheet over Audrey's face. She does not find that unforgettable smell of death that visits her sometimes in her dreams. What she finds is Annie, lying on the bottom bunk, chattering, and Ida rinsing out a towel in the washbasin, and Audrey, propped up against pillows, looking pale and exhausted but focusing, as if she is finally aware of who and where she is.

'I thought,' gasps Lily. 'I thought . . .'

Ida wants to know who is screaming.

'Gives me a chill right through to my bones,' she says.

Edward, who arrives just now, goes to find out and returns, tight-lipped, to tell them the newborn baby down on the Italian deck has died.

The news plunges them all into a dark mood. Edward goes to join Helena while Lily stays in the cabin to fetch glasses of cool water for Audrey, who is still weak and dehydrated and unsure what is happening to her. Lily is relieved that Audrey seems to have turned the corner but filled with irrational guilt that, somehow, by wishing so hard for Audrey to be saved, she has caused the baby to suffer the fate that was meant for her friend. It makes no sense, she knows that. Lily is not fanciful, nor even particularly religious, believing in a general rather than specific way in the existence of something greater than her. But the baby's death has made her fearful. Must other people's suffering always be the price of her own happiness?

Later, Ida and Lily leave Audrey sleeping and go up on deck, gulping in the humid air as if it is the purest oxygen. Teatime has passed, but a sympathetic steward fetches them sandwiches, which they eat slumped on the sofas in the lounge. It's that point of the evening when the sky is deepening from blue to indigo and the swollen, orange sun is dipping towards the horizon. Outside on the deck the passengers chat and play cards and write letters, while from first class there's the sound of a string quartet playing, the searing violin vibrating on the breeze.

Just a few moments later everything falls into a hush and an eerie silence descends, as if the sea itself is holding its breath.

'The engine has stopped,' says Lily, alarmed. 'Has something gone wrong?'

'It's a funeral,' explains the steward. 'For the baby.'

And, sure enough, now there comes the sound of crying and keening. Agitated voices talking in a foreign language at the far end of the deck.

'So soon!' Ida exclaims.

The steward nods and stands up straighter, his expression grim.

'It's because of the heat,' he says.

'Can't have bodies lying around,' Ida agrees.

Lily and Ida go out on to the deck to pay their respects. All the passengers are standing up, heads bent, facing the far end, where the Italian women and a handful of men, clad mostly in black, are swaying and weeping around the familiar figure of the ship's chaplain. A steward, his white uniform contrasting with the sombre colours of the mourners, stands motionless by the railing, carrying a tiny dark box that makes Lily's heart hurt to see it.

She makes a shield of her hand and holds it up to her mouth to stop the cry that threatens to escape.

The string quartet above resumes playing and now there's a low hum as the first-class passengers launch into 'Abide with Me', their voices starting low and tentative but building in confidence and loudness until they are all but shouting the words across the vast, uncaring ocean. Further down the deck the steward turns to lift the box and a woman sinks to the floor like an airless rubber balloon.

'Oh, that poor woman,' says Lily.

'Nothing to do but get on with it,' says Ida.

The sun is now streaking the sky with stripes of blood orange and flamingo pink, the world dressing up in its finest, brightest clothes to see the baby off. And Lily thinks, by contrast, of Mags's funeral. Just her and Mags's mum and dad. Her mum bent over almost to the ground by the weight of her grief and shame, and her dad stood straight as a lamp post, looking stonily ahead, as if he had come to the wrong place and was just having to make the best of it. And Lily herself, still dulled from the horror of that terrible taxi journey to the hospital, with Mags so weak Lily had almost had to carry her, bundled into a long overcoat to hide the blood, with blankets to sit on so she wouldn't bleed into the seat. 'Here's the fare for the taxi,' the abortionist had said to Mags, her face hard and fearful. 'Remember to tell them you did this yourself. At home. And she' – pointing at Lily – 'found you like that. Or we'll all end up in the cells.' The doctors hadn't believed it. But they'd seen it all before. And before long it was all over. *Am I going to die, Lil?*

Right up to the funeral, Lily was washing her hands every chance she got to rid herself of the blood, though it was long since gone. The sky over the graveyard was slate grey and leaden, as if it were too heavy to stay up there and must soon come crashing down to the ground. And the young vicar, so nervous about what he could and couldn't say, calling her 'Margaret this' and 'Margaret that', as if he were talking about someone else entirely. No Robert. Had she really expected he might come?

The music stops, that last word, 'me', stretching out into the encroaching darkness. And with a low roar the ship's engine comes back to life. 'At least that little mite will be spared a war,' Ida says, turning away to return to the cabin. Lily's sadness is wrapping itself around her neck like the gold silk scarf Edward has yet to give back, but still she stands rooted to the spot, with her hands up to her face, gazing along the deck until at last the black figures are swallowed up by the night.

20

18 August 1939

'WASHING! SUITS! Washing! Suits!'

The shouting wakes Lily from a dreamless sleep. Peering out of the porthole, she sees a launch full of dark-skinned people, all either talking excitedly among themselves or calling up towards the ship. Now she notices that the *Orontes* is in a harbour, still some distance from land, surrounded by other ships and smaller boats.

Ceylon. Even the word sounds exotic, the way it stretches her mouth first in one direction then the opposite so there's no chance of just trotting it out like some ordinary name.

Audrey is sleeping. She looks better than yesterday, her colour less vivid, but there will be no chance of her getting off the ship today. Even if the doctor hadn't forbidden it, Audrey is too weak. Luckily, Annie has volunteered to stay onboard with her. That still leaves Ida unaccounted for. Though Lily had found herself softening towards her spiky cabin mate over the previous difficult day, she has no desire for her company ashore. Ceylon is one of the places Lily has been most looking forward to visiting and she doesn't want to risk Ida ruining the experience with her snippy asides and endless complaints.

She hopes to be spending the day with Edward. Now that she has slept properly and is no longer feeling the after-effects of too much champagne, Lily has managed to put her feelings about yesterday's events in perspective. The baby's death was a tragedy but it wasn't her fault, and it certainly has nothing to do with her and Edward. Now, when she thinks back to the deckchairs and the way Edward said, 'I like you so much,' she allows herself to feel a warm glow instead of guilt, and if there's the slightest, slenderest thread of unease about the way he'd said, 'I wish I could be the one to make you happy,' she snaps it off before it can take hold.

Ida is not in her bed. Her pattern is to use the bathroom early before the queues form, so Lily makes the most of her absence, quickly slipping on the lightweight green dress that she wore on the Cairo expedition.

Eliza's peach silk gown is still hanging from the end of the bunk, reproaching her. She ought to have returned it yesterday but, with everything that has happened, it slipped her mind. She runs her fingertips over the smooth perfection of it.

After brushing her teeth at the washbasin, Lily slips out of the door, allaying her guilt by telling herself that Ida will find someone else to go sightseeing with. Up on deck she locates Helena and Ian waiting by the dining room. They chat a little about the sad events of the day before, and Lily resolves not to ask about Edward but almost instantly breaks that resolution, blurting out, 'Is your brother not coming ashore?'

A look passes over Helena's face, too fleetingly for Lily to identify it. Please let her be glad, she thinks. No matter what their parents might say, please let at least Helena approve.

'He's just gone to get more money from the Purser's Office,' Helena says, then gives an anxious half-smile. 'Seems like we are getting through it so fast.'

Lily feels a tug on her sleeve and turns to see Maria standing there, her dark hair pulled back unflatteringly tightly from her face, emphasizing those unusually long features. If anything, Maria is looking thinner even than when the voyage started, and Lily feels a twinge of unease when she remembers that Maria had been wanting to talk to her. When did she become the sort of person who forgets her friends?

'Would you mind if I came along with you?' Maria asks. 'The friend that I was going to explore with is unwell and confined to her cabin and I should so hate to miss Ceylon.'

'Of course not.'

Lily hates the treacherous part of her that wants to say no, to keep herself exclusively for Edward. She slips her hand through Maria's arm and squeezes, noticing how the skin feels like it is papered directly on to the bone, with nothing in between.

Edward arrives, and Lily hardly dares look at him. He greets her warmly, but no more so than he greets Maria, and instantly preoccupies himself with sorting through the notes in his wallet.

They climb on to a launch alongside the boat filled with Sinhalese still shouting out, offering to do washing for the passengers or have suits made up.

'Surely it's not possible to make an entire suit in a day?' says Lily.

'Anything is possible, Lily, if you put your mind to it,' Maria replies.

First impressions of Ceylon are disappointing. Though it's a clear, sparkling day, the harbour itself seems brown and drab, with the buildings of Colombo rising up behind it – no signs of the white, sandy, palm-fringed beaches Lily has been imagining.

She cheers up instantly once they arrive in the town itself, with its colonial-style buildings and streets teeming with activity – rickshaws pulled by men with skin the colour of gravy, wearing only white cloths knotted around their waists like babies' napkins, women in saris as bright as parrot feathers carrying water urns on their heads, groups of half-dressed children chattering and attaching themselves to first one Westerner then another, greeting both kindness and rebuff with the same broad smiles.

'You want guide?' asks a boy with round cheeks and a black mole on his forehead which Lily at first mistakes for a fly. 'I take you bazaar. Very nice. I carry bag?'

No matter how firmly Ian informs him that his services are not required, the boy still tags along.

Away from the main streets, the atmosphere changes. The British influence is no longer obvious in the buildings and there's a pungent smell of fish and rotting fruit coming from the street-market stalls.

Lily, walking ahead, talking to Maria, slips on something. Looking down, she sees to her horror that she has trodden in a pool of blood, the soles of her white sandals now stained with red. She cries out, grabbing hold of the back of Maria's brown dress, and Edward rushes to her side, only to burst into laughter.

'Sorry, Lily,' he says. 'I don't mean to laugh but that's not blood, it's betel-nut juice. The men here mix it with lime and spices and chew it until they've had enough of it then spit it out. That's what we've been walking in. Haven't you noticed?'

And of course, now she's been made aware, she notices for the first time the mouths of the Sinhalese men they pass, their teeth and lips stained red, as if they have been eating raw flesh.

'I feel very foolish,' she says to Maria as they turn around to head back to the centre. 'I am going to keep completely quiet for the rest of the day.'

After consulting the tourist information provided by the ship, the group decide to take a trip to Mount Lavinia. For five shillings each they get to take a drive in one of the ancient touring cars they've noticed around the town out to a Buddhist temple not far from Colombo. They are advised to take an English-speaking guide with them. 'Take me, missy,' pleads the boy with the mole. 'Me best guide in Colombo.'

To prove it, the boy claps his hand and summons a touring car. There is really only room for four in the back but the five of them somehow squash in, with the boy clinging on behind them. Lily is practically sitting on Edward's lap, and holds herself stiffly upright, trying to make herself as slight as possible so as not to put pressure on the point where their bodies meet, which she feels to be scorching hot.

They travel at leisurely speed through the old part of town, the driver honking his horn at natives who get in their way, either on foot or on bicycles. Meanwhile, their guide keeps up an eccentric stream of running commentary. 'In that house very bad man live,' he says, pointing out a shabby, one-storey hovel with a tattered curtain over the doorway. A modern white building a few hundred yards further on, on the other hand, earns the boy's approval: 'This good place British hospital.'

They pass monks in saffron robes and huts with roofs made from the branches of coconut palms outside which squatting figures cook on braziers on the ground. As they drive out of the town, the sights change – peasants, men and women, working in the fields, their heads wrapped in cloth to keep off the sun, carts full of logs pulled by water buffalo.

The temple comes into view, a colourful building set back from the dusty road in the middle of a grove of banana trees. As they walk towards it from the car, they hear raised voices. Turning the corner, Lily's heart sinks to see a puce-faced George Price arguing with a monk, who is pointing agitatedly at a bench next to the entrance. In front of the bench is a small carpet on which are arranged several pairs of shoes.

'The idiot is refusing to take his shoes off,' says Ian. 'Well, I hope he likes waiting around in the sun because they won't let him in if he doesn't.'

George greets them curtly, his eyes skimming over Lily and Maria as if they are made of air. He looks unkempt, Lily thinks, his shirt crumpled, as if he has slept in it.

'These people are trying to tell me I have to take off my shoes,' he complains loudly. 'I'm not walking around in my bare feet. I'm not a savage.'

'That's completely your right,' says Edward sweetly, sitting on the bench to remove his shoes and socks, 'but it seems like a bit of a wasted journey for you. Good job there's this handy bench here with a lovely view of the road.'

Lily bends down, pretending to be engrossed in unbuckling her sandals so George won't see her smile. When she looks up again George is sitting on the bench sullenly taking off his shoes. On a closer look, his eyes seem swollen, the whites angry and shot with red.

'Better say goodbye to these,' he says as he lines up his highly polished brown leather Oxfords on the carpet with the rest of the shoes. 'I don't suppose they'll still be here when we get out.'

The monk who was remonstrating with George when they arrived turns to Helena and Ian. 'Your guide very good boy. He look after shoes. No thieves at Buddhist temple.'

'Think you offended him, mate,' says Ian to George as they enter.

George stares straight ahead, flint-faced and silent, but Lily sees a livid purple stain creeping up from the collar of his shirt.

The monk leads them inside the temple, which is made up of a number of small chambers painted in bright, jewel colours. There are several images of Buddha and even an imprint of Buddha's foot. From one of the chambers comes a sweet, almost overpowering scent. When they arrive they find it carpeted with aromatic frangipani, like a huge, colourful quilt. The monk explains that the flowers have been arranged by the young unmarried girls from the surrounding villages who are celebrating their special festival on this day.

Lily is entranced by the flowers and by the colourful frescos of Buddha on the wall, but behind her she can hear George muttering about how the 'heathen religions' ought to visit a proper British church to see how a place of worship should look.

Back outside, the boy with the mole is taking his shoe-guarding duties very seriously and even insists on helping them put theirs on, making Maria laugh when he lines her shoes up the wrong way around.

'There's not much point in you all squashing into that car. Two of you might as well come with me,' says George gruffly, when they are all once more shod and walking back towards the road. It is a command rather than an invitation.

Lily's chest feels tight and she keeps her face bent towards the ground lest she should meet George's eye and find herself compelled by misplaced politeness to go with him. Next to her, Maria shoots her a wide-eyed glance that is all too easy to interpret. No. Not me. There's a silence that seems to grow out of the dust kicked up by their feet as they keep walking, the *swish swish swish* of their clothes sounding suddenly thunderous in the stillness of the midday heat.

Though she does not look at him, Lily can picture how George's face will be darkening from dusky pink to the colour of under-cooked beef.

It's Ian who answers, finally.

'Thanks, but I think we will all be just fine in the one car. And besides, we're going on to Mount Lavinia next so it's probably best if we five stick together.'

They all know George is most likely heading to Mount Lavinia himself. It's the tour recommended in the ship's guide. Still, Lily is grateful to Ian for finding an excuse.

When they crowd into the car again there's a more subdued atmosphere.

'That was rather awkward, wasn't it?' says Helena.

'Well, he shouldn't be so disagreeable,' replies Edward. This time he is on the other side of the car from Lily, with his sister on his lap. Lily is relieved to be spared the turmoil of being squashed up against him. He seems so distant today, as if nothing has happened between them.

Maria is half sitting on Lily. She hasn't said a word since they were inside the temple.

'Are you feeling all right, Maria?' Lily says softly.

Maria nods but does not answer immediately.

'To tell you the truth, Lily, that man makes me very nervous. The way he looks at me as though I don't have the right to be where he is. I've seen that look before, back in Austria. It frightens me.'

Mount Lavinia is an imposing, white, colonial-style hotel built on a point jutting out into the sea surrounded by tall, slender coconut palms and flanked on each side by pale, sandy beaches. At last, the Ceylon of Lily's imaginings.

They take tea on the terrace overlooking the bathing pavilion and the beach, where dozens of wooden boats are lined up in a row, their simple canvas sails fluttering in the sea breeze. A group of children play in the sand in the shade of one of the trees. Their laughter carries up to the table like soft summer rain.

When the menu comes, there are so many different types of tea on offer Lily feels confused. Not wanting to admit to not knowing what they are, she waits until Helena has ordered and copies her.

'I wish my parents could be here,' Lily says.

'Do you miss them greatly?' asks Maria.

Lily hesitates. Though she doesn't like to admit it, the truth is she goes for long periods of time without her family even crossing her mind. There is so much that is new on the ship, and no associations with home to be constantly reminding her. It's as if she has been reborn without context or history. Home – when she thinks about it at all – is an abstract idea that floats through her mind. Then she remembers Maria's parents in Vienna, holed up with their books and their lovely things, while all around them Jews are being stripped of their civil liberties, banned from public parks and universities, their businesses shut down, synagogues destroyed, and now, for the last weeks, no word of how they are.

'Forgive me, Maria. I'm such a clumsy dolt. I didn't mean to talk about my parents when here you are, worried sick about yours.'

'Don't be silly, Lily. Of course you must be thinking about your family. How about you, Helena? Do you find yourself thinking a lot about your parents in places like this?'

Helena, who has been sipping her tea, which, after all, is mercifully similar to the tea at home, shoots Edward a look that Lily cannot interpret.

'Our parents are quite . . . set in their ways. I don't really think they would feel terribly comfortable here.'

'Father would say, "Why does it have to be so damned *foreign*?"' Edward laughs, but there is a hard edge to his laughter. 'My father doesn't really see the point in other cultures or languages or customs.'

'Oh, that's not true,' says Helena. 'He's not as bad as that.'

'Come on, Helena. The man is terrified of things he doesn't understand.'

'There are some things it's not possible to understand.'

The siblings glare at each other and Lily has the sense of unsaid things reverberating in the air between them.

'Families, eh?' says Ian, in a transparent attempt to defuse the tension.

After tea, they take a walk on the beach. While Ian tells Edward and Maria a long story about the first time he travelled abroad with the Australian military, Helena and Lily take off their shoes and paddle in the sea. When she suggested it, Lily had been hoping

Edward might join her so that they could have some time alone, but he has not even looked her way.

'You don't look very happy, Lily. Is something wrong?'

'How could it be? Look at us, paddling in the Indian Ocean, so close to India itself we could almost touch it. You'd have to be sour as old milk for there to be something wrong.'

Still Helena fixes her with those steady, grey eyes while, on the shore, Ian says something that makes Edward laugh suddenly and loudly, like a dog yelping.

'I can see there is something, so I'm just going to come out and ask you, because I can't bear to see you miserable. Is it Edward? Is he making you unhappy?'

'No!' Lily knows she has spoken too loudly. The three figures on the beach stop mid-conversation, looking towards the sea.

Lily whirls around so her back is to them.

'That is, maybe. Just a little. But it's nothing he's done, Helena. Edward is always a perfect gentleman. The problem lies with me. I just can't seem to work out where I am with him.'

She reaches both hands down and scoops up as much cool water as she can cup in her palms to pat on to her burning cheeks.

Helena stands still, a pained expression on her face, and Lily regrets having spoken.

'Just ignore me. I'm being so foolish. I suppose it comes of being on a ship for so long in each other's company. Helena, forget I spoke.'

'No, Lily. You're right. Edward is behaving . . . inconsistently. And I'm sorry for it.'

Lily feels as if there's something stuck in her throat, as if the leaves from the tea they have just finished have somehow got clogged up in there in one fibrous mass, making swallowing difficult.

'Is it because I'll be going into service?' she asks eventually. She is trying to make her voice light and conversational, but she knows Helena will be able to hear how it breaks in the back of her throat. 'I know your parents are very traditional about such things. You told me as much when you explained why it couldn't work out between you and Ian. Is it because they wouldn't consider me good enough?'

'No! Lily, no!'

Helena leans over and takes one of Lily's hands in hers, turning Lily towards her.

'You mustn't think that. Believe me, my parents would welcome you with open arms.'

'But Ian?'

'The situation with Ian is different. It's different for me.'

'Because you're a woman?'

Helena sighs, a sound that whispers like a wisp of a breeze across the surface of the ocean. A long strand of hair has come loose and she collects it absently with her fingers and repins it without a thought.

'All families have their own ways of doing things, don't they? Their own secrets that they don't want to be known. Sometimes I think our family, mine and Edward's, is built on secrets and without them we'd all just collapse like a house of cards. There are things I can't tell you, Lily, that might make everything clearer. But believe me when I say that, if Edward brought you home, my parents would not object.'

When they go back to the touring car their young guide is waiting for them, sitting back against the trunk of a nearby palm tree.

'You had good tea? This hotel very good hotel. Best hotel in whole world. You tell King of England about this hotel.'

They ask the boy to take them now to the bazaars, which are located just off the main street in Colombo. When they'd passed that area earlier it had looked very colourful and inviting and exotic, with Indian music being piped out of all the shops. But when the car stops to let them off they are appalled to find that the radios are now all playing Western music and they are to do their shopping to the accompaniment of 'Doing the Lambeth Walk'.

'I thought at the very least that would be one of the joys of being so far from home, that I wouldn't have to hear that dratted song ever again,' groans Edward.

'No. This very good song,' their guide tells them. 'Very new. Very modern.'

Lily is drawn towards one shop, which is selling exquisite saris in vibrant colours that echo the flowers from the temple.

'They'll be too expensive,' she decides.

'Don't be so defeatist,' Edward says. 'Let's go and investigate.'

The five of them make for the doorway, squeezing in past the street vendors, who are trying to tempt them with trays of shell necklaces. Lily swallows as she remembers her silk scarf, bought in Gibraltar — how long ago that seems now! — and pictures Edward picking it up, pressing his nose to it as Ida described. She wonders where he keeps it and feels an almost unbearable tenderness towards him. Edward with all his secrets. And now she is one of them.

Inside, the shop is unexpectedly crowded, and Lily recognizes one of the first-class passengers, a handsome silver-haired gentleman with an aristocratic manner and large, flared nostrils. He is waiting outside a closed door at the back of the shop, his whole body leaning forward, as if stiff with expectation.

Suddenly, the door is flung open and Eliza Campbell steps out, resplendent in a sari made from vivid fuchsia silk that wraps itself like a python around her body. She has pinned her black hair up tightly and the shopkeeper rushes forward with a matching pink silk flower that he places carefully behind her ear. The result is mesmerizing, and Lily senses the other customers pausing their conversations to turn and stare.

'What do you think? Will I pass for a native?'

Eliza presses the palms of her hands together in front of her face and bows her head, just as they have seen some of the Sinhalese women doing. The silver-haired man lets out a laugh that sounds like gunfire.

'You, my dear, are an utterly perfect native.'

His voice is deep and rich and sounds vaguely familiar.

'My goodness, that's Anthony Hewitt,' Helena whispers.

'The radio announcer?'

'Definitely so,' confirms Helena. 'My mother listens to him all the time. She says he is the benchmark for how all Englishmen should sound. Isn't that so, Edward?'

Edward nods but he looks tense and nervous, his top lip biting down on the bottom one until it is white instead of pink. Lily hates that Eliza is able to have this effect on him.

Now Eliza spots them across the crowded shop.

'Lily! Edward!'

Within moments they find themselves whisked off to be introduced to Eliza's companion, who is indeed, it transpires, Anthony Hewitt.

'Hasn't he got the most divine voice?' Eliza wants to know. 'I could just eat it up with a spoon.'

Anthony Hewitt is polite and charming, but distant, and Lily gets the distinct impression he resents having to share Eliza's attentions. She herself feels tongue-tied and stupid with nerves, unable to get past the hurdle of how far her life has come. A month ago I was waiting on tables, she reminds herself. Now I am meeting radio stars. Eliza, meanwhile, is in one of her bright moods, where her eyes glitter and her voice is louder than it ought to be.

'Max has gone off in a huff somewhere,' she says. 'He was being very tiresome about wanting to go to a hotel to get a drink. We passed one a few streets back and he got very fed up when we refused to stop and go in, didn't he, Anthony? He's probably propped up at the bar there right now, on his second Scotch, boring everyone to death about his unreasonable wife.'

'Then he's a damn fool,' says Anthony.

Edward drifts off, but every time Lily tries to take her leave Eliza restrains her by asking her a question or demanding her opinion on this sari or that one, seemingly oblivious to Anthony Hewitt's growing impatience. Lily thinks about Maria, waiting for her somewhere outside the shop. Eliza had hardly acknowledged her when she scooped Lily and Edward up to be introduced to Anthony and, when Lily turned to look for her, she had vanished. She hopes she is with the others. It's getting dark now, and Lily doesn't like to think of Maria alone in this unfamiliar place.

By the time she manages to extricate herself and exit the shop after finally convincing Eliza that no, she didn't want to try on more saris and, no, she didn't think the rose-coloured one was just made for her, there is no sign of her companions. She walks in one direction, instantly attracting a crowd of Sinhalese, all trying to sell her something or take her somewhere, and all smiling, as if they are, all of them, sharing together in the most terrific joke.

Immediately, she is back on the quayside in Aden, pushing past the Arab vendors with George Price's ragged breath in her ear, watching the launch preparing to leave without her.

'No,' she says, shaking her head and peering through the crowds for a familiar face. 'No, please.'

'Please,' the Sinhalese repeat, still smiling. 'Please. Thank you. Please. Thank you.'

Panic rises, sweat breaking out on her forehead. When the young boy who has been their guide for the day appears by her side Lily feels she could cry with relief. He speaks angrily to the crowds of people around her, who duly step back, still smiling, but do not go away altogether.

'These bad people. Very ignorant people. These people not knowing how to behave.'

The boy looks genuinely sorrowful at the state of his fellow countrymen and raises his shoulders as if to say, *What can we do, we civilized ones?*

'Have you seen my friends?' Lily asks him.

'Yes. Friends!' He motions to her to follow him and leads the way, shouting at anyone who tries to detain them. Eventually, they arrive at a shop selling tea in beautifully ornate tins. Helena and Ian are inside, marvelling at the array of teas on offer.

'Oh, Lily, can you believe there's a type called gunpowder tea?' calls Helena. Her cheeks have that pink flush that Lily has come to associate with her spending time alone with Ian.

'That'd make breakfast go off with a bang!' Ian dutifully offers up the expected joke with the kind of facial expression that says, *Well, someone had to say it.*

Neither of them has seen Edward or Maria.

Hoping the two are together, Lily hurries out of the shop, accompanied by the boy guide, and stands looking first one way and then the next, in increasing agitation.

She sees Eliza and Anthony Hewitt emerging from the sari shop, he carrying a large package beautifully wrapped in tissue paper and tied with string. She is in the midst of relating some story or other and he, a good six inches taller than her, leans down towards her with his great nostrils flaring, as if breathing in the scent of a low-growing flower. Lily steps back so she cannot be seen. As they walk past, she watches Anthony Hewitt's hand, which has been lightly lying between Eliza's shoulders to guide her through the throng, slide down her back to her buttocks, before she swats it away with a trilling laugh.

Lily doesn't understand the Campbells. She will never understand them.

But though Lily is shocked by what she has seen, she is also, in a way she finds deeply shaming, excited by it. Anthony Hewitt's hand going so freely there reminds her of Robert and how he liked to lay claim to every inch of her until, at the last, she'd hold him back. Not wanting to, but knowing she had to. ('I'll find someone who will, then,' he'd said that last time.) Max Campbell, and even George Price, who makes her skin crawl just to think of him, have also tried to inflict their own urgent agendas on to her. Only Edward, sweet Edward, holds back. And instead of being grateful, now she wonders what is keeping him from trying, why he does not, like Anthony Hewitt, try to probe further, lower, deeper, trusting to her to turn him back.

'Lily! I am so glad to find you here. I thought I should have to go back to the ship alone.'

Maria seems out of breath, as if she's been hurrying. Her hair is messy and there's a blaze of high colour in each of her sunken cheeks.

'It's a strange thing, Lily. I used to be so comfortable travelling alone. It never worried me to walk around a new city by myself, but lately I find myself so nervous. I feel as if I'm being followed wherever I go.'

Lily laughs and points to the Sinhalese who are even now encircling them. 'That's perhaps because we *are* being followed,' she says.

Maria smiles, but it is like a shadow of her former smile.

'Sometimes, even on the ship, I think I hear footsteps. I fear I am turning already into a crazy old woman. There is no hope for me!'

They have arranged with their guide that they will make the short journey back to the ship by rickshaw, just to say they have had the experience. Lily has already written in her head the letters home describing it. How jealous Frank will be when he reads her news. The rivalry they'd had as children hasn't completely faded.

Ian and Helena are here, but Edward is nowhere to be seen.

Their guide tells them he saw him heading off in the direction of the ship and Helena is irritated that he didn't let them know he was going back.

'He can be so selfish sometimes,' she says, and Lily is taken aback by the bitterness in her voice.

The first pricklings of unease come while the guide is negotiating with the man in charge of organizing the line of rickshaws, and Lily realizes that they will each have to have a separate cart. Well, not even a cart, really, more like a sedan chair that has to be pulled like a barrow. Night has fallen now and, away from the bazaar, the streets begin to look dark and menacing. As if reading her mind, Maria turns to her.

'Lily, I'm not so sure . . .'

But now their young guide is here, ushering them into their individual rickshaws.

Lily's driver – what a misnomer that is, 'puller' might be more accurate – is small and slight, and she worries how he will cope with her weight. But at least he is young, not like Maria's, who has grizzled hair and stubble on his face, through which his mouth glistens obscenely, stained vivid red with betel juice as if he has torn raw flesh apart with his teeth.

'It's all right, Maria. I'll be right next to you.'

But as they set off through the near-deserted streets Maria's driver falls further and further behind and though Lily tries to call to her own to slow down, he either doesn't hear or doesn't understand. Every now and then they pass food stalls and the smell of something not altogether pleasant wafts briefly into Lily's nostrils. Apart from the odd oil light flickering, it is completely dark. Shadowy figures loom into view on street corners, groups of men sitting around tables engaged in what looks like some sort of gambling game who pause mid-play as they go past and stare darkly at Lily until she has to look away.

She cranes around, peering into the darkness behind her, but Maria is nowhere to be seen.

Crossing a junction, Lily notices, fifty yards or so off to the left, a tall, run-down building with a lit-up façade and, emerging from it, the familiar broad figure of Max Campbell. So Eliza is right. He has been drinking the afternoon away in a hotel bar. As she watches he is joined by another figure, a woman, in traditional Sinhalese dress, her body swathed in a sari, who stands very close to him, but Lily has only the briefest glimpse before the rickshaw driver moves on and the hotel is hidden from view.

Once again, Lily is plunged into confusion. The Campbells' behaviour leaves her both perplexed and unnerved. This is not the kind of marriage she understands, nor wants to understand. Was it like this, she wonders, before the death of their daughter, or is it grief that has distorted it, stretching it so horribly out of shape?

When they arrive at the ship there is further wrangling between the guide and the rickshaw drivers, who, it seems, are disputing the terms agreed by the man in charge of the queue. As they continue to argue, Lily peers into the darkness, watching uneasily for Maria's rickshaw. When it finally hoves into view her whole body slumps with relief.

'Thank goodness you're safe,' she says, reaching up to hand Maria out of the cart and give her a hug.

But Maria is silent, her features blanched by the moonlight, and when she takes Lily's hand her fingers are trembling.

'What happened, Maria? Did your driver do something to you?'

Maria shakes her head, but the look she shoots the man pulling her rickshaw is one of pure terror. He, in return, grins, his toothless mouth a gaping cavern of betel-nut viscera.

After they pay their young guide a shilling each – 'You take me with you? To America?' – the launch takes them to the ship. The onboard orchestra is playing up on the first-class deck, and the melody of '*Clair de Lune*' wafts down to them as they approach across the moonlit ocean. Unsettled by Maria's odd behaviour and Edward's seeming indifference, Lily's thoughts turn to the possibility of war. Is this the last time the world will be this beautiful? she asks herself. Life, it seems to her now, teeters always on the edge of an abyss, and happiness is so fragile it can break apart in the air for the wind to disperse.

21

FOR DAYS NOW, the passengers have been converging by the railings at dusk each evening to witness the changes in the twilight skies as they near the equator. Gone are the long, languid sunsets of earlier in the voyage, where the sun would sink lazily into the horizon in a blaze of colour. Now there is only day, and then, as suddenly as if a light has been switched off, it is night. And what a night it is, with the constellations of the Southern Cross sparkling like diamonds above the black line of the horizon.

Now all the talk is of the Crossing of the Line ceremony to be held as the ship sails over the equator, followed by a fancy-dress ball in the evening. It is a ritual observed by all the large boats that make this voyage and rumours have been flying around the ship about what the ceremony will entail. One particularly persistent suggestion is that all those passengers who have not crossed the equator before will be thrown into the swimming pool by Father Neptune. Lily does not like the sound of this but is determined to go through with it, if it is all part of the experience. Not so Ida.

'If anyone lays a hand on me I shall be reporting the matter to the police as soon as we land in Australia.'

'No one would dare,' whispers Audrey, who is now quite recovered from her terrifying bout of illness, and goes about the place with a fresh confidence born perhaps of having survived something she didn't expect to.

Between Audrey and Ida there is a new closeness. No, not closeness, for prickly Ida will not welcome or allow that, but certainly a softening. When someone has seen you at your lowest you share something with them that is almost impossible to define and harder still to undo.

With Lily, however, Ida is markedly cool. When Lily asked her, guiltily, how she had spent the day in Colombo, Ida had merely remarked that she'd gone into the town but hadn't much liked the look of it, or more particularly the smell of it, so had come straight back.

'All that red stuff spat in the street, and the stink of fish. Don't know how you had the stomach for it. I certainly didn't.'

Ida makes it sound as if Lily is lacking in discernment. Lily tries not to think of how quiet the ship would have been with everybody gone, how much time Ida would have had to hone her resentment.

The ship is due to cross the line in the early afternoon, and the entire ship, passengers and staff alike, are invited up to the first-class swimming pool to observe the moment. The impressive pool is festooned with flags and bunting. To Lily's relief, it turns out that the only people being thrown into the pool are those who volunteer for the task. The captain is dressed up as Father Neptune, complete with trident, and arrives at the pool clambering over the rails, as if he is freshly risen from the sea.

Two of the stewards have dressed as mermaids and lie on pillows arranged on the deck, flapping their green tails in a desultory manner while various members of staff play-act being pushed or thrown into the pool on a variety of comical pretexts.

As the laughter rings out around the deck Lily scans the crowd, looking for that shock of dark curls that has now become so dear to her. Instead she finds her gaze snagged by a familiar pair of ice-blue eyes.

Max Campbell, a head taller than the woman in front of him, raises one hand in salute. The thumb and forefinger of the other hand comb his moustache top to bottom in an inverted 'V' shape. Next to him, Eliza, wearing her sunglasses so her eyes are completely hidden, turns her head to see who he is waving to. Seeing Lily, she makes a face as if to say, *What is this nonsense we're watching?* Lily scours the faces around her, but Anthony Hewitt is nowhere in sight.

She has been trying not to think about Hewitt's hand slipping down to Eliza's buttocks, or the glimpse of Max coming out of a hotel with a woman not his wife. She can imagine what her mother would say, something about it not mattering how much money you have, if you haven't got morals, you haven't got anything. There was a letter from home waiting for her after they docked in Colombo, and now she has Mam's voice stuck in her head, giving a running commentary on the ship and the people in it.

Mam is still insisting there will not be a war, yet she says she can't help wishing Frank was on the ship with Lily, safely away, just in case.

At the poolside a wooden plank has been balanced over the water on a fulcrum like a seesaw, with a seat at one end where the volunteers take turns to sit and get slathered in foam and then mock-shaved with a huge wooden razor, before being flung into the water. They are then presented with a souvenir scroll to mark their first crossing of the line, while Lily and the other non-participating passengers receive a certificate.

Afterwards they all head back towards the staircase that leads down to the lower deck. Lily can see Eliza coming in her direction and quickly dives to hide herself in the crush of people. She is not in the mood for the Campbells and all their complications. However, Eliza is not to be put off.

'Lily Shepherd!' she calls in a piercing voice, either not noticing or not caring that half the ship's passengers turn to stare.

'Lily Shepherd, stop this minute. I need to talk to you about a matter of the utmost importance.'

Lily thinks about ignoring her and pushing on through, but she is conditioned to obey a summons and, besides, Mam is still occupying her thoughts and Lily's mother would never duck an obligation or an encounter.

'What are you planning on wearing to the fancy-dress ball? You must tell me. My imagination has totally deserted me. I'm thinking of going all in black with a sign hanging round my neck saying, "The death of Eliza Campbell's imagination". Would that work?'

She has the same hard brightness of three days ago in the bazaar in Colombo. Lily doesn't like the way she is reflected back to herself in the black lenses of Eliza's glasses, as if she is floating there in space.

'I haven't really thought about it. I haven't got anything suitable, I don't think.'

'Well, you shall come with me and we shall find something. It's a competition, don't forget. Don't you want to win? Besides, what else are we going to do to amuse ourselves all afternoon? This voyage seems to be going on and on and I am fast losing the will to live. I feel like we've already been at sea for decades. By the time we reach Sydney I shall be a hundred and ten.'

Before Lily has a chance to object they are back in Eliza's cabin, where Max is sprawled on the bed, reading, wearing a pair of black spectacles that Lily has never seen him in before. When he looks up those blue eyes are alarmingly magnified and Lily instinctively looks away.

'I've brought company, darling,' says Eliza unnecessarily. 'Isn't that fun?'

She turns to Lily. 'We always get on so much better when there's someone else around.'

'I'm glad to see you, Lily. We looked for you in Colombo. My poor wife even had to find a new friend to go around with, didn't you, Eliza? And I was forced to spend the afternoon drinking all alone in a hotel bar. There, don't you feel guilty now?'

Lily doesn't feel guilty so much as deeply uncomfortable. The image of Max emerging from the hotel with a woman is all too fresh in her mind.

'Any ideas on costumes?'

Her clumsy attempt at changing the subject sounds false to her ears, as if she is imitating one of those women she used to serve in the house in London who'd come in groups of three or four and talk at each other back and forth in bright, breezy voices, as if they were batting around a tennis ball.

'I think I shall wear the sari I bought in Colombo,' says Eliza. 'It's a bit of a dull choice, but where else will I wear it? Now, let's have a look in my dressing room and see what we can find for you.'

She flings open the wardrobe door and starts riffling through the dresses on the rail, frowning as she pauses at first one and then another. Getting to the end, she stands still, thinking. Then:

'Got it!'

Eliza is grabbing something from one of the hangers. It is the fox-fur stole that Lily picked up off the floor the last time she was here.

'Here.' Eliza loops the stole around Lily's neck. It is heavier than she imagined, lined on the underside with satin and weighted down at the nose.

'Quite hideous in a way, isn't it?' Eliza whispers, pausing to consider the dead creature. 'Max bought it for me so I have to pretend to like it.

'And now this.' Eliza has found a turban in a matching russet colour to the fox and places it carefully over Lily's hair. 'Finally, for the *pièce de résistance . . .*'

A long silver cigarette holder is placed in Lily's hand, and she is propelled back into the cabin.

'What do you think, Max? Guess who she is? Imagine dramatic make-up, eyebrows higher, lipstick, a plain black dress. Come on, it's obvious.'

Max doesn't appear to find it obvious, so Eliza elaborates.

'Film star. You know. *Swedish!*'

'Greta Garbo,' say Lily and Max at the same time.

Lily looks in the mirror. It's ridiculous, of course. And yet, there is something about her eyes, the way her hair curls out of the bottom of the turban.

'It's perfect,' Eliza declares. 'By the time I finish your make-up, even you won't be able to tell yourself apart from the real thing.'

'What about me?' Max asks. 'If you're both getting dressed up, I don't want to be left out.'

Now it is Max's wardrobe that is impatiently picked through, and then picked through again, without Eliza finding anything that suits. How impossible it is to come up with something creative, here on the ship, when one's resources are limited to the contents of three large trunks.

At last inspiration arrives.

'You shall wear my robe.'

Eliza removes a floral satin dressing gown from a hook on the back of the dressing-room door. Ignoring Max's dubious expression, she presses on.

'Oh, this is too good. See how I have these three hats that are virtually the same?'

She produces three almost identical pillbox hats, in black, blue and a deep green, two with veils, one without.

'You and Edward and – oh, what's the name of that Aussie chap Helena seems so smitten with?'

'Ian?'

'Exactly so. You and Edward and Ian will wear silk robes, belted to look like dresses, and these hats, and we will make black wigs out of something – I have an old black shawl that will do – and put on plenty of make-up, and you will go as the Boswell Sisters.'

Lily smiles. With Edward, there might be a chance, but it's almost impossible to imagine big, broad Max Campbell or ex-outback farmer Ian Jones passing themselves off as members of the celebrated American trio of singing sisters. Still, she has to admit the idea is a comic one, if they can get Edward and Ian to agree. Not that she has any influence at all over Edward, who increasingly appears to Lily to be as slippery as mercury, sliding through her fingers every time she thinks she has hold of him.

The rest of the afternoon is spent in a fervour of excited preparations. Ian and Edward are tracked down and made to agree, with varying degrees of reluctance. Helena is once again in bed, unwell, but Eliza fusses around Lily as if she were her own special creation, a piece of pottery or a painting of which she is most particularly proud.

By the time the ball begins even Lily has to admit she bears a passing resemblance to Greta Garbo. Eliza has shaped her mouth with a special pencil so that the upper lip dips down deeply in the middle, like a filled-in letter 'M', while the bottom is full and perfectly semicircular. Her eyebrows have been painted into two perfect high arches and her cheeks have been shaded in, emphasizing the bone structure. The combination of the turban and that fox stole with the cigarette holder give her a sophisticated, film-star glamour, and Eliza has added a pair of long diamond earrings to complete the look. Lily insisted on wearing her own dress, at least, a plain black woollen one she keeps for formal occasions. It's fully lined and she knows she will be sweltering before the night has even begun, but she feels it is important not to be dressed from head to toe in Eliza's clothes. Eliza won't be denied when it comes to footwear, though, lending Lily a pair of high-heeled black mules, which, being backless, get around the problem of Lily's feet being a full size smaller than Eliza's own.

Eliza herself is wearing the pink sari they'd seen her trying on in Colombo. ('Utterly divine,' Anthony Hewitt had said.) She has the pink flower wound into her black hair and she has put a pink teardrop-shaped mark over the bridge of her nose, as Lily has seen Indian women wear in books.

When they are quite happy with their outfits they summon the men, who have been lurking around outside Max and Eliza's cabin, smoking, from the smell of it. Much is made of Lily's transformation. 'You're the very spit of Garbo,' Ian declares, while Edward takes the opportunity, when no one else is listening, to whisper, 'How beautiful you look tonight.' He is in that strange mood she has noticed before when he is around Eliza, taciturn but also tense, as if on the alert for some kind of sign.

In general, though, there is an atmosphere of almost feverish anticipation, as happens in situations where people are forced into each other's company for extended lengths of time and will seize on any diversion on offer.

Now it is the men's turn.

Lily has lent her robe to the enterprise and is secretly thrilled when Eliza decrees Edward should wear it, being the slightest of the three. Ian will wear Helena's, spirited away by Edward while his sister was sleeping, and Max has on Eliza's, stretched almost to splitting point over his shoulders and arms and ending well above his knee.

Eliza and Lily have cut up the shawl (although Lily almost cried to do it; such a lovely thing, with nothing at all wrong with it) and made makeshift wigs which are held in place by a combination of hairpins and the hats. Then Lily and Eliza get to work on the make-up. Lily is half relieved, half disappointed when Eliza says she will start with Edward. It is such an intimate thing, this painting on of lips and eyes and cheeks. She does not know how she would have been able to do it without giving herself away.

How funny they look, the three men, in their ridiculous wigs and clothes. A camera is produced and photographs taken, first of the men, then of Lily gazing enigmatically to the side in typical Garbo style.

Max, who is taking the photograph, murmurs, 'Ravishing,' and Eliza shoots Lily a tight-lipped look which could be either proud or annoyed, it's impossible to tell.

Outside on deck, the passengers mill around, exchanging compliments and laughter. There are a good few Julius Caesars, wearing sheets purloined from the ship's laundry and draped over one shoulder. A group of Aussies have blackened their faces and come as Aboriginals, while some New Zealanders have made grass skirts from raffia and are performing their version of a Maori war dance.

There is food and music and a night sky that is studded with stars that seem so much nearer from up here on the first-class deck, so that Lily feels as if she should be able to reach up and pluck them like silver apples. Best of all, Edward stays by her side as if he has been glued there, even when Max complains he is ruining their fancy dress by keeping himself so separate from his 'sisters'.

Lily sees George dressed in some sort of uniform and ducks behind someone so that he does not notice her. She chats to Audrey and Annie, who have dressed up as Spanish señoritas in long black skirts and lace mantillas and hold colourful fans bought in one of the ports en route. They tell her Ida has refused to come up on deck, claiming the party will be full of drunks, but they think it is because she has nothing to wear but the same old black dress. Lily catches sight of Maria, standing with the Jewish couple she met before, the three of them not dressed up at all but wearing their usual drab, everyday clothes. Maria looks pinched and tired. Remembering how upset she had appeared after the rickshaw ride, Lily goes over to talk to them.

'How wonderful you look, Lily, just like a real film star.'

'And you, Maria, how have you been?'

Maria's smile fades, and her companion, Mrs Neumann, answers for her.

'I am afraid Maria has had bad news from home. A neighbour in Vienna says her parents have been removed from their apartment and taken somewhere. A prison camp of some sort, although nobody knows where or for how long they will be detained.'

Lily can imagine how anxious Maria must feel, being so far away and now knowing that her parents have had to leave their home and been taken to some unknown place. Yet she cannot help thinking that, if this is the worst that happens, it is not so bad. The word 'camp' makes her think of tents in the countryside. To be sure, it won't be comfortable. She has no illusions about that. But surely it is only until things settle down and the German government decides whether they will be allowed back or sent to join their daughters in England.

The fancy-dress competition is judged and the prize given to an elderly man from tourist class who has transformed himself into the cartoon character Popeye, principally by donning a sailor's cap and removing his false teeth and sucking on a clay pipe. To everyone's amusement, Max and Edward and Ian are declared runners-up and curtsy deeply to the other passengers while collecting their boxes of chocolates.

This is it, Lily thinks to herself, breathing it all in – the laughter, the *th-th-th* of a saxophone playing softly, the intoxicating scent of perfume as a woman in a satin gown sashays past, the feeling of Edward's arm, warm and solid, against hers. This is where my real life begins. Here in the Indian Ocean at the very mid-point of the world.

Lily excuses herself to go to the Ladies. She feels self-conscious using the toilets on this deck so makes her way downstairs, where she feels more at home. She is hurrying along the upper deck on her way back to the party when she all but bumps into the elderly woman she met in the gift shop in Pompeii.

'I see you ignored my advice,' the woman says disapprovingly, pulling her chin back into the ample pillows of her face. 'My husband says I should let you make your own mistakes, but I can see you're young and probably have no mother travelling with you, so I will once again warn you to stay away from the Campbells.'

Lily, emboldened by two glasses of champagne, dares to reply.

'If this is to do with the death of their daughter, I already know all about it.'

Now the woman looks confused.

'No. I know, of course, that their baby died, which is all very sad, but it's nothing to do with that.'

Lily remembers now how Eliza had told her Max's family had hushed up the details of exactly how Olivia had died.

'Then what?'

The woman purses her lips. She isn't wearing fancy dress and Lily can see she has on a corset under her clothes. Lily herself is sweltering in her woollen dress and she hates to think how constricting a corset would feel.

'I am not someone given to gossip. However, you should know the sort of people the Campbells are, the sort of woman Mrs Campbell is. Contrary to the story they are putting about, they are not here on some sort of second honeymoon. The truth is, they had to leave London quickly. She – Mrs Campbell – entered into a *liaison* with a married man. And not just any married man but the husband of Lady Annabel Wright, a second cousin to the king and, more to the point, a relation of Max Campbell's.'

She pauses, as if waiting for Lily's expression of shock. Well, let

241

her wait. Perhaps being dressed as Greta Garbo has gone to her head, for Lily, who would normally have been waiting on such a person, unable to leave unless dismissed, now starts to turn away.

'Thank you for letting me know, but I really should be getting back to my friends.'

'She died.'

'Pardon?'

Lily is caught in the act of turning, one shoulder already facing the way she wants to go, to where Edward waits for her by the ship's railings, the other still pointing towards her interlocutor, so she swivels from the waist.

'The young woman. Lady Annabel. She took her own life. Could not bear the shame, I shouldn't wonder. Well, the Campbells had to leave town sharpish after that. They wouldn't have been welcome anywhere. Lady Annabel's husband was still chasing Mrs Campbell, if you can believe it. I heard he even followed her to the docks.'

Now Lily remembers the gilded young man who'd stood on the quayside looking up at the ship. *Don't leave.* What kind of person would pursue another woman, with his wife so recently dead? It can't be true, Lily decides. The woman is talking from jealousy or spite. Such things do not happen. Something of it would have shown in Eliza or Max's demeanour.

'I really have to go,' she says, and rushes away before the woman can say any more.

All the way back to find her friends she tells herself to forget what the woman said. She is someone with an axe to grind, most likely, someone who wants to spread nasty rumours. Lily will not let it spoil her evening.

Edward is standing slightly apart from the others, nursing a drink with a tight 'good sport' smile on his thickly made-up face. He looks relieved to see her.

'Where have you been? I thought you'd run away and left me here looking like this! Are you quite all right, Lily? You look pale.'

'I was talking to one of the other passengers, who told me a most distressing rumour about –' Lily breaks off to look meaningfully at the Campbells. 'It's not true, of course, but still.'

Edward moves forward to take her hand but, just as he is pulling her towards him, there is a commotion and he is jolted away.

'What do you think you're doing?'

Helena stands not more than two feet away, shaking with barely suppressed rage, and gripping roughly on to her brother's arm. For a moment, Lily thinks she is talking to her, but then she realizes her furious question is directed at Edward.

'After everything that happened,' Helena continues, glaring at Edward, oblivious to everyone around, 'everything I've been through.'

It is as if Lily is invisible. As if she is carved from wood. And Lily understands with sickening clarity that, despite what she's said before, Helena is ashamed to find her brother here on the first-class deck, embracing a former maid.

Edward, instead of standing up for Lily, seems to crumple under the force of his sister's anger, snatching off his wig and hat as if embarrassed at being caught out having fun.

'I'm sorry,' he says. 'I didn't think.'

'You never think, do you, Edward? You never think about anyone else. You never think about me.'

'I'm sorry,' he says again, reaching out his hand, as if he might smooth away the lines scored deep in his sister's face. 'Forgive me, Helena.'

Then, just like that, the two Fletchers turn and walk away towards the staircase that leads to the lower deck, leaving Lily standing so perfectly still she may as well be as dead as the fox she wears around her neck.

22

25 August 1939

NOW THERE IS nothing but ocean.

It is there each morning when Lily gets up and each night before she goes to sleep. Water upon water upon water, with no land in sight. It is as if the ship is now all that there is. Despite the vastness of the seascape in every direction, the world itself has shrunk to the size of the boat they are on.

Lily feels as though she has been hollowed out like a pumpkin, her soft, pulpy insides dug out and discarded.

The day after the fancy-dress ball, Edward hadn't appeared at all. Helena had come up to breakfast looking drawn and kept her brother's empty chair between them. He was indisposed, she'd said. He'd been so ill back in England, the slightest over-stimulation was apt to bring on a recurrence of bad health. Afterwards she'd tried to talk to Lily on their way out of the dining room.

'I'm sorry about last night, Lily. I'd like to explain.'

But Lily does not wish to hear Helena's clumsy explanations.

The following day, when Edward had finally reappeared, his eyes sunken like moss-covered stones in his chalky face, he could hardly bring himself to look at Lily, although, like his sister, he did make an attempt at an explanation.

'I have behaved unfairly towards you, Lily. I wish I could explain it properly. It's just . . . Helena has given up so much to look after me.'

'There's no need,' Lily said. She even managed to smile, as if a small misunderstanding had been satisfactorily cleared up.

At mealtimes she now talks to Clara and Peggy Mills, as if their complaints about the heat and the manners of the Australian men, and the noise of the Italian babies, one of whom is in the cabin under theirs, are the most absorbing topics of conversation. Sometimes George Price joins in, although he tends not to converse but rather to lambast, seizing on words or phrases they have used and co-opting them into his own relentless narrative, so from talking about Clara's worries about living in a country so lacking in culture as Australia they find themselves suddenly treated to a lecture on the insidiousness of Jewish culture and the necessity of keeping British culture separate, all delivered with that disturbing, unblinking zeal.

So much has happened since that unpleasant encounter when George tried to kiss her out on the deck that Lily finds herself questioning whether it ever happened, though if she looks too long at his purple, glistening lips, she can still remember how they felt wet and spongy over hers, like the nose of a dog, and how, for hours afterwards, she kept wiping her fingers across her face, as if it still bore the snail trail of his saliva.

The turban and the fur stole languish, abandoned, in Lily's cabin. She tells herself she doesn't have the energy yet to return them, not when Eliza will have no use for them until they arrive in winter-bound Australia. The Campbells will be taking it easy after the excitement of the fancy-dress ball, she reasons. They all need a break from one another.

She does not allow herself to think about Lady Annabel Wright, whose heart was supposedly so broken by her husband's affair with

Eliza that she took her own life. 'Please, don't leave,' begged the young man on the dock, his face painted gold by the sun. But no, she won't think about it. And if she doesn't think about it, it cannot be true.

So the fox stays hooked over the end of her bed and watches her while she sleeps, with its dead, black eyes. One night it even made it into her dream, wrapping itself tightly around her neck, until she woke up convinced she was being smothered.

On the deck, looking for a quiet place to write her diary, she bumps into Maria, her head bent over a letter she is writing. By the time Lily notices how the ink has run in places where Maria's tears have splashed on to the paper, it is too late to withdraw.

'No, stay, Lily, please.'

Maria reaches out to grab Lily's hand and Lily tries not to look at how the skin around her eyes is pink and puffy or at the wet tracks on her gaunt cheeks.

'Excuse my ridiculous display of emotion, Lily. I'm writing to my sister. Look at how blurry the words are. She will struggle to make sense of anything. I can hear her now: "You were supposed to be travelling *on* the sea, Maria, not *in* it."' Maria has exaggerated her accent and adopted a lugubrious expression that makes Lily smile. But soon she is serious again.

'Is there still no word from your parents, Maria?'

A shake of the head, that unruly hair now so dry that the sun picks out the individual ends, frayed like straw. Chapped lips pressing together.

'I am sure they will be fine, Maria. Austria is a civilized country. They would treat older people with respect.'

Maria looks at her sharply and opens her mouth as if to speak, then snaps it shut again.

'And you, Lily? How are you getting on? I haven't seen you around so much with Edward Fletcher recently.'

'Oh, that turned out to be nothing. Just a shipboard dalliance. A way of passing the time.'

Lily's mouth stretches into a painful smile, like a rubber band pulled too tight.

'I hope you haven't been too much hurt by it.'

'No. Not at all. I am perfectly fine.'

She tries to hold Maria's gaze, until, without warning, Maria's face contorts into a grimace and she folds her arms over her stomach, head bent.

'Maria? What's the matter? Are you ill?'

There is no answer.

Should she do something? Lily casts her eyes around the deck but the only other passengers around, a quartet of Aussie men, are engrossed in their card game and haven't noticed.

Just as she is thinking she must fetch help Maria's tightly coiled body relaxes and she unfurls, looking pale but composed.

'Sorry, Lily. How strange you must think me. I have been getting these stomach pains. They come out of nowhere and it feels as if someone has put his hand inside me and is twisting it around.'

'Have you talked to the doctor?'

'What would I say? Unless he happens to be here when it happens, there is nothing to show him. Besides, it is probably nothing. Just the change in the weather or the food.'

Lily walks away, feeling uneasy. The alteration in Maria since she first encountered her those few weeks ago is too marked to ignore. Physically, she has lost weight, but then, many of the passengers have. The heat makes eating a chore sometimes. No, it is more a change in herself. Ever since the night she was assaulted on the deck something has been lost, a certain levity, that keen interest she seemed to have in everything around her. And now this sudden crippling pain coming out of nowhere. Lily is frightened about what it might mean – and how powerless she feels to help.

George Price intercepts her as she makes her way towards the lounge, causing her heart to plummet. He wears a khaki shirt that is soaked with sweat, and sweat drips also from the ends of his hair, which he has allowed to grow so long he is constantly having to flick it out of his eyes, spraying droplets into the air.

'I would like to explain,' he says, his face the colour of a beating heart.

Lily stops, clenching each of her muscles in turn, fortifying herself. Everyone, it seems, has something they wish to explain to her.

He guides her over towards the railings. She is taken aback by how agitated he seems, his body constantly on the move, fingers clutching at his hair or at the fabric of his trousers, shifting his weight from foot to foot, even his facial features in perpetual motion, a tic in his left eye, a habitual sniff that wrinkles up that wide, bent nose.

'I just . . .' he begins, then stops, shrugging one shoulder up to his left ear as if trying to dislodge something.

'I only thought it was what you wanted. The kiss. You seemed to be game.'

Over his shoulder a line of birds sew a black seam across the blue fabric of the sky.

'You thought wrong,' says Lily, and makes to leave, but he steps forward as if to stop her.

'You think me a coward, Miss Shepherd.'

'No. Why should I?'

'Because here I am on a ship, headed for New Zealand, when all the signs are that Britain could soon be at war.'

'No!' The denial escapes before Lily can stop it. 'I've been look- ing at the noticeboard. There is nothing that indicates we are any nearer to war.'

'Of course there isn't. The captain doesn't want a full-scale riot on his hands. Think of all the Ities on board. None of us would be safe in our beds.'

'My mother's letters –'

'Were sent days ago, weeks even. A lot can change in that time.'

Lily doesn't believe him, knows him to be a fantasist. 'There are people who fantasize about war just as there are people who fantasize about sex,' Robert had told her, all that time ago, when it first appeared as though Britain might be edging closer to reopening old wounds with Germany.

And yet.

'I need you to know that this is not my doing. It's my father who insisted I had to leave. I would have gladly stayed. He is a difficult person. As I told you before, there is no saying no to him.'

'It's all the same to me,' says Lily.

Now there is a change in him, a hardening of features which are already hard enough.

'It's because of her, isn't it?'

'Who?'

'Don't play games. I've seen you with her. Everyone on board has seen you with her. The Jewess. You were not like this at the start of the voyage. You were open. Kind. It is she who has poisoned your mind.'

Finally, Lily walks away, turning in the opposite direction so that he cannot prevent her.

George is mad, she thinks. And the thought, now it has entered her head, will not leave it. Frank had warned her about it before she left, the particular madness that comes from being cooped up on a boat with no way off, seeing the same people all the time. He'd heard of someone, he said, who'd tried to kill all his shipmates with an axe. They'd had to lock him up in a cabin until they got to the next port.

Thinking about her brother, she feels a sharp pang of regret.

How she should love to see him, now that everything onboard has turned strange and unhappy.

Lily finds a seat on the other side of the boat which is empty, owing to being in the full blast of the sun, and sinks into it. Within seconds the heat begins to prickle on her bare arms. Somehow, despite everything, she falls asleep, and her unconscious mind takes her to that room in a backstreet in Basingstoke and Mags: *Am I going to die, Lil?* And blood. Who knew there could be so much blood?

She wakes with her heart racing and the skin on her face scorching, knowing that, later, it will be red and angry.

She decides to seek out Audrey and Annie. They alone of all the passengers on the voyage have remained constant, full of excitement and wonder. But a search of the lounge and bar proves fruitless. She stumbles upon Ida, who is on her way down to the laundry. 'Your posh friends deserted you, then?' she asks. Up here on the deck, in the white light of the sun, Lily notices the shocking state of Ida's teeth, yellow like old custard.

Eventually, defeated, her face stinging, Lily makes her way down the staircase to the welcome dimness of the cabin. For once, she does not even mind the stale smell or the sight of Ida's greying petticoat hanging at the end of her bed.

She finds her wash cloth and wets it under the tap in the sink before climbing up to her bunk and lying down, not even bothering to remove her shoes. Laying the folded cloth carefully against her now flaming cheeks she closes her eyes and wonders why she can still feel the fox watching her through the tissue of her eyelids.

23

27 August 1939

THE ISLAND APPEARS as if from nowhere, a flat disc of land broken up only by a few palm trees – or at least that's how it seems standing on the ship's deck. They have been told that beyond it there are more islands – an atoll made up of a cluster of islets – but these are not visible to the watching passengers.

One of the three rotund brothers, always at the head of the cake queue, is the first to see it.

'Australia!' he yells excitedly. 'We're here!'

'What a complete berk you are!' chortles one of his brothers.

Soon everyone is at the railing, pointing and exclaiming, and an excitement spreads, out of all proportion to the island's size and importance. It's a relief to finally see land after all these days of only sea, to realize they are not, after all, the only people left in a vast, wet, empty world.

Lily and the Fletchers are back on civil terms, although there is something that sits like a boulder in the very centre of their relationship so that all conversation has to find a way around it rather than flowing freely, as before.

'The Cocos Islands,' Edward reads from the printed literature given out by the stewards. 'Home to the Clunies-Ross family, descended from Scottish captain John Clunies-Ross.'

'And not just him, from the looks of it,' says Helena, eyeing the little boats manned by islanders who have come out to collect their mail, which the ship's staff lower down to them in wicker baskets.

'But how can they live there, so cut off from everything?' Lily wants to know.

She can see how the islands might be considered beautiful, idyllic even. The water is turquoise and so clear she can see fish swimming far below the surface, and white sand lies over the island's beach like a freshly starched tablecloth. But there is something about its isolation that chills her, despite the wet, tropical heat. What would it do to a person to live out here, cut off from everything? What would it do to a society?

'I'm worried about Maria,' she says. 'She does not seem herself.'

'It must be very hard living with such uncertainty,' says Helena. 'No wonder she's anxious.'

Lily doesn't state the truth, that she is afraid this is much more serious than anxiety, doesn't explain about the worrying violet shadows under Maria's brown eyes.

In forty-eight hours' time they will be arriving in Fremantle, their first stop in Australia, with just another week before they are due in Sydney. How can it be true that in less than two weeks she will be working again – cleaning, cooking, taking orders, watching the world through a pane of glass in someone else's house?

The Campbells appear, unannounced as always, except by a change in the energy on the deck, a stirring up of the hitherto torpid air, a hissed whisper that might come from the other passengers or from the sea itself.

'We have missed you. What purgatory it has been up there.'

Eliza is wearing her shorts with a striped top that is slashed across her neck and clings to her body as if painted on. Her eyes, those peculiar, shade-shifting eyes, are today an intense blue, as if they have taken on the colour of the sea, and Lily squirms uncomfortably when they alight on her, wide and unflinching.

'Lily, where did you disappear to at the end of the fancy-dress ball? We looked for you everywhere.'

As ever, Lily finds herself thrown into a state of confusion by the fact of Eliza. How loud she is, how careless of people's feelings, how exhausting. And yet how dazzling. When she is here it's as if everything that has gone before now was in semi-darkness, like when the day fades so gradually you don't realize you've been sitting in the dark until suddenly someone switches on the light.

Max trails behind her, smoking a cigarette. Today it is he who is wearing sunglasses, and Lily is glad not to see those ice-chip eyes. She thinks about what the woman told her at the dance. *That poor girl!* Then immediately she pushes it from her head. It's not true, she thinks. They would have mentioned something.

'I'm glad you're here. I need to give you back your things,' she says to Eliza. 'I don't think I will have any call to be Garbo in Australia.'

Eliza makes a lazy gesture with her hand.

'Keep them. They looked far better on you. Anyway, that fox gave me the chills. I felt like it was judging me.'

'Perhaps it was, darling,' says Max. 'Now wouldn't that be interesting. Eliza Campbell held to account at last.'

There is a silence that stretches taut across the group like the skin of a drum. Then Eliza's laughter, shrill and savage.

'Rest assured, my love, you will have a front-row seat on Judgement Day.'

There is something about her today. Something wild.

'My darling wife hasn't slept properly since the dance,' says Max. 'Just in case you might all be wondering why she is so fidgety and talking such nonsense.'

'Really, Eliza?' Helena is concerned. 'That's so bad for you. You should ask the doctor to give you something to help.'

'Ah, but she doesn't want to!' Max is mocking. 'She thinks not sleeping makes her invincible.'

'Not invincible, Maxie. Just alive.'

They all go into the lounge, out of the sticky heat.

'Heavens, Lily, what have you done to your face?' asks Max, taking his sunglasses off and peering at her closely as they take their seats on the sofas.

'Burned it. That'll teach me for falling asleep in the sun.'

To Lily's huge embarrassment, he reaches out a hand and strokes her cheek, which she knows to be still livid pink. She turns away from his touch and finds herself locking eyes with Edward. He immediately arranges his features into a smile, but not before she has registered the look on his face. He is jealous, she thinks. And the realization sends something warm and liquid shooting through her veins.

Cards are fetched, games played. But Eliza keeps throwing down her cards, jumping up, moving around. The air is too stifling, she says. The voyage too long. She can't wait to get to Sydney, she declares. New people. New life. New parties.

'I'm afraid you might find yourself disappointed,' says Ian, who has joined them at Helena's insistence, though he normally steers clear of the Campbells. 'Aussie society is not what you've been used to. You'll find us a very unsophisticated lot.'

'How long are you staying there?' Helena asks.

'Until my wife gets bored,' says Max.

Though she tries not to, Lily thinks again about the woman from first class with her corsets and her disapproving face nestling into pillows of flesh. No one will have them, she'd said. Though Lily doesn't move in those circles, she knows enough from working in large houses to imagine how this might be true. The British upper class operates like the sea itself: a stone in its centre will send ripples reaching to its furthest edges. Once one or two key people – key women – have refused Eliza and Max entry to their dinners and salons and weekend house parties, they will be closed out of every house in the land. So what then? Keep moving? What a desolate thought.

Lily's face feels dry and sore, and she excuses herself to go back to the cabin to apply some more cold cream. She is hoping they will all play on without her, but they insist on waiting until she returns.

'Everything is much duller when you're not around,' says Max.

'You seem to find so many things dull, Max,' Edward says in Eliza's voice, both sardonic and hard.

Max gives Edward a look that leaves Lily feeling strangely chilled, although his words are harmless enough. 'I'm easily bored. That's why I seek out distractions. But you know, old chap, even the distractions soon become dull.'

On her way back to the lounge Lily finds Maria huddled into a deckchair. She is looking even thinner than the last time they met, her cheeks sallow and sunken into her face. Still, when she smiles Lily can just about recognize the bright, alert woman of a few weeks before.

'Are you still unwell?' she asks, aware of how she is looming over her friend but too conscious of the others waiting for her in the lounge to sit down.

Maria's smile fades, replaced by an anxious, pinched expression.

'Oh, Lily, I hate to be always complaining, but the pains are getting worse. And now my head aches also. I'm afraid there is no hope for me. I am falling apart like a sandcastle. When you see me next I shall be just a pile of sand in a chair.'

'But what could be causing the pains?'

'I think it's the salt tablets. They don't agree with me, so I've stopped taking them.'

For a moment Lily is confused. Then: 'They don't agree with you? But surely it's dangerous *not* to take them?'

They are all still taking salt tablets to keep their salt levels up and ward off dehydration.

'Have you spoken to the doctor?'

Maria nods, and Lily notices for the first time a bald patch on her head, just behind her ear, the size of a shilling. She looks more closely and sees another at the crown.

'He has given me something for the pain. Tablets. They make me feel so queer, as if I am in a – I don't know the word for it – the glass box where fish live? I am in there, looking out at the world through the thick glass. I didn't tell him about not taking the salt tablets. He is not the kind of man who encourages confidences. Will you sit with me a while, Lily?'

'I wish I could, but I have to get back.' Lily waves her hand vaguely in the direction of the lounge.

'Of course. Anyway, I think I might have a sleep now. I'm so tired. The nights are very bad at the moment.'

Back in the lounge, and still deeply troubled, Lily cannot concentrate on the game and comes last three hands in a row.

'That funny little couple keeps staring over here,' says Eliza, who has once again laid down her cards and sits there, looking around.

Lily follows her gaze and sees the Neumanns, whom she met first with Maria, standing at the entrance to the lounge. Mr Neumann has taken off his hat and is holding it tightly in front of him as if it is a good-luck talisman. Mrs Neumann catches Lily's eye and waves.

The Neumanns make their way over to the table, delicately stepping around the sofas and tables and easy chairs where passengers make themselves at home in an attempt to escape the humid heat outside.

'Oh, my goodness, he looks like an undertaker,' trills Eliza. 'Do you suppose he's got a tape measure in that jacket pocket, and he's planning to whip it out and measure us all up, just in case we should run into stormy weather?'

Lily says nothing, but the sore, lumpen skin on her cheeks burns.

'Miss Shepherd?' Mrs Neumann seems tinier than ever in the grand environs of the lounge with its high ceiling and outsized furniture. 'We can converse?'

Her accent is thick and harsh, and Lily senses Eliza's amusement from across the table.

'Of course.'

She follows them back out on to the deck. They are wearing the same clothes as the last time she saw them, and Lily remembers Maria saying that many of the Jewish passengers have only one set.

'We worry for Maria,' says Mr Neumann once they are outside. 'She has much pain.'

'And since a few days, she has not taken her salt,' says his wife.

Lily tells them she knows, and briefly describes her conversation with Maria.

'You will talk to the doctor?' asks Mrs Neumann, although, when she says it, it sounds more like a command than a question.

'Me? But I—'

'Our English is not so good,' says Mr Neumann. 'He will listen more to you. You will tell him about the salt. Ask him what he gives her for the pain.'

How can she refuse? The Neumanns are asking only out of concern for their friend. Besides, Lily is still thinking of Maria's face when she said, 'Will you sit with me a while?' The momentary flicker of hope in her hollowed-out face.

Outside the doctor's surgery, Lily has to pause to take a few deep breaths. She comes from a family where doctors are venerated, and consulted sparingly, if at all. She is not used to calling on them as if she was just passing and fancied a chat. She is not used to calling on them at all.

Dr Macpherson is sitting at a desk, writing in a ledger. He is a squat middle-aged man with a bald head that is pink as a cooked lobster shell and gleams when Lily opens the door and the sunlight catches it.

'I am not in the business of discussing my patients, Miss Shepherd,' he says in his disapproving Scottish way, once Lily has haltingly relayed her message. 'However, in this instance, I will make an exception, out of concern for the lady's welfare.

'The fact is, I do not consider these inexplicable pains to be of a physical nature.'

Lily stares, uncomprehending.

'But I have been with her when one of the pains came on. She was in agony. She has even stopped taking her salt tablets in case it's they that are causing it.'

'I'm not saying Miss Katz does not experience pain, Miss Shepherd. Just that I believe its source is psychological rather than physiological.'

'But you gave her medicine for her stomach?'

Dr Macpherson shakes his bald, pink head.

'I gave her medicine for her nerves, Miss Shepherd. From what I understand, it is not the first time on this voyage that Miss Katz has exhibited signs of psychosomatic behaviour.'

'I don't understand.'

'I believe she reported she had been attacked while sleeping out on deck earlier on in the crossing?'

'Yes, but –'

'And the captain was subsequently informed by a nearby passenger who had been awake the whole time that at no point had anyone gone near Miss Katz.'

A dark shape. Footsteps. Already Lily's mind is converting what she imagined she saw and heard, questioning the order in which it came. Could the shape have been Maria herself? And the footsteps

Mrs Collins or one of the other passengers summoned by Maria's scream? No. But.

'She wasn't – isn't – the kind of person to be affecting a crisis just to get attention.'

'Not attention, Miss Shepherd. Not necessarily, anyway. I know that Miss Katz has been worried about the safety of her parents. Most of us are able to manage our fears effectively by processing them in our minds but, unfortunately, some people – some women – cannot. In these cases, their concerns manifest themselves in physical ways – a mystery ailment, or an unwitnessed assault upon their person.'

'You're saying she's –'

'I'm afraid she is an hysteric, Miss Shepherd. That is my diagnosis. However, rest assured, the medicine I've given her is quite potent and she should soon be feeling much calmer. And you should encourage her to resume taking the salt tablets. In fact, failing to take them could result in her developing for real the very symptoms she has been complaining about!'

Afterwards, when Lily goes over the conversation in her head, it's the word 'hysteric' – that hateful label first levied by Clara Mills – that lodges there, like a chip of bone in her throat.

When she sees the Neumanns waiting for her out on the deck, Lily slows down, rehearsing what she might possibly say. But when she gets twenty feet away from them she stops altogether. Then she ducks back into a doorway before they can see her.

24

29 August 1939

AUSTRALIA.

What has she been expecting?

Lily doesn't know. Only that it wasn't this.

At first it is just a line on the horizon, a sense of land rather than anything concrete. The passengers gathered on the deck strain their eyes, looking for landmarks. 'Where is it, Mama?' asks a small girl standing next to Lily. 'I don't see it.'

Now a shape distinguishes itself. A lighthouse. And behind that a smudge of something else. The small girl is disappointed. 'Is that it, Mama? Is that Australia? It's smaller than home!'

But now a shoreline is materializing and beyond it a town. More a collection of buildings, really. Nothing big or impressive.

'The nearest city is Perth, and that's half an hour away,' says Ian, as if he has to apologize for his homeland's lack of grandiosity. 'That's just Fremantle you can see there.'

Nevertheless, Lily can't help feeling let down by her first impression of the gateway to Western Australia. Even the wharf, as they get closer, reveals itself to be a modest, sleepy-looking place, nothing like as impressive as Tilbury, from where they'd set off, and with none of the industry and frenzied activity of the other ports they've stopped at.

I'm here, she thinks. This continent will be my home for the next two years. But though she forces her mind to process the words, she feels nothing. No sense of excitement or awe or of a new chapter starting.

It's early afternoon and, ever since she woke up that morning, she's been aware of a shift in temperature. It's still hot and sunny, but further out to sea there was a fresher feel to the air, and even here, approaching the dock, it's clear the extreme stickiness of the last few days is absent. Still, Lily is taking no chances and has borrowed a wide-brimmed straw hat from Helena to protect her sunburned face. And if it also means she feels shielded from the Neumanns and Maria and George Price, well, that wasn't her intention. No, really, it wasn't.

There's a small crowd waiting on the quayside to greet some of the Australian passengers whose voyages finish here. As the ship draws near, Lily is taken aback to hear a chorus of strange sounds coming from the waiting families and friends. 'Coo-ee!' 'Coo-ee!', and now the same sound is being echoed back from the Aussies on the boat. 'Coo-ee!' Long on the first syllable, with the second just an afterthought, a flick of the tongue, an old lady's 'Eh?'

'Don't look so shocked, Lily.' Ian is laughing at her. 'It's a typical Aussie greeting, that's all.'

He insists that Lily and Helena have a go at emulating the sound, which prompts the little girl who'd been disappointed at the scale of Australia to join in, and they all end up clutching their stomachs with laughter. All except the girl's mother, who sniffs and looks away, as if trying to imagine herself somewhere else.

The ship is to spend the day in Fremantle, so many passengers are preparing to take the train into Perth. The trains run every hour so there is plenty of time to explore. The Fletchers are heading into Perth. Ian is keen to show them around their first Australian city. But Lily decides not to go with them. Though things are, on the surface, back to normal between them, there is a residue of tension that did not exist before.

Fremantle looks at first glance like a pleasant enough town in which to while away a few hours ashore – clean and quiet, with the sun not too hot, just the equivalent of a lovely English summer's day. The buildings squat low and flat to the ground, and there are bursts of greenery, but a different green to the measured, school-uniform green of English trees. This is the vibrant, almost luminescent green of only just ripe apples.

As she queues to descend the gangplank Lily's eyes dart around the deck, looking for Maria or the Neumanns. If she sees them, she will offer to spend the day with them, she resolves, to make up for the guilt she feels at hiding from the couple instead of reporting back what the doctor had told her. She catches the eye of George Price, who is also queuing to get off, and his face instantly flushes the colour of red wine. He looks away, making a strange, jerky motion with his head. The Neumanns, though, are nowhere to be seen, and Lily feels heavy with relief.

It is a peculiar feeling, setting her feet down on Australian soil. Or rather on Australian decking, knowing that, beyond this town, lies the continent she must learn to consider home. Lily remembers a seaside holiday with her family when she was a child. Dorset, she thinks. Or perhaps Devon. She and Frank on their hands and knees in the sand, digging with toy spades. 'We're going to keep going until we reach Australia,' she'd said, and Frank, that much younger, had believed it possible, not wanting to stop until they could see kangaroos for themselves. And now here she is. She has left them all behind.

The others are dismayed when she announces she won't be joining them on their trip to Perth. 'Please come, Lily,' Edward whispers as they stand on the corner where Lily will turn off to go into town while they continue on to the station. But she has made up her mind. Besides, Edward is in a strange mood still, jumpy and introspective, with little sign of the easy charm he showed at the start of the voyage.

Walking through the town alone, she feels liberated. It is so long since she was on her own, and she finds she has missed her own company. The houses she passes are colonial-style bungalows, painted pretty colours with verandahs running the length of the front and set back from the road behind small lawns. Lily has already heard about the poinsettia trees with their large red leaves, but there are also hibiscus bushes, aflame with blooms of red and orange, and huge clumps of pampas grass with whiskery, biscuit-coloured plumes shooting up out of a skirt of green rushes. She feels her spirits improving with each step.

The shops are also low-slung. Lily passes a greengrocer's full of exotic-looking produce, its owners chatting away in Italian to a group of Italian passengers from the boat, who look relieved and happy to have found some friendly faces on their first foray into their newly adopted homeland. Some of the women, who, on the ship, seemed far older than her, burdened down with babies and washing and a clinging poverty, here reveal themselves to be young and, in several cases, beautiful, with black hair that gleams in the sunlight and eyes wide with excitement.

As she walks along the broad pavements Lily can't help staring at the passers-by, comparing them to the people she'd see walking around in London or Reading. Surprisingly, their accents don't immediately jar. Rather, it's the small differences she notices – the fact that the young women are wheeling their babies in pushchairs rather than bassinets, with shopping baskets attached to them. The placards and billboards on the sides of the buildings are advertising a bewildering mix of the familiar, like Oxo, and the completely unknown.

She buys a newspaper and some postcard scrolls – six colourful views of the town and environs concertinaed together with a space for writing on the back. Passing a smart-looking hotel, again with a colonial-style verandah and saloon doors into the bar, she decides to go in and have a drink and read her newspaper and write her letter home.

The lounge of the hotel is lovely and cool, with horsehair sofas and large pots containing small palm trees. Lily sinks into a leather armchair and orders a ginger beer from a garrulous waiter who, hearing her accent, insists on giving her the low-down on where to go (Fremantle, obviously, and Sydney, but not Melbourne or New Zealand, which are deemed too English and formal). Finally, he is called away and she is left in peace to read her newspaper, which seems still to be sending out confusing messages about the likelihood of war. As the voyage has gone on, so the news reaching the passengers by way of the noticeboard has slowed to a trickle. Now, as Lily catches up on political events she has missed during the long days adrift on the Indian Ocean, her mouth feels suddenly dry, her stomach tight. Germany, it seems, has signed a non-aggression treaty with the Soviet Union, promising that neither will ally itself to the enemies of the other. Before she'd left it had seemed certain that Russia would make a pact with Britain and France, so this step seems ominous. And a few days ago Chamberlain in turn signed a pact with Poland, promising it protection should Germany invade. And yet still there is hope. The opinion of the newspaper's editor is that the new British treaty will make Hitler think twice about continuing his campaign of expansion.

As Lily is nearing the end of the editorial she is surprised by a hand reaching over her shoulder and folding the newspaper shut.

'You shan't read any more. I forbid it. The news is very bad for your health.'

Eliza flings herself down into the chair opposite Lily. She has on her big, floppy hat, and again her sunglasses cover her eyes. Lily automatically glances towards the entrance, expecting to see either Max's broad-shouldered frame or else the silver mane of Anthony Hewitt, but there is no one.

'He's not here,' says Eliza, not specifying who 'he' might be. 'I gave him the slip once we got on the train. Pushed on ahead of him, and then came straight out of the next available door!'

She seems to be waiting for Lily to make some sort of expression of admiration, but Lily refuses to oblige so Eliza presses on.

'I really need to get rid of him. He's becoming so tiresome.'

Ah, so they are talking about Anthony Hewitt. Eliza's next statement confirms it.

'You know, Lily, I think I was so in love with listening to his voice it stopped me realizing how little I cared for what his voice was actually saying. The man is an ass. Utterly in love with himself and how he thinks he appears to the world. You know, when we were in Ceylon the hotel manager approached him with the bill and he thought he was being asked to sign an autograph!'

Eliza summons the waiter and, before he can launch into further travel advice, demands a gimlet, which seems to confuse him into silence.

Lily is just about to ask her what has happened to Max when Eliza whips off her hat and glasses.

'Oh, my!' Lily clasps her hand to her mouth. 'What on earth –'

The flesh around Eliza's left eye is livid and purple, like chicken liver, and the white is not white at all but a lurid pink.

Eliza makes a face. 'I know. Ugly, isn't it?'

'But what happened?'

'Oh, you know. Max.'

Lily doesn't know. She doesn't know at all. She thinks of Max Campbell and his glass-chip eyes and broad, thick hands. But still. Not this.

'He hit you? On purpose?'

Eliza smiles. 'Oh, Lily, don't be so dramatic. Yes, he hit me. I wanted him to. In fact, I goaded and goaded him until he did. Look!'

She shows Lily her right hand, turning it upside down to reveal the red-raw knuckles.

'I had to hit him a few times until he retaliated. It bloody well hurt.'

'But why?'

'To feel alive, Lily. Why else? I'm so tired of it all. Tired of looking, always looking, for that thing that's going to make me feel something – that new thing, that new person. Never sleeping in case I miss it. Do you know what it's like to be always searching for something you know you'll never find? Something that will finally make everything mean something? Sometimes I take Max's razor into the bath and make cuts in my skin just to feel pain, to feel *something*.

'So I goaded him until he hit me and, you know, for a moment it worked. Right at that second when my eye socket exploded, I actually felt alive.'

Lily sits back in her chair, aware of her heart pounding in her chest, her mouth still open as if trying to formulate a word that might make sense of what she has just heard. How little she understands of life. She had thought, because of what happened with Mags, that she was so worldly-wise, and yet she knows nothing of this, of how men and women might act towards each other, of how elastic a marriage can be, stretching itself into shapes she had no concept of.

'Don't look so shocked, Lily, please.'

Eliza sounds drained suddenly. Defeated, almost. The waiter approaches with her drink and she holds her hand up to her head, shielding her eye.

'You know, I admire you so much, Lily,' she says once he has gone. 'You're so much braver and stronger than I am. No, you are, look at you. Taking this huge step, embarking on this big adventure, all on your own. I wish I had your courage, but I don't. I don't have the courage to leave Max, even though I know we will end up destroying one another. Isn't that silly?'

'Do you really hate him so much for what happened to Olivia?' Lily asks.

Eliza looks at her as if she has said something incomprehensible.

'I could never hate Max. Not really. He's my husband. I love him. But I will never, ever forgive him. That's why I can't make love to him. It drives him crazy.'

For a while they sit drinking in silence. Eliza's drink has a twist of lime and she picks it out with her fingers and presses her teeth into it, wincing at the sourness. She has lost some of the manic energy of the previous few days and Lily feels emboldened to ask her, at last, about the dreadful rumour the woman from first class had told her.

Eliza listens in silence, flicking the tip of her tongue around the rim of the glass that is raised to her lips. Finally, she sighs.

'Poor Rupert.'

'Rupert?'

'Rupert was the husband. I'm surprised you didn't see him on the dock as we were leaving. A rather beautiful man. You couldn't have missed him.'

'But I –'

'The fact is, I *am* sorry about Annabel. Of course I am. She was a sweet person, really, just very highly strung. But I liked her.'

'So why?'

'How old would you say I was, Lily?'

Lily finds herself wrong-footed by the sudden change of topic, floundering to regain her balance.

'I don't know. Twenty-nine?'

Eliza laughs.

'You're very sweet. I'm thirty-four, nearly thirty-five. For practically my whole life I've been defined by the men who have wanted me. But men aren't going to keep looking at me for very much longer, and then what? What will be the point of me?'

'There are other things, Eliza.'

But all the things Lily thinks of saying don't seem to apply. Eliza will never need to get a job. She cannot have more children. She does not even seem to have any hobbies. Once, when she saw Lily with her nose buried deep in a book, she told her she hated reading because after a few minutes the letters seemed to dance across the page and wouldn't keep still.

'I know you're looking for remorse – about Annabel Wright, I mean – and I really am sorry about it. I was devastated. But, you know, she would have done it anyway. If not because of me then because of the next woman, and there would certainly have been a next woman. Rupert was just that sort of man. He loved being in love too much.'

'But why couldn't he have stayed in love with his wife?'

Lily is aware how naive she sounds. How foolish. Yet she cannot help herself. She sees in her mind the young man on the quayside, with his smooth, toffee-apple skin, and she wants to turn him around and rewind time and send him back to his wife, to his home, to the time before he set eyes on Eliza Campbell. She wants the world to be just as her parents had led her to believe it was. You fell in love, you stayed together, in sickness and in health, for better, for worse.

'Men do carry on loving their wives,' she says hotly. 'Max is in love with you.'

'Which is why I can't be in love with him. Don't you see? In every relationship there is a lover and a beloved. It's just my beastly luck to be the one who is loved and not the other way round. At least if I was the one who loved I would have a function. Good job Max doesn't want for female attention to bolster his self-esteem. There's nothing more attractive to a certain type of woman than an uxorious man.'

She glances at Lily sideways as she says this, and Lily looks determinedly away.

When they've finished their drink, they decide to go outside and find the nearest beach. Eliza is growing bored of being stared at on account of her eye, which, even in the dimness of the bar, has a luminescent sheen on the skin beneath it that draws attention.

Just a few moments' walk brings them out on to a long, sandy beach, sheltered by a row of trees at the back and virtually deserted, despite the perfect temperature, with only a few women sitting together, watching their young children playing in the shallow surf.

'Let's give them a wide berth,' says Eliza when she sees them. 'Who can bear all that screaming young children do?'

But when they settle on a spot twenty yards further along, Lily notices how Eliza's gaze is drawn constantly back to the group of women, two of whom are dancing babies upon their laps; notices the hungry look in her eyes.

Despite herself, despite all the heartbreak Eliza has caused, Lily feels her own heart creak and crack like an over-fired pot.

To distract them both, she starts to tell Eliza about Maria and her inexplicable pains, and what the doctor has said, then immediately she feels guilty for using Maria's troubles as a conversational aide.

'It doesn't in the least surprise me,' says Eliza, who has taken off her shoes and is paddling in the shallows in front of where Lily is sitting. 'They are inclined to histrionics, her people. You should hear some of the fanciful stories they've been circulating about what the Germans are doing to Jews in Austria and Czechoslovakia.'

'But couldn't those stories be true? Some of them, anyway?'

Under the floppy brim of her hat, Eliza makes a face, her nose wrinkling so her sunglasses move up and down.

'Lily, darling, only barbarians could do the things they're accusing the Germans of. Let me tell you, I've known a fair few Germans in my time and, though I haven't always agreed with them, they've all been at least moderately civilized. No, it's a fact, I'm afraid, that the Jews have highly active imaginations. I'm not saying it's your friend Maria's fault. It's in her blood, probably.'

A figure approaches from the other end of the beach, small and slight and dressed in black. Lily groans softly to herself as recognition dawns.

'So this is where you've got to,' says Ida. 'Glad to see you decided to give Perth a miss. Can't see why anyone would bother spending the money on a train when there's a perfectly good little town right here.'

She is addressing her comments to Lily, as if she cannot see Eliza standing, right there, in the shallow waters where the sea meets the sand.

Lily freezes. The moment stretches out, long and painfully tight, Ida hesitating in her long, black dress, a wet patch along the hem where she has got too close to the sea even now drying into a salt-bleached stain.

Lily thinks about inviting Ida to sit down on the sand next to her, turns the words over in her mouth, but somehow they won't come out. Instead, Eliza speaks:

'Yes, there is a perfectly good town. You're absolutely right. I think you'll find it most amusing. It's that way.'

She points along the beach in the direction from which she and Lily arrived. Her meaning cannot be misinterpreted, and Ida's dark eyes harden to little black stones set into her parched, pinched face.

'You ought to be careful,' she says to Lily, her mouth like the twist of lime from Eliza's gimlet. 'Now we're here, in Australia, you need to pay more attention to what you do, and who you do it with. Remember, in less than a week's time you'll be looking for work. You don't want prospective employers to hear things about you that might put them off.'

She sets off down the beach, and though Lily is shocked by what she has just said, and how boldly she has said it in front of Eliza, as if she weren't even there, she is also grudgingly admiring of Ida's straight-backed walk, the way her sharp chin is thrust out towards the direction she is going, as if leading the way.

'What an unpleasant little person,' says Eliza. 'I don't know how you can stand to be in the same cabin as her.'

As if the choice is Lily's to make.

Lily thinks about what Ida just said. About it being a less than a week until she will have to be looking for work. Then she looks at Eliza, with her sunglasses and her expensive pale blue dress that she is so carelessly splashing with sea water. There was a moment today when she felt like they were practically friends, she and Eliza. But now she sees there's a gap between them as big as the Indian Ocean itself.

25

30 August 1939

'Lily?'

The voice is hardly louder than a sigh and at first Lily thinks she might have mistaken the sound of the wind blowing up from the now unsettled sea for the whisper of her name. But then she hears it again.

'Lily.'

She looks around, puzzled. She is once again at the far end of the deck, to which most passengers can't be bothered to trek and, up to now, she has assumed herself to be quite alone.

To her surprise, a heaped pile of blankets in one of the deck-chairs begins to stir and Maria's disorderly hair emerges, followed closely by the rest of her.

Lily swallows back a gasp at the sight of her friend. Maria has always had a sallow complexion but now her yellowing skin is mottled by a violent purple rash and her eyes are huge and glassy.

'What has happened to you, Maria? Surely you are not still unwell? Are you taking the medicine the doctor gave you?'

Maria nods, and even that slight movement, it seems, is painful, for she places a hand flat against her bony chest.

'Oh, Lily, what is happening to me? I am taking the tablets and yet

I feel worse. It is them, I think, that are giving me this terrible skin on my face.' Her fingers trace her raised, discoloured cheeks. 'My mind is all the time jumping ahead of itself, as if I have no control at all, and yet my body feels to be closing down, slowing, until I am like those creatures you have in the garden. Black and disgusting. How do you call them? Yes, slugs, that's right. My body is like a slug.'

'And the pains?'

'Yes, those are still there, but you know, Lily, now they feel almost like a relief. It sounds strange, yes? But that pain, it tells me I still have a body, I'm not this slug that has no feelings.'

Now Lily is reminded of Eliza and what she'd said in Fremantle about cutting herself with Max's razor just to feel something. How queer that both of them should be having such similar thoughts, though with Eliza it's a pain she has afflicted on herself.

And with Maria? asks the treacherous voice in her head. Could she be choosing to imagine herself afflicted, as the doctor had suggested? For a moment Lily thinks about telling Maria what she knows, that the tablets she's been prescribed are for her nerves rather than for whatever she thinks is ailing her. Now it occurs to her that perhaps the tablets themselves are producing some of Maria's symptoms – the rashes, the racing thoughts. She remembers some medication her dad was given that made his skin so itchy he'd scratched it till it bled, and gave him nightmares that left him crouching, terrified, in the corner of the bed, pointing at creatures that weren't there.

And now another thought suggests itself:

'Could your symptoms be a result of your body being short of salt since you stopped taking the salt tablets?'

Maria shakes her head, wincing as she does so.

'I am taking them again, Lily. It's not that. But you know the worst thing, even worse than the pain? I'm beginning to fear for my state of mind. All the time now, I'm feeling like I'm being watched, and the nightmares I told you about where I am being chased? Those are getting so bad I no longer sleep.'

'Lily? There you are. I've been searching and searching.'

Audrey looks out of breath, as if she's been running, her cheeks rosy, hair curling with heat.

'Oh!' She has only just noticed Maria there, under the blankets. Her pale blue eyes widen in shock.

'Mrs Collins sent me to fetch you, Lily. There's paperwork we need to fill in ahead of Sydney. Forms and that.'

Lily turns to Maria and holds up her hands in a helpless *What can I do?* gesture, though part of her – a big part of her, if she is honest – is glad to have an excuse to leave. Maria is scaring her, with that livid rash across her face and her sunken cheeks that look as if there is a drawstring attached to the inside of them, pulling them inwards.

Maria's hand shoots out, her bony fingers around Lily's wrist like a vice.

'Meet me later,' she says urgently. 'Please, Lily. I cannot stand to be so much alone. I used to love solitude but now my own company scares me. Please say you'll come again.'

'Of course.'

But Maria is not satisfied. She tightens her grip.

'When, Lily? This afternoon? Here? At five?'

'Yes. I will.'

'You promise, Lily?'

'I promise.'

But as Lily sits in the lounge while Mrs Collins, the chaperone, hands out various papers that need to be read and signed, and explains to them again about the procedure for procuring jobs when they arrive, she feels a creeping sense of dread. The deterioration in Maria's health is so extreme. Might not the doctor have been too hasty in insisting the illness is all in her mind?

At the end of the session, while the other girls are filing out of the lounge, Mrs Collins puts a hand gently on Lily's arm to stop her getting up.

'Can we have a little chat, Lily?'

Lily sinks back down into her seat.

'Is everything quite all right with you, my dear? I have tried not to interfere in your onboard friendships. You're young and unmarried and it's only natural that you should want to let yourself loose a little bit on a voyage such as this. I imagine it's the first extended leisure time you've had since you left school, and why shouldn't you enjoy yourself? However, I have been greatly concerned about the amount of time you have spent in the company of the Campbells and of Miss Katz. To be frank, I don't consider either of those parties to be appropriate friends for a girl in your situation.'

Lily feels herself blushing, as if she is back at school again, being admonished by the teacher.

'I'm sure you've heard the shocking rumours about Mrs Campbell and the husband of that poor girl who died. And Miss Katz, I think, too, has misled you. All that bad business in the middle of the night up on deck. And it turns out to be nothing, just a figment of the young woman's overactive imagination.'

'But we don't know that. No one knows for sure.'

Mrs Collins blinks in surprise.

'There was a witness, my dear.'

'Yes, but how do we know they're reliable? We don't even know who it is.'

'That's not true. Surely you've been told.'

'Told what?'

Mrs Collins blinks again and leans back into a shaft of sunlight that illuminates the soft blonde down on her cheeks to which stubborn flecks of face powder cling like grains of wet sand.

'It was your own friend who saw it. Your cabin mate. Ida.'

Lily does not know what to make of this. Why has Ida not said anything to her? She cannot understand it. Her mind feels befuddled, as if her skull has been wadded tight with cotton wool, leaving no space for thought. She tries to remember that night up on the deck, tries to visualize who was in the beds nearby, but her woolly brain won't allow her to picture it or to make the connections about what it all means.

After she leaves the lounge she heads outside, making her way blindly down the deck in the opposite direction to where she last saw Maria.

'Here she is. The very person.'

Edward has intercepted her by putting out an arm, so that she walks into it like a barrier at a railway level crossing. He and Helena are standing under the awning beside the swimming pool, which is empty today, owing to the choppier conditions. Edward is smiling broadly and his green eyes are alight, as if there is something metallic glittering on the surface of them. Helena, meanwhile, looks strained. Her arms are folded tight across her chest as if to stop herself escaping.

'Eliza has just been down. She needs another pair for cards and Helena is being a spoilsport and refusing to go.'

'We talked about it. We agreed.'

'Yes, but this is just sitting down in the lounge surrounded by other people. And I'm so bored of this deck I feel that if I have to spend one more afternoon looking at the same old faces, I'm going to explode.'

Edward doesn't sound like himself. He sounds, in fact, like Eliza. Lily registers the similarity with a dull thud of recognition. Despite everything that has happened between her and Edward, it is still Eliza who provides his reference points, Eliza upon whom his unconscious mind fixes.

'Edward. You've heard the rumours. Everyone has heard them.

You know what happened. A woman is dead because of Eliza Campbell.'

'We don't know that for sure. Anyway, I thought you never listened to gossip. Didn't you say that to me?'

Edward is glaring at his sister, and there is something hard and tight between them that is made from iron and cannot bend. Now he turns to Lily.

'Will you come, Lily? Please. Or would you rather spend the next few hours looking at the same old sea through the same old railings while the same old people walk past, saying the same old things?'

As soon as he says it, Lily realizes she does want, more than anything, to be away from here. And though she's in no hurry to see Edward reduced to a nervous schoolboy in Eliza's presence, those hours spent with her in Fremantle have made Lily feel there is, if not a friendship, then at least an affinity between them. She glances at Edward's watch, which sits loosely on his narrow wrist, the round, silver face bright against his golden skin.

Three thirty in the afternoon. Plenty of time to go upstairs and play a few hands of cards and breathe a different kind of air before meeting with Maria, as she has promised. 'I will come, but only for an hour,' she says. But as she and Edward head for the staircase, Helena's disapproval follows her like a shadow.

As always when she hasn't seen Max Campbell for a few days, the reality of him comes as a shock. The size of him, the breadth of his shoulders. Those blue eyes like a pick, chip chip chipping away at you until you crack like eggshell. The power of him.

He is in an ebullient mood, presiding over the cards table as if he is hosting a dinner. Even Eliza seems in thrall, sitting quietly by his side, concentrating on the play, not losing patience when she and Max forfeit three hands in a row to Lily and Edward. At one point Lily sees the corseted woman who'd taken her aside to warn her about the Campbells enter the lounge and stop dead as if she cannot believe what she is seeing, before turning sharply on her heel.

'I can't wait to get to Adelaide tomorrow,' Eliza says. 'A sliver of civilization at last. Well, relatively speaking, anyway.'

'What will you both be doing? Have you decided?' Edward asks the Campbells.

Lily wishes he didn't sound so eager. He gives himself so much away, she thinks. And then she thinks, before she can stop herself, if only I had been enough.

'We're going to go into the city and we're going to find the nearest bar and we're going to order the biggest, most expensive bottle of champagne and we're going to drink to being off the bloody boat, if only for a day,' says Max.

For the first time Lily wonders what the Campbells will do when they arrive, finally, in Sydney. How many bars can they sit in, how much champagne can they drink, before they grasp it's still just them, the same two people they were before they left England?

'That sounds like fun,' says Edward, and Max turns his smile on him, though Lily can see that his jaw is set tight.

'Oh, I don't think it's your scene, old chap.'

They play on, and Lily watches the clock on the wall as it passes half past four. 'I must go,' she says. But she says it in the way people say things they wish to be persuaded out of.

'Don't be such a bore,' says Eliza. 'There's still plenty of time.' In twenty minutes I'll make my excuses and leave, Lily tells herself. And yet the clock gets to four fifty-five and there she still is. Just five more minutes. After all, it doesn't take any time at all to get down the stairs and along the deck to where she agreed to meet Maria. Still, she watches as the minute hand moves. Three minutes past. Now five minutes. It won't matter if she's a little late. Ten minutes. Fifteen.

'I'm late,' she says, making a half-hearted effort to gather her things together. 'I promised Maria.'

'Your friend isn't a child,' says Max.

'She's altogether too needy,' Eliza adds, forgetting, perhaps, all the occasions where she has declared herself unable to survive another second without Lily's company. 'You need to detach yourself from her, Lily, or you will get to Australia and find you cannot be rid of her.'

'No. That's not true. She is getting off at Melbourne. And besides, I don't want to be rid of her.'

But still she remains seated.

At five thirty Lily finally admits to herself that she is not going. She cannot face seeing Maria again. Not just yet. There is something so monstrous about the change in her, that livid purple rash, the way her wasted fingers clamped around Lily's wrist.

When she and Edward go downstairs for dinner – too late for a bath tonight – she casts around for her friend. Already she is regretting not keeping her promise, wanting to explain. But Maria is on the earlier sitting and doesn't appear.

Now that the end of the voyage is so close, less than a week away, there's a strange mood at the dinner table. Clara Mills, having spent the journey lamenting being a lone woman in charge of a child, is now worrying about being reunited with her sweet-shop-owning husband.

'He has been in Australia for so long I worry he might have lost some of his refinement. What if he has friends I cannot get along with? And he has taken a house quite some distance from the city. Peggy and I shall be quite alone.'

Helena is hardly speaking to either Edward or Lily and spends most of the meal with her back turned to them, engaged in conversation with George Price. Well, as engaged as she can be. George is, if anything, more jumpy even than when Lily was cornered by him out on the deck. His hands don't stop moving, picking up cutlery, putting it down again, smoothing his hair, plucking at the skin of his arm as if he is testing for quality. His eyes roam around the room without settling, even as Helena tries to solicit his thoughts on his forthcoming venture in New Zealand.

'How long will you be staying in Sydney before leaving for New Zealand?'

'Not long.'

'A day? A week?'

'A night, I think.'

And all the time his fingers roaming around from head to knife to arm to face and back again, as if there will be some price demanded for staying still.

She is relieved when dinner finishes and they file out of the dining room, but her improved spirits soon sink again when she sees a familiar couple standing by the railings, anxiously scanning the passengers as they emerge.

'Miss Shepherd? Over here.'

As ever, Mr Neumann has his grey felt hat in his hands and is rotating it like the wheel of a ship. The outer edge of the brim is dark with grease where it has been touched so often.

Lily feels the weight of her guilt compressing her so that she walks like a smaller person. She should have reported back to the Neumanns about what the doctor told her. She should not have ducked back and hidden from them. What has happened to her? She used to be so straight in her dealings with people, was known for it in the café where she worked. 'Ask Lily, she'll give you an honest answer,' her fellow waitresses used to say when one or other of them was locked into an argument about whose turn it was to clean out the coffee pots or wait on the table with the man who always gave everyone the heebie-jeebies, even though he never quite said anything that could get him slung out.

Little bird-like Mrs Neumann steps forward and, suddenly, Lily can't bear to hear the reproach she is about to deliver.

'I'm sorry,' she blurts out, desperate to forestall her. 'I know I should have come to find you the other night, but –'

Mrs Neumann has raised her tiny hand, delicate as a dried leaf.

'Not the doctor. No. Not that. We look for Maria. She was not at dinner.'

'Perhaps she's in her cabin. When I saw her earlier she wasn't feeling very well.'

'No. We have been to her cabin.'

'She might have been asleep.'

'No.' Mr Neumann shakes his head. 'We asked her friend. Not her friend, really. The woman who lives in the room with her. No persons have seen her.'

Edward joins in now.

'There are so many places she could be. The laundry. The library. Asleep in a chair somewhere hidden away. I'm sure there's no need to worry but, to put your minds at rest, we'll help you look for her.'

It is decided that the Neumanns will explore the lower deck, where the laundry rooms are, while Edward and Lily scour their own deck.

'It's touching, isn't it, Lily, how concerned the Neumanns are for their friend?' says Edward as they emerge Maria-less from the library.

Lily nods, but her throat feels too constricted to speak. Fear is closing up her airways, making it difficult to breathe, and there is a weight of judgement crushing her chest.

When they arrive at the far end of the deck there is no one there, only the pile of blankets where Maria once was. The tightness just below Lily's ribs turns into a pressing ache.

Edward has a brainwave.

'You said she was unwell when you saw her this morning? Perhaps she is with the doctor.'

Lily wants this to be true so she ignores the voice that reminds her how dismissive Dr Macpherson was of Maria's illness, how unsympathetic. She cannot imagine Maria taking refuge in the doctor's surgery for all this time. And, indeed, she is proved right when she sees that the doctor's surgery is all locked up and a passing passenger tells them that the doctor is currently in the first-class dining room, having dinner with the captain.

They meet up once again with the Neumanns, who have had no luck searching down below, although one of the Italian women told them they had seen a woman matching Maria's description at the far end of the deck earlier on.

'She was standing alone, looking.' Here, Mr Neumann puts a hand to his forehead and turns his head this way and that way, miming how one might search. 'The Italian said she was waiting for someone.'

And now the ache becomes a pain, sharp and intense. Edward volunteers to look up on the first-class deck, although no one can imagine why she would be up there. When he returns ten minutes later Lily closes her eyes so she can't see the furrow above the bridge of his nose.

By now it is pitch black out on the furthest reaches of the deck away from the lights of the lounge and the dining room. Helena and Ian, who have joined them, insist it is time to involve the ship's company and Ian goes to find the captain, who grudgingly orders a search.

'He made it clear he didn't really want to,' Ian reports later. 'Suggested that, judging by her past history, she would most likely be hiding somewhere enjoying the drama.'

Word spreads around the ship and soon the other passengers also join the search, scouring the deck with oil lamps and torches, poking in dark corners and raising tarpaulins on the lifeboats, to the embarrassment of more than one courting couple.

A shout goes up from the end of the deck where Lily met Maria earlier in the day. Something has been found by the railings there. The item is brought to the lounge, where Lily and Edward are talking to the captain. Lily gasps as she recognizes Maria's tortoiseshell spectacles, one lens cracked.

By eleven o'clock there isn't one inch of the ship that hasn't been searched. The captain and the purser take Lily and Edward and the Neumanns into the Purser's Office to file an official missing-persons report. He asks for details of when they last saw or spoke to Maria Katz, and when they realized she was missing. When the Neumanns talk their English is more broken than usual, perhaps because of their distress, or because they are nervous speaking in such a formal situation. Belatedly, Lily becomes aware of the uniform worn by the captain and the purser and wonders how much that is responsible for the way the Neumanns' accents have become thicker and more impenetrable and they cast around for words that previously appeared to come more easily.

When it is her turn she describes how Maria seemed earlier in the day – the rash on her face, her alarming weight loss. She leaves out the arrangement they had made to meet at five. The words form in her mind, only to burst like bubbles in her mouth. That she left Maria to wait for her in vain while she played cards and drank tea up on the first-class deck. That Maria's need repelled her, that she worried the other passengers would think her somehow less because of their association.

So she stays silent. And Edward, too, stays silent. And their silence is a balloon that swells painfully inside her and leaves her gasping for breath. Whisky is produced in a crystal decanter retrieved from a mahogany cupboard.

'You've had a shock,' says Edward, anxiously watching her drink. 'No wonder you're upset.'

'What will happen now?' she asks eventually, unable to bear the feeling of so many eyes upon her.

'We will radio on ahead to the police in Adelaide,' says the captain kindly. 'They will want to talk to you. All of you.'

'And Maria?'

'I'm afraid, given the evidence, we will have to report Miss Katz as missing at sea.'

Lily sways in her seat and Edward puts his arm around her shoulders.

'Do you think it's possible someone could have pushed her?' he asks, voicing Lily's thoughts out loud. 'The broken glasses might indicate some sort of struggle. No?'

The captain exchanges a sideways look with the purser.

'We will, of course, report any concerns to the police. However, you must remember that Miss Katz was, by all accounts, a woman of a nervous disposition with a history of imagined assaults.'

The Neumanns have been trying to follow the conversation, and it takes them a few seconds for the captain's meaning to sink in. Now Mr Neumann becomes agitated.

'She would not jump from the ship. She was not that sort of person. She was good person. Intelligent.'

'I'm afraid I have seen this happen before,' says the captain. 'There are some people who cope very badly with being at sea in such a confined environment for any length of time. They start to experience delusions. Sometimes they want to do harm to themselves or to other people.'

'It's not common,' says the purser, 'but it does happen.'

Lily sees once again Maria's frightened face, that horrible rash, the wild look in her eyes. Oh. But. Lily has let her down. Just as she'd let Mags down. *Am I going to die, Lil?* Blood on the walls. Blood on the carpet. Blood even in Lily's hair so that when she washed it out at home over the bath the water ran pink.

'It's my fault,' she says to Edward as he walks her back to her cabin at the end of that terrible, nightmarish evening. 'I was not a good friend to her. And now she's gone and I won't ever be able to say sorry to her. I don't think I can bear it.'

At the bottom of the cramped stairwell Edward takes her into his arms and holds her so close that she can't tell whose heartbeat it is she is feeling – his or her own. And when, finally, he tries to pull away, Lily clutches on to him more tightly because she knows that when he lets go she will be left alone with herself, and she's the very last person she wishes to be with.

26

31 August 1939

BY THE TIME Lily wakes the next morning, groggy from the whisky, they are already docked in Adelaide. There is a brief moment of excitement, then she remembers Maria and is hit by a crushing wave of horror.

'Are you feeling all right, Lily?' Audrey is solicitous but nervous, as if Lily's proximity to tragedy has elevated her to a different social plane.

Even Ida seems affected, shooting anxious glances at Lily as she gets dressed.

'It's a terrible thing,' she says. And for once there's no undercurrent of disapproval in her voice.

Now Lily remembers something.

'Why didn't you tell me it was you who was the witness that night up on the deck?'

Lily has never before seen Ida look guilty, but now the sallow skin which is stretched tightly over the bones of her face is stained dark red.

'It was supposed to be confidential. They shouldn't have said.'

'I still don't understand why . . .'

But Ida is gone. Out through the cabin door in a rustle of petticoats and a waft of sour air.

And soon her cabin mate's strange behaviour is forgotten as Lily arrives up on deck and finds that, overnight, the world has changed. Gone is the sultry heat of just a few days ago. Now, despite the sharp sunshine, there is a definite chill in the air and Lily wraps her white cardigan around her.

'Lily, the Adelaide police would like to interview you.'

Edward has rushed to her side, as if he has been waiting for her. His solemn expression extinguishes Lily's last, secret hope that Maria might have materialized during the night, perhaps nursing a lump on her head where she fell and knocked herself out somewhere so hidden that no one could find her.

'They're here already?'

Her mouth feels dry as dust and, as Edward leads her up the stairs to the upper deck, her legs are almost too heavy to lift.

The police are waiting in the captain's private office, a large, square room with several upright leather armchairs on one side and an imposing oval table on the other. The Neumanns are seated at the far end of the table, appearing dwarfed by the heavy furniture, like the little figurines Lily used to have in her dolls' house when she was young. The thought almost makes her laugh out loud and she claps a hand to her mouth to stop herself. She is losing control.

'Ah, Miss Shepherd.' The captain's voice is grave and Lily imagines him selecting it that morning from a hanging rail of voices as if he were choosing a shirt, and again she wants to laugh. 'This is a tragic business. I hope you managed to sleep.'

The two policemen are introduced, one in his late thirties with blue eyes set so close together he appears to be all the time gazing at his own nose, the other young enough still to have a spray of pebbledash acne across the lower part of his face. Lily remembers

Maria's rash and a sound escapes her that is like a low moan and she covers it up with a cough.

The facts are gone over, Maria's last known movements described. This time Lily admits to the arrangement she made with Maria and failed to keep.

'You made no mention of this last night,' says the purser. His handsome, leonine features look momentarily sorrowful.

'I was ashamed,' says Lily.

'Why didn't you go?' asks the older policeman. 'You said she didn't appear to be quite herself. Why didn't you go to make sure she was all right?'

Lily tries to swallow but finds she cannot. She glances at Edward. Appealing.

'We were playing cards,' he says, coming to her rescue. 'With some friends on the upper deck. We didn't notice the time.'

It is a lie. And everyone knows it.

'You will investigate,' Mr Neumann says, addressing the policemen directly, 'if someone has done something to hurt Miss Katz? Remember the assault in the night, the broken glasses. It could be possible.'

The policeman frowns and avoids looking at the captain or the purser.

'We take all allegations seriously,' he says, 'but we must also look at the facts. Miss Katz had been behaving increasingly erratically. Sometimes the sea will do that to a person. And we mustn't forget she had added anxiety about her family back in Austria. These are difficult days for many people. So much uncertainty. I wouldn't be surprised if we didn't see a lot more of this sort of thing.'

After they leave that phrase goes round and round in Lily's head. *This sort of thing.* As if Maria disappearing off the ship into thin air was part of a movement, or a fashion, like wearing shorter skirts or listening to jazz music.

'I'm so sorry, Lily,' Edward says as they make their way back down the stairs. 'We should never have prevented you from going to meet Maria yesterday.'

By 'we', of course, he means Eliza and Max. Edward himself had not said a thing. But then maybe, Lily thinks, she and Edward were just as complicit in their silence, their inability to stand up for what was right.

She remembers now how, at the gala ball, Ian had warned her about the Campbells, saying, 'They are damaged people. And damaged people are the most dangerous because they have nothing to lose.'

And now it turns out that it is she, Lily, who is the dangerous one.

They rejoin Helena and Ian, and Lily allows herself to be persuaded to go ashore.

'The change of scenery will do you good,' Helena tells her. 'The boat is full of reminders.'

'You can't go ashore like that,' says Ian, gesturing to Lily's thin cardigan. 'Don't let the sunshine deceive you. It's chilly onshore, especially after the temperatures we've been used to.'

'I'll fetch you some warmer things,' Edward volunteers, and disappears below deck, reappearing some time later with Lily's lightweight navy linen jacket and Eliza Campbell's fox-fur stole.

Lily does not have the energy to protest and obediently puts her arms into the jacket sleeves and wraps the fur around her neck. As they file off the boat she sees the Neumanns watching from the end of the deck, their expressions impossible to read from this distance, faces pale ovals of blankness.

Later, when Lily looks back on this day out in Adelaide, she will view it like a montage of images in someone else's slide show, not a place she once visited herself. She will see in her mind the train that took them the short distance from the dock to the town. Then Adelaide itself, clean and bright and whitewashed with wide streets and colonial-style buildings and trees covered in dazzling lilac flowers that Ian informs her are jacarandas. A neat shopping centre. A smart new art gallery.

Women wearing cotton dresses in the gayest of colours, pinks and mint greens and pale blues, despite the cool wind, so that Lily, feeling over-dressed and frumpy, takes off the fox fur and stuffs it into her bag.

Adelaide isn't a huge city and they inevitably bump into other passengers at some of the more touristy spots. There's George Price sitting at the window of a restaurant, head bent over his newspaper so that his nose is practically touching it. And the Campbells stand-ing in the art gallery, gazing in amused bafflement at some Aboriginal paintings. *We heard about your friend, Lily. How beastly for you. Come here.* And finding herself suddenly in Max Campbell's bear-like embrace, looking up after a while – seconds? minutes? – to see Eliza's look of irritation and Edward's expression snapping shut like a trap.

Lunch is eaten at a large modern fish-and-chips restaurant where, rather than ordering from a waitress, you're expected to serve yourself, which, normally, Lily would have found intriguing, storing it up to describe in her next letter home. Today, however, it's just one more detail that passes her by, even though the fish – bream, not cod or plaice – is delicious, as are the little scallop potatoes fried in batter. All the time, people are talking to her, and Lily is talking back to them in turn, although afterwards she will have no idea what they discussed.

Back at the docks the police are still there, talking to a knot of stewards and kitchen staff. A couple of the Australian passengers who are disembarking at Adelaide are in tears saying their goodbyes to friends they have made onboard, while a band of Scottish musi-cians, complete with bagpipes, have gathered to see off a group of Scotsmen preparing to make the relatively short trip from Adelaide to Melbourne or Sydney aboard the *Orontes*.

Normally, Lily loves this aspect of the voyage – watching the greet-ings and the farewells, the tears and the joy, people baring their feelings as if a layer of skin has been stripped off, leaving them newly, briefly, vulnerable. Yet, today, she hardly notices.

Now there are suddenly more Aussies on board than Brits, or so it seems. The bar is bursting with Australian men intent on introducing the Poms to the delights of Australian beer. Edward has disappeared somewhere and she finds herself grateful for a break from the confusion being around him always brings. 'Let me buy you a drink,' Ian says. But Lily has seen the Neumanns standing in a huddle of similarly sombrely dressed people at the end of the deck, and she thinks that if she has any beer she might choke.

Lily excuses herself early, claiming exhaustion. She worries what she will say to Ida, dreading a confrontation with her when her own thoughts are so muddied, but the cabin is, mercifully, empty.

To her surprise, Lily finds she is, after all, truly exhausted and, despite the increasingly turbulent sea, she falls asleep the minute she has hauled herself up the ladder and lain down. But she sleeps fitfully, her dreams fevered and disjointed. In one, her mother is sitting at the kitchen table at home, except she isn't really Lily's mother, she is Maria's sister, asking, 'Where is she? What have you done with her?' In another, the policeman with the close-together eyes is driving her somewhere, not speaking, and she knows in this dream that she has done something terrible. Finally, she has the dream she had before, that night up on the deck, where she and Maria are in a small boat drifting out to sea, except instead of Edward being there with them there is Mags, with her blood-soaked skirt. Just as before, Lily wakes up with a start and, for a split second, she is back there on the deck that night, emerging from that dream and seeing, just as she wakes, a shape crouching in the darkness next to Maria's bed, hearing the scream, followed by the thrum of retreating footsteps.

'It did happen,' she says out loud in the dimness of the cabin to the shape in the bottom bunk that she knows to be Ida. 'Just as she said.'

Somehow she manages to hold it in, this new clarity, hugging it to herself through the rest of that night while waves rock the boat and, somewhere outside the window, the coastline of Australia keeps pace with their progress. When, at last, the new day arrives and Audrey slips out of the cabin to use the bathroom, Lily can keep it in check no longer.

'You lied,' she says to Ida, who is still just a mound in the bed.

'I beg your pardon?'

'You lied about there being no one out on deck that night. I remember now, there *was* someone. I saw him.'

'I don't know what you mean.'

Ida is sitting up, her hairnet making it look, in this dim light, as if there is some sort of helmet framing her narrow pale face. Lily loses her temper, all the sadness and self-hatred of the last thirty-six hours rushing to the surface like bile.

'Maria didn't make it up. She was assaulted. It was you who lied, because you're malicious and bitter.'

'She thought she was better than me.'

'What?'

'Making a show of picking me up from the deck when I fell that time, so condescending. "Are you all right?"' Ida simpers horribly. 'Thinking I couldn't see the smirk on her a mile wide. Then all those times it was the two of you, you and her, cosying up to each other, and when I'd come along, all at once you'd clam up, like it was me who was the unwelcome one, like she was better than me. Her. Who's come from nowhere. Who's got nothing.'

From waking up only a few moments ago Ida is already trembling with rage and Lily realizes suddenly that it's because the rage is never far from the surface, like a lining she wears just under her skin. And now something else occurs to her.

'She thought she was being watched. Followed. Was it you? Was it? Did you push her over the railing?'

'Don't be ridiculous. I'm not a criminal. I'd never harm anyone. I was upset when she went missing. Ask Audrey. Anyway, if anyone did anything to her, it would be him.'

'Who?'

'Him that was meddling with her on the deck. Him from your dinner table.'

Lily is so taken aback that, at first, all she can think of is Edward. She's lying, she thinks. He wouldn't. Then, finally, her fumbling thoughts stumble across George Price.

'You saw him? You're a witness. We have to tell the captain.'

'Don't be daft. I'm not changing my story.'

'I'll tell him, then. I'll tell him how you lied to him and made a mockery of this whole investigation.'

To her surprise, Ida laughs. A dry sound that she coughs up from somewhere inside her.

'And I'll tell him that *you're* making it up. Who'd believe you now, after all this time? They'd just think you were as unbalanced as your friend. They'd say you were trying to cause trouble.'

The door opens and Audrey bursts in, seemingly unaware of the tension looming above the tiny cabin like a spider over its prey.

'Can you believe we'll be in Melbourne tomorrow? Then, just another two days, and Sydney. Time is flying past, and I want to just grab hold of it and tell it to slow down.'

Now, finally, she senses something in the air, and her face folds in on itself like dough.

'Oh, Lily. I'm sorry. You're still upset about your friend. I'm so clumsy.'

For a moment Lily considers telling Audrey what she's just learned, forcing her to choose sides. But something stops her. Ida's voice in her head. 'Who'd believe you now?'

'I need some air,' she says, slipping down the ladder in her haste to be gone. When she gets out on to the deck there's a chilly breeze blowing and she gulps it down like water on a boiling-hot day.

27

1 September 1939

IAN IS SITTING in the bar, drinking a beer, even though it's not yet ten o'clock. For once, his eyes aren't creased up with laughter so Lily can clearly see the delicate lattice of lines at the corners, white against his otherwise tanned skin.

'Isn't Helena with you?'

Lily is so used to seeing the two of them together she is scanning the room for Helena, even though it is obvious she is not here.

Ian shakes his head.

'She's upstairs, mixing with royalty.'

'Royalty?'

'The high and mighty Campbells. Doesn't matter that their moral standards are lower than a dog's, or that, if you listen to the rumours, her behaviour caused the death of a young woman. They come from money, and therefore they must be better than the likes of me.'

Ian doesn't sound like himself, and Lily wonders how many beers he might have had already.

'Surely you don't really believe Edward and Helena are swayed by money?'

He sighs.

'Nah. Not really. But their family clearly is. I like Helena. I mean, I really like her.' He looks at Lily meaningfully and she watches as his Adam's apple works its way painfully up and down his throat. 'But she's scared stiff of her father. They both are. And Father would not approve of me.'

'But you've got a good job. You're an engineer.'

'Yeah, but look where I came from, Lily. My dad was a drunk. I left school at twelve and worked on other people's farms in the middle of nowhere. It's only joining the army that gave me the skills to make something else of my life. From what I hear of Mr Fletcher Senior, that's not going to cut it. Anyway, enough about me. How are you feeling today, Lily? I know you were fond of Maria. We all were. She was a nice lady. It's not right what happened to her.'

. For a moment, Lily thinks she might cry. She looks down at the table, concentrating on a perfectly round drop of beer that is soaking into the wood. She thinks about telling Ian about Ida and what she said about George Price, but the words won't come out past the lump in her throat.

Perhaps guessing her feelings, Ian suggests they go outside to get some air. Though the sea is still unsettled and the air fresh and cool, the sun makes everything hard and bright, and Lily's unshed tears dry up in the breeze. Helena arrives, solemn-faced, followed by Edward. He is wearing the expression Lily has come to recognize as habitual when he has been in any sort of contact with the Campbells. Closed off. Agitated. Though his hands are plunged deeply into the pockets of his jacket, Lily sees through the woollen material how they move around, as if incapable of being still.

'Did you have fun?'

If Helena suspects any hidden sarcasm in Ian's question, she does not react to it.

'Not particularly,' she says. 'Eliza and Max have made some new friends – an Australian actor called Alan Morgan and his wife. Apparently, he is quite famous, although I've never heard of him.'

'And you didn't care for them?' Lily asks.

'No,' says Helena. 'Although Eliza seemed very taken.'

Lily does not need to look at Edward's face to know the expression she will find there.

'I don't know why they even invited us up there,' he says. Angry. 'We weren't in the slightest bit necessary.'

'To show off their new pets, most likely,' mutters Ian.

'Not pets. Toys,' says Helena. She shivers as a savage gust of wind sweeps in from the open sea to their right.

Instantly, Ian is by her side.

'You're cold? Shall I fetch you something?'

Lily thinks she might have a cardigan in her bag but, when she opens it up, she finds only Eliza's fox-fur wrap, stuffed into the bottom.

'This will warm you up,' she says, draping it around Helena's neck before she has a chance to protest.

Edward is smoking a cigarette, leaning on the rail so that the ash drops into the sea and the wind blows his black curls back from his face.

Helena and Ian have fallen into conversation about something, his lips close to her ear to be heard above the wind, and Lily is glad of the diversion so that she can tell Edward what she just learned from Ida, but before she can open her mouth he cuts her off.

'Just three more days,' he says, drawing on his cigarette so that his hollowed-out cheeks seem even more pronounced. 'I cannot wait for this trip to be over.'

Lily feels as though she has been slapped. When we arrive in Sydney I won't ever see him again, she thinks. And he is glad of it.

The tears that had been threatening to come earlier now well in her eyes, and she looks away, blinking rapidly.

'I'm sorry you find us all so dull,' she says.

Now understanding dawns, and he holds out his hands. A gesture of apology.

'I'm sorry, Lily. I didn't mean . . .'

But she doesn't stay to hear what he didn't mean. Instead she strides off down the boat, not bothering any more to stem the tears.

Up ahead she sees Clara and Peggy Mills coming towards her and, conscious of the glaze of tears over her face, she ducks into the doorway of the library. It's a small, generally underused room, so she is surprised to find one of the leather armchairs occupied by a man with his face completely hidden by a newspaper. Only once the door has clicked shut behind her and he looks up with a start does she realize it's George Price.

'You.'

The word is a whisper, her voice lost in the back of her constricted throat. She tries again.

'I know what you did. Up on the deck that night. I know it was you who attacked Maria Katz.'

George's peculiarly dull eyes sweep over her and past her like the constantly moving beam of a lighthouse. The hand that doesn't hold the paper goes up to his head, combing through his hair again and again, flakes of his scalp drifting down on to the shoulders of his navy-blue jacket.

'You can't . . .' he starts, and then stops. 'It's not true.'

His voice is thin as cotton and lacks conviction.

'You were seen.'

Now his eyes swing back to her, but almost immediately slide off again, as if they cannot get purchase.

'If someone had seen anything, they'd have said so at the time. You're upset, Miss Shepherd. I can see you've been crying. Your thoughts will be confused. But I would urge you to read the papers, learn what's going on in the world. What happened to Maria Katz is nothing compared with what is about to happen to all of us. War is breathing down our necks. You must pay attention to the bigger picture. We have to be prepared.'

'If war is breathing down our necks, how come you're heading to New Zealand? Running away from it, are you?'

Anger has burned away the tears, and suddenly Lily feels she might combust with it.

'I told you, it's my father's doing.'

'That's convenient for you, isn't it? "Daddy told me I must leave. I didn't have a choice."'

She puts on a high-pitched, babyish voice to mock him and is gratified to see his lips draw together in a tight, furious line. She presses on.

'I know you did something to Maria that night on deck. And I wouldn't be surprised if you had something to do with her disappearance, too.'

George jumps to his feet, letting the paper fall. His cheeks are the colour of black pudding and his whole body quivers. He pushes his face so close to hers that she feels a fine spray of spittle when he speaks.

'You had better be very careful, Miss Shepherd. I know you think yourself very grand, swanning around with your morally corrupt upper-class friends – yes, the whole ship knows what those two did – but don't forget, at heart, you're just a servant. And in three days' time, when they're all going to fancy parties and eating in smart restaurants, you'll be the one waiting on them, and they won't even remember your name.

'As for Miss Katz, don't forget that, when we're at war, half the people on this ship will be our enemies. I didn't do anything to her, but I can't say I'm sorry she's dead.'

With that he slams out of the library, leaving the room vibrating and Lily's breath tearing from her in harsh, painful strips. *I can't say I'm sorry she's dead.* The words go round and round in Lily's already whirling brain until she feels dizzy.

She dashes from the library, determined to find the purser or the captain to tell them what she knows, but, on the way to the staircase, she sees Mrs Collins sitting in the lounge.

When Lily tells Mrs Collins what Ida told her, a deep frown puckers the older woman's face.

'Will she make an official report attesting to this?'

Lily takes a deep breath.

'I don't know. I don't think so.'

The pucker deepens. Ida is fetched. And denies everything.

'Lily hasn't been herself for the last two days,' she tells Mrs Collins. 'I'm afraid she has become very disturbed and upset since Miss Katz's disappearance.'

'And you didn't say anything to her at all about witnessing an attack up on deck?'

Ida shakes her head. 'In fact, I said quite the opposite, that I was the person who had witnessed there *not* being an attack. As I said, I think poor Lily is easily confused at the moment. It's understandable, with what happened to her friend, and with her being so much under the influence of those Campbells, who, from all accounts, are no better than they ought to be.'

'You're lying!' cries Lily. 'You're a liar!'

'There's no call for that.' Mrs Collins sounds sterner than Lily has ever heard her.

Ida is dismissed and now it is just the two of them, seated together on a sofa in the corner.

'She's lying,' Lily repeats. 'I'm going to inform the captain so that he can report it to the police in Melbourne.'

'I cannot stop you doing that, Lily. But I would advise you to think very carefully. Firstly, you are accusing someone of a very, very serious crime. And George Price comes from a good, respectable family. His father works for the government in India, don't forget. And you're accusing Ida, too, of lying to the authorities. And that could have consequences for a woman in Ida's position.

'Secondly, it will come down to your word against both of theirs.'

'I can't just say nothing.'

'Think of your future, Lily.' Mrs Collins lays one of her hands, soft as a floury bap, on Lily's shaking arm. 'If the captain and the police have you down as a troublemaker, it might count against you. I don't need to remind you that, when we arrive in Sydney, in just three days' time, there are interviews set up with prospective employers – all respectable women. A thing like that is going to be very off-putting and, if you fail to secure a job . . . well, you'll be on your own. Destitute. Thousands of miles from home.'

Lily opens her mouth to speak. Thinks better of it. Swallows.

'But if Maria really was assaulted that night on deck, what's to say she wasn't attacked again? What if she didn't jump but was pushed – and I haven't said anything?'

'*If!*' Mrs Collins sounds triumphant, as if with that short, two-letter word Lily has admitted defeat. 'That's just it, Lily. There is a very large "if". And you are staking your entire future upon it. Is that really a risk you are prepared to take?'

Lily is silent, and Mrs Collins clearly senses capitulation, for her voice softens.

'My dear, you have had a terrible shock. I'm sure we all feel just terrible about what happened to that poor lady. But you have excellent references from England. You will have your choice of positions once we arrive in Sydney, I'm quite sure. I think you could do very well for yourself in Australia, make your family proud. I would hate to see you jeopardize all of that for a – frankly – absurd allegation, which, I have to tell you, is highly unlikely to be believed.'

After leaving the lounge Lily makes her way to the far end of the deck and sinks down into the chair where Maria was sitting the last time they met. For a moment she imagines she can feel the imprint of Maria's bones in the canvas, smell her lingering sadness, but the biting wind soon sweeps such thoughts aside. The pile of blankets has gone and it starts to feel bitterly cold, exposed to the elements on both sides. Still Lily remains, staring intently through the metal railings. But she doesn't see the sky, clotted with grey clouds, or the churning, gunmetal sea. Nor does she notice the movement from the upper deck behind her, where Eliza Campbell, standing next to a man with a narrow black moustache and black hair so shiny it looks to have been polished like a leather shoe, is waving her arm, trying to snag Lily's attention. Instead, there's only one image plastered on the inner walls of Lily's mind, only one face she sees as she hugs her arms around her frozen body, fingers digging into her own goosebumpy flesh.

George Price.

28

2 September 1939

LILY SURVEYS the crowd on Melbourne dock through heavy-lidded eyes. Last night, not wanting to risk a further confrontation with Ida, she stayed up far too late, until she could be sure her cabin mate would be asleep. Then she got up early to slip out before the others awoke. Now, though the day is clear and fresh, she feels as if she is seeing the world through a soupy haze.

The quayside is alive with activity. Many passengers are leaving the ship for good, urgently scanning the crowds for a familiar face. Some people on the dock are holding up placards with the names of people they have been sent to meet. They have that anxious, expectant look of people hoping for the best but preparing for the worst.

In addition to the crowds awaiting their own ship, there are knots of people here and there attending on the other ships in the port, so the whole scene is one of great animation.

Beyond the grey industry of the docks the Australian coastline stretches away with long, yellow-sanded beaches and, behind them in the far distance, the grainy peaks of the Dandenong Mountains, strung out along the skyline.

The ship will be in Melbourne for the whole day. Plenty of time for the twenty-minute train ride into the city, so Lily is in no hurry to get moving. Plus, her bones feel so heavy, making her movements slow and sluggish.

Someone taps her on the shoulder, a light, diffident touch.

There stand the Neumanns. He with his hat on, and carrying a battered briefcase that looks suspiciously light. She with her brown skirt and blouse and a jacket of some indeterminate colour between brown and a drab, dull green.

'We leave the boat here, Miss Shepherd,' says Mr Neumann. 'We want only to say goodbye.'

His tiny, bird-like wife looks searchingly into Lily's face.

'You are not so well, Miss Shepherd?' she says. One of those statement/questions that Lily finds so hard to respond to. She is suddenly conscious of her tangled, unbrushed hair and the creases in her navy linen skirt.

She thinks about telling them what she has learned about George Price and the assault on the deck, rehearses in her mind what she would say. Yet she knows she will not say it. Maria is gone, and nothing will bring her back. Lily, however, is still here, about to start a new life in a country where she knows no one and has nothing to offer but the references she brings with her. Mrs Collins is right: she cannot afford the luxury of making claims that cannot be substantiated.

'I haven't slept well. That's all. I didn't realize you would be leaving here in Melbourne. Where are all your things?'

Too late, she remembers what Maria told her about some of the Jewish passengers having only the clothes they were wearing when they left and feels hot with embarrassment.

'We will write to Maria's sister and tell her what has happened,' says Mrs Neumann. 'You will not worry. You were a good friend.'

But as Lily watches them descend the gangway, two diminutive figures with straight backs and shiny patches on their clothes, she knows it's not true. She was not a good friend, and she knows she will always, her whole life, carry a little ribbon of shame sewn on to the inside of her heart.

The Fletchers and Ian Jones join her. They have all arranged to go ashore together.

'Why so serious?' she asks them, noticing that even the usually amiable Ian looks hard-faced and grim.

'Haven't you heard?' Edward is looking pale and nervous, and suddenly so agonizingly young Lily has to look away. 'Someone came aboard with a newspaper earlier. Germany has invaded Poland.'

At first Lily is relieved the news isn't about someone she knows. But then she looks around at the other passengers on the deck, the expressions on people's faces, and a hard nugget of dread forms in the pit of her stomach.

'You know, don't you, that Chamberlain promised we would go to war if Hitler went into Poland?'

'Yes, but that doesn't mean to say that's what's going to happen. He could step back, like he did last year.'

'He could,' Helena agrees.

'But it's not likely,' says Edward.

Now Lily is thinking about Frank and how, when they were children, they used to play with his toy soldiers and he would always get to be Britain because they were his soldiers, and she would have to be whoever the enemy was that day, sometimes Germany, other times France or Spain or even America. She remembers his excited cries of 'Attack!' and the theatrical, long-drawn-out, heroic deaths of his little metal soldiers. Is he now to be a soldier for real? She cannot – will not – believe it.

The news casts a shadow over the group as they go ashore and wait for the train to take them into the city. The friction between Helena and Edward seems only to have grown since the day before and Lily finds herself in the uncomfortable position of mediating, alongside Ian, whose reluctance is obvious in the way he holds himself so tall and stiff and constantly clears his throat as if he is revving up a car engine.

The train is full of passengers from their own ship or the others in the port, and while many of them seem equally solemn and preoccupied, some are resolutely jolly.

'Aussies,' remarks Ian, eyeing a loud group of revellers in their carriage. 'The thing you have to understand is that, though, obviously the ties to Britain are strong, and if Britain goes to war we go too, Europe itself seems like a very long way away.'

'Well, I feel like turning around and going straight back home,' says Edward. 'How does it look for us to be leaving the country at a time like this?'

'Would you enlist?' Lily asks.

'Of course.'

Edward's comment provokes a noise from Helena that is like an explosion of impatience.

'For God's sake, Edward. Don't be so ridiculous. They wouldn't take you.'

Edward tenses as if struck. Watching his expression change from pride to hurt to anger, Lily feels stricken on his behalf.

The remainder of the journey passes almost in silence. Lily leans her forehead on the window and looks at the bungalows of Melbourne's suburbs, all set well apart and of varying shapes and sizes, so different to the terraces of London. As they come into the city itself, the buildings change, with high-rises and office blocks dominating the skyline. Alighting from the train, they find themselves in a busy, thriving city much the same as any city back home, except there are trams going up and down the roads rather than buses.

The main street is full of large stores and there's a cinema showing *Goodbye, Mr Chips*, which Lily herself saw in London what seems like a hundred years ago. Similarly, when they pass a record shop, the song being blasted from the open doorway turns out once again to be 'The Lambeth Walk', followed by Kay Kyser's 'Three Little Fishies', which has long since worn out its welcome back home.

Lily groans. 'I feel like I've crossed half the world only to go back in time.'

Their dark mood dogs them as they make their way along the main street and Lily finds herself lagging behind, gazing into shop windows just to put some distance between her and the others. The clothing shops are all displaying summer clothes – light cotton dresses in pretty colours, and beach wear. Lily finds it so strange to think that summer will soon be starting when her body is gearing itself up for winter.

'Gotcha!'

Lily jolts forward with a start, narrowly avoiding smashing her head on the shopfront, and Eliza claps her hands.

'You should see your face, Lily!'

Eliza is wearing the scarlet dress she had on when Lily first saw her on Tilbury Docks and her dark glasses, which match those of her companion.

'This is Alan Morgan, Lily. He's a film star so you must be very, very nice to him so he can make you one as well. Wouldn't she look divine on screen, Alan? Have you seen those eyes?'

Alan Morgan raises his glasses to better appraise Lily's camera-worthiness. His own eyes are large and chocolate brown, with thick lashes, jet black to match his hair, and his black moustache is thin as a papercut. Lily is acutely aware of her messy hair and the clothes she pulled on just because they were the first things she could find as she made her early morning getaway.

'Very English,' he says eventually.

'Lily!' Max is looking at her as if it has been years since he last saw her. He snatches up her hand and kisses it, his lips pressed hard against her skin. He is standing next to a woman who must be the actor's wife. Not 'woman', really, Lily reassesses as they are introduced. Girl.

Cleo Morgan is a waif of a thing with a handshake so limp it feels like Lily is clutching at thin air.

'I'm an actress myself, actually,' she says in a small, breathy voice. Then when Lily betrays no recognition, she continues, 'My stage name might be more familiar. Cleopatra Bannister?'

Lily is saved by an interjection from Alan Morgan.

'Don't be an ass, Cleo. You haven't been in anything for three years and even then you were hardly the lead. I don't really think your fame is likely to have spread to England, do you?'

They pass a coffee shop, where the customers are sitting on high stools along a bar that looks out across the street, and chefs with tall white hats are frying doughnuts with holes in them. Despite herself, Lily bursts out: 'Oh, I've always wanted to try one of those.'

And so they must all go in, although Cleo declares that she couldn't possibly eat a whole one of those and stares with horror at the one on Lily's plate, as if it is a bomb that might go off at any moment.

'She is a sweet little thing, but so terribly vacuous it's like making conversation with a very pretty piece of wood,' whispers Max in her ear. He is standing behind her, as there are not enough stools for everyone. His breath is hot and wet and smells of whisky. 'I've had to put up with her for two whole days because my darling wife thought it would be fun to hang around with her husband. I can't tell you how happy I am to see you, Lily.'

His lips brush the tip of her ear. The faint scratch of his moustache.

After they leave the coffee shop Max is never far from Lily's side, pointing out things as they walk along the main street – advertising hoardings, an unfamiliar style of dress. Everywhere they go people stare at Alan Morgan and he pretends not to see them. One elderly woman stops and asks for his autograph, which he provides with spectacularly bad grace. 'Why must it always be the old crones that ask?' he complains.

The Morgans have been touring Europe. They stopped off in Adelaide from an earlier ship to visit Cleo's sister and are now on their way home to Sydney. Their travels have soured Alan's appreciation of his home country, which he now finds to be too unsophisticated, too unrefined. 'When we were in Paris,' he says, followed by an unfavourable comparison. 'When we were in Milan . . .' He finds the Australian accent impossibly vulgar and claims all Aussie women have 'peasant hands'.

'See how insufferable he is?' whispers Max. 'And now poor Eliza, having assiduously cultivated the both of them, finds herself stuck with him!'

Certainly, Eliza, walking ahead with Alan, seems very keen to involve the others at every opportunity.

'What are you saying, Max? Why are you two whispering?'

'Nothing that would interest you, darling.'

Eliza glares at him, and then at Lily, narrowing her eyes as if recalibrating something in her head. In response Max moves even closer to Lily, so his thigh brushes her hip.

It isn't only Eliza who seems put out by Max's attention to her. Edward, too, keeps glancing over, and with each glance his frown deepens. The pavements allow them to walk comfortably only in twos and Edward has been paired with the vacuous Cleo. Though Lily experienced a pang of jealousy when she first saw them together, noting how even Edward, normally the slightest of the men, appeared to tower over the fragile, ethereal girl, she soon realized they were struggling to make conversation.

At lunch in a restaurant where the waitress stares so hard at Alan she misses the narrow table and has to bring them fresh cutlery,

Max sits opposite Lily so that their knees are touching, and she is too tired, too bone-weary, to resist. Alan Morgan is telling them about a meal they were served in Capri, where the lobsters were brought alive and snapping to the table for approval before cooking. He drops the name of an Italian film director Lily has never heard of.

'They closed the whole restaurant for us. I thought it was because of Righelli, who is like royalty there, but he said, "No, Alan, it's all for you."'

Under the table Max's knee presses harder against her own.

'Poor Lily has had a hard time. She made friends with a Jewish woman from Germany who turned out to be rather highly strung and jumped off the side of the boat. All rather shocking, so we need to cheer her up.'

Eliza says all this in a conversational, almost sing-song tone, as if she is relating a rather entertaining anecdote, so it takes a second or two for Lily's outrage to catch up with her. When it does it's like a white heat flaring in her chest.

'Maria wasn't from Germany, she was Austrian. And she wasn't like that. She didn't . . .'

For a moment Lily considers telling them about George Price, and what Ida told her, but something holds her back. Self-preservation, perhaps.

'They will all be coming here now there's to be a war,' says Alan Morgan. 'All the people Europe doesn't want. As if this country wasn't backward enough! I suppose you've had a lucky escape.' He is looking at Edward, the end of his papercut moustache pointing towards him like a blade. 'Young, single chap like you would be one of the first to be called up to serve your country if you weren't lying low here.'

'My brother has not been well,' says Helena hotly. 'We've come to Australia only for his health. When he is quite recovered, of course we'll return.'

Edward says nothing but Lily sees his fingers tighten around his knife, and in his cheek a muscle she has never noticed before throbs like a frog's throat.

Getting off the train at the port ready to get back on to the ship, Lily sees George Price walking on ahead, alone, as he always is. She doesn't bother to slow down. He will not wish to see her any more than she him. So she is surprised when George, having noticed them coming up behind him, stops for them to catch up. He is holding what looks to be a British newspaper. Lily shivers as she reads the headline: GERMANY INVADES AND BOMBS POLAND. BRITAIN MOBILIZES. Frank, she thinks. My baby brother.

'Have you seen?' George is tapping the paper. His eyes glitter, as if lit up by a hundred flickering tea lights. 'We are going to war. There can be no question. Now everything is different.'

He seems to be addressing his remarks exclusively to Lily, does not even seem to be aware of the others – the Campbells, the Fletchers, pompous, preposterous Alan Morgan and his flyaway wife.

'We are surrounded by enemies on board. Italians, Germans. I've been telling you all that, but no one would listen. Well, now we're at war. Everything has changed.'

'You're not at war, though, are you, George?'

Lily cannot help herself.

'Your father got you well away, didn't he, so you wouldn't have to get your hands dirty?'

'There's more than one way to fight a war, Miss Shepherd.'

George is moving, moving, moving, hands, fingers, feet, weight shifting, even the corner of his eye twitching up and down as if in a spasm.

'It's just as well we only have two full days left,' says Eliza gaily. 'Otherwise, how should we be able to sleep, knowing we're surrounded by the enemy?'

George does not seem to notice her sarcastic tone.

'I hope the captain will throw them all off now.'

'He can't do that when we haven't declared war,' says Helena, exasperated. 'It might all still be averted. We've come close before.'

George is shaking his head. His hair looks greasy and uncombed.

'It's war. And we have to be on our guard. Now do you see I was right?' He is looking directly at Lily again. Those bulging eyes and fleshy lips. 'Whatever happened to that Austrian woman on board, it means nothing now, not when so many of our own people are going to die. What's one less of them?'

His words are greeted by a general outcry. One of the men exclaims, 'Shame!' in a very loud voice. Lily feels her arm being firmly taken hold of by someone who propels her past George and across the quayside and up the gangplank to the ship. She senses rather than sees the others falling behind them, conscious only of her blood racing in her veins, her breath coming in short gasps.

Once on the deserted deck, she is steered to the opposite side of the ship, facing out to a sea dotted with other smaller boats and fishing craft.

'Breathe,' orders Max Campbell. And she obeys, taking in great gulps of salty air.

And when he puts his arms around her she lets him because Edward is nowhere to be seen and all her fight is gone, and Max, in all his undeniable, physical, pulsing, overpowering, blood-pumping self, seems at that moment to be the only thing that makes sense in the entire world.

29

3 September 1939

'THE THING IS, I know I haven't treated you fairly.'

Edward is pacing up and down in the library, as he has been since he asked if they could go somewhere to talk privately. There is an air of suppression about him to match his curly hair dampened down into coils, always on the verge of springing loose.

'I have been inconsistent and so wrapped up in myself I haven't considered your feelings, and I wish I could take it all back and start again. This whole wretched trip. I'd do everything differently. Everything.'

Sitting in the armchair where, just days ago, she'd surprised George Price, Lily struggles to follow what Edward is saying, but his thoughts seem to be jumping around without a perceivable order. I don't love him, she thinks suddenly. And the realization is like a bereavement.

In the stark morning light Edward seems pale and suddenly too fragile for Australia's wide, unforgiving skies.

'What is it you're not telling me?' she asks him now. 'I know there's something. I can see it in the way you and Helena look at each other, in the things she says.'

Finally, Edward looks at her, and she feels a part of her crumble into powder that dissolves to liquid and seeps, warm, through her veins at the naked appeal in his eyes.

'I wish I could tell you, Lily. I want to tell you. Sometimes the weight of what I'm not saying feels like it's going to crush me so there's nothing left of me. But I can't. I promised.'

'Promised who?'

'My father. What you have to understand, Lily, is that he's a very difficult man. Helena and I have always been frightened of him. Not physically, although he can be violent when he's roused. But he is very domineering. Very quick to anger, with set rules about what is and isn't allowed. He is not the kind of man you go against.'

'But you did? Go against him, I mean.'

Edward nods.

'And lived to rue the day!'

He is trying for light-heartedness. Failing.

'But please know, Lily, that my despicable behaviour has nothing to do with you. You're splendid. You're brave and strong and fair and lovely and you deserve only good things. Which is why I'm urging you to keep away from Max Campbell.'

Ah, so this is it. When they got back from Melbourne yesterday afternoon, and she and Max Campbell had snatched those few moments apart from the others on the far side of the ship, their absence had clearly been noted. Afterwards Edward had retreated into a tense silence while Eliza contented herself with a series of barbed remarks.

Let them, Lily had thought. She was too tired. Tired to the very marrow of her. Max offered her ballast and more than that, he was straightforward in his needs, his wants. She understood what he desired from her and there was no guessing, no looking for hidden meanings. Since Maria's disappearance everything Lily thought she knew has been knocked off course – George Price openly glad Maria is gone, good people like Mrs Collins advising her to do nothing, say nothing. Edward himself, with his advances and retreats, his ardour and his silences. For a few minutes yesterday afternoon on the deck, with Max Campbell's broad arms around her, leaning her face against his jacket, she'd felt unburdened. Light. As if she could breathe again.

It hadn't been long. Lily had pulled away, mindful suddenly of where they were. Who they were.

'I don't really think it's any of your business whose company I keep,' she says now, and is rewarded with a momentary stab of satisfaction when she sees Edward colour, his skin flushing deep red under his light tan.

'You're right, Lily. I deserve that. But believe me when I say I'm only thinking about you. The Campbells aren't kind people, Lily. There's something missing in them.'

'Oh, I see. So I'm to keep away from Max because they're not nice people, but it's perfectly all right for you to moon around after Eliza, is it?'

'What on earth do you mean?'

'Oh, for goodness' sake, Edward. Be honest for once. You're a different person when you're around her. You can hardly speak. You're a nervous wreck. Just admit it.'

'No, Lily. It's not true.'

But she is already moving towards the door. She does not want to hear any more of his dissembling.

'Lily, wait!'

But she is gone. Striding down the deck. Tomorrow, she tells herself. Tomorrow they will arrive in Sydney and her new life will begin, and all this – the voyage, Edward, Maria, George, the Campbells – will be in the past. And when she thinks back to it, it will seem like a dream that cannot possibly have happened. She will work as a maid or a housekeeper and it will not seem credible that she could have kept company with lawyers and socialites and film actors and radio presenters. George Price was right about that, at least: she will go back to her world and they will go back to theirs and life will be once again divided into its correct boxes.

But first there is this last day to get through, culminating in another gala dinner-dance tonight. At first there was some talk of it being cancelled in the light of the news of the German invasion of Poland, but the captain decreed, perhaps with one eye towards his combustible mix of passenger nationalities, that as there had been no formal declaration of war everything should continue as planned.

It is the last thing Lily feels like doing at the moment – getting dressed up and celebrating. However, already preparations are under way. The stewards are busy decorating the dance area with flowers and bunting and all over the ship small farewell parties are being arranged. Most passengers have started packing, as the ship will be arriving in Sydney early the next morning, and there's a bustle of people going back and forth between their cabins and the deck.

'Don't forget to check the laundry,' she hears a woman's voice call down the stairwell. 'We wouldn't want to leave anything behind.'

Outside the door of her cabin Lily takes a deep breath. She has been avoiding Ida for the last two days but now she cannot put her packing off any longer. She is hoping to find the place empty, or at least for Audrey to be there. But to her dismay, there is just Ida, sitting on her bunk, her back upright, so the top of her scraped-back hair brushes the woven slats of Audrey's bed above. She has her suitcase open on the mattress next to her, a battered-looking affair, and in spite of herself, Lily can't help feeling a wrench of pity when she sees how few clothes Ida has brought along for her new life.

Wordlessly, Lily slides her trunk out from under the unused bottom bunk and starts moving around the cabin, collecting her things. Who could have imagined she would have amassed so many? As well as her clothes, there are combs, lotions, little mementos of her visits ashore. Lily remembers now the gold silk scarf

Max Campbell bought for her in Gibraltar and feels a surge of outrage against Edward. Why bother picking it up? It makes her embarrassed how pleased she had been to think of him keeping it hidden in his cabin, handling it every now and then to bury his nose in it, hoping to find some lingering essence of her scent. If Edward has ever felt that way about her, the sentiment is so hidden among his other conflicting thoughts and feelings that it might just as well not exist at all.

She opens a drawer and takes out a small stack of cardigans and begins refolding them in order to pack them into the trunk, conscious all the time of Ida's eyes boring into her back. Twice, Ida clears her throat as if to speak, but says nothing. Finally:

'I never wanted anything bad to happen to your friend.'

Lily says nothing, just carries on refolding the cardigans and placing them into the trunk.

'It's not easy,' Ida tries again. 'It's not easy having nobody but yourself to rely on. No family. No husband. My John has been dead these past eleven years and I still think of him every day. I am not good at making friends. You are lucky you have that gift. I do not. I had thought . . . I had hoped . . . that we might . . . you and I . . .'

Behind Lily's back she clears her throat again.

'Then to have you favour her instead! That Miss Katz. It felt personal. I know it shouldn't have but there you are, it did. But I never wanted any harm to come to her. It's important that, what-ever else you might think of me, you at least know that much.'

Now, at last, Lily turns to face her.

'But you still won't change your witness statement?'

Ida shakes her head.

'What's done is done. I can't jeopardize my finding work. Anyway, that young man will be carted off by his family. There's something not right about him, not right in the head. And now, with the news about Germany, the captain has other things to think about.'

Lily slowly turns back to her packing and after a few minutes she hears the cabin door open and then close again as Ida lets herself out.

Before she has time to reflect on what Ida said there is a knock and, without waiting for a response, Eliza barges in.

'Hide me, Lily! I am on the run from that odious couple.'

In spite of herself, Lily smiles as Eliza makes a poor show of trying to conceal herself behind Audrey's dressing gown, still hanging on the back of the door.

'Alan Morgan is rather too much,' she agrees. 'But Cleo is totally harmless, surely?'

Eliza tosses her head in a dismissive gesture.

'I suppose so, but she makes me feel so anxious. I'm constantly worrying that a gust of wind will carry her off somewhere. I had to tell Max not to blow cigarette smoke around her in case it swept her overboard.'

Eliza's gaze alights on Lily's trunk.

'How organized you are, doing your packing now. I shall wait until the last minute, as usual, or else get the cabin steward to do it. Oh, I'm so relieved this interminable journey is over, aren't you?'

When Lily fails to respond, Eliza's hand flies to her mouth.

'Oh, I'm such an idiot. Ignore me. Of course you're not looking forward to it finishing when you have to go to work in some dreary house for some dreary family. But you know, we'll still see each other all the time. You'll get days off, won't you?'

Lily nods, although, of course, she knows as well as Eliza that it will never happen.

'I suppose you have a full programme of social events once you get to Sydney?' Lily asks, going back to her folding.

'Yes. I think so.' Eliza sighs. 'Oh, but Lily, what if nothing changes?'

Her voice sounds suddenly flat as if it has had all the air taken out of it.

'What do you mean?'

'I keep thinking, *The next party . . . The next city . . . The next love affair . . .* Waiting for the one that changes everything. But what if this is all there is? What if *I* am all there is?'

Lily turns sharply to see Eliza slumped, dejected, on Ida's bunk.

'Anyway,' says Eliza, sitting up straighter and back to her familiar amused drawl, 'let's not talk about that when we have more important things to discuss, like what you're going to wear to the ball this evening. I hope you're intending to wear the peach. It looks so divine on you.'

She is pointing to her peach silk dress, which Lily has left draped over the foot of her bed, ready to give back.

'I don't think so,' says Lily. 'I have a dress that will do just as well.'

'I won't hear of it. The peach was made for you.'

'I said no.'

Lily's words, uttered more vehemently than she'd intended, ricochet off the walls like gun pellets, taking them both by surprise.

'I'm sorry. I didn't mean to sound ungrateful. I just think it's time for me to start remembering who I am.'

Eliza is gazing at her intently with those strange, violet eyes and Lily has the curious notion that she is seeing her for the very first time. Then she gets to her feet and gathers up the peach gown.

'Of course. You're perfectly right, as always. You shall wear what you see fit, and you will look a picture in it, whatever it is. Just one thing, Lily.'

She has headed towards the door and now has one hand on the handle, hesitating as if considering carefully what she is about to say.

'Don't pay too much attention to Max this evening, will you? I know he can be very charming when he chooses to be, but he collects vulnerable people like other men collect butterflies.'

She says 'vulnerable people', but Lily knows she means 'vulnerable women'. Women like her.

'But the thing you have to remember is,' Eliza continues, 'he doesn't know how to stop being in love with me. That's his tragedy.' She pauses before adding softly: 'And mine.'

30

WHEN LILY LOOKS into the bathroom mirror she cannot believe it is her own face looking back at her. In her head she feels as if she has aged ten years during the voyage, yet the woman in the mirror is fresh-faced, her golden skin matching perfectly her amber eyes and sun-lightened copper hair. How impossible it seems that the last five weeks have not been written somewhere upon her skin.

The young bathroom steward is loitering outside. Emboldened by the fact of it being the last full day, he says: 'I'll be glad to get ashore for a while, but I'll be sorry not to see your face any more, miss.'

All over the ship there is the strangest sense of being in limbo between what is real and what isn't, between the departure and the arrival, between the threat of war and whatever comes next. Perhaps that's why Lily smiles and tells him, sincerely, that she is sorry too, knowing that in reality she is unlikely to think of him but if she does it will be with a fondness that far outstrips his role in her life. That's just how it is on board now, little things magnified out of all proportion, huge things, like Maria's disappearance, reduced to nothing, just a whisper on the breeze, the faint sigh of the sea.

She goes down to dinner wearing the cream silk dress that Max Campbell spilled wine over all those weeks ago and says a polite but distant hello to Edward, trying not to notice how handsome he looks in his black tails and white bow tie. I don't love him, she reminds herself. But already her conviction is wavering. He orders a bottle of wine from the waiter and pours her a glass without asking. 'Peace offering?' he whispers as he pushes it towards her.

She can see he is trying to be casual and upbeat, but his hands are shaking as they pour the wine and, once, when he feels himself unobserved, he slumps forward in his chair with his eyes closed and his fingers splayed out on his forehead.

Clara Mills declares herself too nervous to eat. 'I can't sleep for worrying about what we are heading into,' she tells Lily. 'The Australians we have met have been such rough sorts. And Peggy and I will be so much alone.'

The prospect of being sequestered away with her mama seems to do little to improve the spirits of her daughter who pops another chunk of bread roll in her mouth and chews it in sulky silence. She has put on weight since the voyage began, Lily notices again, and feels a wave of sympathy. It's not easy being fifteen and hauled away from everything you know.

She senses George Price's arrival at the table but refuses to look up, not that he seems bothered by it. He has brought a book, some sort of political manifesto, it looks like, and proceeds to read it all the way through dinner, to the distress of Clara Mills, who confides in Lily that it presages the sort of boorish behaviour they can expect in Australia.

The dinner itself is much grander than usual and there are special menus for all the passengers, which are passed around to be signed and kept as souvenirs. Edward lingers for quite a while over signing hers, and Lily feels herself blush when she sees he has written, 'Ever yours, Edward.'

Helena is wearing her dove-grey dress – the one that matches her eyes. Though she joins in with the flurry of excitement over the signing of the menus, she seems generally subdued and, later, when a young man at the next table gets to his feet to announce he has just proposed to the sweetheart he met on the first night of the voyage, and she has said yes, Helena's cheeks stream with tears.

After the food is cleared away one of Ian's Aussie mates sits down at the dining-room piano and all the Australians sing 'Waltzing Matilda', followed by 'Along the Road to Gundagai'. Then one of the British passengers plays the opening chords for 'In the Shade of the Old Apple Tree' and Clara Mills is horrified when some young wag changes the second line to 'There's a hole in your drawers I can see.'

Then they go out on to the deck while the tables are stacked up to make an indoor dance area for those passengers who consider it too cold to be outside. All around, there are knots of people exchanging addresses and hugs and standing in stiff groups to have photographs taken.

'I still have Eliza's fox wrap,' Helena tells Lily. 'I must give it back to her later in the evening. Will she be coming downstairs?'

Lily shrugs in a *Your guess is as good as mine* way, but deep down she knows they have not seen the last of the Campbells and, when she thinks about yesterday and Max's arms around her, she can't help feeling glad about that.

Ian arrives with his Australian friends, who are brimming with excitement at being so near to home.

Though the temperature is cool, the night is relatively still and the sky reminds Lily suddenly of a black velvet handbag Robert's mother used to have, studded with tiny silver beads. The sagging smile of a half-moon hangs heavy in the sky.

'How are you finding your last night? I expect you're anxious to arrive.' George Price is standing too close to her in that way he has, and Lily automatically takes a step back.

'I will be in New Zealand, as you know, but I don't think it is that difficult to get from there to Sydney,' he continues. 'We could still see each other.'

Now George sees something in Lily's face that even he, through his thick impenetrability, must recognize as disbelief because he changes tack.

'Look, I'm sorry about all that bad business. But it's over now and, obviously, the situation with Germany changes everything anyway. People like you and I must stick together, Miss Shepherd. Lily. We do not know for sure who else can be trusted. That's why I'm willing to overlook the fact that you'll be working in service.' Before Lily can process what he means, he presses on: 'My father won't like it but I am prepared for that. I'm an adult, after all.'

Without warning he lunges forward and presses himself up against her.

'How dare you!' She recoils in disgust and her voice is shaking. 'I want nothing to do with you. Nothing. I wouldn't see you again if you were the last man on earth.'

Now he is staring at her, his eyes bulging, lips glistening in the moonlight.

'Oh, I see. I see it perfectly now. You think you can do better for yourself than me. You've got your eye on one of the others, haven't you? Edward Fletcher, or maybe Max Campbell. You really think either of those is going to look twice at you once we're docked in Sydney? When Edward Fletcher qualifies as a lawyer, do you think he's going to introduce you to society: "This is my wife, Lily. She's a ladies' maid"?'

Lily turns on her heel and makes her way back to her group, whose numbers have been swelled by the arrival of the Campbells. Still reeling from the scene with George, and only just fighting back tears, she is dismayed to see that Alan and Cleo Morgan are also here, looking around the tourist deck as if they are visitors in a zoo.

'At last you've come,' says Max. 'Now the party can begin.'

He is louder than usual and Lily sees two empty bottles of champagne on the table next to him. He opens a new bottle and pours

Lily a glass that, in spite of having already drunk wine at dinner, she downs in two or three gulps to calm her still-racing nerves. It is instantly replenished.

Eliza dazzles in a full-length silver dress with spiderweb-slender straps over her shoulders and a back that plunges deeply enough to reveal the two dimples at the base of her spine, just visible beneath the bottom edge of her white mink wrap. Her black hair is pulled back with silver combs, and diamonds sparkle at her earlobes. Now that Lily is viewing her through the eyes of a soon-to-be maid, Eliza looks as unreachable as one of the stars in the night sky behind her.

'Why do they have to come here? Why can't they let us have this one night on our own?'

Edward's voice in her ear sounds strangled, as if he is choking on something, and Lily looks at him sharply. He is always tense around the Campbells, but tonight he is clearly struggling to keep his feelings under control. Suddenly, Lily can bear it no longer.

'Who will dance with me?' she says, turning to face the group, made bold by the alcohol and the knowledge that, it being the last night, she has nothing more to lose. She sees Edward open his mouth, but before he can speak Max has stepped forward, as she knew – and hoped – he would.

'What hot-blooded man could resist?' he says, leading her away to the dancefloor, where the band has just started playing 'Begin the Beguine'.

He seizes her right hand and pulls her to him, holding her far too close, but for once Lily does not care. Let them all stare. Let them disapprove. These are the same people who didn't bother to get to know Maria, who hardly registered her death. The champagne has made her light-headed and giddy and it feels good to have Max Campbell's arm around her waist, tight as a belt, holding her up.

'Edward is looking cross,' she says to Max, and giggles as she hears herself slurring the last word.

'Poor Edward,' he says, glancing over and then pulling her even more tightly towards him. 'Poor, doomed Edward.'

She is just about to ask him to explain when the band launches into a jitterbug, and she and Max are soon helpless with shrill laughter trying to keep up. On the other side of the dancefloor she sees Eliza staring in their direction over Alan Morgan's shoulder.

'Your wife warned me about you,' she says to Max, who seems to find this very amusing.

'Then you only have yourself to blame,' he says.

They dance some more and then stagger off to join the others. More champagne is bought. Nearby, a group of exuberant young Aussies are tossing multicoloured streamers into the air. Lily recognizes Ian's two colleagues with their arms around each other's shoulders, singing something which makes the others roar with laughter. They're going home, she thinks. And the idea is somehow shocking, that this foreign, unknowable place must, to them, represent all that is familiar.

She is surprised to notice Ian also among the group, the oldest by far, and alone in not joining in the celebrations. She looks for Helena, wondering why Ian isn't taking the opportunity to spend this last night with her, and finds her standing miserably next to Cleo Morgan. The young actress is wearing a lined cloak over her satin dress and clutches it tightly around her throat, as if at any moment someone might attempt to rip it from her. Her doe-like eyes dart around, on guard against imminent attack.

Meanwhile, her husband is watching the raucous Australians with a look of aloof contempt, and Edward and Eliza are deep in intense conversation. Edward seems agitated, unable to keep his fingers from combing obsessively through his hair, and Eliza puts a hand on his arm as if to still him.

325

But now Max is taking her champagne flute from her hand and leading her once again to the dancefloor and she is drunker than she has ever been in her life, but at the same time she is glad because she no longer has to think about George Price or Maria or the way Edward Fletcher has chipped away a little bit of her heart so she does not think it will ever be quite whole again. Nor does she have to think about Eliza and the sadness under the surface of her, like when you scratch off shiny gold leaf to reveal tin lurking beneath.

The dancefloor is packed with people intent on sucking the last drop of pleasure out of their voyage. Tomorrow, anything might happen. They might be at war. But tonight they will dance and drink and laugh and tell each other confidences, secure in the knowledge that they will never see each other again.

And in the midst of all this clamour and excitement and noise and movement Max Campbell holds Lily so tight she feels she cannot breathe, and yet she likes being held like that, likes being squeezed so hard she feels somehow outside of herself; someone else for a while. And he murmurs things in her ear with his hot, alcohol-soaked breath, and she wants him to keep doing it because she feels herself melting under the heat of him and that's fine by her.

They are out of sight of the others now, packed in by a scrum of bodies, and Max is pressing closer and closer to her, his moustache grazing her cheek. And now he is leading her through the crowd to the far end of the dancefloor, away from the others, and then they are through the bodies and out the other end, where the deck stretches away into the darkness.

Lily shivers in the sudden cold and, instantly, Max's arm is around her like a heavy coat she can warm herself inside. And he is still murmuring in her ear. 'We are so good together, Lily. Let me make you happy. Just for this evening. Let me give you something to remember while you're doing whatever ghastly job you get in

Sydney. You're so lovely, Lily. You deserve to feel good. Please let me make you feel good.'

His words are like a warm bath she wants to submerge herself in.

They are at the furthest end of the ship, where the lifeboats are – black shapes, hunkering in the darkness. Lily knows what goes on here, has seen couples emerging, clothing awry. Still, she doesn't resist when he guides her to the furthest boat, laughing as they stumble over a coiled rope. And when he raises up the tarpaulin she steps inside the boat as if she's just sitting down to dinner. She lets her body tell her what it wants – to let go, to feel enfolded, to feel desired and wanted and, just for this moment in time, loved.

The tarpaulin is too low to allow sitting, so Max takes off his jacket and spreads it out on the floor of the boat and then, still giggling, he and Lily lie down, his arms around her, his words in her ear, and she feels that liberating sense of being free from thoughts and doubts and moral strictures. 'Lovely Lily,' he whispers. 'You're so good and so calming and kind, and you make me want to be better.' And all the time his hands roving over her body, his kisses on her mouth, his moustache scratching her cheek.

She thinks she hears a noise nearby but she ignores it. This is her chance. This and only this. To know what other people know, to do what other people do.

Now his hand is under her dress, that cream silk that scandalized her mother when she saw it, and oh, now she has let Mam into her mind and she tries to get her out but she's there in the very corner, in her best cloth hat. And Max's hand has reached the top of her leg where her suspender belt meets her knickers and he is pushing his way past, yanking them aside, just as Robert tried to do. And now it's not just Mam who's in her head but Mags also. Little Mags with her heart-shaped face and her big, round handwriting so like a child's.

'If you won't do it, I'll find someone who will,' Robert had told Lily after she shoved him away from her that last time. Mags didn't stand a chance.

'I didn't want to, Lil. I knew he'd broken your heart, but I didn't know I was allowed to say no,' she'd sobbed afterwards, when she came to Lily to tell her about the baby. 'There was never a chance to say it. He never asked. Just did.'

Max is groaning in her ear.

'So beautiful,' he murmurs, his fingers going deeper.

It was Lily who'd asked around, made the arrangements. Robert had given her the money, on condition his name was never mentioned. There'd been that horrible last conversation with him where he had been unable to meet her eyes, but as he'd handed over the greasy-looking notes he'd tried to take her hand. 'It was always you I wanted, Lil. She didn't mean anything to me.' That's when Lily had finally seen him for who he was – a selfish opportunist with a hollow space at his core. And when Lily and Mags had gone to that woman's house Lily had known, just by looking at the woman's disappointment-hardened face, and the sickly green carpet and the unloved back room with no furniture, just a table in the middle. She'd known it could only end badly. And yet she'd let Mags lie down on the table. Let the woman do what she did. Now she questions her own motives. Could she have been wanting to punish Mags? She doesn't believe it. *Will* not believe it. Always knew Mags to have been, if not coerced, then at least overwhelmed. So why hadn't she stopped it?

'Should there be so much blood?' she'd asked the woman.

'It's what happens,' the woman snapped. 'Babies aren't dollies – you girls need to learn that. They're made from blood and tissue, just like you.'

'Let me in,' says Max, his voice thick with wanting, his fingers fumbling at his own clothes.

But now Lily is back in that room and looking at all the blood, and even the woman has stopped saying it's normal. And it's everywhere. On the walls. On the carpet.

'Fuck,' the woman had said, which shocked Lily almost as much as the blood. 'She's haemorrhaging.'

And Mags so small and scared on that table. *Am I going to die, Lil?* Looking only at Lily's face, and Lily holding her hand and saying, 'No, of course not,' while all the time the blood kept on coming out, thick and visceral and sticky.

'You'll have to take her to the hospital,' the woman said. 'She can't stay here.' But it was too late. All too late.

And still Max's hand is grappling with his clothes.

'No,' Lily says, coming suddenly back into herself. But he is big. Immovable.

'Hush, sweetheart, it'll be fine. You'll enjoy it.'

'No, really.' She is trying to push him aside. But it is like pushing aside a boulder, or the ship itself.

Panic courses through her, but she knows she cannot change anything, knows it is going to happen and it is her fault, but just as she tenses herself, preparing for the assault, there is a rustling noise and then a man's voice: 'In here'; and then a different man, closer, saying, 'Here? But why . . .' And then the tarpaulin lifts and a bright light is shining into her eyes, blinding her.

And behind the light is Edward.

31

Something acidic rises up into Lily's mouth and she sits bolt upright, straightening her clothes, her heart hammering in her chest. Shock has turned her suddenly sober and she sees everything only too clearly – her and Max Campbell, a married man and a soon-to-be maid. How commonplace. How tawdry.

The light is coming from a torch which is being held by a second man, and only when he lowers it slightly to the ground so it is no longer so blinding does she recognize him as George Price.

'Now do you see what she really is?' George says wetly, as Lily scrambles out of the wretched boat. 'I've done you a service.'

And he marches off back down the deck, taking his torch with him.

For a second no one speaks, and they listen to the thud of George's footsteps receding down the deck, heading towards the far-off sound of the bandleader crooning 'Heart and Soul'.

Once Lily's eyes have grown accustomed to the lack of light, she can make out Edward's pale face, clammy in the moonlight, and his dark, staring eyes.

'He told me you wanted to see me,' he says to her, and his voice is hoarse and quite unlike normal. 'He never said . . . I'd never have . . .'

Behind her, she hears Max getting leisurely to his feet, smoothing down his clothes.

'No hard feelings, old chap,' he says to Edward, who recoils as if he's been struck. There's something deeply unsettling about the way Edward stares at Max, his eyes black holes that seem to suck the air from around them until Lily is struggling to breathe.

'No hard feelings?' Edward's voice, still broken and strange, vibrates in the darkness. 'You dare to say that?'

Something gives inside Lily as she recognizes the tremble of passion in his voice. *He must really love her.*

'I'm sorry,' she says, her words stumbling over the sob that is caught, like a bone, in her throat. 'Edward. I'm sorry. I didn't know you felt anything for me, or I would never have . . . I wouldn't . . .'

Edward doesn't look at her, and behind her Max seems only mildly inconvenienced.

'Don't upset yourself, there's a good chap,' he tells Edward now, and there is a hint of a smile in his voice. 'You don't want to end up in the loony bin again.'

Lily gasps, unable to believe the casual cruelty of Max's words. To make fun of Edward having been ill, to compare the sanatorium to an asylum.

Edward's head is held rigid. His wild eyes are fixed on Max as if caught there by some kind of force. She tries again:

'Edward, I want you to know that nothing happened . . .'

Edward turns to look at her, but instantly she wishes he hadn't because it is a look filled with such anguish, such desolation, she cannot bear it. She puts out a hand to touch him but he jerks back, out of her reach, and then is gone, hurrying away from them along the deck, a lone figure briefly silhouetted against the stars.

'Lily.' Max puts his fingers on her neck and she slaps them away as if his touch burns.

'Woah!' He raises both hands in mock-surrender. 'Don't worry. Edward won't tell anyone, and no one will believe a word the other fellow says. Anyway, your honour is still intact. More's the pity.'

He is smiling. As if it's been a game and he's inviting her to share in the joke.

'I'm going back to my cabin,' she says thickly.

'Don't be a dolt. If you disappear, everyone will know something has happened. We have to go back and act as if everything is normal. They probably haven't even noticed we're not there.'

Lily doesn't believe him, but neither can she face going to the cabin, probably to find Ida already in residence, knowing that the next time she opens the door they'll be in Sydney, and all of this will be over, and there will be no chance to make it right, no chance to explain.

It is agreed that Max will join the others straight away and Lily will go first to the ladies' powder room before following on. When she arrives there and looks at herself in the mirror she sees she has a pink, raised rash by the side of her mouth where Max's moustache rubbed against her skin, and she douses it angrily with water, trying to make it disappear.

'Are you feeling better now?' asks Helena when Lily finally rejoins the group. 'Max said you had a dizzy spell. You do look a bit peaky.'

'I'm much better now,' Lily manages. 'It was good of Max to stay with me.'

'Oh, that's Max all over,' Eliza says. 'Such a very, very *good* man.' She gives Lily a long, appraising stare and Lily feels herself shrinking from it.

Helena is agitated. She keeps darting glances over to where Ian stands, chatting with his clearly inebriated compatriots. Lily does not know what has passed between the two of them but she guesses Ian has asked if he can see her when they get to Sydney and, in deference to their tyrannical father, who, even from this distance, seems to wield a strange power, she has refused.

'Have you seen Edward?' Helena asks now, turning her hollow

eyes to Lily. 'I thought he was in the bar, but he has been gone so long.'

Lily's heart constricts at the mention of his name.

Now Helena is staring at something behind Lily's shoulder.

'How very curious,' she says, in a new, wondering tone. 'I have the exact same winter suit that woman is wearing. And that brooch.'

Lily turns to see an unfamiliar woman walking towards them from the direction of the staircase, wearing a dark green suit and a matching hat with a veil. She carries a green pocketbook and has on crisp, white gloves, as if she is going on a journey rather than attending a dance. Pinned to her chest is a brooch in the shape of a bird.

Lily turns back to Helena to question her further but is silenced by the ghastly expression on her friend's face.

'No!' Helena cries out as if she has been hurt, and Lily reaches out just in time to catch her as she staggers.

'What's wrong?'

But she might as well not have spoken, for the entire focus of Helena's attention is on the strange woman, who is close enough now for Lily to see something of her features under that veil.

As her brain struggles to process what she is seeing, there comes a sharp intake of breath from either Max or Eliza, who are clearly one step ahead of her.

The woman is Edward.

'Hello,' he says, joining their group, as if it is the most natural thing in the world. His mouth is mapped out with deep plum lipstick, and his normally unruly dark hair is pinned neatly back beneath the hat, which Lily now recognizes as the one Edward borrowed from Eliza the evening of the fancy-dress ball. Looking down, she sees his feet are crammed into a pair of green shoes she remembers Helena wearing earlier in the voyage.

'I think you misunderstood the dress code,' Eliza says smoothly. 'Fancy dress was last week.'

'Yes, run along and get changed, there's a good chap,' says Max, and it seems to Lily that, though his smile has grown wider, the rest of him has become exceedingly tight. Tense. The hand that holds his Scotch trembles so the ice makes a clinking sound against the glass.

Edward fixes Max with heavily kohled eyes.

'Don't you like it, Max? Don't you like me like this? Funny how you liked it well enough when we were in Cairo, and at the hotel in Colombo. Remember that?'

Now Lily remembers what she saw from the rickshaw. A pool of light from a hotel sign. Max standing with a woman in native costume. Nausea builds, horribly, from somewhere deep inside her.

'I think you've had too much to drink,' Max hisses, and Lily sees that the people around them, who hadn't seemed to notice Edward first arriving, are turning to see what the fuss is about.

'I thought you felt something,' Edward says to him, impassioned now. 'For me.'

'Oh, for God's sake, grow up, will you!' Max has lost patience. 'You must stop mistaking appetite for desire and desire for love. A starving man doesn't care what he eats. I love my wife. And if I can't have her, I'll take whatever is there. That was always the deal.'

In the part of her that isn't desperately trying to make sense of what is happening, Lily registers those words – 'I'll take whatever is there' – and she thinks she is going to be sick.

Eliza, whose eyes have been fixed on Edward all this while, as if they might burn tiny holes right through his skin, now turns to her husband.

'What have you done this time?' she hisses. Her voice is hard as bone.

But now something else is happening, something that causes Lily to push aside all thoughts of Eliza and of what happened between her and Max in the lifeboat and everything else that has gone before. Edward has opened the green pocketbook and taken out something long and slim that glints where the light catches it.

The pocketbook drops to the floor and Edward stands perfectly still, holding the paper knife he bought in Aden against his wrist, pushing down the top of the white glove so that the blade presses directly against his skin. A gasp goes up from the onlookers.

'What are you doing?' screams Helena. 'Edward, please. Help, someone. Stop him!'

'I'm sorry,' he tells her, switching his gaze towards his sister and away from Max Campbell. His shaking hand still holds the knife to his wrist but his voice is strangely calm. 'I've brought you only trouble. Maybe this way you can be free to lead your own life. But you know, Hels, I'm glad to have shown you, finally, who I am. And, after all, it's just me, isn't it? And these are just clothes. Not so dreadful, you see?'

Ian has rushed to Helena's side. 'Put the knife down,' he urges Edward in a low, controlled voice. 'Whatever has happened, it will all be forgotten. We're in Australia now. Everything is different.'

'Forgotten?' echoes Edward. 'My father will never forget.'

'But he's thousands of miles away. The other side of the world,' Ian continues. 'No one here knows you. Whatever you've done is behind you.'

Edward wavers, and Lily sees his eyes fill with tears, as if considering for the first time this possibility.

Helena joins in.

'Ian's right. No one knows us here. Life can begin again. We can put it all behind us – what happened in England, whatever happened on this voyage. Everything left behind.'

Edward moves the knife fractionally away from his wrist.

Inches away, Lily senses Eliza relax, as if she has been holding her breath, and step forward towards Edward.

'Just think,' she tells him, her voice dripping amused scorn. 'A whole new start. Perhaps you and my husband might set up home together in Sydney. You make such a handsome couple.'

It is too much for Max. 'Take that hat off,' he says furiously, lunging towards Edward. 'It belongs to my wife. You're not fit to wear it. You look ridiculous.'

Afterwards, Lily will wonder whether her mind has blocked out what happened next, or whether she genuinely did not catch the moment when Edward, seeing Max's hands coming towards his head, raised his own arms to protect himself, forgetting he still held the knife, so that the steel blade took the full force of Max's forward momentum, ending up buried in his chest up to the hilt.

She will remember only Cleo Morgan screaming and turning to see the actress's face sprayed with crimson drops, as if she had measles; Max's mouth rounding into a perfect 'O' of surprise. She will remember Edward himself, standing so perfectly still, and she will think suddenly, wildly, 'He has been turned to a pillar of salt.'

After that, everything speeds up, as if a projector is playing a film on the wrong setting. Max falls to the ground with a horrible cracking sound that will echo in Lily's head through the remaining years of her life. The blade is sticking straight up out from his ribcage, as if it has taken root and is growing there, and there's a neat red ring around it, spreading at a steady, leisurely pace. And now Eliza, with a sound that is not quite human, is on her knees beside him, pulling at the handle of the knife with both hands, trying to wrench it free. Something jolts into life in Lily.

'Don't!' she shouts, but it is too late. The knife is out and now blood is arcing into the air, graceful and delicate as a firework. Eliza tries to cover the wound with her hand.

'I love you!' she cries to her husband. 'I love only you.'

And Max's face still frozen in that look of surprise, as if stumbling across an old flame he has not seen for many years. Bubbles form in the corner of his mouth, turning to a pink froth like the Pink Lady cocktails they drank up in the first-class lounge in what is already seeming like a different lifetime.

The blood is pumping everywhere, despite Eliza's attempts to stop it, just as it had when Mags was on the abortionist's table. Eliza is covered in it, her silver dress made purple and sodden; blood drying on her forehead where she has wiped her hand across her face.

Ian snatches one of the white cloths off a nearby table and uses it to try to staunch the blood, but it is soon soaked through.

'Is he breathing?' Helena asks, her voice cracking. She is standing next to Edward, both of them seemingly frozen like statues.

Then, from Ian, a slight, barely perceptible shake of the head, followed by a ghastly scream, like a fox fighting in the night, as Eliza slumps over her lifeless husband. Her shoulder blades jut from the skin of her bent back like broken-off wings.

By the time the captain arrives on the scene someone has covered Max in a clean white tablecloth, and Eliza has been led away. Meanwhile, Edward has started shivering so violently it's as if his whole body is convulsing.

'Help him!' urges the paralysed Helena to the crowd of horrified onlookers, but nobody moves.

In the end it is Lily who snatches up the nearest thing she can find – the fur stole that Helena has brought to return to Eliza – and wraps it around Edward's shaking shoulders. She is still struggling to make sense of any of it. Max cannot be dead. Edward cannot be a murderer. Instead it must be the rest of the world that has somehow fallen out of kilter, slipping into make-believe. The fault will be found to lie elsewhere.

The captain doesn't know what to do with Edward. There have been onboard deaths before, of course. Killings, even. But nothing like this. No one like Edward.

'We will need to take her . . . him . . . into custody now.' He addresses himself to Lily, as if Edward himself could not possibly understand.

His words unlock Helena and she springs to her brother's side.

'No. Please,' she begs. 'It was a mistake. He didn't know what he was doing.' She grabs hold of Edward's arm, tugging on his sleeve. 'Tell him. Explain it was an accident.'

Edward rouses himself from whatever trance he has been in, his eyes focusing as if for the first time on the chaos he has wrought.

'I'm sorry, Hels,' he says, in a voice so soft Lily does not dare breathe out for fear of missing it. 'I tried. I really tried.'

His gaze turns to Lily, and she thinks that if it were possible to die from sadness, he surely would.

'Lily. Please. Forgive me. I have wronged you.'

But now the captain seems to have made up his mind how to proceed, and two stewards are despatched to Edward's side. The dumbstruck crowd parts to let them through, and when they arrive they stand stiffly at either of his shoulders with their arms by their sides, as if not wanting to touch him.

'Take him to my office,' the captain commands.

As they start to lead him away Helena moves as if to accompany them, but the captain uses his arm as a barrier to detain her.

'I'm afraid you must stay here, Miss Fletcher.' He turns to the watching passengers. 'I am deeply sorry that you have all had to witness such a distressing scene, particularly the ladies. May I suggest you all repair to the lounge, where the stewards will be able to bring you drinks while you wait for the purser to gather your statements.'

The stewards who are accompanying Edward steer him in the direction of the upper deck. As they pass the prone figure of Max, the cloth covering his face already polka-dotted with blood, Edward seems to sway and Lily takes an involuntary step towards him. *Please*, she urges the stewards silently, *please don't let him fall*, but Edward rights himself and they continue on their way.

When they are out of sight the air on deck seems unbearably

dense. Lily sees a movement in the corner of her eye and turns to find that Helena has slid to the ground. Instantly, Ian is crouching beside her, his arm around her shoulders, whispering in her ear.

'Help me lift her up,' he says to Lily. 'We must get her away from here.'

Supporting Helena between them, they start to head towards the cabins, but the purser intercepts them. As key witnesses they are forbidden to leave the scene, he says. Though, in the circumstances, he will allow them to sit separately from the rest of the passengers.

Lily tries to think through what these circumstances are to which the purser is referring, but they seem too preposterous for her logical mind to process. They are ushered into the library, where Helena is deposited in one of the leather armchairs. Lily takes the other, while Ian stands close to Helena's chair, as if bound to her by an invisible tether.

At first no one speaks, although after her ears readjust to the silence Lily can make out the other noises of the ship – the rumbling of the engine, the low buzz of conversation from the lounge. She hears a thudding sound, loud and insistent, which she only belatedly identifies as her own heart slamming against her ribcage.

'I owe you both an explanation,' says Helena at last. She has curled up on the chair with her feet under her, as if trying to make herself once more a small child, exempt from dealing with tragedy.

'There's no need,' says Ian. 'Whatever it is can wait until after this business – this awful business – is over.'

It will never be over, Lily thinks. But she does not say it.

'I want to tell you. There's nothing to hide any more. And if I don't speak, I feel I shall go mad.

'Edward did not have tuberculosis. And he was not in a sanatorium. At least, not that kind of sanatorium.

'He was always different from other boys, even as a child. Delicate. Dreamy. So sensitive to slights I seemed to spend my childhood trying to protect him. As a small boy, Edward loved to dress up in my clothes and Father would beat him terribly for it. Our father has a very short temper and Edward was always terrified of him.

'There were *things* that happened while Edward was growing up that made me concerned about him. He had very few friends, but occasionally he'd bring a boy home from school for the holidays and I could see that the friendship was not quite normal.'

'Not normal?' asks Ian.

'Too intense. Too close.'

A vivid pink stain spreads over Helena's pale face and Lily feels a sinking sense of dread.

'When he started at Cambridge I thought that might be the making of him. I thought perhaps he'd meet a nice girl at one of the other colleges. He always got on so much better with women. But instead he made friends with a group of men who were all actors and artists and dressed flamboyantly. My father forbade Edward to have anything to do with them, threatened to cut him off, but he didn't stop. And then, halfway through his third year, there was a terrible scandal.'

She stops abruptly and swallows.

'I'm sorry,' she says. 'I have never talked about this. It is too painful.'

'Then don't,' says Lily. Whatever Helena is about to say, she knows she does not want to hear it, knows she will not be the same person after she does.

'Poor Lily,' says Helena. 'I'm so terribly sorry, but it will all come out now and it's better for you that you should hear it from me.

'There was a boy, the son of a well-known politician. Edward spoke of him often and brought him to the house during those Christmas holidays, and I could see straight away that it was not a healthy friendship, that once again there was something overly intense about it.'

She takes a deep breath.

'They were discovered. In a hotel room in Cambridge.' Another deep breath. 'Edward was dressed as a woman.'

A metallic taste now in Lily's mouth, and she feels as if she might be sick. Robert once told her about a boy at his school who liked to wear women's clothes, taking any chance to be cast in a female role in the school play. Robert had told it to Lily as a funny story, to shock her. He'd used a specific word when talking about him, and Lily can still picture the expression of disgust on his face as he said it. *Deviant.*

'There was an awful scandal, though the other boy's father managed to keep it out of the papers. My family moved to a different area of the country where no one knew us, and our father had Edward committed to a mental institution. It was that or jail. He has been there off and on for the last five years, undergoing awful, painful treatments. Insulin injections that brought on seizures followed by awful dead sleeps, and just recently experimental electroshocks to his brain that left him with headaches that lasted days. Finally, my mother stepped in and persuaded Father that it would be better to send him away, somewhere no one knew about what had happened. They decided on Australia.'

'And you were sent as his nursemaid?' says Ian. He sounds bitter.

'Or jailer,' Helena replies. 'I didn't mind. After the scandal we moved from Herefordshire and tried to start again on the south coast where no one knew us, but eventually rumours reached even there and Henry, my fiancé, broke off our engagement. He said he was very sorry, but he couldn't marry into such a family. He was sure I understood. At least news hadn't reached the school where I worked, but then one of the parents heard, and the head teacher felt my presence was bringing the school into disrepute, and after that I didn't much care about leaving England. I had nothing left.'

'You must have thought me such a fool,' Lily bursts out. 'You could see how I felt about Edward. Was it a joke to the two of you?'

'No!' Helena looks aghast. 'Lily. You mustn't think that. Edward liked you so much. Loved you, even. He wanted so badly to be normal, to make our father proud. I think he convinced himself it could work with you. And I was so desperate to believe him.'

Lily remembers now how Helena had insisted that her parents would not disapprove of a match between Edward and her. Of course. If Lily was the only thing standing between the Fletchers and more scandal, no wonder she would be accepted with open arms. She remembers also her silk scarf and how she'd imagined him keeping it because it smelled of her. Now it occurs to her he probably kept it to wear himself, when he was alone in his cabin. How silly she has been.

'But Max?' Ian says, and Lily remembers with a sickening jolt the body lying on the deck outside.

'The Campbells are libertines,' says Helena bitterly. 'They played with all of us as if we were toys whose only function was to keep them entertained during the voyage. Max wanted you, of course, Lily, but if he couldn't have you, he'd settle for Edward. And, like a fool, Edward fashioned that into a love story.'

Now it all slots into place. All those times Lily had thought Edward was staring at Eliza it was actually her husband he couldn't tear his eyes away from. When he'd seemed to affect Eliza's manner-isms and style of speech it wasn't in homage to her but in the hope that emulating Max's wife might bring him closer to him. And the times he'd kissed Lily had been nothing but a knee-jerk reaction against his own shame at whatever he'd just done with Max.

'I told him. I kept telling him,' Helena goes on. 'Oh, my God, what will happen to him now?'

She buries her head in her hands, shoulders shaking as she sobs.

Lily expects Ian to comfort her, but instead he is chewing on his bottom lip, as if deep in thought.

'Is this why you've been pushing me away?' he asks now. 'Because you thought I'd be disgusted, like your idiot fiancé Henry?'

Helena nods, her head still bent.

'I knew it would come out eventually, and I couldn't have borne another rejection.'

'Do you really think that little of me? For goodness' sake, woman, I love you. Don't you know that?'

And now, finally, Helena looks up, her grey eyes wide open to him, and despite her misery, Lily sees in her expression a faint spark of hope as Ian sinks to his knees on the floor next to her and gathers her into his arms, kissing her face over and over again.

The moment is so exquisitely, painfully tender that Lily has to look away.

32

4 September 1939

HOW LILY MANAGES to sleep that terrible last night, she has no idea. But sleep she does. She is woken by Audrey shaking her arm, and still half asleep lurches to a sitting position.

The events of the previous evening come back to her one after the other, as if she is being repeatedly struck. Her and Max in the lifeboat. Edward raising the tarpaulin. *No hard feelings, old chap.* The woman in green walking towards her and her suddenly realizing who it was. The knife. Max. *Oh, Max.* Eliza's screams. Then the library, and Helena's shocking revelations, followed by the purser, with all his endless questions. And, finally, back to the cabin.

How is it possible for one night to change absolutely everything?

'What time is it?' she asks Audrey.

'Six a.m. We're arriving in Sydney. Everyone is up on deck, watching. But if you're too tired, after everything that happened –'

'No.' Lily has already swung her legs over the side of the bunk. 'I want to see.'

Now she is awake she cannot bear the idea of lying in her bed, reliving last night on a never-ending film reel.

'Ida is already up there,' says Audrey. 'She didn't want me to wake you.'

344

'I expect she can't wait to gloat, now all her warnings have come true.' Lily is shocked at her own bitterness.

'Honest, Lily, she didn't seem to be crowing at all.'

Up on deck it is that strange hour just before dawn where the world seems suspended between night and day, between dreams and reality. All along the railing are little knots of passengers, either standing or settled into deckchairs, watching the land that's just visible through the grainy grey pre-dawn haze. As she and Audrey and Audrey's friend Annie take up a position along the rail, Lily is conscious of the stares of the other passengers, the whispers that follow her: *She was there. She's mixed up in it all.*

The rising sun casts a yellow glow over the surface of the sea and burns away the haze, revealing the shoreline. An Aussie standing nearby starts to point out the individual beaches as they pass – Clovelly, Coogee, Bronte, Tamarama. He sounds each name out as proudly as if he has made them himself. They pass Bondi Beach, close enough to see the surf thundering on to the sand.

This is my new home, Lily tells herself. But the words mean nothing.

Up ahead an imposing headland made from looming cliffs juts into the sea, topped by a lighthouse, gaily painted in red-and-white stripes like a bathing hut. The sun lights it up like a flaming torch.

'The South Head,' says the knowledgeable Aussie. 'And that one in the distance is the North Head. Welcome to Sydney, folks!'

The ship swings past South Head, keeping close to the land. A mile away, North Head marks the other gatepost into Sydney Harbour. In spite of herself and the horrors of last night, Lily can't help feeling awed by the sheer scale of the scenery, all the small bays and inlets with their pockets of golden sand, the houses nestling between the trees, their tiled roofs sparkling where they catch the newly risen sun.

'Can you believe it?' says Audrey. 'Can you believe we're here?'

The Aussie is now recounting the names of these new, smaller beaches. Watson's Bay, Parsley Bay, Nielsen Park. Already, through the plethora of yachts and dinghies and fishing boats that dot the surface of the sea, Lily can make out the bobbing heads of early morning swimmers. Though it is only just September, still early spring in Australia, the temperature is already such that Lily is quite warm enough in just a thin cardigan.

A small tug comes alongside the ship.

'The *Captain Cook*,' explains their Aussie guide. 'It escorts all the big liners into the docks.'

Lily gazes, transfixed, at the magnificent Harbour Bridge, still less than a decade old, spanning out across the water up ahead.

Suddenly, Lily thinks of Eliza. In all the nightmare of Edward and Helena she has been able to push thoughts of Max, lying dead on the floor, to the furthest corner of her mind. But now they come flooding back, one after the other. His voice sounds in her ear. 'Lovely Lily,' he says, in that drawling, amused baritone. She remembers that scream as Eliza bent over him, and how she'd said, 'I love only you.'

'I must find Eliza,' Lily tells Audrey, and from the way Audrey looks at Annie she can tell they have talked about last night's events between them and agreed not to mention them.

Lily pushes past the passengers behind them and makes her way up to the first-class deck. With most people's attention firmly fixed on the shoreline, she manages to slip down to the cabin level unnoticed. Outside Eliza's cabin, she hesitates, her nerve failing her.

'Yes?'

Lily is so surprised when Eliza answers her tentative knock that she takes a second to respond.

'It's me. Lily.'

When Lily pushes open the door the cabin is in semi-darkness with the blind pulled down over the window and the sun reduced to a hazy glow behind it. Lily blinks in the sudden gloom. As her eyes adjust she sees that Eliza is lying on the bed, wearing a silk dressing gown tightly belted around her waist. Her hair is loose and she has wiped off her make-up but, even in the dim light, Lily can see a streak of dark, dried blood she has missed up near her hairline.

Drawing closer, she notices an open bottle of pills on the bedside table.

'The doctor has given me something to sedate me,' says Eliza in a slow, flat voice.

Lily's mouth feels dry as sandpaper.

'I'm so sorry,' she says, but to her own ears her voice sounds like an actor reciting a line.

'People will think me very careless,' Eliza says. 'First I lose a daughter and now a husband.'

Lily doesn't want to look at the dark smudge on Eliza's forehead, so her eyes scan the room, alighting on a jacket hanging on the back of the cabin door that she recognizes as Max's.

Lily starts to cry, at the knowledge that he will never again wear that jacket, or use that comb on his dressing table, or light a cigarette from that silver case on the bedside table.

Max is dead. And so is Maria. Both of them reduced to nothing, while she carries on. Lily's mind cannot accept it.

'I need to tell you what I did,' she says. 'You see, it's all my fault. If I hadn't gone with Max —'

'Enough.'

Eliza has raised her hands to her ears.

'I don't want to hear. Max made his own choices, Lily. At least allow him that.'

They are silent, thinking of where Max's choices have led.

'What will you do now?' Lily asks eventually. 'Will you go home to London, or perhaps America?'

'Home?' For the first time, Eliza looks almost animated. 'Haven't you heard? Chamberlain has officially declared war. None of us will be going home. I'm afraid we're rather stuck here.'

'Oh!'

Lily claps her hand to her mouth. Though it's not unexpected, the news is nevertheless shocking. Poor Frank. And her poor parents. She thinks of the thousands of miles of ocean that separate her from her family.

Eliza closes her eyes, looking at once both younger than usual and, paradoxically, much older. Still reeling from the shocking news of war, Lily stands for a while, looking down at her in silence.

'You're tired,' she says eventually. 'I'll leave you.'

But as she is about to turn to go Eliza's eyes flutter open again. Such a strange colour they are, even in this half-light.

'You will be fine, Lily. Look at you. You are young and strong-willed and you've already worked out that you make your own luck in this world. Don't let this – what happened – hold you back.

'I wish I had a quarter of your strength. But I don't. I expect I will have to marry again quickly. Don't look so shocked. I loved Max. My poor Max. But I am not good at being alone.'

'I'm so sorry,' Lily tries again, but Eliza has already closed her eyes. She wafts her hand in a vague gesture, though whether of acknowledgement or dismissal Lily will never fully work out.

'Goodbye, Eliza,' she says finally. 'I wish you well.'

As she opens the cabin door Max's jacket swings on its clothes hanger, as if waving farewell.

Mrs Collins is waiting for her in her cabin when she gets back.

'Ah, here you are, dear. I'm glad to see you up and about. That's the spirit. Let's put this tragic business of last night behind us. I've come to refund you the three pounds of your original passage that we kept back for safekeeping. You'll need some of that to pay for your room at the YWCA.'

Lily and Audrey are both booked into the YWCA in Sydney, while Ida and some of the other girls are staying with Mrs Collins in different lodgings.

'Tonight you'll be able to recover a little, and then tomorrow, bright and early, we have interviews set up with prospective employers. I understand there will be eleven or twelve ladies coming, so I'm sure you will have your pick of positions. And, luckily, the captain has kept your name out of any official reports into what happened to poor Mr Campbell. You're down as a witness, of course, but any other *associations* have been left out.'

Lily feels herself growing hot. That word 'associations', so freighted with meaning.

'Your trunk will be sent on to the YWCA, along with Audrey's case, so you can wander around the city this afternoon quite light and unencumbered.'

'I don't feel very light,' says Lily. 'Have you heard the news from England, Mrs Collins?'

The older woman, who has been fussing around with forms and papers, now grows still and presses her lips together, as if preventing a sigh from escaping.

'That we are at war? Yes, dear, I have heard. It seems so impossible to believe that another generation will have to endure what we went through.'

Lily remembers now that Mrs Collins is widowed and it occurs to her that she might have lost her husband during the last war. How unfeeling of me not even to have asked her, she berates herself. All these people, these passengers, each nursing their own private tragedies, and she has been oblivious to it all.

After Mrs Collins leaves Lily finishes packing the light bag she will take with her off the boat, carefully placing inside her stack of letters from home, tied up with a red ribbon, and the diary which contains all her impressions of the last few weeks, and takes one last look around the cabin. She remembers seeing it for the first time with Frank and her parents, and a sharp shard of homesickness pierces her heart.

Up on the deck, all is activity. Passengers shouting to each other, or to friends or family in the waiting crowd on the dock. Stewards bustling around on last-minute errands – a bag forgotten in an upper-class cabin, a bill that needs settling. The young bathroom steward sees Lily and waves, and she almost doesn't recognize him in the full light of a Sydney day.

'We've been told we can't get off the ship yet,' says Audrey, who is standing with Annie at the railing. 'Not until the police have finished.'

Lily notices now, with a heavy feeling of dread, the police car parked on the far side of the quayside.

Oh, Edward.

Her heart feels as if it is swelling inside her, growing painfully full so it presses against the very bones of her.

Ida appears by her side, lays a hand on her arm.

'I expect you've come to say, "I told you so,"' Lily snaps.

Ida drops her hand as if she has been slapped, and once again Lily has the uncomfortable sense of having rebuffed a confidence. She half-expects Ida to stalk off, but she does not.

'I only wanted to tell you that you will survive this, even though you might think that you cannot. You just have to keep putting one foot in front of the other, one step at a time.'

At first Lily is startled into silence, and by the time she formulates a 'thank you', Ida has already slipped away into the crowd. She thinks about going after her but, before she can move, she becomes aware of something happening further along the deck; a hush falling; people stopping still in the middle of whatever they are doing, just like those figures in Pompeii all that lifetime ago.

The crowd nearest to her parts and now Lily sees what has

caught their attention. Two policemen with ruddy faces and fixed expressions are making sedate progress along the deck. The older one is squat and sandy-haired and sweating profusely, while the younger is taller and more awkward.

In between them, his wrists shackled together, is Edward.

To Lily's shock and consternation, he is still wearing the women's clothing of last night – the green suit and hat, the heeled shoes and Eliza Campbell's fox-fur stole. He stares straight ahead as he is led along, as if he cannot see the expressions of the passengers as he passes – the wide-eyed horror, the thrilled fascination. One man covers his wife's eyes as they go by, as if the mere sight of Edward might somehow corrupt her.

And now the mismatched threesome have nearly reached where Lily is standing. So close are they that she can see the trembling of Edward's hands in those white gloves and the patch of ginger bristles on the older man's chin where he has missed a bit shaving. Her swollen heart feels as if it must burst.

They walk past, just feet from where she stands, so close that Lily is sure Edward must be able to hear the rushing of her blood in her ears. But if he does, he shows no sign, his eyes still fixed on a point up ahead.

Finally, before he is enveloped back into the crowd, she finds her voice.

'Edward!' Up ahead, he stops suddenly and turns, wrong-footing the younger policeman so he almost stumbles.

'I'll visit you!' she calls.

And now his face breaks into that sad, sweet, familiar smile and, though the hat's veil covers his eyes, Lily fancies she sees them shimmer with tears through the delicate green web.

'Thank you, Lily,' he says. 'I shall look forward to that.'

Then he turns and sets off once again with his police escort, but Lily sees how his spine is straighter, his shoulders back and, despite catching sight of Mrs Collins's disapproving expression, she is glad she has spoken.

Helena comes to join her, the skin stretched almost translucent over her bones.

'Why didn't they let him at least get changed?' Lily blurts out, unable to help herself, after they have watched Edward and his escorts cross the quayside to be driven away in the back of a police car.

'Oh, they tried,' Helena says grimly. 'They wanted him to – so much less embarrassing for them. But he refused. He said this is his last chance to be the person he really is.'

'You spoke to him, then?'

'Briefly. Oh, Lily. He loved him. Max Campbell. Can you imagine that? Poor Edward. Poor Max.'

'Where will they take him now?'

'To the police station. I will follow him there, as soon as we are allowed to leave the ship.'

'Will you be all right, Helena?'

Ian, who has appeared by Helena's side, answers for her. 'Don't worry, Lily. I will look after her.'

He has his arm around Helena's shoulders, gripping them tightly. Helena leans her head to nestle safely under his chin.

'Did you mean it?' Helena asks Lily. 'What you said about visiting Edward?'

'Of course.'

Up until now, Lily hasn't really considered the implications of what she said, but now she realizes that, whatever happens, Edward is still Edward and she cannot imagine a life without him in it.

'Thank you,' says Helena.

The order has now been given that disembarkation should commence, and the ship is once again full of hustle and bustle and excited chatter. Standing at the railing, Lily sees George Price already down on the dock and her mouth becomes instantly dry as she thinks of Maria and the part he might or might not have had in her disappearance. He is greeted by a tall, thin man dressed in a sombre black suit who Lily assumes to be his uncle. The two shake hands briefly and stiffly and, watching them head off in silence, Lily sees how living on a farm in the middle of the New Zealand countryside with just this man might turn out to be a kind of prison in itself, and she shivers with the thought of how his life might turn out if he cannot lay his demons to rest.

Clara Mills is on the quayside, too, standing nervously with her daughter, Peggy, her bag pressed to her chest, as if someone might try to snatch it from her. She is approached by a solid, dark-haired man in a grey suit who pecks both women perfunctorily on the cheek before swinging the bag over his shoulder and heading off the way he came, leaving wife and daughter to follow after.

And now it is time for Lily herself to leave. She can see Audrey and Annie already down on the dock waiting for her. She takes a last look at the ship that has been her home for more than five weeks, and all of a sudden it is too much and a tidal wave of grief washes over her.

For a moment she feels as if her knees might give way and she clings to the railing, convinced she cannot go on. Then she looks around at the cobalt-blue sky and the sun glinting off the majestic curved steel bridge, and the quayside teeming with life in all its messy, complicated forms, and she straightens up and steps on to the gangway. Fixing her eyes on a point in front, just as Edward had done, she puts one foot in front of the other and proceeds towards the dusty dock that forms the gateway to Australia. One step at a time.

Excerpt from 'A Woman of Means', the 2006 *Sydney Morning Herald* profile of Lilian Dent

'All lines are blurred, all truth becomes, by the act of retelling it, a fiction.' So says Rose Dixon, heroine of *The Voyage*, Lilian Dent's first and still best-loved novel. And no lines are more blurred than those surrounding the inspiration for this book. The death of Max Campbell on board the ship on which Lily Shepherd, as she was then, was travelling to start a new life in Australia, caused a scandal at the time. While she refused, right up until her death in 2005, to comment on it, or her own involvement with the key players, it's clear the events of 1939 had a huge and lasting influence on Dent's writing and on the themes she would return to throughout her working life, as did the mysterious disappearance on the same voyage of an Austrian-Jewish refugee Dent had befriended named Maria Katz. The following documents were uncovered in the Lilian Dent archives by her biographer, Henrietta Lock, who was allowed unprecedented access after Dent's death by the author's notoriously protective children, Thomas and Frances, who are executors of her estate.

Document One is a letter from Arthur Price, uncle of George Price, enclosing a letter from his nephew. Biographical details of George Price are sketchy. We know he was the son of William Price, an official in the British Raj, and that he travelled on the *Orontes* to Sydney and then on to New Zealand, where he lived with Arthur, who owned an isolated farm. Price is now believed to have suffered from psychosis that went undiagnosed and untreated, and killed himself in 1965, prompting the letter from his uncle reproduced here. On the surface, the enclosed letter from George appears to be some sort of death-bed confession, with him claiming responsibility for the drowning at sea of Maria Katz. Price was known to have been a member of the fascist and avowedly anti-Semitic British Union before leaving for Australia, so this would not have been wholly out of character. However, given the apparently fragile state of George Price's psychiatric state in the latter part of his life, such claims must be treated with a degree of caution.

The second document is a hugely significant find – a letter from Edward Fletcher, who was sentenced in 1940 to twenty-two years' imprisonment for the second-degree murder of Max Campbell, and who many regard as the inspiration for Rupert Longbridge, the hero of *The Voyage*. While the letter does not touch on matters of any great importance, it clearly demonstrates the depth of the emotional bond between Dent and Fletcher, and indeed between Dent and Helena Fletcher, Edward's sister, whose family became closely entwined with Dent's own family. The themes of friendship and loyalty being tested were to be prevalent throughout Dent's work.

Finally, Document Three is a brief telegram from Max Campbell's widow, Eliza, who went on to marry Lord Henry Cullen. While it is hard to gauge much from a four-line message, it is telling both that Lady Cullen remained in contact with Dent some years after the fateful voyage on which her husband was killed, and that Dent chose to keep her telegram for so many years. What happened on board the *Orontes* clearly had a profound effect on the passengers, linking them together in fundamental ways that would endure for the remainder of their lives – and beyond.

Document One

Gully Tree Farm
Starvation Hill Road
Oxford, Waimakariri
New Zealand

6 July 1965

Dear Mrs Dent

I am the uncle of George Price, who you may remember as a fellow passenger on the *Orontes* back in 1939, when you were still Lily Shepherd. I regret to inform you that George died three months ago, in circumstances I would prefer to keep private. He left a letter for you, which I enclose with a heavy heart. I leave it up to you what you do with the information it contains.

Yours sincerely
Arthur Price

Dear Lily

I expect you will be surprised to hear from me after more than a quarter of a century and to know that I have followed your movements with such interest since reading a newspaper article about you when your first book, *The Voyage*, was published fourteen years ago. I am glad you have made a success of your life with your family and your books. I envy you. I never married. Living out here, you can imagine the opportunities were limited, and I think my blunt nature has done me few favours. Life has been hard and I will not be sorry to leave it behind.

However, before I do, I should like to unburden myself of something that has weighed on me heavily lately, something that happened on board the *Orontes* all those years ago. You will remember how things were then, on the brink of war. How there was no right and wrong and our fellow passengers became enemies overnight? I think the strangeness of that situation brought upon me a kind of temporary madness. Sometimes I look back on those events and wonder if they even happened at all.

You remember the Austrian woman, Maria Katz? We did not see eye to eye and it angered me that she somehow won your friendship. It seemed to me that she poisoned your mind against me. One night when all the passengers were sleeping on deck, I crept up and laid my hands on her while she slept. This was not a sexual advance, I assure you. I wanted only to scare her, to make her retreat back into herself and leave you alone. I used to follow her also, making sure she could hear me behind her but ducking into doorways when she turned. I had overheard her say how, after fleeing Austria, she had nightmares about people pursuing her, and I realized that following her would play on her fears. When your friendship continued unchecked, I went one step further, substituting her salt tablets with the lithium salts I had been prescribed by a doctor back home in England when I was feeling not quite myself. If you remember, the salt tablets were laid out on the tables for us before we sat down to eat, so it was a simple enough thing to do.

I must impress upon you that this was not sport, Lily. I did not gain enjoyment from Miss Katz's suffering. I saw her then – and see her now – as the enemy. My father had removed me from the proximity to war, yet I still saw myself as a soldier, doing my bit to make the world safer. To make *you* safer, Lily.

Yet she persisted in pressing for your friendship, trying to gain advantage over me. I saw her talking to you that last day, and overheard her begging you to meet her that afternoon. I could tell it made you uncomfortable and, when you didn't turn up to meet her, I decided you needed someone to intercede. I only meant to warn her off, but she was half crazed. She thought I had come to hurt her and she sprang to the railings like some kind of wild creature. I lunged forward to grab hold of her. To stop her, you understand. But she misinterpreted my intention and flew at me. We tussled, and I admit I lost control. It was all over in seconds.

In the days and months and years that followed, I told myself Miss Katz was another casualty of war. To tell the truth, she seldom crossed my mind. There were so many horrors happening in the world at that time, this was just one more. But lately, she has been much more in my thoughts. I see her even in my nightmares. Who would have thought I could remember her face after so many years? Yet I do.

That is why I wanted to make this confession to you now. In the hope of laying the whole business to rest. You were always fair, Lily. I remember this so clearly about you. I know you won't judge me too harshly. Everything is different in war, isn't it?

Your friend
George Price

Document Two

Goulburn Reformatory, 12 February 1951

Dearest Lily

How thrilled I was to receive your letter with all your news. When they moved me from Sydney all the way out here to Goulburn, I worried we might lose contact, so you can imagine my relief when I saw your familiar, messy handwriting on the envelope. (Don't make that face. It *is* messy. Messy but so very dear.)

Lily, I can't tell you how proud I am of what you've achieved. A published novel! I always knew you would put that fine brain of yours to good use. I hope you will still remember me when you are a rich and famous authoress. Perhaps you can send a signed copy of your book for the prison library when it comes out – that would win me some popularity points around here.

Oh, Lily, please don't feel bad about describing your life back in Sydney. It gives me such pleasure to picture you and your husband and Helena and Ian on the beach with all the children on a sunny Sunday afternoon. What a wonderful life you have all built for yourselves. You will have so much to show your parents when they visit next month. I can't imagine how excited you must be.

Please stop worrying about me, Lily. I am fine. Although I hate being so far from you all, my new home suits me well enough. I have been putting my legal training to good use in helping some of the fellows here with their cases and appeals. They call me 'm'lud', which makes us all laugh.

Like you, I cannot believe it has been twelve years since the *Orontes*. In so many ways it feels like yesterday. But you know, dearest Lily, we cannot go backwards. No matter how much we might wish we could. And despite where I am and the terrible thing I did, I am more fully myself here than I ever was in England. I would be lying if I said I was happy. But I am at peace.

Your Edward

Document Three

August 1942

GREETINGS FROM THE NEW LADY CULLEN STOP MARRIED TWO WEEKS STOP SETTING OFF FOR NYERI KENYA TOMORROW STOP IF EATEN BY LIONS MY PEACH SILK IS YOURS STOP ELIZA

Author's Note

At the tail end of 2015 I was nosing around my mum's bookcases when I came across a curious home-printed, spiral-bound notebook with a laminated cover showing a bleached photograph of a smiling young woman in 1930s clothing standing on the deck of a ship. I started idly leafing through what turned out to be a memoir written some years ago by a late friend of my mother's called Joan Holles, who, as a young woman, had taken advantage of a government scheme offering assisted passage to Australia for anyone prepared to go into domestic service in one of the large British-owned family houses over there. At the time there was a shortage of trained young help in the New World, and organizations such as the Church of England Migration Council were helping recruit young British women prepared to act as maids and cooks and housekeepers in return for a chance to see the world.

The memoir was based on the diaries Joan kept during the five-and-a-half-week voyage from Tilbury Docks to Sydney Harbour. In it, Joan chronicles in meticulous detail the various ports they visited during the voyage, what she wore, how much things cost, which musical numbers the ship's band played. She talks of the friendships she made on board, the romantic dalliances, the balls, the fancy-dress parties.

But more than that, with the ship setting sail in July 1938 and arriving in September of that same year, she also captures the social nuances and tensions of a world in flux. Joan and the other young women travelling on the assisted-passage scheme were in tourist class, alongside professionals and 'respectable' middle-class passengers. The upper-class deck was for wealthy families and debutantes, successful business people and the odd celebrity. As the ship passed through Europe, they also picked up – much to the distrust of many of the British passengers – Italians, who crowded together on the lower deck where the laundries were situated, and Jews from Austria and Germany, fleeing the Nazis. In the shadow of World War Two, the ship became a floating tinderbox of political and social tension.

As soon as I'd read the memoir, I realized the scenario Joan described had all the elements of an intriguing historical crime novel. A world teetering on the brink of war. The enclosed world-within-a-world of the ship itself, with its claustrophobic mix of volatile social groups. A young woman leaving behind everything that is familiar and heading for a brave new world about which she knows next to nothing, mingling socially for the first time in her life with people from all strata of society, both from Britain and abroad.

On the ship, passengers are forced together in the infernal building heat, day in, day out, with no way of getting away from each other. Wouldn't tensions rise? Particularly with the threat of war hanging over their heads. What if something happened on board this boat? Something awful. How would a young, naive woman who had never before left England deal with that?

I decided to move the action of the book forward a year so that the ship leaves England in July 1939, when conflict looks likely but by no means inevitable. I made my heroine a high-spirited young woman called Lily Shepherd, who is escaping from a terrible secret but is nevertheless determined to wring every last ounce of adventure out of this once-in-a-lifetime voyage. By the time the ship docks in Sydney five and a half weeks later, two people are dead and the world is at war. Nothing will ever be the same again.

Though I have written other books, this is my first historical novel and I have had to learn to negotiate the tightrope between fact and fiction. While Joan Holles's memoir provided an invaluable starting point, Lily Shepherd's story is entirely her own. Likewise, all the characters she meets on her journey – the Campbells, the Fletchers, George Price, Maria Katz – exist only on the pages of this book.

As always with historical fiction, certain liberties have been taken with the truth. While the ship Lily sails on, the *Orontes*, shares a name with a real passenger liner that served the same route between London and Sydney, its layout and operational routines owe as much to my imagination as to any notion of factual accuracy.

The assisted-passage scheme existed in various forms for decades during the twentieth century. While the vast majority of Britons who took advantage of it travelled to Australia in the thirty years following World War Two, there was targeted subsidized migration during the inter-war period as well, mostly aimed at young people, particularly young women with experience of domestic service. However, while these crossings continued well into 1939, the departure date of 29 July is entirely my own wishful thinking.

While writing the book, I researched the stories of many young women who, like Joan and Lily, made the decision to leave home and family behind and journey to the other side of the world, some earlier, others much later. Their circumstances differ wildly, but their hopes and dreams for the future are all touchingly similar. A better life. Kindness. Adventure.

This book is for them.

Rachel Rhys, October 2016

Acknowledgements

A big thank-you to Joan Holles, whose journal provided the inspiration for this book, and to my mum, who had the very good sense to become her friend all those years ago.

Huge thanks to my agent Felicity Blunt, who said, 'Why don't you try writing something historical?' and was involved in every stage of this novel's evolution, from the opening scene to making sure it found the best possible publishing home. And to Melissa Pimentel at Curtis Brown, who has worked so hard to get Lily's story read in all four corners of the world (well, almost).

Thanks eternally to Jane Lawson at Transworld and Beverley Cousins at Penguin Random House Australia for responding to *A Dangerous Crossing* in the way all authors fantasize about publishers doing. I am so thrilled to be in the capable hands of the Transworld team, especially the incomparable Alison Barrow. Special thanks also to Alison's dad, Bill Barrow, for his valued input. And heartfelt gratitude to Richard Ogle for his stunning cover design.

Thanks to the many people who attempted to answer my often random research queries, especially Holly Pritchard and Jill Chapman at the National Archives of Australia and Rachael Marchese at the Victoria League; also to the Church of England Record Centre. Thanks, too, to Dr Paula Hamilton of the University of Technology in Sydney, who directed me to the oral history collection at the National Library of Australia, which includes fascinating accounts from British women who ended up in domestic service in Australia.

Book bloggers are among the most generous of people, giving up their time to spread the word about the books they love. My thanks to Cleopatra Bannister, blogger extraordinaire, who won a CLIC Sargent charity auction to have a character named after her in this book, and helped raise money for children and young people with cancer.

The final thank-you is to my two earliest readers, Rikki Finegold and Amanda Jennings. The Pink Ladies are on me.

RACHEL RHYS is the pen-name of a successful psychological-suspense author. *A Dangerous Crossing* is her debut under this name and is inspired by a real-life account of a 1930s ocean voyage. Rachel Rhys lives in north London with her family.